secrets of the suburbs

Secrets of the Suburbs

Alisa Schindler

Rocky Road Press
New York

For Bruce,
who knows all my secrets

Acknowledgements

An enormous thank you to my early readers who have supported and guided me with their words, wisdom and friendship – Stacy Deluca, Alyzia Sands, Jackie Stapleton, Pam Gawley, Beth Ain, Emily Preceruti, Christie O. Tate and Samantha Brinn Merel. And special shout out to my cousin and soul sister Mara Wolman who reminded me first, that I could write, and second, that I am good enough. To the blogging and freelance community who I have never met but I love. To graphic art master Heidi Nachimson for her awesome designs and for always being there to chat and chew, brainstorm, and help a friend. To Rachel Costello for my cover art which is totally badass. To my mom who thinks everything I do is a work of genius. Everyone should be so lucky to have a mom like mine as their cheerleader. To my boys for letting me hide away in the computer room to do what I needed to do. Thank you for your grudging patience, sticky smiles and warm hugs. I couldn't be more proud and lucky to be your mom. And to my wonderful, supportive and extremely tolerant husband. You are my one and only. I love you.

You know that tingly feeling you get when you like someone? That's common sense leaving your body. —Sassy ecards

CHAPTER 1

Percentage of marriages where one or both spouses admit to infidelity, either physical or emotional – 41%

In a mild state of panic, Lindsey focused all her energies on the one thing that had always given her a sense of calming comfort and control – herself. She blew out her hair, fussed with her face, and tossed clothes on and off her body, searching for the outfit that would make her look cool even if what she felt was hot and bothered. She knew she would see him later and the thought of it filled her with dread. Delicious dread.

The whole thing was completely ridiculous. Nothing happened. Nothing. So why was she in such turmoil to see a man she had seen practically daily for the last few years? Why was she driving herself crazy reliving that moment? It was so quick. A second. Not even a second. She probably misunderstood and imagined the whole thing. In fact she was certain of it, because she couldn't even begin to contemplate the implications if she hadn't. But of course, it was all she had contemplated since that quick connection, followed by a hasty retreat that left her feeling like she had been struck by lightning.

She had definitely been a little tipsy. She had what? Two Grey Goose and tonics. Or was it three? So maybe she tipped over tipsy into solidly buzzed, and maybe the two of them had been a little looser on the usual restraints, but they always had an easy rapport. He was sharp and funny, occasionally at his wife's expense, but honestly at anyone's.

They both played that game. It was all reasonably good-natured, absolutely good-humored and mildly flirtatious, but there was nothing for the peanut gallery to whisper about.

Besides, Lindsey told herself, they hung out all the time – at school functions, at sporting functions, in the neighborhood, as couples going out for dinner. They were all very comfortable with each other. So they were palling it up by the bar? There was nothing wrong or unusual about that.

Although they were doing a lot of laughing. One upping each other with tales of their children's laziness and trading snarky remarks about random party goers. And when he commented that this woman Lydia was wearing a shirt that looked like someone threw up a parrot on her, Lindsey practically spit out her drink and fell off her chair, just managing to catch herself and instead knocking her bag and half its contents onto the floor.

Still kind of giddy with laughter and vodka, she bent down to collect the contents and he bent down to help.

"I can't believe I just did that." She giggled. "I think I need to be cut off."

"It's no big deal." He flashed a mischievous grin. "Girls have always fallen all over themselves for me."

"Oh right. I can see them from here carpeting the floor. Impressive." She smirked, feeling young, clever and a little adventurous.

"You mock my skills?" He pretended offense, retrieving her cell that had fallen under the table.

"Never." She laughed, but when he returned the phone to her, his hand lingered on hers just a second too long. "Thanks," she said, looking up.

Their eyes met and flashed something completely new to their general easy way; something unsettling, something exciting, something very bad. The noise level was high, full of talk crashing into each other and Adele's throaty, sexy Rolling in the Deep, undulating like a wave. Yet somehow it felt strangely quiet. Time suspended. Lindsey didn't even get to truly process the current she felt in that second because then they were up, and casually, yet quickly deciding it was time to find their respective partners.

She hovered around her husband Mitchell for the rest of the evening, sipping water, feeling agitated. Was it me? She wondered. Did I overstep myself somehow in my drunken state?

On the way home from the party, Mitchell remarked on her quiet state. "Are you okay? You were kind of quiet tonight."

Lindsey was thinking how happy she was that they hadn't carpooled with their friends. She couldn't imagine being in a car with him right now.

"I was just thinking," Lindsey admitted, "how tired I am, and how much we have to do tomorrow."

"What's tomorrow?" Mitchell asked, and Lindsey marveled at his ability to remember the personal and medical histories of 20 consecutive patients daily, yet totally blank out on their weekend obligations.

"Well, Liam has soccer at 9am. You're going to that, right? I promised Riley we'd do a girly morning. Maybe get mani/pedis and a few errands done. She also has a birthday party in the afternoon and Liam has a play date. I was planning on dropping Riley and then stopping by my parents. They're almost ready to move and I need to clean out my old room. You know, I've been putting it off."

"Sure babe," he said easily, and Lindsey knew she'd have to remind him again in the morning. His hand rested on her thigh and Lindsey covered it with hers. She looked up to his glittering hazel eyes and suggestive smile on his strong jawline. I have a sexy husband, she thought, a sexy, doctor husband. Why aren't we having more sex? She wondered. Lindsey gave his hand a squeeze. The night was not over yet.

That night was four days ago. Four days to go back and forth to the point of insanity trying to reconstruct what transpired in that second, if anything. Four days to agonize whether there was a look that somehow crossed the line from proper to improper, appropriate to inappropriate, friendly to suggestive.

Was she just drunk imagining? They had known each other for years. The further away from it she got, the more silly the whole thing appeared. She was getting herself all worked up over nothing and she began to feel embarrassed; mostly because of her own ridiculous reaction, her body's instant response and the last four days of fantasy that she had been guiltily indulging with relish. She needed to put that whole night behind her, especially since they would all probably be seeing each other in an hour at the school art show.

After finally settling on casual chic skinny jeans, heels and a cute off the shoulder burgundy top, Lindsey corralled the kids into the car with only moderate resistance. Mitchell would meet them there, since he was coming straight from work.

They should have been only ten minutes late, but Riley of course wasn't happy with her outfit selection and needed to do a last minute change. Lindsey marveled how into fashion she was even though she was only eight years-old, but she never wondered where she got her tendencies.

Luckily, Liam at ten years-old, had no such inclinations and refused to change the same dirty clothes he wore to soccer practice earlier. Lindsey was going to insist, but ultimately they ran out of time and it was one of those things that had to give. Besides, people generally gave a pass to dirty fourth grade boys.

They rushed in almost a half hour into it, not that they missed anything. There was no structure to the event. It was social and interactive, with art displayed all over the walls of the school, and parents' left to haphazardly search for their child's masterpieces.

Riley half dragged, half pulled Lindsey down the hall where she knew her work was hanging.

"Come on, mom!" she whined in complaint. "You are so slow! Why did you wear those shoes?"

Why did she wear these shoes? Lindsey wondered as well, although she knew exactly why she chose the sexy heels over the ballet flats. "I'm moving as fast as I can," she said, and quickly maneuvered through the throngs of people.

They wove in and around other parents and students, and Lindsey kept her steely game face on the whole time, although every so often she would spontaneously burst into a smile when she passed a friend, rolling her eyes with amusement at being her daughter's pull toy.

"Hey," she called out, tugging at the shirt of Diane Jameson, a queen in her town and also one of her closer friends. "Spin tomorrow?"

"Definitely," Diane agreed. "Then Bloomingdale's? It's the friends and family sale."

"I have some work to finish up tomorrow. Next week for sure."

Diane shook her head. "Okay, but you're missing out. All the good stuff will be mine already."

"All the good stuff is yours already." Lindsey laughed.

Diane gave a smug little shrug that she softened with a compliment. "Well, not that cute top you're wearing."

Lindsey tried to say thank you, but apparently Riley thought they had chit-chat enough.

She saw Marnie and Bradley, Caren Lucci and her husband 'what's his name' and many random parents she was friendly with but continued on, scanning heads, telling herself she was looking for Mitchell, but knowing perfectly well who she was really searching for yet terrified to see. He had to be here, she thought. It seemed like pretty much the whole town was.

She wanted to see his face, felt compelled to, maybe to confirm that they were normal and she was crazy. Or maybe, a tiny part of her brain acknowledged, she wanted to see if she would feel that rush again.

She pushed that disgusting thought away. Somehow in that one second, he had switched in her brain from a friend and friend's husband to a person she needed to see, a person she was thinking about. She needed to turn that switch right off.

They came to an abrupt halt in front of Riley's artwork which could only be described as an organized explosion of nature. Neither of her kids had any real art talent, but Riley, ever the perfectionist, always put in a solid effort. It may not be the prettiest piece on display, but no one could say her "Falling for Fall" montage was anything but respectable, having incorporated both real leaves and sticks into her hand-drawn neighborhood scene. Not a space was left unattended.

After appreciating every aspect of Riley's leaf work and color scheme, Lindsey had to literally force Liam into showing her where his piece was being exhibited. In contrast to her enthusiastic daughter, their trek over to his work was painfully slow, and the moment Lindsey tried to even utter a small compliment, he silenced her with "Mom, please!" So they stood quietly for a minute, appreciating the scene he created of small figures and colorful trees. It was actually quite good, but she wasn't allowed to say anything of the sort.

They were on their way back for some further appreciation of Riley's art, since apparently Lindsey had failed to notice the dog Riley had cleverly hidden somewhere in the leaves, when they ran into Mitchell, looking quite adorable in his button down shirt, chinos and loafers. He gave her a quick peck and a squeeze and then got busy gushing over Riley's masterpiece.

They hung out for another half hour or so, allowing the kids to eat some pizza in the cafeteria and run around with their friends. Then someone who looked remarkably like her son, suggested ice cream and after some jumping and screaming with new puppy excitement, they agreed.

The kids hitched a ride with Mitchell since they liked his car better. Not that there was anything wrong with her car, Liam assured. "It's just that dad's car is so much cooler." Uh, thanks.

"Oh, don't worry about me and my jalopy. I'll just meet you there. You guys go on in your hot ride," Lindsey yelled after them. Friggin Porsche, she thought. I can't believe I let him talk me into that. Doesn't he care that he's an over 40 guy in the suburbs with a sports car? A total cliché, she thought, and then headed out to her Volvo SUV.

She was almost at her car when she spotted them. They were with their kids and getting ready to leave as well. Now, she actually didn't want to see him. She had found some relief to her nerves in the passage of time without a sighting. That, and the half a Xanax she took before leaving the house. But it was too late.

"Lindsey!" His wife, her friend Jeanie, called and hurried over with a kiss and small hug combination. Jeanie worked on two speeds fast and manic. "How are you? I don't know how we could have missed you guys in that madness in there." She laughed but it was a high, affected laugh, one for show. Jeanie was sweet, but also a little sour, the sensitive kind who insulted easily. "Hey, where are Mitchell and the kids?" Jeanie asked, her small, sharp eyes looking past her, darting left to right, as if they'd somehow mysteriously appear in the darkness.

"Oh, they're all in the fun man-mobile. I'm meeting them over at Lucky Dip for ice cream."

Lindsey sensed him in the background and her heart started pumping out less and less blood making her feel faint. Her instincts told her to run from this scene as fast as she could, but there was nothing she could do but finish up their pleasantries and hopefully make it to her car before she passed out.

"That sounds like a great idea!" Jeanie smiled and then turned behind her, addressing her troops, "Hey, everyone! Want to go to Lucky Dip?"

Momentarily distracted by the cheering of her boys, Trevor and Elliot, Lindsey was totally caught off guard when John appeared by her side. "Hey," he said softly, and leaned in to kiss her cheek. She smiled and hoped she didn't look as uncomfortable as she felt.

"Are you okay?" Jeanie asked, eyeing her with concern. "You look, I don't know, maybe in pain?"

Okay then, there it was. Apparently she did look as uncomfortable as she felt. She brushed it off and smiled wide. "Oh no, I'm fine. Really. Thanks. So, I'll see you guys at ice cream." Without waiting for a response, she turned and headed for her car. Once inside she breathed deeply to collect herself. Damn, he smelled good.

***

Lucky Dip was a charming old-fashioned ice cream shoppe nestled in between a popular overpriced seafood restaurant with only marginally good food, a family style Italian restaurant which wasn't much better, a bait and tackle store and a Pilates studio run by a high intensity, low key instructor with a cult following. Out their store's back windows a dock stretched out to nowhere and boats bobbed peacefully in moonlit waters. With its waterfront setting, homemade chunky ice cream and jars of penny candy, Lucky Dip was definitely a shoppe shop. Lindsey had seen the view so many times and it never failed to impress, yet tonight for the first time, she felt the smallness of the town, the water all around her, and although it was irrational, it made her feel a little trapped.

She walked through the jingling doors and immediately saw two other families she knew who obviously got hoodwinked as well. She gave them a quick nod and headed over to Mitchell and the kids, already in line arguing over who was getting the best flavor. Mitchell felt strongly about Blueberry Crumble. Riley was at war with herself between the Chocolate Fudge and Cake Batter, and Liam remained fiercely loyal to his Cookie Crumb Dough, the only flavor he ever chose. Lindsey joined them on line and in argument. They had a kick ass Coffee Chip. She rarely indulged, but since she had dropped a few pounds in the last few days of anxiety, she allowed herself the much needed treat.

They had just placed their orders when Jeanie, John and their kids walked in. Lindsey instantly moved closer to Mitchell who smiled and warmly put an arm around her shoulder. It made her feel even more claustrophobic.

Jeanie and John's boys were the same age as Lindsey and Mitchell's kids and immediately bounced over to converse in the way children do, by doing stupid things and trying to best each other. The adults casually watched, disinclined to intervene unless they become too embarrassingly loud or disruptive to ignore.

It was all completely normal, Lindsey thought. She had definitely over-exaggerated one questionable second and played it out in some wacky desperate housewife fantasy for almost a week now. Pathetic. Totally pathetic. Whatever. No harm done. She was over it. She couldn't even believe what she had been thinking. Not only were Jeanie and John her friends, but she had the most rocking, hot husband out there. She was a mother with two kids. She was happily married. She was a complete idiot.

"Hey, are you guys going to Sean's 40th birthday party next week?" Jeanie asked. "We should go together."

"Sounds great," Mitchell said automatically. "I don't know how Diane is going to top Marnie's party last week but I'm sure she'll try."

At the mention of Marnie's party the week before, Lindsey paled and glanced hastily at John who seemed completely unaffected. Feeling the beginnings of hives starting a slow crawl up her skin, she excused herself momentarily to assist Liam with his dripping cone.

By the time she came back, they were still deep in conversation over Diane's upcoming party. Everyone agreed it would be a good one. Diane was Shore Point royalty, and she didn't like to be one-upped. She was the one-upper. Lindsey could only imagine what she had planned for next week. 'Expect the Unexpected' was her theme and that could mean anything.

"All these young 40 year-olds and their parties," Lindsey added, rolling her eyes and joining the conversation. They were all a couple of years past 40. Only Diane and Marnie and their spouses were at the threshold of that milestone. "When will they grow up?"

"I don't know," John said, "but I'm happy to chaperone these toddlers as long as there's an open bar."

"We'll all drink to that," Mitchell agreed and the two men clinked their ice cream cones while Lindsey and Jeanie exchanged an indulgent, 'girls are so superior' look.

"You'll pretty much drink to anything." Lindsey laughed and gave Mitchell a little nudge.

The kids were all standing on one foot trying to jump in a circle and eat their dripping ice cream cones at the same time. How was it that the adults had finished their cones five minutes prior and the kids were still not even half way done? And more fascinatingly, had lost interest. Liam came over and handed Lindsey his unfinished cone. Another time she might have refused, made a snide comment about not being the garbage and instructed him to throw it away himself, but tonight she appreciated the distraction.

"Hey."

Jeanie startled Lindsey who had just snuck a last lick of Liam's cone before tossing it in the trash. She definitely wasn't herself.

"Hey," Lindsey said.

"So did you see the latest Secrets of the Shore post?"

"No!" Lindsey said, her eyes wide. "Tell me!" Secrets of the Shore, or SOS as it was commonly called, was a secret Facebook page that spread the style and scandal in her town and some neighboring towns. She and her friends were addicted.

"Here, I'll read it to you." Jeanie whipped her phone from her bag and within seconds of frantic finger tapping began to read,

So as I'm sure you all know, and if you don't, well that means that you haven't scored an invite to the hottest party coming to town. It's sure to be the chi chi la la of Shore Point putting all other soirées to shame. So if you're one of the chosen few... hundred, I'll see you there. And if you're not, check in for my full report the morning after. I'm sure it'll be full of stylish social climbers, sloshed suburbanites and if we're lucky some fabulously inappropriate conduct. Stay tuned...

"Oh God," Lindsey beamed, taking Jeanie's phone and going over the words. "She must be talking about Diane!"

"I wish I knew who she was," Jeanie gushed. "I'd invite her to one of our lunches immediately."

"We'll scope out the party and see if we can figure it out." Lindsey chuckled and then noticed the time. "It's getting late. We have to go."

When the sticky hands, arms and faces had been unstuck, they all made their way toward their cars with the kids running ahead. "Well this was nice," Lindsey said. "And..." She looked at her phone for time confirmation. "Just past 8:30p.m.. Not too bad."

"Great. Well, we'll see you guys next week, if not around the block," Mitchell said agreeably and went to open his car for the kids to pile in. "I'll see you at home." He waved an off-hand goodbye to Lindsey, the wife in the uncool car.

"Oh, Mitchell?" Jeanie asked, following him. "I have a question about my back." She probably was waiting to ask that all night, Lindsey thought. In fact, it probably had prompted the ice cream tag along.

Mitchell was always so good about things like that. He never minded offering his 'doctorly' advice. He really wanted to help people.

"Did Jeanie hurt her back?" Lindsey asked, turning towards John.

"Yeah," John answered reflectively. "She was lifting heavy boxes for storage that she shouldn't have. I told her I would do it when I got home, but she can't help herself. She has a need to organize everything and can't wait."

They stood there quietly. They always had such an easy rapport and had never been at a loss for conversation. The quiet grew.

Lindsey was afraid to look at him. "So what, the ice cream freeze your tongue? Can't talk?" She joked awkwardly, trying to be normal and braving a glance up. His eyes were closed off slits, unreadable.

"I'm trying my best here," he answered slowly.

Moments ago they were all laughing easily. All of a sudden there was a shift in the air, and it was suffocating.

He looked stressed, like she had never seen him. His muscles, his whole body in fact, was stiff and tense.

"John, what are you talking about? What are trying your best to do?" she asked, her voice sounding strained and faraway, like it was coming from someone else. She could hear her heart beating, although she couldn't believe it could beat at all. She was almost completely paralyzed with fear.

His eyes opened then and when they looked at her, they were so blue and sad and their quiet, intimate, honesty left her dizzy. "I'm trying not to think about you."

CHAPTER 2

"A good husband makes a good wife." - John Florio

After John said what he said, they both stood in stunned silence, unsure of anything. There were no words, no protocol. The whole world seemed a little off kilter - Mitchell talking to Jeanie, putting his hands on the small of her back, John's kids banging on the window of their car to get their parents attention, her, standing in an awkward bubble of tension next to John.

"Uh, I don't know what to say to that," Lindsey whispered and stole a glance at him, but his eyes and face had retreated back to closed, unreadable slits. With his hands in his jean pockets, he looked at once the picture of easy going casualness and tight control.

"I don't expect you to say anything," he replied, as Jeanie made her way towards them.

"Your husband is a saint, I tell you," she gushed. "He knew just what I had done to myself. Told me to take a couple of Advil and it should be gone in a few days. If not, I must go and see him right away." Jeanie smiled wide, almost clownishly, Lindsey noticed, like her mouth was stretched outside the seams.

"Great. Well, I'm going. See you guys later." Definitely time to make her exit, Lindsey thought.

She walked around to stick her head in Mitchell's car just before he pulled away. "Well, Jeanie thinks you're a saint," she said, trying to be normal.

"Well, how lucky are you, then?" He laughed, leaned over and kissed her cheek. "See you at home."

Married to a saint. Great. Lindsey sighed. With the thoughts running through her head, she was going to need all the help she could get.

Lindsey was relieved to have the ten minutes driving home with only the noise in her own brain distracting her, instead of the kids yelling in the back seat. Plus, she didn't want to be next to Mitchell. She felt too disgusted with herself and guilty. She thought about all the time she and John had spent together over the last few years... the lazy afternoons at soccer games, the school events, afternoons at the park, birthday parties, the dinners out with groups of friends, the parties. Were they dating without realizing it?

They always had such an easy connection. Their conversations were natural, their flirting, light but safe. There was no doubt Lindsey found him attractive, but he was her friend's husband, she wasn't attracted to him.

That wasn't true. She was attracted to him, but she had been attracted to a few men around town over the years and never thought of it as inappropriate. She was happily married and loved her husband, but she still wanted men to be attracted to her; still liked being attractive to men. Was something wrong that, with her? She wondered.

Lindsey reached home, but remained sitting in the driveway, overthinking and chastising herself when a knock on her window made her jump.

Mitchell.

Embarrassed, she opened the door and stepped out.

"Babe?" he asked curiously, brows lifted in amusement. "You

okay?"

Lindsey gave a little cough that simultaneously morphed into a laugh. "Ha. Oh yeah, I was just thinking."

Mitchell automatically put in the security code on the garage and the children ducked under as it was lifting and ran into the house. They stood there for a moment watching them.

"You looked almost like you were telling somebody off. What were you thinking about?"

"Oh man, I'm transparent." She laughed again, struggling to come up with something feasible. "I was re-living a little disagreement I had with that mom whose daughter wasn't nice to Riley? Remember? And when I confronted her about it, she just kind of blew me off? Well anyway, I saw her tonight and I had an urge to go up to her and stick up for Riley and for myself. I am still pissed I let her off without resolution."

Where did she pull that out of?

Mitchell squinted his eyes in concentration. "Oh yeah, I remember. Wasn't that like a month ago?"

"Yeah, but I guess it still bothers me. I just didn't realize till I saw her."

He snickered. "Well, I bet you told her off good."

Lindsey smacked his arm, then closed her eyes, pinched her lips and furrowed her brow.

"What are you doing now?" he asked, amused.

"I'm telling you off," she said. "And I was good."

"Come here," he said, his voice throaty. His arm pulling her towards him.

"What? What are you doing?" She smiled, happily.

"You look very sexy tonight."

15

He kissed her deeply, leaving her surprised and a little breathless. "We'll continue this later," he said and beeped his car locked. Then without looking back, he followed the kids into the house.

Lindsey stood outside alone for a second to collect her thoughts. The ones about her husband make her smile. The ones about someone else's husband make her uncomfortable. They both got her a bit excited, even though she knew that just like the other night Mitchell was more likely to fall asleep than follow through. That was pretty much the way it worked; a nice kiss, then falling asleep on the couch with his lap top. Still, a gal can dream. Tonight, she was just a little afraid of what that dream might be.

Lindsey spent the week avoiding everyone best she could. No lunches with friends. No chatty walks in the neighborhood. Solitary runs instead of the gym. She needed to be alone; to immerse herself in her life with her family and kids. She ran her errands, did a little shopping and scheduled a hair, nail, facial and a massage appointment. It was excessive but you can't put a price tag on looking and feeling your best. Plus, she needed to keep busy. With too much time to think, her brain traveled down dangerous paths.

When her best friend Ellie finally got her on the phone and started harassing her, she sidestepped any immediate plans; blaming her parents' upcoming move and their need of her assistance. It was partly true. She promised her mom she would clean out her old room, take what she wanted and discard the rest, but she hadn't actually done anything yet. Well today was the day, she thought and headed over.

Her mom greeted her at the door with a kiss and two glasses of Merlot.

"Mom! It's 11am. You're drinking?" She pretended offense but it was no coincidence that red was her mother's favorite color. Even as she chastised, she took the glass her mom extended. There was at least three hours before she needed to get back.

"You are too and you're going to need it. The movers came early this morning. Everything is pretty much gone, except for your room. I didn't touch anything just like you asked. Brace yourself."

Lindsey followed her in and what she saw made her even more appreciative of the wine. She took a long sip.

"Wow."

"Yes," her mom echoed, taking a sip of her own. "Wow."

The house Lindsey grew up in was just a shell. It was cleared out. Empty. Vacant. Nothing but walls and a floor. She walked slowly around taking it all in, unable to find any of her memories hiding here. Where was the dresser she banged her eye on at two years-old and had to get stitches because she was being chased by her brother, Liam? Where was the couch she first made out with Danny, the captain of the baseball team? Where was the table she and nana made her famous chocolate chip cookies on every year? Where was their shrine to Liam who died when she was fifteen?

Lindsey slowly took it in and took another sip to soften the blow. This was no longer her home. It was just a house. She may have been forty two years-old, but she wanted to cry.

"Honey it's okay," her mom said, and put an warm arm around her. "This house will always be a part of us, whether we are here or not. Just like your dad and I will always be a part of you, whether we're here or not."

Lindsey almost snorted the wine she sipped out of her nose. "Mom!" She scolded. "Was that supposed to make me feel better? Hey, we'll soon be dead, but don't worry, that'll be fine too."

Her mom laughed. "First of all, I was talking about our move to Florida. You made us dead. And second of all, it worked. You're laughing."

She smiled. "Sorry about killing you off."

Her mom shrugged. "It's okay, I've already taken you out of the will."

"Very funny."

"Well see..." she said with a sly grin, and lead Lindsey to her old room. "Now go on. You really need to get to work. You're lucky that the new buyers aren't set to move in till the end of next month."

Lindsey nodded and took another gulp to drown her emotions. "When are you guys leaving?"

"Two weeks, honey. But don't worry. Florida is not so far away."

"Seems like a whole other planet," she whined. With her mom, she became a little girl again.

"Nope. Just another state. You never were any good at geography." She made an over-exaggerated, disappointing sigh. "Now take a big gulp, stop procrastinating and get to work."

Walking in her childhood bedroom was a throwback in time, a museum to her youth. It still looked like a fifteen year-old girl, albeit one heavily influenced by eighties pop culture, lived there. Pez dispensers lined a shelf; posters of Scott Baio, John Stamos and Duran Duran covered one wall. She was embarrassed to admit that she had a Menudo calendar over her desk surrounded by a self-made collage of her high school friends and boyfriends, cut-outs from magazines like Teen Beat and Cosmopolitan mixed together with scratch and sniff stickers that had been sniffed out decades ago.

Open any drawer and she never knew what she might find – an old note from her H.S. BFF telling her that Nicky N thought she was cute, an old favorite earring whose partner she lost at a backyard party where she got drunk off wine coolers, a Sony Walkman with a Prince cassette tape inside, an ankle bracelet that she wore as a necklace from Danny who she dated for most of ninth grade, blue mascara that should have been tossed decades ago, her favorite old roller skates with the rainbow laces, a picture of her and Ellie wearing matching fringed half-shirts at camp, trophies from her tennis team days... There were so many good memories here that she re-lived every time she saw them.

Lindsey had been somewhat of a tennis phenom early on, playing on the Varsity H.S. team since she was a freshman. She and her brother Liam took lessons together when they were young and all through growing up were each other's best partners and competitors.

He was two years older and could kick her ass, but every so often, she could kick his right back, which she never tired of reminding him. When he died, tennis died with him, although Lindsey didn't actually quit the team. She played varsity throughout high school, enough to get a scholarship to the University of Virginia, but even though her talent was intact, the intensity and edge were gone.

She also harbored dreams back then of being a doctor, but those dreams changed as well because of Liam. On top of everything else, apparently she had a commitment problem. Could she blame that on her dead brother too?

Not that things hadn't turned out well for this girl, she thought. She had a successful, caring, good husband who kept her secure and happy. They had two beautiful, reasonably well-adjusted children. She had satisfying creative work as a freelance producer that she now did on her own terms. Health. Friends. Money.

A major crush on her friend's husband. Yeah, there was that.

An hour later, her mom knocked on the door and entered. She found Lindsey lying back on her bed. She was fantasizing about John, much in the same way she did twenty-five years ago with any number of cute boys who grabbed her eye.

"Oh, so did you enjoy your nap? Looks like you got a lot accomplished." Her mom was the queen of sarcasm, although her friend Ellie could give her a run for her crown.

Her mother's intrusion in her old bedroom was the perfect culmination to her time travel back to the 80's. All of a sudden, Lindsey craved a Hot Pocket or a Pizza Roll, not that she would eat anything like that ever again. "I'm hungry," she replied, sitting up. "Let's get something to eat and I'll come back this weekend."

"Fine," her mother said. "But you'll have to drive. I almost finished the bottle while you were busy not working." Then, she sighed dramatically and shook her head. "I can't believe what you teenagers will do to keep from cleaning up your room."

Lindsey smiled. She really loved her mom.

Lindsey pulled up to her house with 15 minutes to spare before the bus, just enough time to respond to a few emails. Her time with her mom had improved her mood. She felt lighter, like the movers had come and cleared out her brain as well. There was nothing but a few sales promotions and school calendar alerts. She decided do a quick check on Facebook. The screen filled with usual pictures of friends, friends of friends, friends who used to be friends and friends who she would never in a million years call a friend. She scrolled through some interesting essays from bloggers she liked and hoped to read later, some political stuff, a few recipes, pictures of families doing the apple picking thing, a funny 'dogs hugging kittens' video, and a new post on the Secrets of the Shore page. Goody, she thought and immediately clicked to read.

Hello my pretties, especially you gorgeous single or divorced ladies. Word on the street is there may be a hot new addition entering your arena. Yup, another marriage bites the dust. Or at the very least, is choking on it right now. And this one's a shocker. Look left, look right ladies, is it your husband who's sitting there on the fence gazing over at greener pastures? Of course if he is, good riddance, right?

Oh man. Lindsay gaped, sipping her coffee and rereading the gossip when she heard a light rap on the side panel window of her front door.

The minute she heard the knock, she wished she had closed the door instead of leaving it open in anticipation for the soon to arrive bus. First, because it was a bad habit that drove Mitchell nuts, and second because unless it was a friend who would most likely knock, call out and walk in at the same time, it could only be one of three things... a college kid with an earnest smile and some save the world cause, a Jehovah's Witness with a save her soul cause or city kids who came around the neighborhood quarterly selling cheap candy to raise money for a supposed basketball trip. She hated to be so cynical, but was always a bit affronted that these kids came into her neighborhood by bus to solicit money.

"Coming," she called out, got up from her chair and walked toward the open door.

Or, it could be John.

He stood there, hands in his pockets, a closed off expression but with a faint, tentative smile on his lips. His dark green Jeep 4x4 was parked out front. It was a truck that Porsche driving Mitchell often remarked upon with some wistfulness. Apparently, the car is always greener on the other driveway as well.

Taken aback, she stopped briefly before reaching the door, feeling the weight disappear from her body leaving just a jumble of raw nerves and a clump of tumbleweed in her throat. Somehow she breathed, collected herself and found the strength to move forward. "Hi," she said, pushing the screen open, trying to sound casual and keep the stress out of her voice. "What's up?"

It was far from the first time he had been to her house. In fact, it was a pretty common occurrence since he lived only a few blocks away. Often, he walked by with the kids and hung out while they played. There were also countless other times when he came by to drop something off or to pick up something from one of her kids for school. His schedule was the more flexible between him and Jeanie, so he wound up picking up a lot of the parenting slack.

Something hit her, an unlikely yet possible reason for his visit. "Oh, you know what? Trevor left one of his Wii games here the other day. Let me get it for you." The words rushed out of her, high and fast, so different from their usual easy way. Normally, he would have been in the house already chatting about whatever it was, but normally was not normal anymore.

He shook his head. "No, don't worry about it."

"Okay." Her voice trailed off and disappeared. He was making her very uncomfortable just standing at her door like this. It seemed like he wanted to say something, but apparently the guy she spent years conversing easily with had stopped talking to her.

"Listen, I just wanted to say that I'm sorry about the other night, about what I said. I was completely out of line."

She didn't respond. She didn't know what to say.

"Anyway, can we please try to forget it?"

"Sure," Lindsey said, knowing full well that wasn't going to happen. "No problem. It's forgotten."

There was nothing and everything to say and they stood for a couple of seconds saying it in the awkward silence.

"Well, okay." He smiled bashfully. "So, I guess I'll take that Wii game since I'm here. Trevor did mention it." He finally looked directly at her, his blue eyes sparkling with mirth, kind of like his old self.

"Of course. Come in for a sec. I'll get it."

The minute he reached for the door, Lindsey knew it was a mistake. His hand briefly touched hers causing small fireworks to quietly explode in her body, and when he stepped in, his proximity to her was close. Too close. His scent invaded her senses immediately. He must have felt it as well, because he frowned and instantly took a step back. "Sorry," he mumbled, and they were right where they started.

"Let me get that game," Lindsey stammered. "I think it's in the basement. Just give me a second." She hurried away, trying to breathe, trying to collect herself, trying to figure out what the hell was going on.

Downstairs, she located the game on the floor mixed with a bunch of others. Cursing and full of jitters, she almost tripped over the mess and broke all the games, but caught herself by grabbing the wall for support. Taking a minute to exhale, she finally retrieved the game but when she got to the base of the stairs, John was coming down.

"I got it," she said weakly as he moved toward her. She backed away slowly, until she hit up against a wall. He was so close. She could feel the heat from his body surrounding her. Her senses heightened, rushing through her, making her skin electric. "You have to go," she choked out, but couldn't move. Her body was melting from the brain down.

"I know," he said and moved closer.

It was too much. She was lost. His face was close to hers, his smell intoxicating, his desire overwhelming. She wanted him to kiss her.

Hard. She wanted him to push her back against the wall and press his body to hers. She wanted him, more than she wanted anything, she wanted him.

Closing her eyes, she felt faint and dizzy with the kind of desperate need that she hadn't felt in so long, possibly ever. It was how she imagined heroin to feel.

"John," she pleaded. "You have to go." But she said it so weakly, it was pathetic.

"I know," he agreed hoarsely, sounding pained. He didn't move any closer, but he didn't move away either. The air was thick with tense, unthinkable passion. It took all her strength not to take that tiny step toward him; to reach her hand up and touch his chiseled face. "Well," he whispered heatedly, his mouth inches from hers, turned up a little on the sides into a sly grin. "That didn't work at all."

She wanted to smile back, to be cool and funny, but her brain was still under the influence and unable to function. Finally, she looked up tentatively in his eyes and said quietly, "No. Not at all."

They stood there, assessing each other for a moment. His face was lined a bit and sharp, not severely, but enough to make him seem a little bit cowboy. His sandy brown hair hung a little too long, in need of a cut. His eyes captivated her. They were so blue and expressive; tenderness, pain, desire, a little amusement. They held her, and their connection once again started releasing natural drugs into her body. She was on a serotonin rush, reeling in the tangible electricity between them. His hand reached up and gently touched her hair. Somewhere distant in her brain, a voice started screaming, this is wrong! Stop! You can't do this! But she didn't want to listen. She didn't want to listen at all.

But then there were real voices screaming, her children fresh off the bus from school. She heard the door slam and immediately stepped to the side, the spell broken. "Well, here's your game," she said softly.

He followed her up. At the top of the stairs, she found a green knapsack dropped on the floor. Liam's. And sneakers, which had apparently been kicked off at the moment of entrance, lying in opposite corners of the room. Also Liam's. And in true Liam form, he had gone right for his mini iPad and was already lazed out on the couch, playing some game.

In contrast, Riley, ever the perfect child, had placed her shoes neatly by the door, hung up her hoodie and was busy in the kitchen going through her homework folder.

"Hey guys," Lindsey called out. "I'll be right with you." Of course neither responded.

When she turned, John was already at the door so she followed him out.

"I'm sorry I came by," he said. "I knew it probably wasn't a good idea." He grew quiet. "I thought maybe I could, I don't know, apologize and move on, but I was deluding myself."

All of a sudden, it was all too much for her. Whether it was the kids being home or the fresh air smacking her in the face, she needed to get away from him.

"You need to go," she said, sounding hard and very unlike herself. He nodded his head in resigned acceptance. Lindsey didn't allow herself a second to think. She caught a brief glimpse of his miserable expression as she quickly shut the door in his face.

CHAPTER 3

"There are only the pursued, the pursing, the busy and the tired."
— *F. Scott Fitzgerald*

"What are you smiling about, you freak?" Lindsey threw down her trendy Tory Burch tote that cost more than Ellie's whole outfit combined and slid into the booth across from her.

Ellie closed out her screen and put her phone down. "I was having a fabulous conversation with my virtual friends who are never fifteen minutes late. They are always there for me."

"Oh, ha ha."

"What? Did you just get your hair done?" Ellie asked. "It looks great. It kind of has a beachy wave thing going on."

"Uh no," Lindsey answered distractedly, busy with her bling covered phone.

"So what's with the secret meeting? What's going on?"

Lindsey had called Ellie because she needed her as a confidant but now sitting across from her, she could barely meet her eye.

"Are you blushing?" Ellie asked incredulously and Lindsey felt her scrutinizing which only made her blush deeper. "Lindsey," Ellie reprimanded. "What is going on here? As your best friend, I demand to know." She looked good, Ellie thought. Not just her healthy, glowing complexion and shiny auburn hair. Her brown eyes seemed brighter, lit with some inner excitement. All of a sudden, it hit her. "Oh my God! Lins! Are you pregnant?" She kind of shouted it.

"Shh!" Lindsey laughed and immediately looked around. It was still early and there was only a smattering of people. Still, it was a small town and people lurked unseen behind menus, in back booths and in bathrooms. Everyone knew someone and ears and mouths traveled. "No! I am not pregnant!"

Ellie eyed her suspiciously, especially her boobs. "I don't believe you."

"Come on. Liam and Riley are more than enough kids for me. Besides, I'm too old." She caught herself and quickly amended. "What? I'm talking about me. You're like a baby."

Ellie gave her a mildly annoyed look. Lindsey was a whole four months older than she was, and while forty-two wasn't exactly a spring chicken, it wasn't a dead chicken either. She still didn't believe her. She was definitely hiding something. "Order a drink."

Lindsey's eyes opened wide with amusement. "It's freaking noon on a Wednesday!"

"Come on, order a drink," Ellie challenged. "Then I'll believe you."

Lindsey rolled her eyes. "You know what? I could use a drink anyway. But you have to drink too."

"Why not?" Ellie agreed. "Let's be those ladies who lunch today. Besides, Conner was driving me crazy this morning. He was like a baby possessed. Poop coming out one end, spit-up coming out the other. Disgusting."

"Hey, you wanted that poop and spit-up!" Lindsey pointed out.

"Oh, you don't have to tell me. I live for it. I live for his poop and spit-up."

They laughed. Ellie's unnatural journey into motherhood was finally okay to joke about. After ten years, three miscarriages and two failed IVF attempts, she and her husband Benny finally adopted a baby boy eleven months ago. Conner. The day he was put into her arms at the overripe age of forty-one was the day she was finally delivered.

Immediately, Ellie switched from a well-paid, in-house attorney for Gerber Baby Food – an irony that was not amusing – to doing part time closings, small estate matters and essentially mind-numbing work that she was completely over-qualified for and underpaid to boot. It didn't matter, though. Benny was well compensated for his amazingly anal accounting skills and she got the real benefit of being more available to her beautiful, pooping, drooling baby boy.

The waitress arrived and they ordered Sauvignon Blancs and two sushi lunch specials; two rolls, shumai and double salad. Normally, she would pass on the shumai, but today felt like a day to be a little wild.

The waitress dropped off a complimentary bowl of edamame along with their wine and they clinked their overfull, underpriced glasses as they each pulled a salty pod from the bowl to pick on.

"So, do you really think I'd pick sushi for lunch if I were pregnant?"

"Oh yeah, I forgot about that." Ellie shrugged absently, sucking a bean out from her edamame. "So, what's with all the secret spy stuff? What's the big news? What's on the down low? What's the 10-4?" She was trying to come up with another clever – okay, not so much clever as annoying – way to ask what the scoop was, when Lindsey leaned closer and revealed in a hushed, serious tone.

"I'm thinking about having an affair."

Ellie almost choked on her bean, and it took a good minute to try to swallow it down; her eyes tearing as she coughed, while Lindsey frantically waved the waitress over for a glass of water.

Once she cleared her throat and collected herself, she stared at

Lindsey in disbelief. "You're what?!"

Even though the moment was serious, Lindsey gave a half-smile filled with the satisfaction of knowing she dropped a bomb that just hit its mark. "If I say it again, do you promise not to choke?"

Ellie nodded but when Lindsey repeated that she was considering an affair, her brain actually did kind of choke a little; lacking any oxygen to help her process the information. "Uh, wow. You actually shocked me here, and that's not easy to do. You could have just told me you were a lesbian and let me off easy."

"I know. I'm sorry. It's just that I had to tell someone. I was dying to share and there is no one I could really tell. Everyone loves Mitchell. You, I trust."

"Hey, I love Mitchell." Ellie pointed out, feigning offense.

"Yes, but you love me more." She batted her lashes comically.

Ellie shook her head. "You're such a dork."

Of course, it was Ellie who she would confide in. She wasn't just another mom who met Lindsey in the burbs. She and Lindsey had history. They went to sleep-away camp together a hundred years back in the late seventies and early eighties, walking round the lake in satin short shorts and half shirts. They started out braiding friendship bracelets next to each other in Arts and Crafts, and years later playing spin the bottle with the CITs behind the tennis courts. Through all the summer and teen-aged drama - and Lindsey was the queen – she and Ellie remained tight; their names set in Sharpie on the wall in the teen lounge - Lindsey and Ellie BFF 4-Eva!

Back then Ellie was Betty to her Veronica; the sweet sidekick, who would cover for Lindsey while she snuck away in her cute Camp Beverly Hills shorts outfit to make-out in the woods with bad boys in cut off shirts and parachute pants. Only she was a redheaded Betty. Lindsey used to say that Ellie blushed so much that it went to her hair, and the reason she had so many freckles was so she could hide herself. Since no one else in Ellie's family shared her coloring or complexion, it seemed as good an explanation as any.

"Lins, I'm totally speechless. I mean, holy shit." She shook her head in disbelief.

"That's all you got?" Lindsey laughed, her eyes bright with delight.

"No! This is huge." Ellie slammed her hands down on table for dramatic effect, accidentally knocking the dish of discarded edamame over, sending sucked over pods flying across the table. For a minute, they giggled uncontrollably like drunken school girls. The situation had clearly gone to their heads.

"Okay. Seriously. Start talking. When did all this happen?" Ellie asked dumbfounded after they calmed down. Words were escaping her, which under the circumstances was pretty disappointing. She never had a married friend who cheated. She had friends who were cheated on, but never one, at least that she knew of, who cheated. It was so... Ellie wished she could say that the first adjective that came to mind was something like, disgusting or horrible, but at the moment all she could come up with was... exciting.

Just like at camp, Ellie was thrilled to be sitting there listening to Lindsey's tale of adultery and deceit. Yes of course it was horrible. Or, it could be for her family, her kids, her husband, even potentially for herself. But at the moment, right there at the telling, Ellie was fascinated. Horrified but fascinated.

Lindsey shrugged cagily. "I don't know. It's complicated," she answered, looking like she wanted to explode; like every lurid, crazy detail was right there on the tip of her dirty tongue waiting for her to ask.

Ellie and Benny had been married for over fourteen years now. Was it exciting? Not so much. But they had been through the ups and downs of life and infertility. Somehow, what they went through didn't pull them apart, although, there were moments, real bad, low moments when she was in such a dark hole, she couldn't imagine anyone willingly suffering with her miserable self. Ultimately, it brought them closer together, and Conner, their miracle baby.

"Who?" was all she could manage as the waitress placed their salads on the table in front of them. They both stopped and silently acknowledged the waitress and food.

"I've got to eat," Lindsey said and stuck her chopsticks into her bowl. "I'm famished."

"Because you've just come from an... extracurricular activity?" Ellie teased.

She blushed again.

"Oh my God! You did?"

"Shh!" Lindsey ordered. "No! I didn't! Stop it!" She shook her head and looked anxiously around again. "You are so loud. This is serious."

"I know," Ellie apologized, noting that the restaurant had filled in a bit since they arrived. There were even two women just walking in whom they sort of knew. She had no idea what their names were, but they waved when they saw them. "I'm sorry. I really didn't say anything." She over-exaggerated her whisper, "But I need some more information. A lot more. And I need it now."

She looked at Lindsey expectantly, waiting with baited breath for her next words; intent on her pink, lightly glossed mouth that had just parted to speak when a hand on her shoulder made her jump.

"Hey girls," greeted a friendly voice.

It was Caren Lucci, a good friend and neighbor of Jeanie and John's, who also lived in Lindsey's five block radius. Lindsey immediately tensed.

"Oh wow." Caren winked. "Looks like I'm interrupting something juicy." She was one second from pulling up a chair.

"Hey Caren," Lindsey said and rose from her seat. "We were just leaving." She motioned to the waitress to wrap their meals.

Ellie immediately followed her lead. "Yeah sorry," she said, "But we're running late. We'll catch up soon."

Thankfully Caren took the hint. "Okay girls, sounds good. Maybe we can grab Jeanie and all do dinner?"

"That sounds great," Ellie said.

"Absolutely," Lindsey nodded and Caren headed back to her table of friends, who included the two women who recently walked in and waved.

"We definitely shouldn't have this conversation here," Lindsey said, clearly shaken. "How bout we go back to my house?"

"Good idea," Ellie agreed and checked the time. She had an hour more with the babysitter. "Let's go."

Once settled at Lindsey's with their sushi rolls before them, Lindsey tried multiple times to begin but she couldn't seem to start. When she opened her mouth nothing came out, except an embarrassed giggle. They stared at each other expectantly, until finally Ellie couldn't take it anymore.

"Come on already, spill! I am totally, completely floored over here! Seriously, you've killed me. I am dead."

The stalemate broken, Lindsey smirked. "You sure are loud for a dead person."

"I am just shocked."

"I know," she admitted. "I am too."

"So," Ellie asked, with a raised brow. "Who is it?" It was the million dollar question but Lindsey looked away and shook her head. "I'm not going to tell you that, at least not now."

"Come on..." She shined her brightest smile and gave puppy dog eyes to match. Of course she was going to tell her.

"Oh yeah, sure." Lindsey grinned. "I'm helpless to your weird facial powers."

"Come on," Ellie coaxed. "You know you want to."

She shook her head. "I do but I can't."

As far as Ellie knew, Lindsey had never been able to keep anything like this from her. She was the confidant for the Lindsey broken hearts club all through high school and college. But apparently they weren't girls anymore and as Ellie well knew, everyone had their secrets, including her.

"Fine." She was a little hurt and considered pouting, but Lindsey seemed resolute so she had to let it go, at least for now. Instead, Ellie asked a question that bothered her for the whole drive over. "You and Mitchell really seem happy. I mean, I know he's MIA a lot at the hospital. Is that it? Were you lonely?"

Lindsey sighed and looked somewhat distraught. "The truth is we were happy." She corrected herself. "We are happy. Even now. I mean, our relationship is a little on auto pilot and all that, but whose isn't after 12 years? But, I am good with us, even with being on my own a lot. I wasn't expecting this at all. I certainly wasn't looking for it." She paused and considered, "I don't know. Maybe I was. But really, I always thought Mitchell and I were happier than most couples we knew, except of course, you and Benny."

"Of course." She smirked. "Thanks for throwing that in." Great, Ellie thought dismally. They were happy. There was a long pause where they were both lost in their own heads. Ellie was thinking how fragile marriage was. How no relationship was safe, even the happy ones might be doomed. She began to feel a little uncomfortable and popped a piece of her salmon avocado roll in her mouth, even though she no longer had any appetite. She had to do something with herself and there was no reason to waste good food. She would probably wind up eating Lindsey's as well. "So..." she broached tentatively, "do you... do you love this guy?"

Lindsey exhaled deeply. "I don't know. I really don't know. All I know is that I am alive, crazy alive, for the first time in years. It's like I'm driving at 110mph. I know I'm going to crash, but I can't stop. I don't want to stop. I'd rather die than stop and I haven't even started. That's how good it feels."

Ellie slowly chewed her roll, even though it had become mush in her mouth. She had to keep her jaw busy or it would just be hanging open.

CHAPTER 4

"You live longer once you realize that any time spent being unhappy is wasted."
-Ruth E. Renkl

Secrets of the Shore
FB Post

So cats and kittens, I've been thinking a little about adultery and what makes us tick. Here are the reasons I came across in my 'don't quote me on it' research. Reasons men cheat - Boredom. The opportunity presented itself. To prove that he's still got it. His wife let herself go. He feels emotionally unconnected. He doesn't feel supported. To get back at his spouse for cheating.

Now here are the main reasons why women cheat - Feeling underappreciated. Craving intimacy. Feeling bored/lonely. Needing to feel love/passion. He cheated.

So it seems that barring retribution, men are looking for some kind of approval and woman want attention, mostly emotional attention. But really it seems that they are all just looking to be noticed and appreciated, to feel a spark of excitement.

I mean who doesn't want to feel those things, but I guess some people need it more than others. Or maybe to some extent, we're all feeling it but the opportunity doesn't present itself. What if you were somewhere with no ties and you met someone through work and connected immediately. There was a physical chemistry and you spent the day working together laughing and sharing, while doing some very easy flirting. Your hands touch over papers passed. You share some thoughts about who you are and who you hope to be. After hours, there is a very real attraction and a nice level of intimacy between you.

At the end of the 'meeting' you both walk out the door at the same time. You laugh with slight embarrassment but you both are so heavily drawn to each other, and find yourselves in the awkward highly charged position of proximity. Your faces are close. Your bodies are close. You are feeling every emotion at an intensity that you have not felt for fifteen years. You realize you have not felt real desire or felt so attractive and wanted in so long. You want this. You feel desperate for it. No one would know. Except you of course.

Your faces move a little closer. The air around you thickens...

And....?

And... who knows. I certainly don't. You know what they say, wrong place, wrong time in a marriage and wrong things happen. I actually don't know if they say that but I just did!

Just thinking out loud here. Big party tonight!!! Stay tuned.

***

"Babe, you almost ready?" Mitchell called up from downstairs.

"Coming!" Lindsey yelled, put down her phone and took a deep swallow of wine. The latest SOS post touched a nerve, making her even more antsy than she already was. She had been ready for an hour but then changed her outfit four times only to come back around to her original choice. Lesson learned. Go with your gut. Unless your gut is in upheaval, she thought.

In front of her full length mirror, she berated herself for not finding an excuse to give to John and Jeanie to avoid carpooling to

Diane's party together, but it was too late now. For the hundredth time, she gave herself the once over and officially declared herself ready as she'd ever be. The phone rang and distractedly she reached for it.

"Hello?"

A familiar woman's voice responded, but Lindsey couldn't immediately place her. "Can I speak with Mitchell?" The woman asked, sounding crisp and professional. At the same time as she said it, Lindsey realized who she was. "It's Celia from his office."

"Sure, hang on a minute." Why was she calling on a Saturday night? Lindsey wondered in annoyance. The office almost never called the house phone.

She called for Mitchell to pick up the phone. About a minute later a horn honked outside.

"They're here!" Mitchell yelled. "Let's go."

"Coming!" She yelled back, took one last look in the mirror and nodded approvingly. With her hair blown out for the occasion, it looked as shiny and sleek as the off the shoulder silver top she was wearing.

Walking down the staircase, Lindsey had to hold tight to the bannister and go slow. Her nerves were making her as shaky as the impractical stilettos she chose to wear.

Mitchell stopped her mid-way. "Babe, you look amazing. You are definitely the hottest housewife on Long Island." He turned to her number one fan. "Doesn't mommy look great?"

Riley stood next to him, nodding with big eyes. "You do, mommy. You do look fabulous." Lindsey could see her little brain at work. She definitely had to hide her shoes or they might somehow mysteriously disappear from her closet. The little fashion thief.

"What? Only Long Island?" Lindsey laughed and reached her hand out for Mitchell to guide her, as if they were heading down the grand staircase of a formal ball. She probably shouldn't be wearing these shoes.

As if Mitchell read her mind, he said, "You probably shouldn't be wearing those shoes."

"I know. I know. Just help me to the car."

More terrified with each step, she followed Mitchell outside. "Hey," she said, keeping her mind off the car they were seconds from getting into, "what did Celia want?"

"She's in charge of checking the office messages on the weekends and there was a patient who left multiple messages specifically for me even though I'm not on call. I know his case. I'll get back to him from the party."

"Her voice annoys me," Lindsey commented, sliding into the backseat of John and Jeanie's Mercedes.

"Yeah," Mitchell agreed with a laugh, "it annoys me sometimes too."

She wanted to ask why she called the house phone, but the moment her nose breathed in the scent of John's cologne, she forgot everything else. The effect was like doing a shot of vodka. She felt tipsy on impact.

"Hey guys!" Jeanie said, twisting around in her seat to talk to them. "Oh, Lins, you look great."

"So do you." Lindsey returned the compliment, and hoped she didn't sound as nervous as she was.

"So, this should be some party, right?" Jeanie gushed, "I love that it's in her backyard."

"Me too," Lindsey answered, jumping into the conversation with both feet, so thankful for the distraction. She intended to keep up this comfortable girl talk as long as possible. The idea of silence would be unbearable. "So much better than a lounge or club. I'm so over those."

They yammered on a bit and she probably sounded like a vapid idiot, but it kept her from completely suffocating from the situation.

"Hi John," Mitchell finally broke in with a chuckle, but not until they were parking.

"Oh, you're back there?" John responded in good humor.

Then the engine was off, the doors opened and she was outside breathing fresh air. She almost fainted with relief.

Sean and Diane's backyard was naturally impressive, but when they all walked in they were blown away; floating candles lit the infinity pool, Cirque Du Soleil like performers stood on pedestals entertaining the crowds, a sushi chef worked frantically in one corner while Five Guy burgers were being served up in another. Off to the far side of the yard under a white tent, a band rocked Aerosmith's 'Dream on' while guests swayed and danced.

"This is insane," Jeanie remarked as they all stood and gawked at the spectacle and the crowd.

A young man with a top hat walked over and from nowhere produced a small bouquet of red flowers and handed them to Lindsey. "Have a magical evening." He winked and was gone.

"Expect the Unexpected," John said, noting the 'theme'. His nearness and the sound of his voice mixed with a week's worth of fantasy brought color to Lindsey's face. She looked carefully over to him, hoping he wouldn't catch her and when he didn't, she felt keenly disappointed.

"I need a drink," Lindsey announced abruptly, looking around for a place to toss her unwanted bouquet, finally discarding it by the side of the pool.

"There's the bar." Mitchell pointed and they headed toward it. On the way, they bumped into Ellie and Diane. Diane looked exceptionally fabulous in a trendy shapeless shift dress in vibrant blue. Lindsey wondered about the designer, Marc Jacobs, maybe? The girls fawned over her and her party while she feigned humility.

"Oh, stop it," Diane ordered, waving her elegant hands, nails the color of silver; like this whole affair was just another old dress she randomly pulled from the closet. "It was so fun to put together. You know I love this stuff."

While she talked, Lindsey eyeballed Mitchell directing him to continue to the bar, which thankfully he and John did.

"Well, you blew Marnie out of the water," Jeanie said, dropping her voice to a conspiring whisper.

They all smiled but also looked around guiltily. Outwardly comparing one friend's party to another was a no-no. Jeanie never did have a great social filter, but it was no secret that she practically worshiped Diane.

"It is amazing," Ellie complimented, filling in the awkward space. "Is Sean happy? I haven't even seen him to say happy birthday."

"Please." Diane rolled her eyes but was clearly thrilled. "He's got his own cigar bar set up behind Five Guys. I think there's a poker game going as well. He's in heaven."

"There's a cigar bar behind Five Guys and poker?" Mitchell repeated, coming up from behind and handing Lindsey her drink. "Works for me. John?"

"No place I'd rather be," John quipped, and Lindsey cast another furtive glance his way. "Ladies." John gave a gallant nod of the head and Lindsey could imagine the cowboy hat he would have tipped had he been wearing one. Again, he didn't look at her. He looked at everyone, but not her. It was driving her nuts.

With the husbands' disappearance, the ladies mingled and hung out drinking and laughing. Lindsey was trying to have fun, but she kept catching herself scanning the crowd for John. She was anxious and tense, angry at him for ignoring her and angry at herself for caring. She was also somewhat drunk.

On the way to the bathroom, Lindsey's attention was drawn by one of the acrobatic performers; a woman, moving slowly from one position to another. Her body painted in blue and silver clay, she moved like a shape shifter, and Lindsey stood transfixed watching her morph from her backbend position into a ballerina, leg lifted to her head. Lindsey felt stuck there. Or, it might just have been her heels sinking in the grass.

"Hey." His voice came from behind and she immediately felt its impact. She was now lucky her shoes were wedged in the grass or she might have fallen over. John moved next to her and together they watched the woman's slow transformation.

"Hey yourself." She couldn't decide whether she was pissed and why she even would be.

"You okay?" he asked, still looking ahead at the blue woman.

"Not even a little," she answered honestly. She definitely shouldn't speak to him buzzed. That was how they had gotten into this mess in the first place.

"Yeah, me either."

They stood together watching; the unsaid, a charged bubble surrounding them. She was so filled with excitement just standing near him. She wanted to step away, knew she should step away, but instead closed her eyes to let the intensity envelop her. She despised herself, but she loved what she was feeling.

Without the balancing factor of eyes, Lindsey lightly swayed and almost fell into John. He put his arms on her to steady her, and Lindsey's body immediately responded to his touch, burning with such longing, she thought she might combust. Opening her eyes, she looked directly into his. Pure desire. She quickly turned away. She wanted to block him out and for him to kiss her in the worst way. His arms stabilized and weakened her at the same time. She was lost.

After a moment, she braved a look up and found him studying her with care. Instead of shutting him down with a look or word, she steadily held his gaze, feeling the pulsing electricity of their connection. What the hell was she doing? Lindsey finally broke the tension and the eye contact. "Nice party, huh."

"I can't look at you anymore," John said quietly. "At least not with people around."

"And I was angry you were ignoring me," Lindsey admitted with a small self-conscious laugh.

They lapsed into silence again.

"Well, isn't this cozy." Jeanie's sharp tone interrupted and Lindsey quickly snapped to reality.

"Lindsey's had too much to drink." She heard John say from somewhere far away. "You want to stay with her while I find Mitchell?"

And then it was Jeanie's cold hands that were on her, her nails slightly digging into her shoulders as she led her away. "Come on. Let's find a place to sit."

Jeanie sat with Lindsey on a bench, while Lindsey kept her head in her hands, happy for the excuse not to talk or look at her. What was she thinking? What was she doing? Before she could come up with anything, Mitchell was there. And John. Jeanie moved over and Mitchell slid next to her.

"You okay?" Mitchell asked. Lindsey looked up guilty as he smiled down with absolution; a saint, who also seemed to be quite drunk.

"I'm fine," she managed. "I just got a little dizzy there. The shoes didn't help," she added.

"Well, I'm willing to bet you didn't eat much. Sit right here. I'll get you something."

"We'll stay with her," Jeanie announced protectively.

In the time it took for Mitchell to retrieve a bowl of rice and a glass of water, colorful strobe lights started flashing and Persian music piped out from strategically placed speakers. Then from nowhere, half a dozen belly dancers emerged, swinging and gyrating with the crowd and produced a giant birthday cake lit with sparklers which was brought to Sean who good naturedly put out his cigar and appreciated first the gyrating half-naked women and then his wife, whose irritation was only barely perceptible. He blew out the candles, and heartily thanked everyone for coming, before re-lighting his cigar, grabbing his drink and returning to his poker game.

41

"Hey babe," Mitchell asked, "do you mind if I finish the game? Unless you want to leave?" He looked longingly in Sean's direction at a bunch of guys sitting around a card table, smoking cigars, laughing jovially.

"No way am I leaving," Lindsey mustered with enthusiasm. God, I want to go home, she thought. "I'm totally fine. Go," she ushered. "Have fun." Mitchell kissed her breezily on the cheek and bounced off like an eight year-old with a free pass to Disney World. She turned to Jeanie and John. "You guys go on. I'm just going to sit here a minute."

"You sure?" Jeanie asked. "Of course, we'll stay."

"I know." Lindsey smiled. She hoped, somewhat sheepishly. "But I could use a few minutes to regroup. I'll catch up with you in a few."

"Of course, honey. Take all the time you need," Jeanie said reassuringly and turned to her husband. "Come on." It seemed she grabbed John's arm slightly possessively, but Lindsey's perceptions were totally off, so maybe not. Right before they walked away, John caught her eye and they exchanged a brief glance filled with 'who knew what' before Jeanie pulled him to follow. She was better off when he wasn't looking at her.

Alone on the bench, Lindsey slowly breathed in and out, trying to clear her mind and just focus on the steadying rhythm of her inhale and exhale. This was all too much.

"Hey stranger." Ellie's butt gracelessly bumped her. "Scoot over," she ordered. "What's going on?"

Lindsey wanted to tell her. Desperately. When she was younger, her older brother Liam used to taunt her with his little mantra, "Tattle tattle, Lin Lin." It drove her running to her mom in fits of crying tantrums, but it was well deserved. She could never keep a secret. Still, she couldn't mention John to Ellie. She couldn't.

"So?" Ellie prodded. "You're never this quiet. Spill."

"Let's mingle," Lindsey commanded and stood, discarding her water. She needed the movement to distract from this private conversation with Ellie and keep her from talking her head off. "I had a moment," Lindsey offered as explanation, "but now it's passed."

"Uh huh." Elle nodded, completely unconvinced. "Well, I'll accept that for now in this very public place, but I'm on to you. You can't hide from me, sista."

Lindsey pretended she didn't hear her and kept walking till she reached a group of friends to mingle with. There was safety in numbers.

It was close to 2am when they rode home in the back seat of Jeanie and John's car, Lindsey's head resting easily on Mitchell's shoulder. As opposed to the trip coming, Lindsey stayed quiet on the way home, letting Mitchell and John pick up the slack which they did with ease, recalling their apparently heated card game with great amusement. Lindsey closed her eyes and relived every look, touch and scent of John, the untouchable man who was right in front of her.

When they pulled up to Lindsey and Mitchell's house, Lindsey mumbled a goodnight and a thank you but as she reached for the door handle, the car door swung open automatically. John stood before her, his hand extended. She met his eye and waves of longing that she hadn't experienced in so long rushed through her. Quickly she lowered her gaze and smiling shyly accepted his assistance. When she stood, her hand still resting in his, John leaned in and kissed her cheek softly. "Good night," he whispered into her hair and for a moment Lindsey felt young and sexy, like she had just had a fantastic first date and the delicious goodnight kiss was seconds away. Instead, he handed her off to Mitchell.

Stepping carefully, they wobbled towards the house together; Mitchell, because he was drunk on vodka and Lindsey because she was drunk on John and wearing those stupid shoes.

***

The next day was Sunday and Lindsey's parents were coming over to hang out before their big send off to Florida. She had planned on having Mitchell barbeque and making a couple of good side dishes, but the headache Mitchell woke up with immediately put Plan B into action – ordering in Chinese food. Her parents arrived around 4pm and spent some time with the kids; her mom, drawing with Riley and her dad, playing a game of HORSE with Liam and Mitchell outside. The day was beautiful and it was much more relaxing to hang out without the formality and restraints of a restaurant.

Lindsey, her mom and Riley decided to recreate Nana's old cookie recipe in the kitchen for dessert and got busy finding all the ingredients, which surprisingly Lindsey had. It made Lindsey immediately nostalgic and wistful, sitting with her mother and daughter, making her grandmother's cookies. She became even more melancholy when she thought about her mom moving to Florida. It made her so sad for the years gone by. They were all getting older. Her mom was in her late sixties already. She was in her forties. Her kids were growing up. It was all going by too fast.

"I wish we could make these every day," Riley piped in. "This is so fun!"

"I know honey," her grandma agreed. "But that rotten daughter of mine decided to send you kids to school or we could have been the Mrs. Fields of cookies by now. She is such a party pooper!"

Even seeing her grandma regularly and knowing her sense of humor, Riley still looked flummoxed. "Wait!" There was a twinkle in Riley's eye and she looked sideways at her grandma. "You're kidding, right?"

"What do you mean?" She put a hand to her chest and looked horrified. "I would never kid about a rotten daughter."

"You're kidding again!" Riley practically jumped up, almost knocking the flour off the kitchen island.

"Mom!" Lindsey scolded with amusement. "Stop teasing."

"What? And now you're keeping me from getting my feelings out. You're rotten to the core. What did I do to deserve such a rotten daughter?"

"And a rotten granddaughter," Riley happily interjected.

"Yes." Lindsey's mom smiled. "A perfectly rotten granddaughter."

They were interrupted during dinner by the sound of Mitchell's hospital beeper. Today was the start of an on-call week for him. After he called in, unfortunately he had to go, leaving among many hugs and a promise extracted from Lindsey's mother on threat to his life that they would come down to Florida for Thanksgiving break. Then it was grandpa and the kids in the TV room watching a Harry Potter movie and Lindsey and her mom in the kitchen cleaning up.

"What time does your flight leave tomorrow?"

"8:30a.m."

"You'll call me the minute you arrive?"

"Yes, mom," her mom said.

"I can't believe you're going," Lindsey pouted. Her emotions threatened to overwhelm her. She was just so sad that they were leaving, or really that her mom was leaving. She barely spoke with her father.

"Yes, well. We figured we'd wait till you were over forty before we broke the news to you."

"Mom," Lindsey warned, wanting to be stronger, but truly in danger of falling to pieces. She was an adult woman over forty. Why was she such a mess here? It wasn't like they wouldn't see each other. Plenty of retiring parents moved to Florida. They were even coming back for extended summers and staying in a bungalow-type of community in the Hamptons. Really, she was being such a baby.

"Sweetheart. What's going on here?" Her mom's brow furrowed with concern.

"I don't know. I just feel like I need you. And you're leaving me."

"Come on. Sit. I'm going to Florida. Let's not make it a guilt trip." She led Lindsey to the kitchen chairs where they sat down and she patted Lindsey's leg warmly, "I'm not leaving you. I'd never leave you.

Remember? Even when I'm dead."

Lindsey cracked a small smile.

"Now really, what's all this about?"

Lindsey opened her mouth to share. She wanted to tell her what was going on. How lost she felt. How she was toying with adulterous thoughts. Heavy adulterous thoughts. But she knew what her mom would say; what anyone who knew her well would say. That she was doing the same old high school and college bullshit. She had a wonderful husband, a wonderful life and there was something broken in her, something intent on screwing it up, and not being happy.

No, she realized. Her mom would never say that about her. Lindsey would say that about herself. Because it was partly true. Lindsey had always been looking for something else. Or someone else. She was never satisfied. She had amazing boyfriends in high school, even better ones in college; absolutely perfect on paper and in real life. She dated each of them for a couple of years and cheated on them, generally with their replacements. As wonderful as they were, none of them filled the emptiness in her and made her happy enough to forget her dead brother. Or possibly, they did make her happy and she felt guilty. Yep, she was one sick puppy, until she found the right doctor. Mitchell.

Mitchell swooped in with his old money respectability and bad boy rebelliousness. He had a reputation for being quite the player, but she did as well, so he didn't intimidate her. She expected nothing from him but a good time and he gave it to her. They'd ditch proper dinners with the country club crew to drink beers on the golf course. Even though, he was doing his hospital rotations, when they went out he'd always surprise her. Not with the typical wine and dine routine. She had been there for years. No. Mitchell would pick her up on his Harley and they'd ride to a quiet beach. He made her bungee jump. Water raft. Helicopter ski. They laughed and talked endlessly. They were wild without the drama. In fact, they spent hours analyzing how addicted they had both been to drama, excitement and sabotaging relationships, and how easy they were together. And it was good. So good.

But when the kids came along things changed. Life changed. Maybe it was the combination of maturity mixed with the responsibility of taking care of those tiny, needy, terrifying beings, but little by little she lost herself in them. The bike and the all the adventure trips and excitement went on hiatus - and she didn't even mind because the kids were fascinating and she was overwhelmed - and it was good, not great, but really good in a different way than she ever expected. The weeks became months and years. She built a wonderful, typical, enviable life loving her husband and kids, doing a little satisfying work, lunching and gossiping with friends. Until one day she realized that she was just another over forty mom, living in the suburbs who hasn't felt anything deep and thrilling in a long, long time.

What a cliché.

"Uh, what was the question, mom?" Lindsey asked, reemerging from the tornado in her head.

Her mother caressed her hand kindly. "Rotten daughter."

Her parents left an hour later and Lindsey couldn't help herself, she cried. She tried not to, but she felt an overwhelming loss at them leaving. It made no sense. It was irrational, but that seemed to be her state of mind lately. When she finally got a hold of herself, she kept busy getting the kids into bed, which she did with a good amount of efficiency. Then it was 9pm and it was just her, her thoughts and a last glass of Malbec left in the bottle. Her mother was clearly off her game leaving this over, Lindsey thought with affection. Or maybe she left it knowing Lindsey would need it, she realized, and then started to cry again - for her parents' move, for her husband, for herself. She could have cried all night.

CHAPTER 5

The most common age for a woman to have an affair is in her 40's.

She almost expected the knock on the door. In fact she was ready for it. So much so that it took her an extra half hour in the morning after she showered to put on a pair of underwear. She went back and forth between the usual casual cotton briefs from the Gap and a sexier satin and lace number that almost never saw the light of day. It was a near mental breakdown putting on underwear. She was embarrassed by which ones won.

Her mind had been racing non-stop trying to make sense of what she was feeling, to hide it away in the back recesses of her brain. But John wasn't some random person. He was someone close to her, someone she always bonded with, and may have even on a few occasions harbored a harmless fantasy. Not so harmless now, she chided herself.

Something had always been between them, a natural chemistry, but confined by the rules of marriage, friendship and society, they barely acknowledged it existed. Until that moment. And now it was almost totally impossible to pretend.

When she heard the rap at the door, she swallowed the lump in her throat, and walked awkwardly, like a remote controlled robot to answer it.

"Hey," John said, the picture of cool control, from his hands in his pockets to his casual, direct gaze. "Can I come in?"

"Sure," she heard herself say quietly with a shaky voice.

He walked in and pushed the door closed behind him. They stood in the entranceway wrapped in the tension between them. Neither of them moved. It was almost impossible; the air was so thick with anticipation.

Time stopped and they stood looking at each other, feeling the electricity around them. John's blue eyes focused on her with such concentration and tenderness, she felt embarrassed and couldn't hold his gaze. He took a small step forward and his face was so near hers that the air left her body and was replaced with water, rushing water. Again, she was melting.

He didn't touch her, but she desperately wanted him to. Instead, he took another small step closer, deleting almost any space between them. His body lined up with hers, his face inches from her. Her heart raced. She felt faint, desperately needing to feel him on her, to touch him, to be touched by him, yet simultaneously terrified.

All the thoughts she originally had running through her head had run away. Slowly he tilted his head and lifted her chin to meet his lips. Lindsey submitted fully, wanting, waiting, but he denied her the pleasure, choosing instead to lightly and gently kiss her cheek, first one and then the other. He took his time, nuzzling her neck, and her hair, nibbling her ear a bit before he whispered, "I'm sorry."

She heard his words, but the only thing that registered was his hot breath on her ear; the burn in her belly spreading downward. She was spinning in her own desire. His hands cupped her face as his lips moved with deliberate slowness closer to her mouth. "I'm sorry," he whispered again and touched his lips to hers. She ached with such need that when his mouth finally found hers and he pushed his body against her, she closed her eyes and lost herself to sensations so strong her legs almost gave out beneath her.

Those were the two minutes when her brain and body lived in

an alternate universe, one where she lived for her own desire, one where she wasn't married. Then she remembered she was and once the thought was back in her brain, she couldn't expel it. "John, stop," she sighed softly through his kisses.

He pulled back a little and studied her closely. His blue eyes filled with concern. Then, without saying anything, he leaned in again for one more, tender, hungry kiss, which she greedily accepted. His arm wrapped round her waist, drawing her more tightly against him and his mouth grew harder, more insistent. Lindsey pulled at him, wanting no distance between them, wanting to breathe his breath and touch every part of him.

Suddenly he stopped. "Okay." He obeyed and stepped aside, giving Lindsey her space which she completely forgot she had wanted.

She took a deep breath or two to steady herself. It was like when she was ten years-old at the dentist, having a cavity filled and they gave her the sweet air. She remembered spinning around in her own head, vivid colors mesmerizing her. Flying. She would fly. Then, ultimately, the dentist would finish up and change the sweet air back to regular air and after a few deep breaths, she returned to Earth. That was what she was doing now, returning to Earth.

"I need a minute," she managed, trying to grasp what had actually just transpired with her eager consent.

"Come," John said and led her to the couch in her living room. "Let's talk."

They sat down and strangely, even at this precipice of a moment, Lindsey couldn't help but notice Liam's dirty socks sitting on the floor. Could that kid pick up anything himself? She wondered. Then she saw Mitchell's slippers and was brought back to reality. She put her head in her hands.

"I know this is crazy," John soothed. "But once it was out there, I couldn't think of anything else. I found myself taking runs by your house. I drove out of the way just to take the route down your block. Even as I was trying to convince myself to bury my feelings and keep pretending, I knew I couldn't."

Lindsey nodded. "I know. I tried too." Not hard enough, said the voice in her head, but she ignored it. "John, this is bad. Really bad."

His eyes flickered a little. Hurt? "Not so bad," he said and placed his strong hand gently on her face.

She was immediately drawn to him. The blood draining from her brain and rushing to other areas. John moved closer and their lips touched again. Was she doing this? Was she really doing this? Lindsey opened her eyes and looked directly into his. They stayed rapt in each other's reflection, silently contemplating the huge implications of their actions and of their need. Never taking his eyes off her, he lightly kissed her lips, moved down to her chin and her neck and the skin revealed between the open buttons of her top. She closed her eyes and allowed herself to be swept away by desire.

She knew this was going to happen, had decided it much earlier with a choice as benign as underwear. She didn't want to think about consequences or her husband or any of it and brought his mouth back to hers to keep herself from talking.

His tongue tasted like cinnamon. His scent invaded her. Their kisses grew deeper, more hungry, and left nothing unsaid. His hand moved to her breast which was practically bursting to be released to his touch. Then his mouth moved down too, ravenously kissing, nibbling her over her clothes. She ripped at the top buttons of her shirt and pushed herself into his mouth. When the cool air touched her breast, fresh from the warmth and wetness of his mouth, she gasped and pulled his entire body down onto her.

She was an unstoppable animal in heat. She cared about nothing, not Mitchell, not herself, not her marriage, not her whole life. Not the goddamn socks on the floor, or the slippers next to them. There was nothing but this minute, this man and this desperate need that she had never felt before.

She reached for the zipper of his jeans, but his hand stopped her and she felt angry, like a child who had been denied the cookie put out before him.

"Lins," he said, panting. "Are you sure?"

She put her mouth on his to stifle him, kissing him hard, desperately, and in answer, unzipped his jeans and pulled out what she wanted. There would be no stopping her now. He groaned as she stroked him and drew him to her, happy she wore her tennis skirt, which slid easily down. When he entered her, they were already so far gone. She arched her back and his cries of pleasure matched her own. They came together almost instantly, her body contracting with such force, riding wave after wave of intense desire fulfilled.

"Holy shit," John muttered, when they could breathe.

"What?" Lindsey asked with concern, all of a sudden feeling insecure and strangely worried that he was having second thoughts. "Are you okay?"

He looked at her with an amused expression and a raised brow. "Yes, I'm okay." He laughed. "I meant holy shit that was the best fucking thing I have ever done in my whole fucking life." He grinned wide and kissed her long and hard and happy. "Thank you."

"Thank you?" she asked, playfully, "Like I've just given you a gift?"

"Yes," he said, grabbing her hand and instantly serious. "I was dead and you brought me back to life."

Lindsey nodded thoughtfully. "Well, you're welcome. I guess since I saved your life you're now forever indebted to me, huh?"

She was teasing, but he was still serious. He grabbed her hand and kissed it. "I have been yours since the day we met."

She almost faltered at that, unsure if he was kidding or not. A rising unclear apprehension caused her to pull back a little, but then he started kissing her again slowly and it just dissolved into a puddle from the heat.

***

General functioning had become a challenge. She screwed up the kids' lunches, giving Riley, Liam's turkey sandwich and Liam, Riley's cream cheese and jelly. They missed the morning bus for the first time ever and she completely forgot to show up at the Art Room on the day she volunteered to help out with the kids' fourth grade project, making a mural dedicated to bully prevention. She was a distracted mess; half the time giddy with excitement, relieving every moment of her encounter with John, and the other half of the time beating the shit out of herself for it.

Thankfully or not, she actually had work to get done this week and was spending the day at an animation house in the East Village producing a commercial for Skittles candy. She had copy, an approved voice over, footage of the product and still photography. She had worked with this team before and liked them. It was the second spot in a campaign that was roundly approved both by the client and focus groups, which made it even more approved by the client. It was pretty seamless and fun and the spot was total eye candy. Plus, there was lots of real candy.

It had been three days since John. Three days since she lost herself in his scent, his hard body and intense need. Three days and nights filled with fantasy, putting her right back at that afternoon.

She felt guilty. She did. She was struggling with the guilt and the excitement and having a hard time being honest with herself about either. She wanted to believe she was guiltier over Mitchell than she was excited over John, but she didn't know if that was true.

She knew she didn't want to lose Mitchell. They had it all and they had it good. Her brain wouldn't even go there or acknowledge it as a possibility. It was like what was going on with John was completely separate from her real life. Clearly, she was a master of denial. And she wasn't feeling nearly guilty enough.

They took a last look at the final Skittles edit and she and the team declared it a winner. Now all Lindsey needed to do was wait for a few copies of the cut for herself and the client.

She was heading straight home to get a few things done before school let out; mainly take a quick shower and freshen herself up. Her kids were actually set to have a play date over at John's house. Not of her doing or John's. Jeanie had called the day before – which, she of course, could not bring herself to answer, but when she heard her message asking for a play date with the kids, she texted back her okay. She couldn't ignore the irony of Jeanie creating a meeting for them when she had spent the last few days obsessing about when and where she would see him again.

John worked erratic hours, often leaving the house by 5am. Most days he was home by bus time for the kids, but often he was not. They employed a nanny named Ronnie, a nursery school teacher who worked a few hours each day from 3p.m.-6p.m. just in case John didn't make it home in time or had work to do.

Lindsey was dropping the kids with the sitter for an hour and a half after school. She tried hard not to get ahead of herself, but she fantasized about John opening the door, somehow maneuvering all the kids down into the basement with the caretaker and them running upstairs for a totally different kind of play date. The thought of going to his house and seeing him, filled her with excitement. She could barely stand still.

"Ate a little too much sugar?" One of the animators commented, handing her the copies.

"I guess so." She gave a small grin and gathered her folders to leave. "What can I say? I can't say no."

"It's a problem for us all," he commiserated, and lovingly rubbed his ample belly.

"You have no idea," she responded.

"Well, you hide it well." He nodded, giving her an approving man appraisal.

"That's what I'm counting on." She laughed and exited the room.

Traffic on the LIE was light and she got home pretty quick. The combination of sugar mixed with the expectation of seeing John filled her with jittery nerves, and she fussed with herself to pass the time while waiting for the bus. After a while, she ran out of hairs to tweeze, body parts to moisturize and things on her face to pick at. She wasted some time at the computer, checking emails and playing on Facebook where she found a new SOS post about Diane's party. She quickly read through it.

Without any further ado, the party rundown. Cirque du Soleil under the stars. Five Guys, sushi and designer clad housewives dancing dirty. A smashing success with so many smashed guests. Highlights included, an end of the evening impromptu pool party started by a statuesque blonde giving an 'accidental' push to her ex-husband, a certain Housewife downing white wines and frantically searching for someone who was definitely not her husband, and a prominent doctor engaging in so much PDA he made half the party sick.

And of course, my top three fashion disaster sightings from that evening –

The nude colored body hugging dress. Terrible. Yeah, I'm putting a ban on the entire color. It's not attractive people. At best, you look naked. At worst, you look fat and naked.

The body stocking dress made for a 12 year old. If you're going to show off the boobs, do not show off the vagina. Unless you're on a pole, choose only one of your private areas to go public.

The 'Seriously? Did she think that was flattering?' Outfit. Loud prints on the bottom and the top make you look like ugly wallpaper.

I just call it like I see it. And an embarrassing shout out to many, you know who you are (wait, you actually probably don't) but - please get a bra that fits ladies, double boobs, uni-boob, belly-button boobs – not attractive. Honestly, just cause y'all have money doesn't mean you have style. You're welcome.

Even distracted, the post got a smile. She knew exactly who was wearing all those outfits. Afterwards, she went through the mail and picked up a few things around the house. She walked from room to room wondering why she was there. By the time Liam and Riley walked in, Lindsey's ants in her pants were also up her shirt. She was on the edge of her seat. There was nothing left to do but to drive her kids crazy. She hovered over them annoyingly, helping with their homework and passing out snacks, ushering them back into their shoes and practically pushing them out the door. "Let's go. Let's go. Let's go."

"Sheesh, mom!" Liam exclaimed, "What's the rush?"

That stopped her. "I'm sorry sweetie," she apologized. "I was caught in my own head. Work stuff. You know sometimes when I'm there part of the day, I'm in a different mode and then when I come home, I forget to switch back from work me to mom me. Do you get that?" She looked into his confused eyes in earnest.

He looked back like she was from another planet, "Sure, mom. Whatever. I'm ready."

"Me too!" Riley sang, dancing her way over, holding her art portfolio. "I'm going to show Elliot my work. He's a good artist too."

"I think that's a great idea, honey." She smiled at her with affection. "And Liam? I picked this up for you this morning." Lindsey reached into her bag and handed him the new Madden game for X-box.

"Whoa! Mom! You're the best!!" Liam grabbed the game and studied the back. "I can't wait to play Trevor! This is so cool!"

"And?" She hinted, searching.

"And....?" Liam repeated, searching as well. "I love you?"

"That's good. But how about, thank you."

"Thank you!" Liam gushed and gave her a giant hug that almost lifted her off the ground. Her little boy wasn't so little anymore, she thought wistfully then frowned for a second remembering the last thank you she received from John, but then guiltily smiled at the memory. She was completely conflicted. She must look like a lunatic. Good thing children live in their own world and barely notice their parents except on a need to need basis.

"Let's go!" Liam ordered. Apparently, now he was ready.

"Uh mom?" There was the tug on Lindsey's shirt that she had been waiting for.

"Yes, honey?" she asked, playing innocent.

"How come Liam gets a present for no reason and I don't?"

"Well, it's not for no reason. Liam was a great, supportive teammate on his last soccer match. Plus, for the last few nights he has been doing his reading before bed without me even reminding him."

"Oh," Riley said, deep in thought. Lindsey could see the wheels of her brain turning. "But Mommy, I always read before bed without you telling me."

Always so beautifully reasonable and sincere, Lindsey reflected with pride. "I know," she agreed and pulled another box from her bag.

"Sparkly colored pencils!" Riley squealed and Lindsey loved her for it. She was so good and easy to please.

They bounded out the door, little puppies with their bones. As she locked up, she worried about her intentions with those unexpected treats. What had prompted her to make today the day she doled out gifts? She shook her head like a wet dog trying to remove the excess heaviness from its fur and like that the thought disappeared.

It took two minutes to get to John's house, five short blocks over. It took less than ten seconds for the hives to start forming.

"Hey," Lindsey called out to the open house when knocking received no attention. "Hello?" She looked back questioningly at Riley and Liam, who shrugged. Then they heard them, or more accurately heard what sounded like a circus of children instead of two boys and a tired, but indulgently smiling woman.

Liam and Riley ran in front of her into the house where they practically knocked into Trevor and Elliot to show off their new goods. Within seconds and without a backward glance, they all raced off to play.

"Thank you for coming!" Ronnie, the babysitter grinned. "Those kids were wearing me out."

Lindsey nodded cordially, still standing in the hallway looking expectantly around. "I know," she said, stalling, waiting for John to walk into the room. "Who would have thought adding kids would make life easier, but it does."

"Sure does," the nanny agreed.

They stood there awkwardly for a beat, while Ronnie waited for her to leave.

Not one for small talk or uncomfortable pauses, Ronnie took control and ended their longest conversation to date. "Okay then, so you'll be back in about an hour and a half?"

Lindsey nodded. "Yeah, that's perfect."

"We'll see you then." She started walking toward Lindsey, forcing her to move toward the door. And that was goodbye.

Lindsey stood outside feeling she don't know what. Rejected. Stupid. Annoyed. Disappointed. Pissed.

That was it. She was pissed. Of course, she shouldn't be. Really, seeing John in his house with all the kids was totally inappropriate. She knew that. She did. But she couldn't help what she was feeling, which was like a teenaged girl just ditched for prom.

She walked back to her car and sat for a few minutes trying to figure out what to do, wanting to cry for what she had gotten herself into. Was she really using her children as a means to see a man who wasn't her husband? The whole thing was horrible and a huge mistake. This was a sign, she thought.

She should go home, but she didn't feel like it. Out of the corner of her eye, Lindsey noticed Caren Lucci power walking down the block coming her way. Immediately she started the engine. She wasn't interested in having a conversation with chatty Caren or anyone. She made a snap decision to drive the fifteen minutes to her parents' place, and pulled away from the curb just as Caren reached her house two doors down from John's.

Taking the key from under the mat, Lindsey unlocked the door. It was so strange to walk into her old house without anything in it; to hear the clip clap of her feet echoing loudly on the wood floor. "Hello?" She called out and heard a smaller version of her voice respond. Lost and alone with no one to guide her, she put her face in her hands and cried.

The floor creaked with the sound of feet approaching but before Lindsey could turn he was behind her, his hands feeling up and down her body, his lips on her neck. She fell back into him, her heart thumping hard, anxiously, as his hand found its way up her skirt and slid into her underwear, while his other hand kneaded her breast. She was locked to him, helplessly restrained.

She tilted her head back against his neck and inhaled his intoxicating smell. She tried to turn, to move. She wanted to see him, to touch him, to feel him on her mouth, but he pulled her more tightly against him and wouldn't let her. His hands and lips worked her from behind until she could take no more. "Please," she begged. "I want to feel you."

He squeezed her nipple. "You will," he whispered huskily in her ear as he played. "You will feel every inch of me." She came hard, wanting more, wanting so much more.

When he finally released her, she turned to look at him. "Hi," she said shyly, a little embarrassed by their new dynamic. Was this the same man she chatted with at the soccer fields recently about the Common Core and fifth grade bullies?

"Hi," he repeated, his intense blue eyes on her.

He kissed her mouth greedily, biting and toying with her bottom lip. She tasted his tongue and returned his kiss with fervor, biting his lip right back. He groaned with pleasure, pushed her back against the wall and pulled her tee-shirt over her head as she pulled off his. When their naked skin touched it singed her senses, making every nerve burn with need. She wanted to pull him as far into her as possible, but he pulled back.

"What?" she asked, breathless for his mouth to make her more breathless.

"I want to look at you."

Oh. She immediately felt embarrassed. She hadn't been scrutinized by a man in well over a decade and she squirmed under his gaze, holding in her stomach a bit, putting a self-conscious hand over her C-section scar which he gently pushed away. Finally, he dropped to

59

the floor and put his mouth on her stomach, sliding down her skirt at the same time. "You're so beautiful." He sighed, pressing his face to her belly.

She pushed her fingers through his hair as he kissed down her stomach and continued the sensual assault over her lacey panties, freshly bought. No way would she be caught dead in the cotton briefs now. He carelessly tucked a finger inside the seam causing her to gasp.

"No," Lindsey said, finding her voice and taking some control. "Come on." She took his hand and led him down the hall, leaving their discarded clothes. He followed without a word as she brought him to her bedroom.

He gave the room an amused once over, but quickly lost interest and refocused all his attention on Lindsey. He lifted her up, pressing her to him, and she wrapped her legs around his strong body. They kissed the way new lovers do, with care, emotion and intensity.

Laying her down on her comforter and ran a gentle hand down her body. "Let's do this right," he said, eyes dark with desire. "We're not in a rush." He glanced at the clock by her bed and Lindsey pretended it wasn't Hello Kitty. There were forty minutes before they had to get back, "Well, not too much of a rush."

He loomed over her and she was without words, absorbing his strong features, his hard body, his overwhelming need. She let him kiss her everywhere. She let him tell her how beautiful she was over and over. Their mouths and hands and tongues explored every inch of each other. They couldn't seem to kiss enough. Lindsey just wanted to touch him all day long, until she wanted him inside of her. Then she wanted nothing else. She moved out from under him, turning over until she was on top, licking his body up and down. His face contorted with pleasure so good it was painfully sweet. Then, she guided him inside of her and sat on him without moving, letting the tension build, leaning forward to bite his lip and kiss his mouth. She rode him slowly, pressing hard, feeling him deep inside of her. Her brain thought of nothing but him and his overwhelming desire for her. It had her at the brink, but right before she lost herself to him, he picked himself up and pushed her back at the same time. Now he was on top, pushing himself deeper and deeper into her. She ripped at his back, pulled him as far into her as possible and burst to the heavens with a rush of endorphins so powerful, it lifted her high over herself. She wasn't even in her body any longer. She had never taken Ecstasy, but this was fucking it.

They laid there, panting a bit, taking a moment to come to their senses. "Why is it so good?" Lindsey wondered out loud. "Is it the whole forbidden fruit thing? The doing something we're not supposed to do?"

John turned toward her, tenderly brushing a strand of hair away from her face. The simple, intimate gesture caused a sudden surge of feeling that made Lindsey want to cry. Her emotions were all over the place.

"I'm sure that has something to do with it," he said. "But I like to think it's because we are good together."

"Oh, you." She playfully nudged him.

He sat up. "No, seriously, I've been in..." He stopped, reconsidered and began again. "I have had feelings for you for a long time."

Lindsey's heart started beating hard again but for a different reason. She didn't like where this was going and was unsure why. She felt very connected to him, but she couldn't begin to define those feelings. She wouldn't. She tried to lighten the tone, and teasingly traced her fingers down his naked torso. "Obviously, I feel the same."

John caught her hand and held it. "Do you?" he asked uncertainly, a spark of hope lighting his eyes.

She pulled back a little, afraid of his intensity. "I'm... I'm not sure what we're talking about here," she said cautiously.

Sensing her withdrawal, John stepped back. "Yeah, me either. Just talking." He casually changed the subject. "Hey, do you think you could sneak away for bit, maybe tomorrow so we could get to spend a little more time together?"

Lindsey hesitated a minute, feeling the gravity of what she was doing. This was no longer spontaneous. Now they were planning their rendezvous. While every brain cell told her to say no, every fiber in her being was counting the seconds. They were still together and she couldn't wait to see him again. She blushed and nodded. "Okay, once the kids are in school."

She was rewarded with a wide, boyish grin that would have charmed the pants off of her if he hadn't already done that and a kiss that would melt a marshmallow. "Good," he said then pulled away leaving her gooey. "We've got to go." He arched a brow toward the clock. "Kitty says time's up."

***

It was after 11pm when Mitchell came home, showered and crawled into bed. Lindsey was already half asleep, consciously dreaming about the afternoon with John, going over and over it again with as much detail as possible. She breathed in his imagined scent. She felt his hands on her. She tasted his mouth, visualized his strong body. She wanted him right then. She could barely wait till tomorrow.

"You awake?" Mitchell whispered, his voice just a distant dream in the dark.

For a moment Lindsey debated feigning sleep. She was so deliciously drenched in her reverie, so completely lost to John and of being someone beautiful and passionate and desirable that she resented Mitchell's intrusion. His presence automatically put her in a different head, a defensive, guilty one.

"I'm still awake," she mumbled faintly, sleep blurring her words.

"Sorry I'm so late," he apologized. "I got caught up." He pulled her back in an embrace against him and Lindsey immediately woke up. What if he wanted sex? She panicked. What would she do?

He was her husband and even though Lindsey knew their sex would probably be better tonight than usual thanks to John's overwhelming presence in her brain, she ironically felt wrong about it. Generally Lindsey entertained fantasies during sex without care or a shred of guilt, but John wasn't just a fantasy anymore, he was real. If she now thought about John while having sex with Mitchell, it took on all new implications. She wasn't prepared for any of this.

He was her husband.

He felt damp and shower clean and it was so warm under the covers. They hadn't been together in too long. She wanted to have sex. She loved him. She felt his long body layered all along the length of hers. All she had to do was turn around.

She pushed her body a bit against his in response and he threw an arm around her pulling her in even closer, two spoons. He kissed the back of her neck under her hair and Lindsey felt an illicit thrill. Full of excitement, she was about to turn when he mumbled, "So tired" into her shoulder, gave her one last squeeze and flipped over to sleep.

It was exactly how it usually happened, but tonight Lindsey felt the rejection even more keenly. She didn't really want to have sex with him, but why the hell didn't he ever want to have sex with her?

The next morning, Mitchell didn't even blink when Lindsey casually mentioned that she would be in the city all day finishing up some last minute revisions on the Skittles job. When she had a project, she was in and out of the city all the time. It was thankfully, an easy, believable excuse.

She took the train in like John had suggested and hopped a cab over to the Gansevoort Hotel on Park Avenue. The whole ride she was on pins and needs, vacillating wildly between guilt and longing. She thought of Mitchell and her heart clamped up; strangled with self-reproach. She thought of John and it opened as wide and lush as a valley. Needless to say, she spent most of her time thinking about John.

The hotel entrance was impressive; very chic with ultra-modern furniture and a black and white art deco, zigzag floor.

Lindsey took it all in, unconsciously twirling the side of her long gypsy dress up in her fingers as she was checked in by a pretty blonde girl with some sort of Scandinavian accent. "Hi. My name is Shore." She said awkwardly, using the fake name she and John had come up with; a play on their town. She couldn't bring herself to say Mrs. Shore.

The pretty young thing was all business, typing away at her computer. "Oh yes, here you are, all taken care of." She dangled a key in front of her like a carrot. A dirty carrot. "Room 1207."

"Thanks," Lindsey replied, grateful for her sunglasses. She didn't care if she was inside. This was New York City, indoor sunglasses were the norm. "Just take the elevator on the right," the girl called out as Lindsey hurried away.

She rode the elevator up to the twelfth floor and tentatively stepped out into the darkened hallway, taking a few deep breaths, wondering why she felt so anxious. They had already had sex, more than once. She had lived through him seeing her naked, but for some reason, coming to a hotel felt like a turning point. It was so calculated. She was choosing to have an affair and actively pursuing it. The immense reality of her situation stopped her again. What was she doing? She felt momentarily stuck as the elevator doors closed behind her. Breathe, she reminded herself.

She looked at the number of the nearest room and counted the doors down to her destination. Five. Five doors to John. Alone in the darkened hallway on this sunny morning, it seemed unreal that he was in there waiting; that she was now slowly walking toward him. When she reached room 1207, she nervously slid her key in the door, close to shaking.

The room was modern, spacious and open, with a large white bed and a wall of windows that opened up to the city. The art on the wall was strangely raunchy, a series of sexy shots of a man and a lingerie clad woman in the act. Lindsey found it a little weird, unless John had requested the sex suite, which of course he hadn't. There was a couch, a desk, and an eating table with two chairs. On the center of the table was a bottle of champagne chilling in a bucket of ice, and a plate of fruit. Lindsey absent-mindedly picked up a grape and popped it in her mouth.

The shower, which was running, all of sudden shut off and her insides twisted anxiously. She placed her bag down in the corner and leaned up against the wall. It felt awkward. Instead, she sat on the bed which was by far the plushest, cushiest mattress ever, but that felt wrong too. Ultimately, she decided to stand by the open window and look out at the view, which was magnificent.

But not as magnificent as John, she realized as he emerged and she watched him walk toward her with only a towel wrapped around his trim waist, the sun from the window making him almost glow. "Hey," She said softly, still feeling uncomfortable about being there.

He barely smiled and moved toward her with determination, pulling her roughly to him, crushing his lips to hers. All thoughts fell out of her head as he pulled open the tie straps around her neck causing the top of her dress to fall down, exposing her naked flesh. With a small shake, the loose fabric of her dress dropped to the floor in a pool around her feet. She stood there naked except for a pair of pink silk panties and he stopped. "That's better," he appraised, his rapt eyes taking all of her in.

She took a step closer to him, touching her chest to his. They kissed long and slow before he lifted her up and carried her to the bed. "I want you more than I ever wanted anything," he whispered hoarsely. "And now I'm going to make you want me more than anything."

She lay breathless as he spread her legs. She had never been comfortable having someone down there and closed them reflexively. "John, I don't really like that." She tried to pull him up toward her, but he refused to budge.

"Oh no," he scolded. "That won't do." Again he spread them and went to work.

Except for a few awkward times many years ago, Lindsey had never really experienced that before, certainly not in a way that would give pleasure. More it was a messy affair which she had been relieved to see end. When Mitchell never showed much interest, she had been happy for it. Only now did she realize what she had been missing.

Just as she was on the brink of explosion, he stopped. She almost cried with frustration and pushed him back down. He laughed, lay down next to her and started stroking her gently, then more forcibly, kissing her everywhere, until her body was like an out of control live wire. It was too much. It was all too much. She was almost frantic with need. "How bad do you want me?" he asked.

"I want you," she rasped. "I want you."

"How bad?" he repeated, leisurely stroking her up and down.

"Desperately," she cried out and in one motion he was on top of her and they were one, slowly moving together towards rapture.

Afterwards, he stayed on top of her for a moment or two kissing her neck. "I'm glad you came," he said and smiled mischievously.

"Stop it!" She giggled and pushed him off.

"No," he grinned, "I mean it. I'm glad you came. Until you walked in the door, I wasn't sure if you would."

"I wasn't sure either," she admitted. "But I did."

"Oh you did alright."

"Stop it!" She hit him playfully, and jumped from the bed. All her nerves about coming were gone. This was where she belonged; stress-free and happy, really feeling desire, passion and alive for the first time in so long. She no longer felt guilty, she felt entitled. "I'm taking a shower."

"I'm coming," he laughed and followed.

They wore the plush hotel robes and ordered an early lunch in the room, talking easily about themselves. John told her how unhappy he had been for so many years, how wrong he and Jeanie were for each other. He talked about his kids and how much he adored them. In contrast, Lindsey admitted that she had been reasonably happy and how good Mitchell was. Hearing her words out loud, again left her silently question what she was doing. But she pushed it away. She might have been happy enough with Mitchell but she was ecstatic with John.

"It's surreal being here together," he said contemplatively.

"You could say that."

"I mean, I just never could have imagined this would happen."

"Well, me either," she agreed.

"But I'm so glad it did."

Lindsey didn't answer. In the silence, his blue eyes searched hers. "Are you?" he asked gently.

She nodded, a tear falling from her face. "I am. I know this is wrong but really, nothing has ever felt so right." Feelings she had pushed down started to bubble at the surface. "I just wish it didn't have to be like this. I wish there weren't so many other people involved. It's just so hard."

He nodded in understanding and opened his arms, gesturing for her to come and sit on his lap. She immediately left her chair for his, and found genuine comfort in his embrace. He hugged her and she snuggled in tightly. "Oh Lindsey, Lindsey. What am I going to do with you?" He said and kissed the top of her head.

"Whatever you want," she answered, looking earnestly into his eyes and meaning it.

He leaned down and kissed her forehead and nose and she tilted her chin up to offer him her mouth. He placed his lips gently on hers and their kiss became deep and soulful. It was a kiss full of promises; a kiss that meant something.

Then Lindsey's cell phone rang.

Quickly, she scrambled off his lap and ran to her bag, worried it would be the school. It was Mitchell, who almost never called her during the day. She had a brief panic attack that led to momentary brain loss where she almost unconsciously pushed send and took the call, but quickly realized what a bad idea that would be. Shaking slightly, she let it go to voice mail.

"God," she exclaimed, exhaling deeply. "That kind of freaked me out."

"Are you okay?" John asked, concerned.

"Yeah," she reassured him. "I'm okay. But it's almost 1pm. There's a 1:38pm train I need to catch. I'm going to get dressed."

She gathered her things and dressed in the bathroom because she needed a few minutes to collect herself. The call from Mitchell had her rattled. She wanted to get outside so she could listen to his message with a clearer head and call him back from the street if she needed to.

Within ten minutes she was ready and they stood at the door quietly. She knew she had to go immediately if she wanted to catch the train, which she had to catch, but looking at him made her want to stay and never leave. She felt her heart ripping.

He pulled her to him and hugged her close, wrapping her in a cocoon of contentment. "I don't want to go," she said honestly and stood on her tiptoes to kiss his lips. He put a hand in her hair and pulled backwards so that her head was back and her neck revealed. He kissed down it hungrily, making her shiver. "You'll be back," he said. "I can wait."

CHAPTER 6

"We are what our thoughts have made us; so take care about what you think. Words are secondary. Thoughts live; they travel far."
— Swami Vivekananda

"So what is up with Lindsey?" Marnie asked and looked over at Ellie expectantly. "Have you heard from her?"

They were sitting at Yaki, waiting for their sushi lunch specials.

Diane shrugged. "Not me. She blew off our usual spin class yesterday and hasn't returned my calls."

"She's been MIA for me as well," Ellie said off-handedly. "I spoke to her briefly the other day, but she was in a hurry. I think she's been busy helping her parents with the move and all."

"I thought they moved last week," Marnie asked with confusion. "Didn't they move last week?" she repeated, looking around the table for confirmation.

"She's missed the last two lunches. It's so unlike her. Do you think everything is okay?" Diane probed with both her radar and her eye brow raised. She didn't like being out of the loop, any loop.

"I think so." Ellie hesitated a second, treading the waters

carefully, working hard not to seem evasive, which Diane would pick up on in a second. "I mean, I'm sure she is. If something was wrong, I'd know about it."

"Well get to the bottom of it," Diane ordered. "Something is definitely up."

"Ay ay Captain! I will do some detective work and report back." Ellie saluted Diane.

"On a totally frivolous but more fun matter," Marnie interrupted and changed the subject much to Ellie's relief, "Did you guys read the SOS post on your party?"

Diane rolled her eyes. "Ridiculous nonsense," she said, but was obviously pleased with the coverage.

That was all it took. Within seconds, Diane and Marnie were heavily rehashing the party that they had already been hashed to death. But with so many people in attendance there was so much entertaining stuff to analyze and gossip about, and Diane never tired of discussing her own fabulous affairs or other people.

Ellie quietly pulled out her phone to secretly text Lindsey.

"Where are you?!! And why have you ditched lunch again?"

Within seconds came her reply.

"Sorry, caught up. Let's talk later."

"When?!" She wrote back.

"Come over later with Conner? Whenever. Mitchell's on call."

"7?"

"Works."

Ellie put the phone away and rejoined the conversation, but her mind was on Lindsey. What the hell was she doing?

Benny had plans to go out with his friends from work, relieving Ellie from the burden of preparing dinner. Usually she enjoyed cooking but was happy for the break tonight. She had indulged too much at lunch, finishing off Marnie's shrimp tempura avocado roll. Skipping a meal wouldn't be a bad thing. She struggled enough with five extra pounds. No need to add to that.

Without the pressure of multitasking Conner's nightly ritual and Benny's train schedule, Ellie leisurely bathed her baby, gave him a fresh diaper and dressed him in his new PJs, the light blue ones covered in lions, giraffes and monkeys that he looked totally delicious in. Then she fed him his last bottle before bed. It was 7pm and if he didn't fall asleep on the way to Lindsey's, he would soon after. She shoved all of his crap (most of it completely unnecessary for a reasonably short visit where he should be sleeping) into an oversized monogrammed LL Bean tote bag that had been one of Lindsey's gifts to her and then bundled Conner into his car seat. He yawned with his whole face then smiled up contentedly. Oh my baby loves me, she thought, or he just farted, either one.

Conner was such a good, easy baby. He slept just as easily in his car seat as he did in his crib, so going to hang out with Lindsey for a while wouldn't mess with his schedule in any way. She grabbed an extra bottle and a jar of formula just in case and headed out.

When she arrived at Lindsey's ten minutes later, Conner had drifted off and if her luck held, he would stay asleep till 6am. That was of course, if he wasn't awakened by the screaming going on at Lindsey's. Apparently, Liam and Riley were in the middle of a heated argument over who had been more helpful over dinner.

Lindsey looked hopelessly at Ellie and her eyes rolled in amusement. "Every night," she chuckled. "They fight about everything." She nodded at sleeping Conner. "Enjoy this peaceful, yummy time. Why don't you put him down in the living room, and I'll deal with loud and louder."

Lindsey disappeared and a few minutes later, both Riley and Liam crowded in the living room quietly oohing and ahhing over a sleeping Conner.

"Aw, he's soooo cute." Riley beamed with delight at the living toy. "I wish I could hold him!"

"Next time," Ellie assured her, smiling proudly at her baby and feeling all sorts of warm fuzzies for Lindsey's kids.

"Definitely."

"Alright guys," Lindsey interrupted, "time to get upstairs and shower. Please show me that you can wash up without me refereeing between you. When you're finished, I'll have a good snack ready for you both. Now go."

Liam and Riley both raced loudly for the stairs, taunting each other the whole way.

"That should give us about thirty seconds," Lindsey announced. "Come into the kitchen with me for a few minutes. I'm going to make them fresh ice cream cookie sandwiches."

"Yum," Ellie said, and followed her footsteps, panting like a lap dog. "Coming."

They sat at her kitchen table as Lindsey pre-heated the oven and placed blobs of cookie dough on a sheet. "So what's up?"

Ellie shot her a give-me-a-break look. "Really? Playing clueless."

Lindsey hesitated and appeared to be biting her lip. Finally, she sighed and looked at her helplessly. "I don't know where to begin."

"Well," Ellie prompted, "are you still considering? Or have you moved past that to... um... involved?"

"Involved." She lowered her head guiltily. "Honestly El, I don't exactly know what is happening here. It's like I'm not me. Or, I'm pretending to be someone else. Someone not married. Or someone married who cheats on their husband. It's so weird how I really don't see this having anything to do with Mitchell. That's weird, right?"

Always diplomatic, Ellie stepped gingerly around the shit that was coming out of Lindsey's mouth. "I can't say anything is weird or not. I'm not you, nor have I ever had an affair." She whispered affair like an old woman would say cancer. "But you know, it does have everything to do with you and Mitchell, whether you admit it or not."

Lindsey distractedly arranged the dough on the sheet. "I know, I guess, you're right. I just feel like I can't stop." She placed the cookies in the oven and then sat at the table by Ellie. "He's like a drug. I'm totally addicted to him. I feel like a teenager. I feel sexy and attractive. I feel so desired, so alive."

As much as Ellie wanted to hear every bit of detail, she also wanted to slap Lindsey, to bring her back around to reality and to Mitchell. "Don't you feel that way with Mitchell? You guys seem so great together." It was a stupid, naïve thing to say and she knew it the minute it left her mouth. No way she felt like that with her husband of over a decade. It wasn't a fair comparison.

Lindsey shook her head and her eyes pleaded for understanding. "Of course. I love Mitchell. And our sex life is fine I guess; a little standard and not as frequent as we probably should but, you know how it is."

"How often is not so frequent?" Ellie asked, curious.

"Well, with work and the kids, we could easily not have sex for a month or more before we realize it." She seemed embarrassed, "But what can you expect after fourteen years, right?"

Ellie didn't know. She and Benny had sex at least three times a week, sometimes four. She knew it was more than most couples, but it worked for them. "Sure," she said, reassuringly.

"So what are you going to do?" she asked. "I mean, you can't keep up a double life for very long."

Lindsey got up to check the cookies. "Hopefully, long enough to figure it out."

Now Ellie really wanted to scream. Long enough to figure it out? Was she crazy? She was going to fuck up her whole life and her kids too. She was always a self-centered girl, but this was so selfish and arrogant to think she could get away with it.

"I wouldn't count on that," she said, trying hard to sound more maternal than judgmental. "The longer this goes on, the harder it's going to be to stop. And you're not the only one affected here. You have other people to consider."

"I know," Lindsey huffed defensively, "but I'm a person too. I get to count too. I'm not just going to throw myself under a bus for the sake of everyone else." All of a sudden, she felt ready for a fight or to break down and cry.

Ellie backed down, unsure what to do with this fragile and aggressive Lindsey. They stewed in the uncomfortable, contemplative silence with the scent of fresh cookie growing more and more delicious around them, until the timer on the stove dinged, sending them back to their corners.

"Hey, did you see that last SOS post?" Lindsey asked, gingerly attempting a lighter tone as she shut off the oven.

"Yeah."

"I'm sure I'm being crazy but you know when she mentioned the housewife frantically searching for someone other than her husband…? You don't think she meant me, did you?"

Ellie's eyes widened with interest and she grabbed at the dangling bait. "So are you telling me that the guy was there at the party? He's not someone you met through work? He's a neighborhood guy?"

"I didn't say that," Lindsey quickly denied. "I was just being paranoid, I guess."

"Uh huh." Ellie just looked at her skeptically.

"Whatever. Come on. I didn't look like I was frantically searching for someone other than my husband, did I? I mean, I'm being crazy, right?" She looked hopefully at Ellie.

"Well, you were kind of distracted for most of the night." She paused. "But I wouldn't say you were frantic or drew attention to yourself in any way. Don't worry. That could have been any number of people. I mean, did you notice how Caren hung out at the poker table all night? Or how that girl Nicole, Diane's friend practically ripped her husband's head off and then stormed off never to be seen again? There was a lot of questionable behavior going on. I think you're safe."

Lindsey considered Ellie's words and visibly relaxed. "Yeah, you're right. Okay, enough of this. It's time for a snack break." Lindsey pulled the hot, sweet, goodness from the oven.

"What flavor ice cream you got?" Ellie asked, her former resolve to eat less forgotten.

For now, they had had enough of the complicated. It was time for simple and sweet. Together they put together the homemade ice cream sandwiches, tabling the whole conversation, and talking instead about the all the annoying, adorable and amazing contradictions that are motherhood.

They were laughing and eating – Ellie, an entire ice cream cookie sandwich and Lindsey, four stolen chips picked out of some leftover raw dough – when Riley and Liam appeared in the kitchen, having floated down on the aromatic powers of fresh baked goods. It is true that in life there are just some things that are beyond our control.

***

With bleary eyes, Lindsey tried to make the numbers on the clock come into focus. 6:15 am. Barely morning. Okay, barely morning for her. She looked over at Mitchell's sleeping form. He must have come in pretty late because she hadn't heard him.

Since meeting with John in the city, Lindsey was wild with emotion. The voicemail message from Mitchell had been no big deal, just a quick call to let her know he would be home late; that he was covering someone's shift. But even if Ellie couldn't see it, she was totally shaken by how easy it was for her to fall into this thing with John.

She could hardly sleep anymore. Her brain was reeling, a constant whirlwind of emotions and thoughts, justifications and reproaches. Each morning she woke up and looked at her beautiful, sleeping husband and was so disappointed in herself that she wanted to scream and cry and shake him awake to beg forgiveness.

But of course, she wouldn't do that. She wasn't stupid. She spent half of her young adult and adult relationships dabbling in extra - curricular activities. Not that she was proud of her promiscuous behavior and two timing ways, but for the most part, none of her boyfriends' ever found out, and she never felt the need to dispel her own guilt by laying it on them. She never understood the purpose of that. Why would she torture someone she cared about by sharing such hurtful information? To her it seemed like adding insult to injury, an absolutely selfish thing to do.

She could shove whatever guilt she had down and either move past it or break up with the guy without disclosing the real reason. She didn't know if it was conscious blinders by them or blind faith, but apparently she was pretty convincing.

Seeing Mitchell's long, lean body relaxed in sleep. His wavy deep blonde hair too long now and falling over his eyes, she felt a pang of regret and self-loathing. So, things weren't so passionate anymore. So they didn't talk, laugh and connect like they used to. So he worked a lot. He was a damn good husband. He took care of her and their kids. He was kind. He was caring. He was supportive, hard-working and trusting. He was an amazing person and a good father. She was a shit.

Lindsey quietly slipped from the bed, wanting him to get as much sleep as possible and tip-toed down the stairs to sit and continue her onslaught on herself, except with coffee. She may be an adulterous asshole but she wasn't a sadist.

In her younger relationships she never experienced much guilt about her infidelities. Entwined in each other on the beach drinking Coronas, she and Mitchell had a pretty deep conversation about it early on in their relationship. Both certified cheats, they agreed that monogamy wasn't natural and felt reasonably justified in their behavior. They could respect each other and their own sensibilities without conforming to societal mandates. They were above that. They were different they vowed, clinking their beers, and drinking to each other.

Although she had been faithful these last fourteen years, deep down she still believed it. At least she thought she did. It was harder to be as black and white in your forties, especially with all the grey in the world – and in her hair. Regardless, she couldn't afford those liberal views. Back then, she didn't have her whole life on the line. Mitchell wasn't a boyfriend anymore. He was her husband, the father of her children. She had them to think of as well. She needed to stop this nonsense. She wasn't in her twenties. She was middle aged. She seriously needed to get over herself.

An hour later she was still at it, back and forth like a tennis match when Liam and Riley sauntered in. Riley was already dressed and alert, having laid her outfit out the night before, while Liam still wore his sleep shirt with a pair of shorts and a half dazed expression.

"Mommy! There you are!" she chided, like she had been looking hours for her. "I need your help with my braids. They refuse to braid!"

She smiled, ready for a good distraction. "Come here," she said. "Hug first, braid second." She looked at Liam, who appeared as though he was asleep standing up. "Chocolate chip pancakes third!"

That perked him up and her as well. This was what she loved to do. This was a life worth protecting. Having seen her children, she felt a new resolve. She hoped it wasn't bullshit.

By the time Mitchell woke, the kids were already off to school. She heard the shower going and toyed with the idea of surprising him up there, but ultimately decided against it. She didn't want to shock him into a heart attack. Instead, she stayed downstairs and set the table with coffee, the chocolate chip pancakes and some fresh cut melon.

When he walked into the kitchen, fresh and clean at 10 am and saw the table laid out before him, he immediately looked skeptical. "Okay, what did you do?" he asked, sitting down to his steaming coffee.

"Nothing!" she protested. "Why can't I set out breakfast for my fabulous husband?"

"Uh huh," he said, sipping suspiciously and taking a bite of pancake. "So, what did you buy?"

"Come on! You know I make chocolate chip pancakes all the

time."

"Yeah, but you don't try to sweeten me up with them."

"Fine," she pouted, "I just felt like I haven't seen you and I thought it would be nice."

He softened a bit. "You're right. It is nice. Thank you. Come, sit. Tell me how your week has been."

She sat down and started to tell him about the kids, but he was only half listening. She could tell. This might have been okay a month or so ago, but unfortunately she now remembered what it was like to have someone's undivided attention. Mitchell really wanted to be reading the paper and milking this bit of relaxing morning before his office hours. She didn't blame him, but of course, she did.

"I'm going to go do the laundry," she mumbled, and he nodded absently, his eyes on the paper. She silently fumed, wondering how he didn't notice the puffs of smoke piping out of her head. As she got up to walk out, the phone rang. Lindsey checked the receiver. It was a city number she was not familiar with. She answered automatically.

"Hello?" It was her, 'I'm already bored, why are you bothering me' voice.

"Hey Lindsey. It's me, Jeanie. How are you?"

Alarm bells immediately sounded in her head. Jeanie never called her from work. "Uh, good. Just been busy with my parents' move and all." Shit. Shit. Shit.

"Yeah, I heard about that. So, I was just wondering if you wanted to meet me and maybe Caren later to take a walk around 6pm? It's been a while."

"Oh, sorry. That sounds so nice, but Mitchell is coming home early today and we're going to dinner."

Mitchell raised a questioning brow. Lindsey threw her hands up in a gesture of annoyance and helplessness.

"Well, then how about you and me Saturday morning? And

don't say no, or I'll come to your house and stalk you. I haven't seen you in a while. Come on, it will be nice to catch up."

"Okay. Sure," she agreed, knowing it was a huge mistake even as did. "Usual time."

"Great. See you then," Jeanie chirped and they hung up.

"Jeanie," Lindsey said as explanation to Mitchell, although he already knew who it was. "Trying to secure a walk. I don't want to go, but somehow I got roped into agreeing."

"Hey, I forgot to mention," Mitchell interrupted. "Jeanie called the office the other day and set up an appointment for next week. Remember she said her back has been acting up?"

Another small wave of panic flared. It was too much Jeanie in one five minute period.

"Huh," Lindsey grunted, busying herself by flipping through some random mail. "She didn't mention it."

"Who knows?" Mitchell said casually, "Jeanie's a funny one."

Lindsey looked at her husband sitting at the table and felt a rush of emotion, possibly fear. She came back towards him and positioned herself on his lap, interrupting his coffee and breakfast. She couldn't tell if he was happy or mildly annoyed.

"What's all this?" he asked.

"What do you mean?" she said a little sharply, growing more and more attuned to his rejections. "Is there something wrong with me wanting to sit on your lap?"

"Nope. It's just hard to drink hot coffee."

She ignored him and cuddled her head on his shoulder like a cat. She wanted to suggest a morning dalliance, but she didn't want to as much as she did. She figured sitting on his lap put it out there. The decision was in his hands. He decided to chastely kiss her cheek and give her butt a little squeeze as he pushed her off.

Well that answered that.

"I'll be home early tonight," he said before he completely returned his attention to his newspaper. "Do you want to get a sitter and go out for dinner? I wouldn't want to make a liar out of you."

"Sure," she responded, unsure whether she was annoyed or relieved by his rebuff. Both, she decided and headed off to do the laundry for real this time.

By the time Mitchell was ready to leave for the office, Lindsey had had a hundred mental conversations with the washing machine and was feeling reckless and desperate; a combination that generally led to positive, productive behavior. She gave him a kiss on the cheek and watched him walk out the door with her heart pounding. The minute his car was out of sight she texted John.

"Play date?"

His response was immediate.

"Yes."

She puttered around her house trying to get a few things done while she waited in a state of excited anticipation. She was being careless and crazy and she knew it. About a half hour later, she heard the front door, which she had left unlocked, creak open and then ominously shut, closing them in, leaving them to their own bad choices.

She padded down the stairs in yoga pants and a tank top, the everyday outfit of the suburban mom. He stood in running shorts and a tee-shirt, looking strong and masculine. She smiled at his outfit and he shrugged and grinned.

"Is that your cover?" she asked, moving closer to him.

"I thought I'd get some exercise," he said, wrapping his arms around her.

She stood inches from him, their breath mingling, luxuriating in their closeness and on its dizzying effect. "I think that's a great idea," she agreed, her voice thick with desire.

They kissed eagerly, desperately. She ran her hands up his shirt, feeling his strong chest, wanting to see it, needing to feel his skin on hers.

He took her possessively in his arms, carried her into the den and laid her down on the carpet. She wanted him fast, hard and immediately. Her brain and body were so turned on since she made that first move and texted him that no foreplay was necessary. She was hot on her own boldness. She wanted to finish what she started, but he wouldn't allow her that pleasure. Instead, he insisted on kissing lightly and slowly, removing her pants and rubbing her gently till she moaned.

She tried to grab for him, determined to force him into her, but he pushed her down undeterred and continued his onslaught of slow teasing, light petting and gentle licks and nibbles in all the right places. She squirmed with growing urgency and need.

"Please," she practically cried. "Please." But his face was a mask of concentration and he would not stop. Her body was one giant nerve ending, a swirling sensation of rapture. She was past the point of any thought other than her desperate need to have him when he finally spreads open her legs and entered her. He pressed his hardness in her again and again, strong and deep; the heat of his body finally on her, she teetered right over the edge and exploded with release so strong she feel lifted to ecstasy.

"Well, fuck me," she said, beyond words.

He smiled a roguish cowboy grin. "Thought I just did."

She just looked at him speechless, experiencing a rush of so many feelings; she could not come to terms with them. She did not know what they were. Lust certainly, but it was all so mixed with tenderness and true caring. She felt like she was in high school, infused with that witches' brew of fresh hormones and emotions that made you ride around stalking a boy's house, or waiting casually and pathetically by your locker for him to walk by with his friends just for a passing hello. It made you pathetic. And stupid. And careless. Young love was powerful stuff. Even in middle-age. Probably even more so, because you knew how rare those feelings were, making them even more special; something to cherish, something worth fighting for.

81

When she looked into his face, she just wanted to kiss him. She wanted to feel him on her. She wanted to lose herself in him. She never wanted to leave him. It felt dangerously close to love.

Sensing her vulnerability, he pulled her to him and wrapped his arms around her. "I know," he whispered and buried his face in her neck and hair, uniting them in their depravity and the hopelessness of their union, somehow strengthening the ties even more. "I know."

She wanted to cry but his smell was around her and his lips were on her neck. Unbelievably, she wanted him again.

"Jeanie called me this morning," Lindsey said, successfully and immediately killing their buzz.

He looked heavy in thought and she moved off his lap to put some distance between them. After a moment, he asked, "Why?"

"Just to schedule a day for us to walk together," she said. "The only thing out of the ordinary about it was that she called me from work to ask, which she's never done. Usually, she'll text or we make a plan based on random encounters. Why? Are you concerned?" Lindsey questioned nervously. He certainly looked concerned.

He shook his head. "No. I mean, I'm not concerned about me. I'm concerned about you."

He had her attention now, and she distractedly grabbed at her clothes on the floor and started dressing. "What do you mean?"

"I mean, Jeanie cannot hurt me. We were headed where we were headed even without you." He softened and touched her face, "Not that you haven't made it so much easier and sweeter."

"You mean...?" She was trying to process all he was saying and not saying.

"Yeah, it was just taking longer than it should have. You know, it's easy to get stuck, especially with the kids."

Lindsey nodded, but then her head flew up in terror, "Wait, do you think she knows about us?"

"No. I don't think so. I really don't. But, I can't be sure about anything with Jeanie. She surprises me with how sharp her antennas are."

"Okay well, we're meeting for a walk tomorrow morning. I am sufficiently freaked out."

"I'm sorry," he said sincerely, and the words brought her back to their first time. "I know this is a mess for you. You and Mitchell aren't anything like me and Jeanie."

"No, I guess not," she thought sadly. "It would be a lot easier if we were." That left them contemplative.

"I've been struggling for weeks," he confessed, "hating myself but unable to stay away from you."

"I know how you feel," she agreed.

"So what do we do?" he asked, but then almost immediately realized his mistake. "And I wish to hell I didn't just ask that out loud."

Lindsey looked at him miserably. "But you have," she sighed.

He reached for her. "Can I take it back?"

She was bereft. She heard Ellie in her head. She saw a vision of Mitchell sleeping in their bed; their children, chocolate smeared on their faces while eating pancakes just this morning. She shook her head. "The right answer is we should stop before there's no turning back."

"I'm already at that place," he said sadly. "There's no going back for me." They drifted into silence. "So, you want to stop?"

Lindsey looked up at him, but he had gone to that guarded, unreadable place. She didn't want to stop. She didn't want to stop at all. She moved toward him and curled up in his embrace. "I don't want to. I have to," she whispered. He nodded and even as he wrapped himself around her, holding her close, she could feel his tension, his hurt.

"I'm sorry," she blubbered, tears pooling in her eyes, and starting to drip down her cheeks. "I'm lost here, truly lost. I don't know what to do." His eyes, warm and blue like a tropical pool, looked down at her and she felt him relax a little. He leaned in and kissed her wet, streaked cheeks. She tilted her head up, a mechanical force not of her own. They kissed meaningfully, slow and long. A final kiss. It sent sweet waves of longing, heightened further by emotional turmoil, rolling throughout her body. She truly never wanted it to end. But it had to and it did.

Sadly, she removed herself from his lap, allowing him the space to get up. And then they stood there awkwardly in the hall, two neighbors, friends, whatever.

"Okay then," he said soberly. "I think I need to take that run now."

Lindsey walked him to the door and held her hand up in a gesture of farewell, watching him run away with her heart. She lingered, gazing mindlessly out into the street until she noticed one of her neighbors, a woman with kids near her children's age standing by the corner with her dog looking her way. Immediately apprehensive, Lindsey gave a wave and quickly shut the door. She had just found her heart and it was now pumping wildly to go along with the lump in her chest.

CHAPTER 7

79% of men and women believe they are destined to find their soul mate.

Later that night when they went out to dinner, Mitchell was sweet and adorable, pulling out some of the old charisma he now reserved for new patients and nervous moms. Normally, it thrilled her to see this side of Mitchell but now she could only smile wanly as he playfully teased her about being her alibi and ordering exactly what she wanted without even asking. She felt herself holding back, refusing to succumb to his charms. She needed to relax and try harder, whether she felt it or not. With a glass of wine under her belt and another on the way, she babbled on about the kids and the week he basically missed on call. They talked a long time about the fact that she hadn't yet cleaned out her room at her parents' house. Mitchell thought she was unnaturally attached to the past and her mom, and her room was symptomatic of that. She couldn't let it go. He gently suggested that it all had something to do with her brother. When he said it, Lindsey immediately got defensive but since all of a sudden she also felt on the verge of tears, she quickly changed the subject.

They got home around 10p.m., not too late, but after that second glass of wine and the effort of enthusiasm among other things from the day, she was exhausted. She worried that Mitchell might want to cap off their evening with a little something extra, which would make sense because it had been a nice night and she could barely remember the last time they had sex. The thought of it at the moment bordered on repulsive. She could still feel John's hands on her. A wave of regret weakened her, and it wasn't guilt, it was loss.

As it turned out, her worry was for nothing. Mitchell wasn't interested either. She should feel lucky she guessed with more than a little bitterness, because as usual when she said she was tired and going up to bed, he gave her a fetching, rueful smile along with his standard, "I'll be up soon," and planted himself on the couch with his laptop. He even blew her a little kiss.

The last thing Lindsey did before drifting off to sleep and dream about John was text his wife and cancel their morning walk. There was no way she could do it.

In the morning she received a text from Ellie.

'Never let the things you want make you forget the things you have.'

'Thank you, Confucius,' she texted back.

'Words for the wise,' she wrote.

'Then clearly, you are not talking to me,' Lindsey responded.

She was still in bed and could hear Mitchell already in the shower. Usually she was up by then, having a morning walk or run, but lately, she had been lax about her usual obsessive exercising. Now she was strangely disinterested and not even a little guilty, something she hadn't experienced for decades, not even through her pregnancies. She guessed, she thought smugly, she had taken guilt up a notch. Lack of exercise was no longer a big deal.

The shower turned off and Mitchell emerged, saw her awake and smiled. "Hey there." He sat at the edge of the bed, clean and naked but for one of their navy towels around his waist that Lindsey couldn't help but notice looked washed out and frayed. She wanted to want her husband. She wanted to want him bad but her brain focused on towels and was already sending her to Bloomingdales. He was good looking. She loved him. He loved her. What happened to their passion? She wondered miserably. What happened to them?

Mitchell noted the funny, yearning expression in her eyes and took it as an invitation, which maybe it was. She didn't know what she was doing, but she knew that she needed to get things right with her husband, even though as she kissed him, she felt like she was betraying John. It was all kinds of wrong, but no less true.

She had been kissing Mitchell for over fifteen years. She had been kissing John for barely a month. How had John so quickly replaced all those years, many of them very good, of kissing? Her mouth was as disloyal as the rest of her body.

Still, their kiss was nice, like returning home on a crisp day after a weekend away. He was clean and shower damp. Mitchell was more tall and lanky, than strong and muscular like John, but the good doctor had kept it together well. She was sure half the nursing staff at the hospital had a crush on him, and as far as the husbands went, Mitchell was definitely the one getting all the eyes.

Her thoughts of Mitchell mingled with those of John and her kiss went deeper. Mitchell pulled back and looked at her funny. Had it been that long since she kissed him like that? Maybe it had.

"Wow," he said, "that was nice. If the kids weren't up..." He let the promise hang. "Later?" He grinned suggestively and gave her a flash of his goods, which were not nearly as shabby as her towels. She gave his butt a slap and got up to dress wondering if she actually could somehow fit Bloomingdales into her day. It felt good to be normal. It felt right.

All of a sudden, Riley raced into the room. "Mommy!" She called, "Someone's here to see you!" Lindsey exchanged a mildly quizzical look with Mitchell, at least she hoped it was quizzical since her heart was pounding like the gig was up and they had come to take her away, ha ha.

"Who is it?" she asked, but Riley had already disappeared. "Okay, I'll be right there," she said to herself, and pulled on a pair of yoga pants.

She hurried down the steps and saw Riley with her face pressed up to the door. When she replaced Riley's face with her own, her blood drained. Jeanie.

She opened the door and came face to face with her small tight lips opened in a smile, and her short blonde hair pulled back severely in a small bun. "Hey!" Jeanie greeted. "Ready?"

Lindsey forced a smile. "I guess you didn't get my text."

Jeanie looked at her blankly. "Nope. Let me see." She took out her phone and within seconds started nodding. "Oh, I guess I missed this. I conked out early last night and then just came." She looked Lindsey up and down. "But looks like you can go."

She opened her mouth, but nothing came out. "Great," Jeanie enthused, "I'll wait right here. Go put on your sneakers."

Stunned into submission, Lindsey put them on. By the time Mitchell descended the staircase, she was ready. "Uh, I'm going for a walk with Jeanie," Lindsey said flatly. "I'll be back in around an hour."

"Unless I kidnap her." Jeanie laughed.

Why was she afraid?

"Okay," Mitchell replied and waved. "See you in the office next week, Jeanie. Watch your step."

He turned his attention away from them and to the kids. "So, who wants pancakes?"

Lindsey walked out slowly, closing the door on the cheers of her children.

"He's great," was the first thing Jeanie said as they started down the street.

She nodded. "Yeah, he is."

"I would be so grateful to have a husband like that." She sighed. "I would keep him close and never let him go."

Okay, that was a weird thing to say, or was Lindsey being overly sensitive.

"What do you mean? John is great."

Jeanie shook her head harshly. "I'm sure it seems that way to you. You guys always hit it off, and to be honest, since the day we met, he's had a crush on you."

Lindsey literally swallowed her tongue. Choking, she finally coughed it up. "What? Stop it. That's ridiculous."

Jeanie gave her a don't play me look that Lindsey was sure scared the shit out of the peons under her at work. She and Ellie always joked that they'd never want to work for Jeanie. She'd be some tough boss.

"Don't tell me you never noticed," she pressed.

"I never thought about it," she stammered, "Why are you telling me this?"

Jeanie exhaled deeply as they passed her block, "I don't know. I just think he's cheating on me." She spit it out emotionless, like a bulldog discarding a chewed over bone.

"I don't know what to say," Lindsey said. She was afraid to look at Jeanie but stole a quick glance. Jeanie looked rigid as a board, her face flat and hard. Lindsey stopped walking. "Jeanie? Are you alright?"

"Have you seen that last SOS post?" Jeanie asked abruptly, without breaking stride, forcing Lindsey to jog for a minute to catch up.

"No." She broke into a cold sweat. "Why?"

But Jeanie power-walked on without explanation. "Come on, I've got a surprise for you."

Now Lindsey was truly terrified. "Jeanie, I think we should talk." They reached the Long Island sound that bordered their town and continued on along the water.

"What for?" she said puffing and Lindsey struggled to keep up. "Honestly, I think I've talked enough for now. Let's just walk."

They moved in unison, each of them in their own thoughts. Lindsey was sweating profusely, mostly from the talk, not the walk. In her head, she was trying to remember everything she had just said to figure out if Jeanie was insinuating what she thought might be. And what did that Secrets of the Shore post say? She had worked herself up into a frenzy of fear.

When they reached the Dunkin Donuts, Jeanie slowed down and motioned her over. "Come on," she said and walked in. Having no other choice, Lindsey followed and found Marnie, Diane and Ellie all sitting there.

She faltered, completely thrown. Was this an intervention? She must have looked baffled and maybe terrified because Ellie came over and put her arm around her. "Hey stranger, we haven't seen you in so long, we thought it would be nice to catch up."

All of her friends' faces smiled, even Jeanie, in her tightly wound way.

Could it be okay? Feeling like a skittish cat, Lindsey allowed herself to be led to a seat. "Wow. You guys all met here for me?"

"Well, you refused to meet us for lunch," Marnie huffed.

"Or spin class," Diane chimed in with her perfect brow arched accusingly.

"When Jeanie mentioned that you were walking, we thought we'd crash," Ellie explained, probably the only one to note her genuine discomfort. Lindsey was going to beat her silly later for not giving her a heads up.

"You've been totally MIA," Diane said, assessing Lindsey coolly, looking for cracks in the armor, signs of weakness or distress. Diane liked things a certain way, with her parties and her body, her clothes and her friends. She didn't appreciate things being remiss. "Is everything alright?"

"We know your parents' move has been difficult for you," Marnie added sensitively.

Lindsey semi relaxed. It was just her girls missing her, wanting to catch up, being concerned. Just what she needed, she thought, more guilt.

After everyone got iced coffees, they sat around laughing and chatting, talking over one another and about each other; just a jumble of girl gaggle and giggle. They made plans for an upcoming lunch and a couples' dinner for the next Saturday night.

Lindsey was happily back in the fold, engaging with the friends she almost forgot she cared about. She had been so consumed with herself lately. And John. It was a bubble she needed to pop.

They finished up and headed out; all shoving in Marnie's minivan for a ride home. While they all discussed whether to attend an upcoming school social, Lindsey surreptitiously checked her phone, going immediately to Facebook and the SOS page.

It seems Suburban swinging is in full schwing! A marriage on the rocks, a secret affair under our noses, another soon to be ex-husband spotted out to dinner one town over with someone he introduced as his cousin who apparently enjoys licking the food from his fingers... Well you know, some families are super close. Looks like a few people right here in our town are looking for love in all the wrong places.

Lindsey felt sick. Without thinking, she cast a glance over at Jeanie and caught her looking back at her, not angrily, just sort of curiously. Lindsey realized she had barely said a word since they entered Dunkin Donuts. Lindsey gave her a small smile. Jeanie returned the sentiment, and then turned her head away toward the window.

When Marni dropped Lindsey off, she found Mitchell and the kids in the backyard kicking a soccer ball. She watched them feeling emotional. Riley's ponytail flopping, her face, a wide blissful smile revealing her two missing front baby teeth as she dodged around Mitchell trying to get to the goal. Liam, determined and showing off, coming from seemingly nowhere to kick the ball away from her. Riley screaming in frustration. Liam apologizing but clearly not sorry. Mitchell rolling his eyes. They were all so beautiful. They almost never had a Saturday morning with nothing to do. She immediately felt desperate to do something together as a family.

"I've got a great idea!" she said with almost manic enthusiasm. They turned, noticing her for the first time.

"Mommy!" Riley called out and ran over.

"No! We don't want to go shopping!" Liam whined.

Lindsey flashed him a stern look, "I wasn't going to suggest shopping."

"Do I have to go with you to the gym?" Riley asked, "Cause I think I'll stay with daddy."

"No! We're not going to the gym," she retorted sulkily. "Gee, is that all you think I do? Go to the gym and shop?"

"You get your hair done!" Liam offered.

"And your nails," Riley added helpfully.

Mitchell tried very unsuccessful to hide his amusement. Lindsey sent some evil glares his way. "Okay, guys." he chuckled. "Let mommy finish."

"Thank you." She exhaled her minor annoyance. "I just thought we could do something fun together. You know, as a family."

"That sounds lovely, mommy! You want us all to go shopping and get manicures?"

"Uh, no," she managed to remain calm, even though her family apparently thought very little of her. Did no one know she worked? "I was thinking more like mini-golf or bowling."

"Mini-golf!" Liam cheered just as Riley screamed, "Bowling!"

Then the fighting began.

Mitchell looked at her semi-amused, "Enough family time for you?"

Lindsey blew a piece of hair out of her face in frustration but she was smiling; determined to make this work. Somehow with the kids' activities and their school stuff, sports and friends and work, they had lost a little bit of 'family' along the way, and a lot a bit of them. They needed to re-connect, all of them.

"Okay! Enough," Lindsey finally yelled. "We are going to mini-golf first. Then getting lunch and going bowling. If we haven't killed each other by then, we'll grab dinner and see a movie! How's that for a good day?"

She bowed to the sound of their cheers.

As far as family days went, Lindsey had to say this one was a hit. No-one smacked anyone with a golf club. No one dropped a bowling ball on anyone's foot. They had lunch at Chow Chow, a local Chinese restaurant and dinner at La Parma, family style Italian. Too tired for a movie out, they headed home and had their own movie on the couch.

Lindsey looked at her exhausted kids, now showered and in pajamas, splayed out on the carpet shoveling in popcorn and engrossed in, *Back to the Future*, her choice. She and Mitchell watched as well. One big happy family, cozy together, on separate couches.

All day, Lindsey tried in her own way to move closer to Mitchell and he responded with a brief arm around her shoulder, a smile, a perfunctory kiss on the cheek. It was all nice. It certainly looked good for the cameras, but whether he realized it or not, they were not connecting.

It brought her down a bit, but she remained committed to moving them closer. Going against the grain, she decided to join him on his couch. When she surprised him with her intention, he seemed both pleased and mildly inconvenienced. Now he had to move his feet, which had been up resting. Now he had to turn and sit in a more uncomfortable position. For Lindsey's part, she found herself leaning away, resting on the arm of the couch instead of the arm of her husband. It was like trying to part your hair left when it naturally went right. They were no longer going in the same direction.

She was hyper aware of their distance, even this kind of unconscious one. They didn't feel together. She wanted to feel together, but there were walls that they spent years building and even decorating that had become as much a part of their lives as the real ones. Some walls were necessary of course. When you're together a long time, you need a wall or two for self-preservation, but too many walls and you've locked yourself in and other people out. It was time for some reconstruction, but they needed to move carefully; some walls were weight bearing and some just in the way.

They had sex that night. Lindsey couldn't say who initiated. It was mutual. She was still smarting over feeling unconnected, but she knew it was important to their relationship. They hadn't since John, so they really needed to.

It was nice. Easy. Satisfying. She knew Mitchell. Even with their random off weeks, or even at certain times like now, months where they had gone without, when they came back together, their lovemaking was always true; never earth shattering, but warm and comfortable and good. She tried hard not to think about John, but he made his way in, heightening her pleasure in a way Mitchell just couldn't. Was it bad to use him like that in her brain, she wondered, but she didn't worry too much about it. At this point, she'd accept a bit of fantasy adultery as long as she was with her husband in reality. If she could be happy like that, she was willing to leave her brain to its own devices.

Monday came quick as usual and they were back to the routine. Her Skittles project was wrapping up and there were only a bit of loose ends to tie, so she wasn't bogged down with work. On Wednesday, she met the girls – minus Jeanie since worked in the city and rarely joined - for lunch for the first time in over a month. They laughed as they always did and she took a good ribbing for being MIA for so long. It reminded her that she had yet to clear out her room. She could only ignore her mother's increasingly hostile messages for so long. She really was running out of time.

When they had all finished up their lunches, and as usual Ellie took Lindsey's leftovers home in a doggy bag, they exchanged kisses and lingered for some more random chat. After re-committing to their Saturday night outing, Lindsey walked with Ellie toward her car. Ellie had been shooting her meaningful glances through lunch and Lindsey knew she was dying to get her alone.

"So," Ellie asked eagerly, the minute they were out of ear shot. "What's going on?" Her red hair was braided a la Wendy's girl; a look she regularly adapted in her younger years but now indulged in less frequently. They all pretty much gave up the braids a few years back, but Ellie could still pull it off without somehow looking like she was trying too hard to look younger.

"It's over," Lindsey said.

Ellie's eyes widened. "Really? What happened?"

"I'm not sure. I really don't know, but we both realized what we were doing was a mistake." Why did she sound so miserable saying that?

"Wow. Well, that's good. I'm really glad to hear that. You know it's the right thing." Ellie put her arm on Lindsey's shoulder and rubbed gently. Lindsey guessed she must have looked miserable as well.

"I didn't want to break-up my marriage..."

"Or anyone else's," Ellie added.

"Yes, that either." Lindsey somewhat grudgingly agreed. "Although I think that marriage was doomed way before me. But," she struggled for words, unsure what truths she wanted to put out into the universe. "I have..." She stopped and changed her mind. "had..." Then she shook her head and reverted back to the honest, original statement. "I have really strong feelings for him. I miss him."

Ellie nodded sympathetically as Lindsey continued. "It just feels like there's a big hole in my life and in my relationship and I'm trying desperately to fill it up by doing good things with my family and Mitchell; doing the right things, and just hoping at some point the hole will close up and heal. But right now, it just feels like I'm trying too hard and it's exhausting." She took a deep breath. It was more than she intended to say.

"I think that's better than filling a void in your marriage with someone who's not your husband." Ellie somehow managed not to sound judgmental, which Lindsey really appreciated.

"I know you're right," she agreed, grateful to have such a good friend. It helped more than she could have imagined having someone to talk to and confide in. Somehow when it came to her emotions, she had an amazing capacity to bottle them up, close off and not share; often giving others the impression that she was cool and aloof. There were a lot of old emotions from old wounds Lindsey locked deep away. She probably would have benefited by talking with someone back then. Maybe she should talk to someone now, she considered. "It just doesn't completely feel that way," she finished. "But I'm still trying."

"I think the longer you try the more normal it will seem."

Ellie was so wise. Lindsey knew from experience that you can lose yourself in who you're pretending to be, all you have to do is commit to it. Then after a while, it doesn't seem as though you're pretending at all. It becomes who you are. With some effort and denial and a busy schedule, she could do it. She could become the good wife again. She just had to want it more.

"So are you impressed at my restraint? How I haven't asked you who?" Ellie conjured some mock pride, but she was not so subtly fishing for more than a compliment.

"Oh my God. So impressed," Lindsey gushed. "You're the best." she added, playfully knocking her on the shoulder.

"Doesn't that make you want to reward me? I don't know... maybe with some... information?" Ellie threw her line deeper, hoping to catch something.

"Hmm. Uh, no." Lindsey laughed.

"Biotch! You know you're going to spill!"

"Sorry. It's over. Locked away. Moving on. Remember?" She answered playfully. Spilling something like that would make quite the mess for both of them. Lindsey certainly didn't intend to drag Ellie into a situation with Jeanie. Sharing was one thing, but over-sharing was just stupid.

"Biotch," she quipped again, sensing she wasn't reeling anything in. "Come on, you don't want to leave me to my imagination. No telling where that could go."

"Um, I think you might need some more work on your restraint," Lindsey pointed out.

"Seriously? Well, how's this for restraint?" Ellie agreeably flipped Lindsey the bird as they said their good-byes.

"Like I said..." Lindsey sang as they head off in different directions.

When Lindsey arrived home, the first thing she did was call her mother. She picked up on the first ring.

"I knew it was you," she said, before Lindsey said anything.

"Showing off your psychic abilities again?" Lindsey joked.

"Nope. Just reading the caller ID."

"Very funny. So, how are you?"

"I can't complain, pussy cat. It's like camp down here. I play tennis and cards with a bunch of old fakaktas."

"Is everyone old?" she asked.

"Yes! They are all my age! But, who can complain? When someone farts at the card table, no one can hear it."

"Ha!" Lindsey snorted. Her mom's sarcastic, easy humor gave off calming pheromones, even across the state lines. "Well, I guess you need to choose your seat carefully."

"I have been but they can still smell me."

"Mom!" She was thoroughly amused. "Sounds like you're next in line for home coming queen of the retirement community."

"That's the plan, sweetheart. But how are you?"

"I miss you!" she whined. She didn't intend to say that. Why did that come out?

"I miss you too."

"Please come home," she added, only half joking.

"Lindsey, what is this nonsense?" Her mother asked, suddenly serious, "What is going on with you?"

"I don't know, Mom. I just feel like I'm coming apart a bit lately."

"Well, I'm going to send you some super glue." She kidded, as usual, using her humor and wit to brush things over or sweep them entirely away. Her mom didn't have a lot of patience for foolishness, even her daughter's, but she softened her tone a little and said, "Sometimes life kicks us in the tuchus, we just have to kick back. You let me know if there's anything I can do."

"Move back?" Lindsey pouted, refusing to let up.

"I'll send you a picture." Then her mom changed the subject and turned the tables on her. "So, you clean out your room yet?"

"Uh…" she stammered. "I'm going to do that tomorrow."

Lindsey heard her sigh deeply and probably bite her tongue. "Chop chop girl. Get it together. Time's a wasting."

She couldn't be more right.

***

The next day, after the kids were off to school and Mitchell was off to the office, Lindsey took a quick run, avoiding John and Jeanie's block because she felt magnetically drawn to it. She didn't want to see him because she was afraid of what would happen if she did. It was a good run. She did three miles, quick and easy.

The only annoyance of running in her neighborhood was

running into the neighbors which today included, Caren Lucci power walking with one of her friends, her neighbor walking her dog, two stroller moms strolling and another runner mom who passed her outright. Her competitive nature briefly stirred, Lindsey picked up the pace a notch until she realized that either she was in terrible shape or that other runner was younger. Much younger.

Two blocks from home, Lindsey saw John running towards her, sending her heart racing but her body automatically slowed. His pace was fast and stride strong; his arms pumping, the muscles in his legs flexing. Lindsey stared at him hopelessly, wanting desperately to make some connection, willing him to notice her, to not turn down any blocks before reaching her. As if hearing her silent prayer, he looked her way. Lindsey watched his eyes light with happiness, but just as quickly he shook his head and his expression closed off. Still they both came to almost a complete halt across from each other on opposite sides of the tree-lined street.

They were too far to speak without yelling and coming any closer to each other was even more dangerous, so they stood there for a moment just looking, sucking in as much of each other to hold on to for later when they were alone. Lindsey attempted a small smile but he didn't return it and she felt herself fill with desperation. Seeing him was possibly more torturous than not seeing him.

The sound of nearby women chatting alerted them that their time was over, but Lindsey was unable to move even as John nodded solemnly and continued on. Moments later, Lindsey was greeted by Caren and her friend.

"Hey there stranger." Caren laughed. "Run out of gas?"

Lindsey looked at her confused and then realized she was standing in the street a block from her house. "I just got lost in thought," she apologized.

"Hey, are you okay?" Caren asked. Her whole tone changed, filling with concern.

"I'm fine," Lindsey said. "I'll see you later." She walked away toward her house in a bit of a daze. Caren and her friend now stood in her vacant spot in the street watching her. It was only after she reached her house that Lindsey realized that she had been crying.

After she showered and unsuccessfully tried to wash that man right out of her hair – what a stupid sentiment, she hopped into her car and headed immediately to her mother's house with full intentions of getting something done. She walked in to the cavernous space and once again, immediately felt an overwhelming sense of loss and misery. Why was she having such a hard time with this move? Sentimentality was one thing, but this seemed really immature, kind of ridiculous and possibly a real mental issue. She stood there for an extra moment, letting the well of emotions subside until she realized that she was no longer lingering in nostalgia, she was waiting for someone. For John.

Seeing him only hours before had refreshed and heightened every memory of him. She could almost hear the sounds of his footsteps behind her, could almost feel his hands on her body, his smell wrapped around her. She could picture his eyes, full of need and desire, taking her all in. Lindsey breathed deeply, waiting, but of course he wasn't here. It was only her and the empty brown boxes outside her bedroom waiting to be filled with all things she used to love.

She sat on her bed, looking around at all her childhood knickknacks that still held such meaning: her cheer-leading pompoms, the collage of teen-idols, she and her old friend Suzanne had put together in the sixth grade, the last tennis trophy she and Liam had won in a Jr. Mixed Doubles Tournament at their tennis club. She picked up the trophy, clearly remembering that day, which happened only weeks before he died.

They were so good together, especially that day, and wiped the floors with every team they came up against, ultimately sweeping the championship round, 6-0, 6-0. They were winners. They knew it and everyone in that tournament knew it.

She rummaged through her drawers and found the picture of them taken that day. Lindsey, 15 and beautiful, her auburn hair braided down her back, a sweat band around her head and a tennis skirt so short, it almost gave away the prize, and Liam, 17, lean and gorgeous with dark sandy hair and blue eyes, his face, a masculine version of hers. Both of them smiling triumphantly. She sighed and held the picture to her chest, feeling the tears sting her eyes. Almost 25 years and it may as well have been yesterday. She definitely needed to find a therapist.

CHAPTER 8

1 in 10 married adults sleep alone.

Secrets of the Shore
FB Post

So it seems that the majority of people who cheat on their spouses are – get this – happy! Maybe not ecstatic, but certainly not miserable. That's really not saying much for marriage is it? From what I can deduce, it boils down to the fact that people are bored. Can you believe it? I guess, having been married for a long time, I can. Sort of. But wow, if that's not a kick in the pants. The happy spouse is not really that happy. So all you people out there married to miserable, cranky bastards, apparently you're good. As a completely related aside, I hear that the 'affair' may have fizzled, the questionable marriage is still in question and get this, there's a woman in town who likes to let her dog poop on their neighbor's lawn. There are some overlapping lessons here. I'm not sure I can tie it all together except to say there's a lot of shit happening.

***

"So our reservations are at Tavern MP. 8pm. Do you guys want to hitch with us? We'll pick you up. No problem," Ellie asked Lindsey on Saturday afternoon over the phone.

"Sure," Lindsey answered absently. For the past couple of days since Lindsey realized they were all going out this Saturday night and that included Jeanie and John, she had been a bundle of nerves. For almost a week, she had survived without any contact or sightings. It helped some, but if the run in told her anything it was that unfortunately out of sight does not mean out of mind; and her mind would screw her in a minute. Not to mention what it would do it him.

"But Mitchell can drive, if Benny wants to drink. I think he has hospital hours in the morning, so he wouldn't be drinking anyway."

"Sounds good," Ellie said, enthused. "I'm really looking forward. It's been a while since we all got to hang out together. It'll be like a party."

"Yeah, a party," she mimicked.

Ellie picked up on her down tone. "Are you okay?" she asked, full of concern. Ellie had always been so mothering and attuned to her moods. Early in their friendship, whether subconsciously or consciously, Lindsey gravitated to her at sleep away camp because she knew she was someone who would protect and care for her. Ellie never let her down.

Lindsey thought it was the ultimate irony that the woman who most deserved a baby couldn't have one; whereas she, on the other hand, had absolutely no issues physically getting pregnant, yet had a million emotionally. She never craved children; not that she wasn't thrilled to have them. She just wasn't that girl who saw a baby and gushed, who babysat and goo-goo'd over their sticky fingers and pudgy faces. She guessed, she was always a bit of the baby herself and didn't like the idea of sharing the spotlight. She knew how self-absorbed that sounded but she grew up a bit spoiled, at least until Liam.

"Sorry," Lindsey lied. "I got distracted by a work email. I'm fine. All good. We'll see you around 7:45p.m.."

"You sure?" Ellie asked, skeptically. "Is there anything going on that you want to talk about?"

"No worries." Lindsey sighed, sounding somewhat worried. "Just still trying to fill up the hole."

"Don't worry," Ellie promised. "Tonight we will fill it with wine."

Lindsey hung up. "Who was that?" Mitchell asked, walking in the kitchen, opening the refrigerator and emerging with a container of juice.

"Ellie," she said. "We're driving them tonight."

"Sure. I've got early hours anyway. Can't really drink."

"That's what I said."

"So, I've been meaning to ask. Have you got your room finished over at your mom's?"

It was funny how Mitchell picked up her habit of referring to her old house as her mom's, instead of her parents'.

She shook her head no. "Every time I go, I have the best intentions, but I just can't seem to make myself box anything away. I'm running out of time before the new family moves in. What is wrong with me?" she asked, not really expecting an answer.

"Well," Mitchell said, placing his glass in the sink. He really was a good husband. "I think it has a lot to do with your ability to pretend things don't exist, like your brother being dead and your distant relationship with your father. I think your childhood room preserves young you, before bad things happened, before you were damaged and changed. And, my beautiful forty-two year-old wife, there might just be a touch of mid-life crises thrown in."

Lindsey raised a brow at his frighteningly astute analysis. Just when she thought he wasn't paying any attention, he comes out with something like that. Sometimes Mitchell really did surprise her. "Why thank you, doctor."

He gave a little nod of the head. "You're welcome. See me after hours for a more thorough analysis." He winked suggestively and left the room. All in all, it was a pretty good exit. Mitchell loved a good exit.

They arrived at Ellie and Benny's at 7:45p.m. and waited for them in the car for ten minutes before Ellie came rushing out with Benny walking leisurely behind her.

"I'm so sorry," Ellie babbled. "Conner was having a moment, you know, and I needed to soothe him."

"Of course. No problem. Besides," Lindsey lifted a plastic red SOLO cup filled with wine to show her. "I was prepared."

"Nice," Ellie approved, "but what about your best bud here?"

"Come on." She laughed. "Give me some credit." And she produced a matching cup and handed it to her.

"You rock."

"I try..." Lindsey said and then turned back around in her seat. She was having such nerves getting ready that the drink, her second now, was more a necessity than an indulgence. She was shaking so much she couldn't even do her eye make-up. The drink absolutely calmed her down but now she was downright giddy. "And succeed," she added, posturing and doing a little car seat dance. She could hear Ellie's, "Oh, dear" and practically see her shake her head tolerantly.

"Music?" Lindsey asked but didn't wait for a response before cranking up the tunes. Carrie Underwood's, 'When He Cheats' blasted, and even though she loved that song, she immediately changed the station. No good. The next song she hit was Katy Perry's, 'Firework'. She had some issues with this one as well, but let it stand and started singing along. She could hear Ellie inquiring to Mitchell about her general well-being, but it didn't bother her. For the first time in almost two days, she was feeling good. She wasn't about to ruin it now because she knew that in just a few minutes, her buzz would be killed by sobering reality.

They walked into the restaurant; amazingly, the last to arrive. Mark and Diane usually held that honor, but having come with Marnie and Bradley who were generally early arrivers, they managed to come on time. Diane was probably pissed about it.

John and Jeanie were also there, apparently having come by

themselves. They were all at the bar engaged in multiple conversations, but the talk stopped when they arrived and the kisses hello and greetings began.

Lindsey worked her way through them, terrified. She caught sight of the back of John's head while saying hello to Bradley, causing her to linger in her greeting with Marnie, which then grew to include Diane and Jeanie. The words coming out of her mouth probably made absolutely no sense but it didn't matter, she had effectively stalled enough and avoided saying hello to John before the hostess called them to their table.

As they made their way over, Lindsey felt a light hand on her waist, a small gesture with huge meaning. She knew him by his touch which made her shiver, and also because all the other men, including her husband, she could see walking in front of them.

"Hey," he said, and she turned to face him. For a brief moment, looking at the emotion in his eyes made her want to touch his face and kiss his lips, but thankfully, she collected herself before she actually did either of those things. She could not be near this man, especially under the influence. His influence was overwhelming enough on its own. His eyes flickered back to casually distant and he leaned in and gave her a quick kiss on the cheek, "You didn't say hello."

"Hello." She smiled awkwardly, breathing in his scent. Really she was about to break out in hives. Worse, her nerves had just shut down her internal organs. There was a very good possibility of her dying right there.

"Shall we?" he said gallantly and gestured toward their group milling around a long rectangular table in the back, the kind Lindsey generally hated for a larger party because you only spoke with the people right next to you.

"I need to go the bathroom," she blurted out. "I'll be right there." For a second, his eyes flashed so many things she couldn't begin to sort them out, but he gave a small accepting shrug and moved toward the crowd.

Okay, she told herself, you can get through this night. You can do it. That was the hardest part. Lindsey took a big deep breath to center herself, looked up and saw Ellie staring at her slightly horrified, her lips clearly mouthing, "What the fuck?"

She was about to say something to explain or defend herself, although she had no idea what, when she noticed the person standing behind Ellie with a blank expression on her face. Jeanie.

"Hey guys," Lindsey said, and forced herself to look them in their faces. "I'm just going to the bathroom. I'll see you at the table."

"Sure," Ellie replied dryly. "We just came from there. I'd recommend it."

Lindsey smiled lightly and brushed past them, concentrating on keeping her face a mask and her gait from breaking into a run. Once she pushed open the women's bathroom door, she almost collapsed and vomited. It took her a minute to collect herself, again breathing deeply and talking herself down from the ledge. She had no idea if Jeanie saw anything. There really was nothing to see but a quick glance and she was behind him. So maybe it was okay. Ellie definitely suspected something but she could deal with Ellie. She just needed to get her ass out there before someone had to come in looking for her. That would be more of a scene than she could handle. Staring at her reflection in the mirror, she concentrated on fluffing her hair and fixing her gloss. She looked pretty good for someone about to fall to pieces, she thought. A small consolation but it helped. Finally as ready as she'd ever be and with no choice left, she headed back to the table.

She walked into the party already in progress. Only Ellie looked up when she took her seat beside her. Thankfully, the long table she found distasteful for dinner groups worked to her advantage tonight. Queen Diane had decided to hell with pretense and made an executive seating call, placing the men on one side of the table while the women sat on the other.

She swallowed her anxiety and signaled for the waiter's attention. The moment at the bar sobered her up quick. She needed to rectify that immediately and ordered a Skinny Mojito. She should save time and just order two.

As the dinner and drinks progressed, the incident seemed a lot less important. Maybe she even dramatized it a bit in her own head. It was possible. She was prone to drama. Once she even braved eye contact with Jeanie who returned it casually, certainly not like someone who thought she was sleeping with her husband, which Lindsey took as a good sign.

Somehow she managed through dinner, but right before dessert Marnie brought up the Secrets of the Shore post. "Have you guys been reading SOS? I mean there's some crazy stuff going on around town."

"Yeah, crazy," Ellie said, catching Lindsey's eye. She almost shrank from its intensity putting her brain in a whole new swirl of insecurity.

"And I know it's a side bar," Marnie continued, "but seriously, who would let their dog shit on someone else's lawn?"

They all laughed, for the moment enjoying a light tangent, but Lindsey couldn't handle any more. She interrupted them all and apologized, claiming she didn't feel well or maybe drank too much or possibly both. She got Mitchell's attention and motioned that she wanted to leave. To add to even more notches in his good husband belt, he didn't balk for a second, stood immediately, handed some cash to Bradley to cover their bill and gave their good byes. With Ellie and Benny secured in Jeanie and John's car for a ride home, they left amid much well wishes to feel better. She truly did feel sick.

"Not a bad exit," Mitchell whispered as they head for the door.

They drove in relative silence for most of the way home. Lindsey let Mitchell contend with the sitter and headed straight upstairs, guzzled a bottle of water, took two Advil and went to bed. She couldn't even begin thinking, and she definitely didn't want to talk to Mitchell. Within minutes she was out cold.

She slept late. Unbelievably, she didn't wake when Mitchell left. By the time she walked downstairs, it was 10a.m. and Riley and Liam were both eating a bowl of cereal and watching Sponge Bob.

"Hi mom," they both said together in between mouthfuls of

Captain Crunch, their weekend treat cereal.

She gave them each a kiss on the head and went to the kitchen to guzzle some more water, rip off a piece of bagel and make a cup of coffee.

She checked her phone. There were six messages from Ellie.

"Call me."

"Call me."

"Don't make me call you!"

"Are you seriously ignoring me?"

"I'm waiting!"

"I am standing right here by the phone and if you don't call I'll be at your door soon."

The last text was sent fifteen minutes ago. Lindsey quickly picked up the phone and dialed, afraid the door bell was going to ring simultaneously.

Ellie picked up on the first ring.

"Are you joking?" Were her first words, "Seriously, tell me this is a joke."

"I'm sorry. I literally just woke up." Lindsey was not sure what she was referring to but thought it best to go with less scary option.

"Uh huh." Long uncomfortable pause. "So, you want to talk about last night?"

"No. Not really." Her voice sounded a bit high and agitated.

"I'm sure you don't," Ellie said sarcastically.

"What are you talking about?" Even to her own ear, Lindsey sounded defensive. "I didn't feel well so I went home." Her heart was thumping slow and hard in her chest. Was she going to admit this to Ellie? Was she going to lie to her? She needed her coffee to be finished brewing ASAP. She needed a little clarity here.

"Lindsey. Don't play with me. I know what I saw."

"What did you see?" She challenged, completely backed into a corner. She was a frightened animal but she couldn't decide whether to lunge or to curl up in a ball and give up.

"I saw…" Ellie hesitated a moment, formulating an answer, "I saw body language."

It hung in the air. Lindsey thought maybe she could wiggle her way out of it. She could leave Ellie doubting, but in her heart she would know. It would always be there between them. "Please," she responded lamely, "I was tipsy and you know I'm a big flirt. You're making something out of nothing."

Ellie's voice was measured and cool. "I know you Lindsey, better than anyone. Remember that."

Lindsey sighed, her resolve caving. There were only so many lies she could tell. "I know."

"And you know I'm your friend no matter what fucked up thing you did," she pressed.

"I know." Lindsey felt the tears welling up. She was on the verge of a small breakdown.

"Just don't lie to me. I can't have that."

"Okay," she whimpered, sounding small like a child. Mom Ellie was so strong but steady. "But can we not talk about this now. I'm seriously not up to it. Please? Come over during the week, when my kids are in school and we can talk, okay?"

Lindsey heard Ellie take a breath, considering. "Okay," she finally agreed, "I'll be there tomorrow. Wait, no, I've got a closing tomorrow and Tuesday. Shit. Let me check my calendar." She put the phone down and I heard papers rustling. "Okay, possibly Wednesday but Thursday's a definite."

"Okay. I'm open. I'll see you then. And thanks for being a good friend Ellie. I don't know how I'd get along without you."

"Clearly, you'd fuck everything up even worse if that's possible. See you soon."

She hung the phone up exhausted, ready to go back to bed. It was a good idea, she thought, took her coffee and padded back up the steps.

"Mom!" Liam called out, which stopped her half way up.

"Yeah?" Please don't ask me to make you something, she thought. But it was worse than that.

"What time are we leaving?" he asked.

Shit. She walked back down. It was then she noticed that he was wearing his soccer uniform. Mitchell generally took him to his Sunday games or she had a pre-arranged ride, neither of which was happening today. "Right. Sorry honey, I blanked. What time is the game?"

"11:30a.m., but we have to be there by 11a.m.."

Well, that gave her a half hour to get it together, get dressed and get down to the field. Going back to bed just got bumped. It was such a nice idea. "Okay, honey. Let me get dressed and we'll go."

By 11a.m., they pulled up to the fields. She had miraculously gotten snacks and water bottles for the cooler, grabbed Riley's craft box so she could busy herself making rainbow loom bracelets, and stopped to get a large coffee and a healthy egg and cheese English muffin from Dunkin Donuts for herself and a couple of bagels and munchkins for the kids. She had their spectator chairs in place on the sidelines by 11:05a.m..

Liam joined his team warming up and Riley went off kicking a ball with two other team siblings with no other choice but to be there as well. Hanging out at the field was actually a nice thing to do, especially on a beautiful fall morning.

Lindsey opened her book while she waited for the game to begin, but first casually scanned the field. She saw a few parents of

Liam's teammates. All casual acquaintances who she was friendly with but not really friends, already engaged in conversation at the other end of the line. There was no one she needed to speak with, thank God. For now she could sit here hopefully invisible and blank out. She doubted she would be able to concentrate enough to read but it was a good cover regardless.

Then she saw him. Immediately her throat tightened and a flutter of excitement swelled in her body. He was walking towards her talking with Bradley, Marnie's husband, which of course made sense since both their boys played on the team.

They stopped when they reach her.

"Hey guys." Lindsey forced the words out like a hairball from her constricted throat. "Sorry to break up the three amigos but Mitchell has hospital hours this morning."

"You'll do," Bradley said easily and opened up his fold-away chair, just as John did the same. Much to her relief and annoyance, Bradley placed his chair next to hers and John sat next to him. The closeness was as unbearably tangible as their distance. As in life, he was so close but completely out of reach.

"So how are you feeling?" John asked. "You left us a little early last night."

"Much better, thanks." Could you feel claustrophobic outside? The air was choking her. "Did I miss anything?"

"Only Diane dancing on the table." Bradley chuckled.

"Oh yeah, I could totally see her doing that." Well-mannered, socially perfect Diane was the least likely to ever dance on a table.

"I'm just kidding. It was me. Sometimes, you just have to dance." Bradley said it seriously, eyes lit with amusement.

"Well, I'm sorry I missed that."

She chatted with them a bit but after a few minutes opened her book to further distance herself and allow them to engage in their own banter without feeling any responsibility to include her. She stared at the words on in her book but they were just a meaningless jumble of letters. She stared at them harder and they all blurred together.

Lindsey had a hard enough time pushing John to the back of her brain without seeing him, but having him in front of her was something else entirely. There was such a strong connection between them. It was like when the neighborhood lost power, except for that one house on the corner which seemed to stand out in unnatural illumination, like it was covered lawn to roof in holiday brightness instead of just the front porch light being on. In a sea of darkness, that light was a flashing neon sign.

The game was just about to begin and Riley checked in from her sideline play for a juice box. Glowing with a light sheen of sweat, she exuded youth and energy, and flashed Lindsey a smile of perfect, uncomplicated joy before running back to join her friends. Lindsey sighed wistfully, remembering a long time ago when life was that good and easy.

They boys were tied 2-2 nearing the end of the second half. Liam had played well, but bungled a penalty shot that would have given them the lead. Trevor, John's son, wasn't as strong of a player and generally played his position without helping much, but without hurting either. But Charlie, Marnie and Bradley's boy, was a star. He was the offensive attacker, the kid who always got hold of the ball and dribbled impressively down the field with a lot of showy footwork. He was the one to watch.

Bradley spent the entire last half of the game on his feet, pacing the sidelines, shouting at the boys, putting only an empty chair and a current of electricity between Lindsey and John. After feigning intense interest in the game which she barely had any idea what was going on, she finally snuck a glance over at him. His eyes were also on the field, but as if so keenly in tune with her movements, he turned his head toward her at the exact same moment. Their eyes met. Goal! Score! Win! Crap. Her stomach did flip flops. Her mouth went dry. She wanted to climb over the chair to get to him. Fuck. Yep, that too.

It was too much. She placed her head in her hands and covered her eyes. She wanted to cry. All of a sudden, cheering erupted from the sidelines, apparently Charlie was driving the ball down in scoring position, but she didn't care at all. She was lost.

"Lins?" She heard him say and then felt him closer. He had moved into Bradley's chair. "Lins, look at me."

"It's too much," she refused sadly, but lifted her head anyway. If anyone looked, Lindsey was certain her face revealed her every feeling. Thank goodness everyone's attention was on the field. At least, she hoped that was the case. This was way too public for a meltdown. She heard what sounded like a goal. Abruptly, she got to her feet to clap. John followed suit and soon the team raced off the field jumping all over each other like happy puppies.

She packed up their stuff amid the thrill of victory, which was way better than among the agony of defeat. Riley and Elliot whooped around them, begging for a play date. Lindsey immediately put the kibosh on that. "Not today, honey. We'll make a plan for during the week."

Both kids turned to John who shrugged, and gave the 'don't look at me, blame her' cop out face. Lindsey gave him a dirty look. "Seriously kids, not today. I'm not up to it."

"I can take her," John offered. "It's not a big deal. We're not doing anything for the rest of the afternoon."

"Then can Liam come too?" Trevor asked hopefully.

Four sets of little bugged out, frog eyes silently pleaded with her to agree. "Are you sure Jeanie won't mind?" It was a loaded question if ever there was one.

John shook his head. She'll be fine. She has some work to finish up, so at least the kids will be occupied and out of her hair."

"Fine, they're yours." She sighed, giving in. "I'll drop them at your house."

Cheers almost as loud as from winning the game ensued. Lindsey rolled her eyes and gave John a playful shove. "Well, you were really helpful."

"I aim to please," he said, and this time her sigh was internal. She knew that all too well.

Lindsey followed John home and let the kids out without leaving the car, watching as they raced into the house. She called out to John, "I'll call in a little bit and we'll figure out a pick-up time. Okay?"

John walked over and stuck his head in the passenger window. "I need to see you," he said seriously.

"Does Jeanie know?" she asked, and then gritted her teeth and held her breath.

"Maybe. I don't think so, but she suspects something."

"About us?"

"I don't know. She's just fishing now. We're at a critical point here. She knows it's over. It's just a matter of how easy she lets that be."

"John, I'm terrified."

"I know. I'm sorry. I never meant for this."

They looked at each other across the seat. He looked so sad; she wanted to curl on his lap and bury her face in his neck. He was a man who could make it better, she thought, and then instantly admonished herself.

"You'd better go," she said quietly, feeling the tears well.

"I know." He nodded. "But we still need to talk." As he stepped away from the car, she saw Jeanie with a sour expression standing at the front door watching them. Fuck me again.

"Hey, Jeanie!" Lindsey called out, sounding surprisingly natural. She really made herself sick. "Is it okay for the kids to be here?"

Jeanie gave her a wave. "No problem," she called, glaring at John. It seemed all her darts were aimed at her husband.

At 3p.m., Mitchell came home and Lindsey sent him to pick up the kids. She couldn't handle another interaction like that. It was all too heated and intense. She always thrived on drama in her youth, but she didn't have the stomach for it anymore. This whole situation was out of control. She decided to go with her earlier plan and spend the rest of the day in bed. With Mitchell back home, she changed into sweats, told him and the kids she had a headache and hibernated in her room. It was the best thing she could have done for herself. She fell right to sleep and didn't stir till after 6p.m.. When she ventured downstairs at 6:30pm after a refreshing shower, she found the house blissfully empty. A note on the table said that they had gone out for pizza and would be back around 7:30p.m..

Lindsey ate a container of Greek yogurt mixed with some cereal and blueberries and went back upstairs to bed. By the time they got home, she was halfway through an episode of the Real Housewives of Orange County. Full of drunken screaming fights, betrayal and gorgeous clothes, it kept her mind happily occupied on other people's ridiculous drama. It was damn good television.

She put the show on pause and resumed her roll of wife and mom; helping the kids wash up, double checking their knapsacks for school the next day, making sure they didn't forget anything that was due. After spending twenty minutes picking out Riley's outfit for the next morning, and enforcing the mandatory when-it-worked-out reading time, it was finally lights out by 9p.m. for Riley and 9:30p.m. for Liam.

Still exhausted even after a day of sleep, Lindsey joined Mitchell on the couch – the one adjacent to him, not the same as him. She learned not to mess with certain personal space comforts that had been mutually agreed upon over the years. She refused to believe that relaxing on different couches was really one of their issues. Sometimes, after a long day you just need a little room to breathe.

"So, how was work?" she asked.

"Good." He nodded distractedly, still paying attention to his laptop.

"Do you think maybe we could talk a little without the laptop?"

She tried, working really hard to hide the annoyance she felt. She always shared Mitchell with his work. It was the third person in their marriage. Before she added the fourth, she thought, guiltily.

His time at work, both at the office and on the couch, had never bothered her much, but since John, all their flaws glared. It was like when she put on a crisp white tee shirt but found a tiny yellow stain in a corner. Once she saw it, it was all she saw and she'd need to put the shirt in her pile to give away. Or maybe, she was looking for stains; searching like Riley did for the minuscule shred of green hidden in her food and then declaring the entire dish inedible.

Mitchell glanced up. She could tell it wasn't a good time. He seemed stressed. "Listen babe, I've got a ton of labs to go through tonight. Do you think we could catch up later?"

"I guess, but it would be nice to, I don't know, connect a little? I feel like I haven't seen you."

There was a pause in his typing, and he looked up searchingly, "We've seen each other as much as we always do."

She had his attention and there was an opening for a possible conversation. "Well, maybe it's not enough. Maybe we should work on seeing a little more of each other." She felt like she put something major out there, but Mitchell didn't take it that way.

He smiled smoothly. "Of course. Absolutely. We'll make a night out just the two of us, okay? Next Saturday?"

"Sure," she agreed, barely disguising her disappointment.

"We'll talk about it later." He smiled guiltily. "After I get through all this." He picked up a pile of papers, as if to document proof of his busyness.

"Of course, honey." She let him off the hook. There was no way it would happen later. It almost never did. By the time Mitchell came up from his doctor bubble, she was almost always asleep, and tonight was no different.

CHAPTER 9

57% of those in unhappy relationships still find their partner extremely attractive.

Lindsey needed to keep her mind occupied but had nothing going on. The Skittles job was done and she didn't have another freelance project anywhere on her upcoming calendar. She generally averaged two to three jobs a year, which suited her just fine. Enough to keep her in the game and give her a little sophisticated edge, but not enough to overwhelm her life.

She had vowed not to think about her relationship with Mitchell, the flaws that must hound every marriage, the taking for granted, the assumption of security, the casual dismissals, the diminished sex. They were patterns many couples fell into over the years which were balanced out by having someone always in your corner. It was the shared baggage that came with a life time together, companionship, family and love. Any relationship under a microscope could be picked apart. She needed to throw away the microscope, stop focusing on the bad and concentrate on the good. Sexy, good man, she repeated, because it was true and she needed to hear it over and over.

Even though it was the perfect thing to do, and the thing that she needed to do, she still didn't want to go to her mother's and do her room. But she didn't want to think about that either. So as a distraction, she made the mistake of checking the SOS Facebook page for any updates. She found one and read horrified.

Holy Toledo! Or more accurately, Holy Shore Point! What is in the water over here?! Apparently, the marriage on the rocks and the affair are connected, so look for another marriage to be heading to those rocks real soon. This is all way too Peyton Place. "Oh hello, can I borrow a cup of sugar. Forget it, I'll just take a piece of your hunka husband." Man, I can't take this! I'm running out of nails to bite!!

Oh my GOD. This had to be about her and John. It couldn't be! It had to be!

She read through some of the comments, there were almost a hundred. Most were gossip whores, many of whom she knew, jumping all over the mystery, but a few comments were quite scathing like, "Mind your own business bitch." From Heidi Burnett. And, "You're playing with people's lives. What are you doing?" That one was from her friend Diane.

She felt manic, like she main-lined her coffee and chased it with a shot of Red Bull. She briefly wondered if she was having an anxiety attack, but put that ridiculous notion out of her mind. She needed to run. She needed to run right now. She threw on a pair of cropped running pants, a tank and a long sleeved tee shirt, which she would inevitably take off and wrap around her waist when her body warmed up. Although she already felt hot and she hadn't even started; it must be her brain racing like a crackhead hamster on the wheel.

She hadn't been officially outside yet but knew it was a nice day from the sun pouring through the windows and the crisp breeze she had felt when she waved the kids off to the bus. Exiting through the garage so she could pull in the garbage cans, she tapped her feet waiting for the automatic door to roll up, impatient to get moving and feel the fresh air. She watched the sunny outside slowly leak in as the door rose, then took a quick startled step back noticing a pair of men's shoes. Slowly, the door continued its upward momentum revealing pant legs around the ankle, then knees and thighs. Her first instinct was to run back into the house and lock the door. It would be the normal thing to do just in case it was a killer waiting to kill her, or Jeanie. But somewhere inside she knew.

The door continued rising along with Lindsey's heart rate, waiting to find out what was the prize behind curtain number one, but she didn't have to wait any longer because John ducked under and stood before her.

"Close it," he ordered and Lindsey pushed the button to reverse the doors' motion. They stood locked in an eye embrace, waiting tensely for the door to bang to its finish. He moved toward her in a rush and kissed her long and deep. She kissed him back almost as greedily before she remembered they weren't doing that anymore. His hands were already on her body which was a hundred percent behind her betrayal. "John. Stop," she whispered, but his mouth was crushed against hers.

"I've missed you so much," he said in between his sensual assault. "So much."

Somehow Lindsey managed to slow down the force of his need by pushing him back a little and kissing him tenderly and unhurried. It calmed him a bit, but did nothing to extinguish their mutual desire. "John," she tried again, "Stop." He heard her that time and listened, but their faces and bodies were so close she could almost taste his mouth and she could definitely feel his hardness against her. It was denying a force of nature to keep them apart, but she did.

"Okay," he said, but still took one long, sweet, open mouthed kiss full of slow licking and gentle biting before he released her. "Sorry," he offered slyly, causing her to smile despite herself. She was almost giddy with happiness to have him near her. It was bad.

They went inside and sat down on the living room couch. The same couch where their relationship officially began. "Maybe we should talk... in the kitchen," Lindsey suggested uncomfortably and quickly got up. He followed her, a satisfied grin settled on his face, until she punched him in the arm. "Not funny," she scolded and pointed to one of the chairs around her island. The cool, efficient kitchen felt safe, although one would have thought the cluttered, dusty garage was safe as well. "Come on, can I get you a drink. Something cold?" She raised a brow.

"Sure. Whatever you've got."

Lindsey poured both of them a cup of water and leaned against the counter, trying to figure out where to begin with this conversation.

Finally, she sighed and asked the right question; the one she actually didn't care about the answer to, but had to ask. "What are you doing here?"

"You don't seem unhappy to see me," he countered. "Not now, not at soccer, not at dinner."

She nodded. "You're right, but that's exactly the reason why we can't see each other. Clearly we are extremely attracted to each other. And we're good friends. It's a combination that is becoming emotionally out of control really fast." Her words sounded cool and detached; such an insulting contrast to the warmth and genuineness of their connection. She was trying hard to say the things she was supposed to, which were not the things she wanted.

"It already is for me," John argued, as overwhelmed with feeling as she was subdued. He sprang from his seat and pinned her against the counter. How did the kitchen become so hot so quick? "Lins, I can't imagine not seeing you, not being with you. I feel alive and complete with you."

He had her locked again in his embrace and his words. Fuck me, she thought angrily at everything and everyone. Fuck Mitchell. Fuck my picture perfect life. Fuck this man. She couldn't help but respond to the heat emanating from him, pushing against her body and her heart. He lifted her up onto the counter and pulled off her shirt, nuzzling his head into the crown of her breasts. He kissed her again and again as he opened the fly of his pants and she struggled out of her leggings.

"I am so in love with you," he whispered, and even though she knew it and felt it and wanted it, the honesty and reality of his words stopped her cold. She pushed him back breathlessly. "John, stop."

"Now?" He groaned, but took a step back. "We have to work on your timing."

Again, he made her smile and she hopped off the counter. "Come on, sit."

"With this thing?" He smirked and pointed to his extended crotch area. "You're kidding."

She resisted the urge to help him with his problem and instead hit him on the shoulder, which was getting to be kind of fun and a good release of pent up energy.

"Ow." He pretended injury.

"I was just trying to divert your blood to another location."

"Gee thanks." He pulled up his pants and managed to close them, although it looked pretty comical, while she retrieved her leggings and pulled them back on.

"This is bad. You can't be..." She was embarrassed to say it.

"In love with you?" John offered easily without awkwardness.

"Yeah, that." She couldn't maintain eye contact, but he lifted her face to his.

"Honestly, I've been in love with you since we met and it has only grown stronger in the years we've gotten to know each other. Us fitting together so well is something I never expected. Not that I ever expected this to happen at all."

"I can't believe it happened either," she said. "I didn't see it coming."

"Do you regret that it did?" He winced a little, afraid of her answer. "I mean, I would understand if you did. You have a lot to lose here."

She looked up into his eyes. She also had a lot to gain, she thought miserably. It wasn't an easy question to answer and she said so, but her gut instinctual answer was no. No, she didn't regret that it happened. She couldn't regret feeling this connected and alive. She did regret the implications of it and the complications. She regret betraying her husband and Jeanie, but being with him? No. She didn't think she had ever felt more right with someone ever. If she could go back and do it again or not, she would. She wanted to be with John, there was no denying it, but even having said that, she knew that she loved Mitchell too.

"I don't want to break-up my marriage," she said miserably, trying to convince herself as well. "Which is why I can't see you, no matter how much I want to. No matter what feelings I have for you." She didn't know where she was channeling the strength to do this. Ellie probably.

"Because your feelings for Mitchell are stronger?" John asked searchingly, which was not even a remotely fair question.

"Because he's my husband and the father of my children." Lindsey answered simply and turned away at the expression in his eyes.

He nodded regretfully. "I told Jeanie I wanted a divorce last night."

Even knowing it was inevitable, it still threw Lindsey for a loop. "Oh my God. Really?"

"Yeah. It shouldn't have come as a surprise given our relationship and recent discussions, but apparently she wasn't expecting it. There was a lot of broken glass."

Her hand flew to her mouth in shock. "What about the boys? Were they there?"

"No. They were at her parents for the night. That's one of the perks of having in-laws who live in the same town. You get your mother and father-in-law a little too close, but you also get built-in babysitters. I have the cleaning woman there right now. I already filed. So it's done. No going back, not that I would ever want to. I swear, after filing and telling her, it was the biggest relief, like I was holding my breath for years and I finally let all that air out. I feel like someone has just given me a get out of jail free card. Although, it'll be anything but free. Jeanie will make sure of that."

"So is Jeanie home now?" All of a sudden, Lindsey was afraid she was about to knock on the door. Her brain flipped like a pancake, between feeling bad for them to feeling worried for her. She was like a mood ring, constantly changing colors.

"Nah, Jeanie's a professional." Then he intoned a sarcastic, bitter charge, complete with a small fist pump. "When there's work to be done, Jeanie will do it."

It sounded like something he had said often. "So what do you do next?" Lindsey asked.

He shrugged. "I don't know. Wait for the lawyers to tell me if I can move out of my house, I guess. I hope it's going to be soon. I really can't wait, especially now. It's not going to be easy living together for too long. It was hard enough when we were pretending to like each other, now we have to pretend not to hate each other." He quickly amended, "Not that I hate Jeanie. I don't. She's a good person and a good mom, and I wasn't the husband for her, just like she wasn't the wife for me. We both pretended too long for our own reasons, the kids being a huge one. It's still going to be hard on her to get over this. You know her. She's not one to swallow a pill easily. She always secretly thinks everyone has it out for her. Her friends, her job, me... it's like she's always just sitting there waiting for the other shoe to fall so she could say, 'Aha!' and cross the offender off her list. I don't know why she didn't divorce me sooner."

"I'm sorry," she said, because she didn't know what else to say.

"Don't be," he smiled. "This is the best thing that could have happened to both of us. I know divorce is terrible and I don't take it lightly, but I've given well over a decade of my life to Jeanie and it's time for me to be happy too. It's really a good thing for us both. I've spent a lot of my life taking care of other people, sometimes you have to take care of yourself."

Lindsey nodded, thinking about what he said. It spoke to her on so many different levels. His needs were important, just like hers were. Maybe it was time to look at her own life a little more closely. Not that she was comparing John and Jeanie's marriage to hers and Mitchell's. Not in the least. They were obviously unhappy; while she and Mitchell could continue on in their contented apathy probably until they died. But there was no denying that at the moment, both physically and emotionally, Lindsey wanted a man who wasn't her husband much more than she wanted her husband.

A small part of her was even a little bit excited that he was getting a divorce, because, not only was there a higher possibility that they would both be happier, but pathetically, it left the door open for her, if she should so choose. Lindsey was always a girl who liked options but that was just a tiny ugly part of her brain and she quickly shoved that thought under the rug. John needed to start a new life and Lindsey needed to figure out how to get hers back. "Well, okay then," Lindsey amended. "I stand corrected. I am happy."

He smiled, warm and sweet. "Good. That's how I want you." Then, he grabbed her hand and squeezed it. "Listen, I'm going to go, because if you truly don't want to break up your marriage, you're right, I shouldn't be here. It's just too hard for both of us. No matter how much I like Mitchell and want to be a good guy here, the truth is I love you. I want us to be together. I know there's something exciting about this sneaking around crap, but I'm not that guy. I want you in my life for real, and if you're not in the same place, then it's better for us both that I really do stay away, as difficult as that may be."

He stood to go and even though it was exactly what she wanted, it certainly didn't feel that way. Not even a little bit. All of a sudden, the thought of losing him made her desperate to keep him. Panicked, she threw her arms around his neck and hugged him tightly to her.

As expected, their hug immediately assumed greater implications. It was a sensation she wanted to hold on to, to be branded in her soul - desire, attraction, passion, someone who longed for her, a genuine connection without the complications of real life. But that wasn't real, was it? All of those things weren't really sustainable in the face of real life. Lindsey looked up at him, filled with emotion and held him even tighter against her than before. "I don't want you to go," she cried.

He sniffed back his pain, gently touched her face and hit her with the truth. "But you don't want to leave either."

And there it was. She lowered her eyes and felt the tears mount, sliding down her face in slow, quiet rolls. He looked at her sadly. "Don't," he pleaded. "Don't make this harder than it is."

She nodded, knowing he was right; that she was not playing fair. "Could it really be harder?" she asked, wiping her face with her sleeve. She was just so afraid of losing him and these feelings; so potent she literally glowed when she was with him. She couldn't imagine anymore going back to the bland, non-descript existence she was living. Her eyes were open and she couldn't help but see the beautiful man and the potential life that was right in front of her. She was torn straight down the middle, pulled apart by love on both sides. "You're right," she sniffled. "I know. I'm sorry."

He tilted her head up and they looked at each other in raw despair. His lips touched hers and she tasted her own tears. "See ya around," he said with a wistful wink and walked out of the kitchen toward the front door.

"See you around, cowboy," she whispered quietly to herself as the door closed firmly behind him.

CHAPTER 10

Lindsey - 1986

"Mom!" Lindsey screamed. "Where are my Big John jeans?"

"Wherever you left them," she screamed back.

"That's not helpful!" Lindsey screamed back down.

"Help yourself!" her mom screamed back up.

"Moooooooommmmm!" she whined loudly.

"Try under your bed," her mom yelled. "You're unbelievable."

Lindsey rummaged around, pulling out her roller skates with the rainbow pom pom laces, one blue Reebok sneaker and... her Big John jeans.

"Thank you!" She yelled back down, but her mother stood in her doorway; small, fit and dark haired. She seemed much younger than forty-five years-old, with two teenage kids living at home.

"So where you headed tonight?" her mom asked.

"Maryann's house. She's having a big party."

"Yeah, a senior party, doof. Not for little sophs like you." Her brother Liam barged his annoying face into the room, right next to their mom, who he kissed sweetly on the cheek.

"I'm going," Lindsey said defiantly. "All my friends are."

Liam brushed his sandy hair away from his eyes. He wore it surfer long lately and with his lanky athletic frame, it suited him, although it annoyed their mother, who always threatened to cut it in his sleep. He shrugged and warned, "Just don't let me catch you hitting on any of my friends."

"Ha! Why don't you tell your dirty old friends to stop hitting on me," Lindsey considered a moment, "Except Billy. Billy can hit on me."

He pointed a threatening finger in her direction. "Stay away from Billy."

"Sure." She smiled slyly. "But will Billy stay away from me?"

"You!" Liam trounced into her room and pushed her on her bed, mock beating her.

"Mom!" Lindsey screamed. "Help!"

"Help yourself. I'm out."

Their mom left them to playfully beat each other, which went on for a loud, ridiculous minute until Lindsey finally shoved Liam away. "You're screwing up my hair!" She yelled. She had already spent over a half an hour with a curling iron to get it right.

Liam gave her a final noogie and sauntered out, the essence of senior cool. "Just remember Tattle Tattle Lin Lin, what you see at the party, stays at the party. Got it?"

"You don't see me, I won't see you," she agreed, as he exited.

"Deal." He flashed a wide toothed grin, which had all the girls in his high school falling over themselves to kiss. "Except, I'll be watching everything you do, so you better be good."

Lindsey threw the blue Reebok at his smiling face.

"Your aim is about as good as your serve!" he taunted, and left to go to his room down the hall.

Lindsey and her friend Tracy got a ride with their friend Carly, a junior who already had her license. Lindsey had an 11p.m. curfew, with the possibility of extending it to 11:30p.n., if she called and begged. When they pulled up at 8:30p.m., she could tell this was a party which was already out of control. It would be lucky to last till 10p.m., much less 11p.m..

Cars were parked up and down the residential street. The music blasted so loud the house seemed to pump with the beat. They needed to turn that down or someone would be calling the police pretty quick, Lindsey thought. They found a spot and walked to the backyard gate where a high school senior named Troy stopped them. "It's a $5 cover."

They all looked at one another. A cover? What kind of a party was this?

"Five bucks?" Lindsey stammered. "For what?"

"To get in," Troy said. He was obviously in practice for a career as a bouncer. "There are also kegs back there."

"Oh." They all started rummaging through their purses.

"Hey, aren't you Liam's little sister?" Troy asked and she nodded. "Well, why didn't you say so? You're in. No problem."

"Thanks," she smiled coyly.

"No problem cutie," he said and gave her a wink. Her cut off Madonna shirt must have looked even better than she thought.

With the party in full gear, they had to push and slide their way through the largely drunk crowd. Lindsey's eyes were wide, taking it all in. She was no stranger to parties, but this one was bigger and badder than usual.

Mary Ann's backyard was huge. There was a pool and tennis

courts, not unusual in upper middle class Dix Hills, but always nice. Some kids she recognized had set up their band in the corner and were blasting out a not too terrible rendition of 'What I like about you' by The Romantics. They mingled a bit and lost Carly to her boyfriend Jimmy, last seen heavily making out on a lounge chair in the pool area.

Lindsey and Tracy each got a blue Solo plastic cup, and made their way to one of the kegs. "I wonder where Mary Ann's parents are?" Tracy asked.

"I wonder who Mary Ann is?" Lindsey laughed. It wasn't unusual to show up to neighborhood house parties like this and have no idea who was hosting.

"How you doing with that?" Tracy asked amused, gesturing to the keg that Lindsey was trying to make sense of.

"Not so good." She had never pumped a cup of beer from a keg herself and it didn't seem like that was going to change tonight.

"Can I help you there?" The voice came from behind her. Lindsey turned around and saw Billy and bit her lip in happiness. There was nothing she wouldn't do to hook up with Billy Mason. Well, almost nothing.

"That would be great," she said, handed him her cup and shrugged cutely, she hoped. "I really don't know what I'm doing."

"Ah, a first timer." He smiled, a toothpaste commercial, all American jock smile.

She and Billy had been flirting on and off for almost a year, since he and Liam became good friends. Billy was on the tennis team and they played basketball together. Liam had always come between them, but Lindsey decided tonight to pretend that she wasn't Liam's sister.

"Maybe you'll show me how?" she asked innocently, while Tracy mock gagged behind him.

"Sure." He placed her hand on the lever and covered it with his own. "You just pump it like this, not too slow and not too fast and angle your cup under here."

They stood bodies close, hand over hand for the thirty seconds watching the golden liquid fill the cup but really watching their attraction rise. When it was full, Billy handed her the beer, which he said had the perfect amount of foam. She hadn't had a sip, but already felt a little dizzy from their contact.

Billy got a cup for Tracy and one for himself, and then they stood together awkwardly. "Want to hang out with me over there?" he asked and pointed to where a group of seniors were sitting on a bunch of patio chairs. Lindsey saw her brother among them. She also saw a few juniors, two other sophomore girls and even a freshman hanging out. "Sure, why not?"

"You know," Tracy interjected. "I see a couple of our friends over there." She pointed to where a bunch of fellow sophomores they knew were hanging out. "I think I'm going to go say hello."

Lindsey felt immediately torn. She wanted to be with Billy, but her group of friends had their own comfortable appeal. She looked at them and then back at Billy, who smiled at her encouragingly. "I'll meet you over there in a little bit," she said to Tracy. Billy smiled and grabbed her hand. Happiness.

"I'm a little afraid of my brother." Lindsey admitted as they walked slowly over. He had seen them coming and fixed her with a dark don't-you-dare stare.

"If you're uncomfortable, we can go take a walk or something." His offer hung there appealingly, but she was feeling rebellious.

"After. Let's go hang out first," she said and all of a sudden she was dragging him over.

They joined the party easily and hellos were exchanged all around. Nobody cared that she was there, except Liam who refused to say anything to either her or Billy, and seemed a little drunk. She tried to speak with him more than once, but each time she approached him, he just held up that warning finger and fixed her with a look that kept her back. She didn't want to embarrass him. Or herself.

"Fine," she finally muttered and leaned back into Billy who put his arms safely around her. She wasn't going to let Liam ruin her night. It was after 10p.m., and the party, miraculously, hadn't been broken up yet. She was sipping her second beer, still enjoying the buzz of the first. By her count, Liam had downed three beers in the past hour, and that wasn't including what he drank before she joined them. He had become loud and showy in the past half hour, daring his friends to do stupid things.

She walked over, a little off balance from her own alcohol consumption and whispered in his ear. "I think you're drinking too much."

He sneered and gave her a little shove. "Lins, go back to the kiddie pool."

She knew he was drunk but still his words stung. She and Liam bantered back and forth a lot but they were always allies. She never expected a public reprimand. It was humiliating and she reacted exactly like a fifteen year-old by leaning into his friend Billy and making out with him in front of Liam. The explosive look on Liam's face could have started a fire. "We're out of here," he announced, standing unsteadily. "Let's go." A few of his friends rose to follow him, but they all looked equally wobbly.

Lindsey stopped immediately and went over to him. "Liam. Please don't go." He ignored her. "I'm sorry," she called out but he walked past, and off-handedly shoved Billy who immediately stood at offense. She gave Billy the stand down look and followed Liam to the party exit. "Liam! Stop!" she yelled but he just kept walking with his friends toward the street. He got into an old Chevy Malibu with three equally inebriated friends and slammed the door in her face.

"Liam! You guys! You can't drive." Lindsey was growing a little hysterical and Billy stood away from her unsure of what to do. She banged on the car hood. "Hey!"

Finally, Liam rolled down the window. "Don't sweat it, sis. It's okay. Just remember, no Tattle Tattle Lin Lin, Okay?" He gave a wolfish grin, banged the roof of the car and after some loud rotating wheels, they sped off.

It was the last time she ever saw Liam alive.

CHAPTER 11

"Sometimes the things you are most afraid of are the things that make you the happiest."—Kiara Leigh

"So, Jeanie came in to see me today," Mitchell said casually. He had just come home from work, changed into house clothes and was sitting at the kitchen table flipping through mail while Lindsey finished up dinner. She was stirring the sauce and automatically stopped mid-stir, a feeling of anxious paralysis creeping through her body. Realizing this would seem a strange reaction; she picked up the pot by the handle, turned around and continued her unhurried mixing.

"Oh yeah? How's her back?" She really, really hoped she sounded normal.

Mitchell didn't answer and took his time opening a piece of mail in front of him. Was he playing with her? She fretted. Would she normally wait patiently for him to finish with the mail or make some remark about being ignored? She was so out of sorts, she had no idea how to act, so she just repeated herself, pretending she thought he hadn't heard. "So, how's Jeanie's back?"

Mitchell looked up at her blankly. There was no smile in his eyes today. "Is there something you want to tell me?"

Lindsey felt the walls closing in. She didn't even feel the pot slip from her hand to the floor. It crashed with a loud bang, red sauce splattering everywhere. "Oh shit!"

Mitchell was up immediately. "Did you burn yourself?" he asked with a concern she took comfort in.

"Not really. A few splatters won't kill me." She looked around. "What a mess." It was amazing what one half pot of sauce could do. It looked like someone had been murdered. The thought gave her an involuntary shiver. As she unrolled paper towels to start wiping up the spill, Mitchell arrived with the mop. He really was smarter than she was. "Thanks," she said. "Why didn't I think of that?"

"Why didn't you think of getting a mop?" Mitchell snorted. "Do you even know where the mop is?"

Lindsey puffed out like an Angry Bird with indignation and grabbed the mop. "Of course I do!" She was lying. She didn't. Or at least she'd need to think about it. She had a housekeeper come in twice a week. She couldn't remember the last time she looked for the mop.

Mitchell just stood there snickering. "Oh yeah, you and the mop, you seem like you spend a lot of time together." It was hard to maintain an aura of mopping prowess when she couldn't figure out how to wring out the water.

"Arrgh!" She yelled in frustration that probably had nothing to do with the mop, but she took it out on the inanimate object anyway and left it sticking out of the sink, refusing to use it again. She crouched back on the floor with the paper towels. She was frustrated and aggravated and practically spit, "So, are you going to tell me what happened with Jeanie or what?"

Mitchell relented. "Looks like she and John are getting divorced. She said you knew and was surprised you hadn't mentioned it."

"Wow," Lindsey said, because she didn't know what to say. "I mean, I had heard that possibility but I didn't know it was really true. We were just out with them last week, but obviously it is if Jeanie is just coming out like that and sharing. That's crazy."

"She was pretty sour, already talking about financial

compensation and all that. Jeanie's pretty aggressive to begin with. This is definitely not going to be pretty."

"I just hope they're smart for the sake of Trevor and Elliot."

"I said that and she just looked at me sideways with a bitter smile and an equally sour tongue and said, and I quote, 'If I were you I'd be smart about Lindsey. John's always had the hots for her.'"

Lindsey's mouth went a little slack and Mitchell raised a brow. Nothing pretty about that comment. Jeanie's guns were out and she was already shooting around. "She said that? What did you say?"

"I didn't say anything and returned the conversation to her back issue."

Oh. They stood there wordlessly until finally Lindsey handed him a wet paper towel and he joined her around the floor wiping sauce. After a few moments of silent contemplation she asked, "So, how is her back?"

"She's fine. A minor herniated disc, a few pinched nerves. She's completely tense and tied up in knots. She needs to relax, take some hot baths, use some cold compresses, do the exercises I gave her, but somehow I don't see any of that happening."

"Not likely," she agreed.

"So, John has the 'hots' for you, does he?" Mitchell repeated and Lindsey felt the intensity behind his eyes.

"If Jeanie said so," she answered easily, like she could lie all day. Then, she smiled picked up a soiled paper towel and attempted to lighten the mood. "Well, can you really blame him?"

Mitchell didn't answer and continued to help with the floor.

Lindsey wasn't sure what was going on in Mitchell's head. He had a strange faraway look in his eyes making her extremely nervous.

After the mess was cleaned and the table set, they all sat around the table eating Lindsey's chicken cutlets, broccoli and spaghetti, sautéed with butter, garlic and oil, since the sauce was toast.

Liam and Riley kept the conversation alive with their constant bickering over who was and wasn't eating what was on their plates, who liked the chicken the most, who typically eats more spaghetti; although obviously the term conversation was very loosely employed. More like distraction and noise. Still it was better than silence.

"Why don't you guys ask Daddy about work?" Lindsey suggested. "Maybe he has a good bone story to tell you?"

Since the kids were little, Mitchell had told them fabricated stories about his work with bones, somehow becoming an animal specialist of the neighborhood. They would go for walks around the block and the kids would excitedly point out dogs to him. "Did you give that dog a bone yet, daddy?" Mitchell would crouch down, give the dog a scratch and either nod his head happily and say something like, "Oh yes, that dog really likes shoulder bones." Or he would shake his head contemplatively and say, "No, not yet. Thank you for reminding me. I'll put him on the list." For years, the kids probably thought their father was either a veterinarian or a butcher.

More recently, Liam, especially, was fascinated with real medical stories which Mitchell offered him at times in age appropriate terms. Liam might actually follow in his dad's footsteps. He was the kid who when he needed to have blood drawn, watched the vile fill with fascination, and at the pediatrician asked precocious questions about his shots; what they were and why they were necessary. But today it seemed there would be no stories.

"Sorry guys," Mitchell apologized with a shrug. "Daddy's tired."

That wasn't like Mitchell at all.

Lindsey spent the evening keeping busy with laundry and being on top of the kids, making sure their homework wasn't just done, but done perfect. She got them to bed about a half hour earlier than usual, hoping and dreading for some alone time with Mitchell.

At around 9p.m., she sat down on the couch across from him. You would think that just entering the room and sitting down on the couch might register a reaction from her husband, but not tonight. Still, not completely out of the ordinary. She had had run-ins with him and his iPad before. "Hey," she said and the sound of keys clicking halted.

"Hey," he answered.

"I just thought we could talk more. You seem... I don't know..." Her voice trailed off.

"Lins, I've got a lot of work to do."

She was really tired of that old line. "I know, but you always have a lot of work to do."

"You married a doctor. Part of the deal," he said flatly.

"And you married a woman," she shot back. "I need some attention."

He sighed loudly. "Fine. You're right. But I've had a busy, bad day. I just need to unwind." He forced a smile that just looked impatient and annoyed. "Could we table it for tonight? I really am not up to any conversation. I just want to relax."

She didn't know what to make of that response. It was beyond frustrating being shut out. Even when the potential conversation was terrifying, she was more afraid of the unknown. "Sure," she said, having no other recourse and stood up to leave him be. "I'm going to go up then."

He nodded seriously but it was directed at his computer. "Okay. Good night."

She was almost clear of the room but couldn't help a last question before she left. "But just tell me, are you okay? Is everything alright?"

This time he didn't lift his head from his screen when he answered. "Remains to be seen."

Crap. It was a killer exit line.

She spent the rest of the evening in a state of heightened

anxiety. His words haunted her. Losing herself in television was impossible. She just couldn't concentrate and kept drifting back to her own drama. After flipping channels mindlessly, she gave up and decided to take a shower, then to scrutinize her skin. Afterwards she started going through clothes in her closet. She couldn't sit still. Mitchell came up around midnight and even though she was waiting for him, she pretended sleep because having any sort of interaction at that moment would only be worse.

That night, she didn't think she slept even a minute, but when Mitchell got up in the morning, took a quick shower and dressed, she still pretended that she was. As per his usual Wednesday routine, he headed to the gym early, before the office.

After she heard him leave, she got out of bed and dressed. Out of habit, she put on her gym clothes, but she didn't think she had the strength. She made herself some coffee and checked her phone. There were twelve new texts. Apparently, the word on Jeanie and John was officially out and Diane, Marnie and Ellie had a group text going sharing their dumbfounded shock.

It was basically,

"OMG! Did you hear?"

"Is it true?"

"Oh, it's true!"

"I can't believe it!"

"I can't believe it either!"

"Me too!"

"WTF?!"

There were a few more enlightening, articulate interactions like the above which finally concluded with a scheduled emergency lunch at Yaki. Ugh, Lindsey groaned, she really needed a shot in her coffee this morning.

She got the kids off to school and headed to the gym, intending to do a half-assed workout but instead joined a Zumba class and walked out covered in sweat, expelled toxins and natural endorphins. She felt so much better. After a brief stop at the supermarket where she amazingly didn't run into anyone she knew, she went home, put the groceries away, showered and with much trepidation, headed off to meet the girls for lunch. All of a sudden, she was starved.

Lindsey was the first to arrive which was unusual. She was typically one of the last, sliding in right before Diane, who took pride in being the most late. Lindsey actually thought on more than one occasion that Diane stalked the restaurant and watched them all arrive only to casually saunter in a few minutes later. Lindsey wouldn't put it past her. It was all about appearances.

She pulled her book from her bag, once again attempting to read, and once again realizing it wasn't happening. Luckily, she didn't have long to wait, the doors opened and the girls walked in one after the other, talking excitedly.

They all kissed hello in between exclamatory bursts of amazement – I know! Can you believe?! It's crazy! Totally floored! Once seated, they immediately started in on the gossip which when talking about friends doesn't qualify as gossip as much as concern and commiseration.

"I'm still in shock," Diane said, "Really, really in shock. I mean, I talk with Jeanie often and I knew they were in trouble but I didn't realize how much. Did any of you guys know?"

She looked directly at Ellie who shrugged. "Well, I knew what you did. That they were in trouble." Ellie turned to Marnie and filled her in. "I was over Jeanie's one day a few months back with Diane and she confided that they had some major issues."

"And does anyone know anything about this potential affair?" Diane scrutinized each of them at the table, first focusing on Ellie then around to the rest. They all shook their heads like puppets for the scary puppet master. No, they had no idea.

"Just because a stupid post insinuated it, doesn't mean it's true," Marnie said. "I mean, we don't even know if it was about them."

Was Lindsey being paranoid or did Diane's gaze linger on her for just an extra beat? Lindsey quickly looked away and checked herself. Get it together, she scolded herself sternly. They're all just talking. She took a mental breath and refocused.

Diane sniffed in offense. "Oh, I think we know."

They all nodded sheepishly.

"You're probably right," Marnie agreed.

"That post has sunk to a new low. I used to be amused by it... the neighborhood gossip, the party scenes, the style watch... But lately, it's just nasty innuendo that can destroy lives," Diane said, and Lindsey felt the strength of her conviction.

"Do you think they'll move?" Marnie wondered.

"I guess it's possible, but I would think it's more likely that John will just move out," wise council Ellie offered. Lindsey hadn't yet made eye contact with Ellie. She knew they were supposed to have their own private lunch today or tomorrow, but obviously the group gathering and the explosive news trumped them. Now, no matter how uncomfortable, it was important for Lindsey to make both eye-contact and actively join the conversation.

"What a mess," Lindsey added, shaking her head.

"Yes," Ellie repeated a little sternly. Lindsey felt heat rising from the back of her neck and prayed it didn't travel round to her face. "What a mess."

The waitress took their orders in between their comprehensive dissection and analysis. Marnie, Diane and Ellie had all spoken with Jeanie and as a running dialogue they pieced together what they each understood had happened. Lindsey listened to how John had sat Jeanie down on the couch and handed her a glass of wine. How he had arranged for her parents to take the kids for the night.

"Jeanie said she thought they were going to have a real discussion. Yes, she knew divorce was on the table but was completely thrown that he had actually already filed." Marnie said.

"That's when she screamed, threw the glass of wine at his head and flipped out," Diane added.

"I approve of flipping out after screaming and throwing glassware," Ellie said.

"And back to the potential affair..." Diane lowered her voice for dramatic effect, which totally worked. They all leaned in to hear better. "I don't know if she mentioned but it's not just the stupid post. Jeanie is convinced he is having one."

The entire table took in this information with a quick intake of breath, which must have been laced with helium, since each of them pulled immediately back and sat straight up. The truth was out there.

"Whoa," Marnie exclaimed wide-eyed. "Huge."

Ellie flashed Lindsey a knowing look, which she felt across the table like a harsh smack in the face.

They were figuring out the bill, when Ellie pulled her aside. "I'm coming over now." There was no asking. It was an order.

"Uh sure," Lindsey said with heavy skepticism, and handed over her $20 contribution for lunch.

Lindsey avoided her scrutiny by feigning unnatural interest with her phone which dinged with a new message. When she saw it, the color must have drained from her face because Ellie immediately looked concerned. "What? What it is? What's happened?"

"Listen, I've got to go," Lindsey apologized to the girls, still purposely avoiding Ellie. "I'm sorry. I forgot I agreed to help out in Riley's class at school and I'm late. I'll see you guys." She quickly gathered her stuff and headed for the exit. She thought she had made a clean getaway when there was a tug at her arm.

"So you think you're dodging me?"

"Ellie, seriously, I'm late. I'm not making it up."

"Uh huh," Ellie just nodded her head and coolly studied her. "I'm wise to you missy and you are going to have to fess up sooner or later."

"Great. Later," Lindsey agreed and gave her a quick peck on the cheek. "Promise."

Lindsey walked briskly down the street until she was locked in the safety of her car before pulling her cell back out and re-reading the text. It said, "I'm home. I know you're at lunch. Meet me here as soon as you're finished." It was from Jeanie.

A million possibilities ran through her head, but only one really made sense. She knew and she wanted to have it out with her. Terrified didn't even begin to describe how she felt.

Ellie

Was Lindsey kidding? Ellie wondered. Leaving her standing out there on some bullshit pretense? Ellie didn't know who that text was from but it certainly wasn't the school. Lindsey's face had morphed from golden to albino faster than Ellie could ask, 'Are you gonna finish that?"

This whole thing was so insane. She felt like she truly was living in an episode of reality television. Lindsey's was having an affair with their friend's husband and now they were getting divorced. That's the ugly truth that she was terrified to admit to but which Ellie already knew. And she knows I know it, Ellie thought in frustration, so why won't she talk to me? She felt a little like the ditched lover; acting pissy, waiting for her call, hoping she'll see her. The world had gone mad.

Diane and Marnie ambled out of the restaurant still deep in conversation, noticed Ellie and walked over. "I see you got left holding the bag again." Diane smirked, and for a quarter of a second Ellie looked at her like she was a witch. How does she read people like that? She was scary. But then she looked down and realized Diane was referring to the bag of leftover food she was holding. It was a running joke how she lets nothing go to waste. What could she say? She was practical to the point of embarrassment. Luckily after years of fertility treatments, it took a lot more than a doggie bag to mortify her.

"Yup, diaper bag, doggie bag, laundry bag... bring it on," she said.

Diane cracked a smile but it was barely a chink. She got to her point real quick. "So what is up with Lindsey? She's been, let's just say, not herself for a while now."

Marnie nodded in agreement. "She does seem a bit off lately. Is everything all right?"

Shit. The last thing Lindsey needed was Diane's small, sharp did-she-or-didn't-she-have-a-nose-job-nose sniffing around.

"I really think her parents' move messed with her." It was the only plausible, legitimate excuse Ellie had for her. "I know it's crazy but Lindsey is so attached to her mom and you know her history and all."

Was she making sense? Why were they looking at her like she had food hanging from the corner of her mouth? She couldn't help it. She wiped at her face just in case.

"What do you mean?" Diane asked, ears perked, "What history?"

The woman was a blood hound. "Well you know about her brother and all," Ellie said and the looks on their faces confirmed that they didn't. "Oh. Well, Lindsey had a brother who died when she was a teenager which totally messed her up. I just think that her parents' move is bringing a lot of old stuff back up and she's having a hard time dealing."

Both Marnie and Diane nodded with understanding and compassion. Even though it was all true, Ellie felt guilty using it as an excuse. But not that guilty.

"How did we not know this?" Diane asked.

"I don't know," Ellie shrugged. "It's not a secret, but it's not something that comes up every day. Anyway, I'm supposed to have a heart to heart with her today. I'll make sure everything is okay."

"Let us know if there's anything we can do," Diane said.

"Totally," Marnie agreed.

"I really can't believe what is going on here," Diane said, referring of course to Jeanie and John.

"But if they really weren't happy..." Marnie began and then trailed off.

Ellie was nodding, about to verbally agree when Diane cut her down. "He should go fuck someone else?! Are you kidding?"

Marnie and Ellie both gulped and nodded dutifully. Yes, yes, we were kidding. Then, Diane sighed, releasing the tension in their strings. "I just hate when things get so screwed up."

"I know. It's sad," Ellie agreed.

"Are you sure you don't know anything about this affair business?" Diane asked pointedly. "I know there's something you're not telling us."

"Believe me. All I know is the same rumors you've heard... We've all heard. If I hear anything different, you'll know about it."

"I don't doubt that." Diane rolled her eyes and blew one of those fake kisses before turning with Marnie and heading off.

***

Lindsey had pushed any feelings about Jeanie even further down than those about Mitchell, so she really hadn't come to terms with the depth of her betrayal. She honestly was too wrapped up in herself, John and Mitchell to give much attention to Jeanie, but now she had no choice. She had to face the music and there were going to be a lot of sour notes. This meeting would not only destroy their friendship, but could take down her marriage as well. Jeanie was in a strong position of power and Lindsey knew from experience that Jeanie was not someone who took disloyalty lightly. You didn't want to mess with Jeanie, and it couldn't get much worse than messing with her husband.

Lindsey remembered the poor woman who made the mistake

of not inviting Trevor to a party in kindergarten. They didn't even know the woman that well, but Jeanie took it so personally that she actually called the mom, told her off, got Trevor invited and then of course didn't go. If she was left out of any dinner plans, she talked Lindsey's ear off about it for the entire length of their hour walk. No amount of soothing would calm her affronted soul.

It took all of seven minutes to get to Jeanie's house, and then another five sitting out front, trying to talk herself into getting out of the car. She had no excuses. No plan. No idea what to say. She was going in on a wing and prayer, but she had no option but to get it over with. With extreme apprehension, Lindsey turned off the ignition and headed to the house.

A film of sweat coated her body as she rapped with a light shaky fist on the open front door. "Hey?" she called out. "Jeanie?"

"She's in there," Caren Lucci said, appearing before her.

Completely taken off guard, Lindsey faltered a little. "Oh hey, how is she?"

Caren assessed her coolly, shrugged and brushed by. "How do you think?"

This was getting worse every second, Lindsey thought and she walked slowly in, but all she found was a composed Jeanie sitting on the couch, small and unassuming; her short blonde hair falling loosely to her chin in a stylish bob. She was an attractive woman, except for her disposition, and a petite woman, except of course for her big mouth.

Lindsey was so uncomfortable and unsure of what to do, but she did the only thing that made sense. She sat down next to Jeanie and compiled her guilt in the worst way by attempting to care about her and her feelings. "Jeanie, I'm so sorry. How are you doing?"

"I'm sure you know how I'm doing," she responded flatly. "In fact, I'm sure you girls have been talking it up for the last hour or so, am I right?"

"Well," Lindsey admitted, "we did meet for lunch and it was discussed. But not in a gossipy way, more concerned and upset for the both of you." She was as quick on the defensive as Jeanie was on offensive.

"Right," Jeanie scoffed with disbelief. "Concerned and upset, please." She sounded so angry and bitter. "Not that I blame you guys, I mean if it were one of you, I'd be right there too. How can this not be big news in a small town, right?"

"You should have come," Lindsey said, but Jeanie just waved it off as the most ridiculous of suggestions. Lindsey could barely take this banter. She needed to know what Jeanie wanted, if she was being baited. There was no way that the girls' lunch was the reason for her requested visit. "So," she broached tentatively, "how are you holding up?"

"I guess as can be expected. But you probably know more about that than anyone, right?"

Lindsey froze and stammered, "I don't know what you mean."

"Of course you do, with you and John being so close and all." Jeanie sneered then grabbed Lindsey's hand, making it impossible to back away without an obvious scene, while every instinct in Lindsey's body screamed to withdraw.

"Sorry?" It was the only word Lindsey could push out, since her throat had started to close.

"You know, because you guys are always hanging out and all." Jeanie's face was blank with just the hint of aggression, but Jeanie was naturally a Pitt Bull, Lindsey still had no idea of her intentions. Slowly, she extracted her hand on the pretense of scratching her face.

"Jeanie, of course I wanted to stop by and see you and all, but what is this about?" Might as well get it over with, she thought and braced herself.

For a flash, Jeanie looked hurt. "What do you mean? Aren't we friends? I wanted to talk with you?"

Lindsey bumbled over herself in apology. "Of course, of course, but this just happened and it's so sensitive, I guess I just thought that you'd call Diane to just talk. You're so close with her, and..."

She stopped but unfortunately Jeanie finished her thought. "And, you're closer with John? Is that what you were going to say?"

Shit. Yes. No. It wasn't what she was going to say exactly, but it may have well been, because it was true. Recent events aside, Lindsey was always closer with John. He was more present during the day and they connected. For years, she had been hanging out with him on play dates and in the park.

It was a gender reversal, but she and John were the real friends, while she and Jeanie were the significant other friends. But of course, they all pretended otherwise. It was a female thing that left the wives to bond socially since it would be inappropriate to do it with husbands. "I guess I was," Lindsey admitted, wincing.

"Well, that's what I wanted to talk with you about."

Lindsey waited, holding her breath. Was this it? Was this when her life completely hit the fan? She could almost visualize Mitchell and the kids flying in all directions, with her cut up in little pieces.

"I figured since you were such good friends with John, maybe you could speak with him on my behalf."

What? Really? That couldn't be it. Lindsey looked at Jeanie skeptically, waiting for the other shoe to fall and hit her in the head. If it would only knock her unconscious it would be worth it.

"I just thought," Jeanie continued with uncharacteristic earnestness, "that maybe he'd listen to you. If you could convince him that he would be doing a terrible injustice to his kids. I can't talk to him at all."

Lindsey pulled back uneasily. "Jeanie, I don't think that's a good idea. I really don't feel comfortable doing that."

Jeanie was immediately offensive and dangerously intense. "Why not? Don't you want to see us reconcile?"

"Uh sure," she hesitated. "I just don't think that's my place.

That's between you and him. It's not my business."

"Really?" Jeanie threatened; her blue eyes bright with fight. "Not your business? You want to go there?"

Immediately, the hairs on the back of Lindsey's neck and the tiny microscopic ones in her throat stood at attention. It was actually amazing how a body responded to stress and panic. Lindsey realized that she was not a fight or flight person, she was a just roll over and die on the couch kind of person. She really might pass out any second now. "I don't know what you mean," she somehow managed.

Jeanie looked at her long and hard. "You made it your business when you decided to be closer with my husband than me. You made it your business because he looks at you the way he should be looking at me."

Lindsey flushed crimson. Did she know? Didn't she know? Her head was spinning. Jeanie had her all twisted in knots with no idea know what to say. Lindsey had been side-stepping here for too long and if she stayed any longer she felt sure she'd hit a landmine. Resigned, she agreed. "Sure, Jeanie. I don't think it's a good idea, but if that's really what you want."

Jeanie frowned but nodded. "Good. Just consider yourself lucky you have such a great husband, not a piece of shit like mine."

Lindsey could not have gotten out of there fast enough. The minute she hit the street she practically gasped for breath, like she had just exited a burning building and barely survived. She stumbled a little to her car and drove home. Those few blocks now seemed way too close.

Inside the safety of her house, Lindsey made coffee which she was too jittery to drink and paced instead. Thankfully, there was still an hour before the kids came home. She felt like a caged animal. Should she call John? Should she call Ellie? Should she call her mom? She grabbed the phone and called Mitchell. She didn't know why. He was always so busy, she almost never called him at the office, but she desperately needed to hear his voice now.

Celia, the receptionist who called her house the night of Diane's party answered and put her on hold. As usual, she was too sharp for her liking. Within a minute Mitchell picked up the line.

"Hey, what's the matter?" he asked abruptly.

"Nothing," Lindsey quickly assured him. She probably shouldn't have called. "I just wanted to check in and see how you are. You seemed not yourself last night."

She heard him sigh. "This isn't a good time. I'm in between patients."

"Oh sorry." She really shouldn't have called. "Okay, I'll see you later."

"Great," he said distractedly and hung up.

Wow. She wondered, feeling like she had been smacked in the face. Was that how he typically spoke to her from work? Was that why she stopped calling him at the office? How had she not noticed this before? Or, more accurately, when did she decide to accept it?

At some point over the years, Lindsey realized that Mitchell was always busy and stressed at work and didn't like to be interrupted. So she naturally tapered off her calls unless it was something important, until finally, there was this huge part of his life that had nothing to do with her.

When Lindsey considered the truth, she realized that Mitchell spent more time at the office or hospital where she barely spoke with him, than he did at home. Even at home, there was barely time when they really connected. Most of their Saturday nights were booked with other couples. On weekends, they divided and conquered with the kids. During the week nights, they each relaxed basically in their own way, separately. They had sex very inconsistently.

When she put it all together, she was almost shocked. There was so much of Mitchell that she didn't know. Their relationship, so perfect on the outside, was really just two people who got along reasonably well, going through the motions, living their lives together separately.

Was this what marriage was supposed to be? Had she been willingly sleep-walking through her relationship? Filling in all the gaps with shopping, spin class and lunches... and now John? She felt punched in the gut, like she was going to throw up. Everything was a mess.

Her phone dinged, alerting her to a new text. She checked it and sighed deeply. It was from Ellie.

'You can run, but you can't hide.'

Ellie was wrong. Lindsey had been running and hiding for years.

Lindsey's next call after Mitchell was to her mother, who lucky for her wasn't home. She didn't even bother trying her cell because even though she had one, somehow when her mother spoke on it, she was every inch the stereotyped caricature of a senior screaming into the wrong end of the phone and then hanging up on you. Even in Lindsey's current state, it was not worth the aggravation.

She considered calling Ellie. She owed her a conversation, but as much as Lindsey wanted a confidant, she still wasn't sure how much she was willing to reveal. Or more honestly, she was worried that if she spoke with her, she'd come clean with the whole thing. What if Ellie stopped speaking to her? What if she didn't stand behind her or at least next to her? Ellie was her best friend; the person she could always count on, who really knew her and loved her, flaws and all, her female husband. She couldn't lose her.

Which left John, the only person Lindsey could truly confide in about everything, the only one with whom she didn't have to pretend, the only one she was dying to call, but of course shouldn't. Jeanie had strongly directed her to speak with him, although using that as a reason was just a transparent excuse. Still, she considered, she couldn't ignore Jeanie, could she? That didn't seem like a smart idea. Lindsey felt a dangerous swirl of excitement in her belly. What choice did she really have?

CHAPTER 12

Lindsey - 1986

When the police came to their door at 12:25a.m., her mother's screams could be heard across the neighborhood. Lindsey was awake upstairs when the bell rang and immediately ran to the edge of the steps to eavesdrop. When she saw the police, her heart died and when she heard her mother scream, she wanted to die as well. What happened? She needed to find out. Extremely slowly, she padded down the stairs, her dead heart beating loudly.

She heard bits and pieces of fractured conversation. "Car crash... hit a tree... driver was impaired...two dead. Two critical. I'm sorry..."

"Mom? Dad?" Lindsey heard herself speak, her voice sounding foreign and far away. Her mother was huddled over in tears; her father a contorted mask of pain. She stood there lost, alone and bewildered, until a policeman approached.

"Hey there," he said kindly while she continued to stare dumbly ahead, panic rising in her brain. What was happening? What was happening!? What was happening!! "Are you Lindsey?" he asked. She heard him, but was stuck in her head. "Lindsey?" he said a little more forcefully, and touched her shoulder. She reacted to the touch and jerked back as if burned. "Hey, it's okay," he said gently, "I just want to ask you a question or two. Okay?"

She nodded.

"Good. Now you were at the party tonight with your brother, weren't you?"

She nodded again.

"Was there alcohol at the party?"

Again she nodded.

"Was Liam drinking?" Her eyes darted away nervously, but the officer put a calming hand on her shoulder. "You're not going to get in trouble here, honey. We're just trying to figure out what happened." She nodded. "Were you drinking?" Again, she looked around for help, but there was only another officer standing nearby writing things down and her parents, looking stricken and staring blankly at her. "Okay, honey. You need to tell me what happened. What you saw."

"He... he... got into a car with his friends Jimmy, Nick and Tommy. I told him not to go. I begged him not to go! Is he... is he going to be alright?!" she asked, still uncomprehending.

The officer didn't get a chance to answer. Her father, his face distorted in rage, lunged forward and screamed with heightening hysteria, "Alright?! Alright!? Your brother is dead because of you! He's dead! You let him go? You let him go!!!! And he's dead!!!!"

Lindsey fell back on the floor. Not hearing or seeing anything. He's dead? Liam was dead. Her brother was dead, and she may as well have killed him.

The funeral was held two days later. Countless family members and friends flew in from everywhere to be with them. So many faces she didn't know; they all blurred together in her tears. The entire town was in mourning. Two teens had died, one was still in the hospital and Nick, who had suffered a concussion, two broken ribs, a broken leg and multiple lacerations, had just returned home and was said to be recovering at home and not wanting or willing to speak with anyone.

Lindsey went through the motions stoically, feeling as dead as her brother, wishing it were her. She replayed the night over and over in her head, knowing it was her fault, that she instigated his departure, knowing she could have prevented it.

Her vital, beautiful mother looked shrunken and overwhelmed in her own grief. And her workaholic father, who always bought her everything she ever wanted but gave her no time? She didn't think she would ever speak with him again. Lindsey felt herself sinking, deeper into her misery, wrapping it around herself like a warm, protective coat.

It was a tough year. At school, she saw Liam's friends every day. She saw them move on with life. She saw them laugh, except around her of course, but she saw them. She couldn't even look at Billy. Whenever she saw him in the halls, she turned and went the other way. Liam and Tommy were dead, but life had to go on. Unless you lived at her house. She was trapped in her house of grief, Liam's room just a door down from hers. Stuck.

Her father went back to his workaholic ways with a vengeance and the only saving grace of those days was that they barely saw one another. It was just Lindsey and her mom blindly pressing their way through the thick, unrelenting grief they were drowning in. They ate in silence. They cried in silence. They spoke in silence. Still, Lindsey was grateful to have her there. Her silent presence was a giant comfort.

After a few months, the weight lightened enough for Lindsey to breathe without suffocating. She knew that she needed to get out of her town and her house. When summer came around, she practically begged her mother to send her back to sleep away camp where there were distractions. She buried her feelings along with her brother, and threw herself into camp with a vengeance. For that entire summer and long after, Lindsey pretended she was someone else; someone who went with too many boys, someone who had fun, someone who didn't have a dead brother. After a while, she wasn't pretending anymore. It was just her.

CHAPTER 13

Nearly 60% of both men and women who were unhappy with their relationships say they would still be happy to spend eternity with their partners.

Should she call him or shouldn't she? Lindsey paced the floor like a lion till she almost wore a hole in the carpet. The thought of seeing John again was so overwhelmingly appealing that she knew it was an absolute mistake to call. She shouldn't want to see him that badly. She needed to calm down. She was too over-excited from her lunch with the girls and her meeting with Jeanie. She needed to think and not make a snap decision.

But it was really hard to think when she couldn't sit still or concentrate. In fact, she couldn't do anything but freak out. Relax, she told herself, but it wasn't her strong point under less dramatic circumstances.

Distraction. She needed distraction. Automatically, she went to her closet and started cleaning things out. Folding, organizing, and discarding. It soothed her a little and her brain calmed enough to at least think semi straight about her whole crooked affair. She bounced from her and Mitchell to John and Jeanie to her and John, back and forth, because a love triangle apparently has many sides.

She replayed her meeting with Jeanie to the point of nauseam. It was just so strange, everything about it, the vibe, the logic, Jeanie. Of course, it could just be her discomfort skewing her perception, she thought. Normally Jeanie scorned on a much lesser level was strongly reactive and defensive. Jeanie seemed to nurture her slights, almost reveling in them, like they verified some personal internal, preconceived notion that people were bad and out to get her. It was only a matter of time before they proved her right.

Not that any of that helped her current predicament. Jeanie had asked her to speak with John on her behalf. Clearly, that wasn't going to work, but did she put up the pretense? Did she follow through as she asked? She certainly couldn't lie and tell her she did when she didn't, at least not without John knowing about it and backing her up. So she had to speak with him, she decided logically as she folded a cute white top with tags that she forgot she even owned and placed it back in the drawer, probably never to be seen again.

She pushed the fact that she desperately wanted to see John to the side, as an unfortunate incidental which she would have to deal with. Oh, the things she does for her friends, she thought, not without a heavy dose of sarcasm and self-loathing.

Thankfully, she couldn't dwell too long because it was bus time. Lindsey pulled herself off her closet floor and went down to greet her kids, trying really hard to focus on them instead of herself. It wasn't easy, but there was more than enough to do to keep her occupied. Liam had to be dropped at soccer practice and Riley had a friend coming over. There was homework to finish and dinner to make. Before she knew it, the clock struck seven and Mitchell was home. She breathed deep and prepared herself for whatever was coming next.

"Hey," she greeted, as Mitchell walked in the kitchen where she was finishing up dinner. He came over and kissed her lightly on the lips. Still distracted, Lindsey sensed.

"Hey," he returned. "I'm going up to change. Where are the kids?"

"They're doing some secret spy stuff. They've got themselves dressed all in black. Every so often they sneak down and fly past me and I pretend not to notice."

He gave a small smile. "Cute."

"So don't worry. If you don't find them, they'll find you."

"Okay." He nodded, looking tired. "I'll be down in a few."

"Are you okay?" she asked before he walked out, partially wanting to push the words back into her mouth. She really was a glutton for punishment, but her rising concern over his distance and her guilt were playing into each other making her extra paranoid. She wanted to go over to him, but was extremely aware of the unspoken wall between them, so she stayed by the stove and tried to reach out with her words. "You don't seem yourself."

He stayed there, not saying anything, looking as though he wanted to but finally just shook his head resignedly. "I might just be a little under the weather. I'm sure it's nothing."

"Oh." Lindsey felt a surge of tenderness. "You want Tylenol or something?"

"Lins, I'm a doctor. I think I can medicate myself." He smiled a little too self-assuredly, effectively eliminating her empathy.

Later, after the kids were sleeping, Lindsey once again tried to engage Mitchell in a conversation, but he once again shut her down. She was quickly going from hurt to angry, even though she recognized that she had no business being angry given her indiscretions. Still, she couldn't help feeling rejected. Grabbing her book and her heaviest feet, she trudged upstairs. She wasn't sure what he knew or didn't know, but he was definitely acting strange and pissing her off. Or, she considered as she washed up for bed, maybe he wasn't acting strange. Often he brought home work from the office and essentially ignored her, but she had gotten used to it, so much so, that she didn't even seek out his company as much anymore.

Up until now, she was okay with this arrangement. Some days were exhausting with the racing around and the kids. It's was a pleasure not to have to pretend with someone at the end of the night; to breathe easy and know that you didn't have to do anything else for anyone but yourself. That you could watch your show or read your book, call a friend or even masturbate without hassle. It was all so easy, good even.

But was that how a marriage should be?

Her affair with John had all of a sudden highlighted all the complacency in her relationship; the taking for granted, the obvious boredom with each other, the lack of connection, both physical and emotional.

Lindsey exhaled deeply overwhelmed and exhausted with her internal struggling. The truth was that until John, life was pretty good. On a scale of one to ten, she probably would have given herself and Mitchell a seven or even an eight. She guessed it was the old ignorance is bliss thing, but it was true, what you don't know can't hurt you. Unfortunately, now that she was no longer ignorant, she didn't know how to go back; to disregard what she rediscovered in herself, to want more out of life and her partner. But did she want it with Mitchell or John?

Lindsey took the night and slept on it as she knew she should, even though there wasn't much sleep. Her initial reaction had been to call John immediately, and after a thoughtful, excruciating, sleepless night of mental Olympics, her mind had not changed. She needed to see him.

She waited impatiently for Mitchell to leave. He still seemed a little tenuous, again claiming he didn't feel well, lingering with her in the kitchen and apologizing for being short the night before.

"I know I've been a bit of an ass," he admitted. "I've taken on Dr. Field's patients this week while he's on vacation and the extra workload is wearing me out."

Lindsey accepted his apology and his bear hug before he left, which seemed both genuine and aggressive. She couldn't figure out which.

She was probably over-thinking this call to John, but for obvious reasons she didn't trust herself. For her, being with him was like wearing glasses in the wrong prescription, she couldn't see anything else clearly.

She shouldn't call him. She knew it, but right after her final wave goodbye to the kids at the bus stop, she texted him.

'Can we talk?'

His response was instant. 'When?'

'Now?'

'Where?'

Good question. She debated in her head. Not here. The only place she could think of was her mother's house or in public. Both had their benefits and potential hazards. Being in public would keep them honest, but it was always risky to be with a man who wasn't your husband with people around. The house was private, which was good, but also dangerous. They did not have a great track record.

'My mother's house'

'Half hour'

Lindsey got there first and left the door unlocked. She clicked through the empty rooms, purposely avoiding her own. There was no need to see her ineptitude.

As she was leaning against the doorframe of Liam's old bedroom gazing in, she heard his footsteps approaching. He found her there and leaned against the frame opposite of her.

"Hi there," he said, blue eyes smiling but cautious. "You rang?"

She tendered a faint smile. "How are you?"

He shrugged. "Could be better, could be worse."

"Better how? Worse how?" Lindsey asked softly, curious how he was doing, but too distracted by him and by everything for a real conversation.

"Better with you. Worse with Jeanie." It was a matter of fact, carelessly tossed her way. She nodded thoughtfully. "How are you?" he asked.

"Could be better, could be worse," she answered, with a small wink.

He raised a brow. "How so?"

Now she was in trouble. Her flip, cutesy response now required serious back up. She thought for a moment and said, "Better with you, worse with you."

John nodded. He didn't need further explanation and accepted this at face value. They stood silently, looking at the floor, and around the empty deep blue room, thinking their own thoughts.

"Whose room?" he asked.

"My brother Liam. He died." Lindsey rarely ever spoke those words out loud, and it sounded funny to her ears.

He seemed surprised and looked at her carefully with concern, "Oh. I didn't know you had a brother who died. I'm sorry."

"It was a long time ago..." She drifted off in memory. "And a Lindsey far, far away."

"Will you tell me about him sometime?" he asked gently.

Before she knew what she was saying, the words spilled out. "It was a car accident when he was seventeen. He was drinking at a party. I saw him drive off but couldn't stop him. At the time, my father blamed me."

"Oh Jeez. That's horrible," John said. "I can't even imagine how difficult that must have been for you."

She nodded. It was horrible and difficult. Not just what happened but what happened after, the blame, the glossing over and the silence.

She hadn't spoken about Liam in years. Mitchell knew about him of course, but he always respected her space regarding him, which she had insisted on; although if he had tried a bit harder and with more interest, she knew she would have opened up to him. But the one person with whom she desperately needed to talk about Liam was her mom. He was the only thing they never talked about, and the one thing they needed to.

"I've been working through it for the last twenty-five years, give or take." She smiled but it was full of pain.

"I'm here if you ever want to talk," John offered seriously and Lindsey's spirits lifted. It felt good to talk about Liam. She wanted to remember him more out loud; to say his name, to deal with the burden of his death and let it go, to enjoy his memory.

"I just might take you up on that offer," she said, and then they lapsed into silence again.

"So, what are we doing here?" he asked, with only the slightest hint of mischief. Lindsey wished that was the reason.

With no other choice, she just put it right out there. "Jeanie asked me to talk to you."

John's eyes opened wide. "What do you mean by that?"

"I mean, she summoned me over and then pleaded with me to speak with you on her behalf."

John's face distorted in skepticism and anger.

"It was definitely weird and totally freaked me out," she continued, "But I didn't know what to say or do."

Suddenly, John grabbed her arm and pulled her. "Shit. Come on. Just walk with me into the living room to talk, but keep your distance from me," he warned. "Just casual conversation."

She walked behind him nervously. "What's this about?"

"I'm not sure, but Jeanie is not someone to trust and I'd be remiss if I didn't tell you she's been jealous of you for years and has always known on some level my feelings for you." He turned toward her, and she caught a glint in his eye that automatically made hers glimmer. "Nope." He smiled. "None of that look. No sir. That will not work at all, especially if there are cameras."

That stopped her in her tracks. "What do you mean cameras?" She asked in alarm.

"I don't know if there are any, but if Jeanie sent you to talk to me, it was for a reason. It definitely wasn't to see if you could talk some sense into me. We've known each other a long time. I know how her mind works. At best, she's messing with us completely. At worst, she's trying to set us up."

Lindsey swallowed hard. "She would do that?"

"In a heartbeat."

"So she knows?" Lindsey flustered, trying desperately not to look traumatized just in case she was being photographed and Jeanie was standing right outside the window.

"I can't be sure, but she's been throwing around a lot of insinuations."

Lindsey felt punched in the gut. "I thought it was extremely weird, and her whole vibe with me was so wrong. But I was just hoping it was because she was messed up and my brain is messed up too. I can't figure out how I'm supposed to act. Not with my friends or my husband. I don't know how to be me anymore." She felt so lost and confused, and ironically, alone.

"How bout with me?" John asked gently and immediately Lindsey wanted to cry. John was the only person she felt free with, the only person she wanted to see, the only person she felt like herself. She could actually feel his hand longing to grab hers. Or maybe it was her wishful thinking because instead he lifted his hand and pointed at the wall away from the window.

"Look over there," he ordered.

Confused, she listened immediately. "What?"

"Your face was so raw and open, I could hardly look at you without kissing you, and I didn't want anyone else - if there even is an 'anyone' else - to see that expression because," his tone softened to a caress, "because it says more than any words or actions could."

"I need to go to the bathroom," Lindsey abruptly announced and walked purposefully in the other direction.

John stood there quizzically for a beat before he quickly followed.

The bathroom down the hall away from any windows was only a small half bath and they stood in it awkwardly, John with his back to the wall and Lindsey with hers to the sink.

Their heavy breath mingled in the small space creating delicious anticipation. When he slowly touched her hair, she was surprised he didn't get one of those small shocks, like when she was a kid and would rub a balloon on her head to then stick to the wall. Lindsey felt those sparks popping like firecrackers in her whole body. They each took one step closer. "We can't stay in here," he reprimanded, but a sly grin spread across his lips.

"I wouldn't dream of it," she spoke heatedly, all those sparks lighting her up.

His other hand caressed her face and she leaned into him. "Just one kiss," he warned.

"Just one," she repeated dutifully and tilted her face to his. The moment their mouths met, her whole being went limp, almost sighing relief. Their tongues and lips danced while their bodies hummed with energy.

"I can't stay away from you," she groaned, lost in his touch. "I can't." She put her hand on the band of his jeans but he stopped her.

"No. It's not a good idea."

"Fuck her," she cried desperately, "I don't care. I want you. I need you."

John pulled back a little, a question in his eyes. "But there ain't no way you're ever gonna love me?"

Lindsey gave a small, playful smile. "Two outta three ain't bad?"

John looked down hurt and she immediately chastised herself. "John, I was kidding. It was a bad joke. I'm sorry. Really."

His hand reached for the bathroom door. "I know you think you were kidding, but I'm not so sure."

She pulled at his arm insistently before he walked out, "John! I'm sorry." She repeated again pathetically, "You know you're so much more to me than that. More than I feel I can say out loud. It's all so complicated and I'm terrified. I'm really doing the best I can."

John turned and nodded sadly, leaning his head down to rest on hers. Lindsey closed her eyes and inhaled their closeness like oxygen. They stayed like that for a minute before John finally broke away. "I'm sorry too. Come on, let's go."

She followed him out and grabbed her things. "Let's go get a cup of coffee. Okay? Can we? Please?" She felt desperate to stay near him. "It's really not that crazy, two old friends chatting over coffee? We used to do it all the time."

"Uh, before we did it?" John smiled boyishly, and she was practically giddy to be back in his favor.

"Come on." Lindsey rolled her eyes and pushed him out the door.

They each walked casually to their cars while someone sat watching, eyes fixated on their every move.

Twenty minutes later, Lindsey and John were back in Shore Point sitting at Small Comforts, a cozy, little bakery/coffee shop off Main Street with lounging couches and an easy, unhurried vibe. It wasn't Starbucks or Dunkin Donuts, so there wasn't as much traffic, but it was still in the center of town and people came and went. It was hiding in plain sight.

They had coffee, shared a giant chocolate chip cookie and talked and talked. They avoided any tricky topics like spouses and focused on enjoying each other's company and their conversation, which was almost as stimulating and attentive as their love making.

Lindsey learned about his family and his childhood dreams of playing ball for the Yankees. She shared with him about her family and opened up a little about Liam; not about his death so much as his life; how special he was to her, how strong their bond was.

An hour flew by quickly and the second one even faster when John looked at his watch. "Crap. We have been here a long time." There was only one other patron there at the time, an older woman sipping her coffee and reading the paper. Still, people were in and out, a few vaguely familiar, and they were conscious of themselves, their conversation and their body language. "We have to go," John advised quietly. "Random married neighborhood friends of different genders don't hang out in coffee shops for two hours shooting the shit."

"Yeah," she soberly agreed. "I know." She gathered her belongings and headed to the door behind him. He didn't walk her to her car, instead patted her arm genially. At some point, she felt him slip something in her pocket. With a casual wave goodbye, she headed down the street, trying not to skip with joy or to turn around to catch one more glimpse of him. She hid her smile inside and walked on air to her car.

She drove to the supermarket, wanting to get at least one errand for the day accomplished, and floated through the aisles like a little girl with a pocketful of candy. She bought extra snacks for everyone and picked up some fresh salmon to make for dinner.

Home, waiting for the bus, the groceries unpacked, the salmon marinating in the fridge, she nuked the baked potatoes to soften them, and was casually folding laundry when she remembered to check her pocket. She found the light fleece zip-up she had been wearing and pulled out a crumpled up napkin. Slowly, she opened it and felt her heart open as well as she read his simple words. "Best first date ever."

Fuck, she was screwed.

CHAPTER 14

More than 33% of men and women say they have watched a TV show or movie that affected them so much they considered breaking up.

Mitchell walked in under a dark cloud which made Lindsey's silver lining even more grotesque. As usual, she was in the kitchen finishing up dinner. The salmon was perfect, the baked potatoes were crisping up a bit in the toaster oven and she had just thrown in some spinach to sauté. She felt like a real Martha Stewart, only cuter and a little less scary. She tried not to think about her need to create perfect family dinners in spite of the fact that her situation right now was anything but perfect; that her family was threatening to fall apart. Just like with that magnifying mirror that she made the mistake of buying last year to better scrutinize her skin, only to be horrified and quickly return it, she realized she shouldn't always look at herself too closely if she wasn't going to like what she saw.

She waited for Mitchell to walk in and give her, her usual quick kiss hello before going up to change his clothes, but the only one to walk into the kitchen was Liam.

"Ew. It stinks in here," he complained and held his nose dramatically.

"That stink is dinner and it's good! You're gonna love it." Liam screwed up his face, expressing some serious doubts. "Hey, where's daddy?" she asked.

Liam shrugged. "I guess he went upstairs." Then sticking his tongue out and mock gagging, he ran out of the room.

Mitchell always walked in the kitchen before going up to change, Lindsey thought. Always. Something was wrong. She turned the stove and oven down to low and walked up the stairs nervously. When you know you're guilty, every scenario you can think of turns out badly.

"Hey," she said brightly, entering their bedroom and watching him change into a pair of lounge pants. "How are you feeling?"

"Shitty."

He didn't make eye contact. "Oh. I made a good dinner, maybe that'll help?"

"I'm not really hungry." He brushed past her and moved to the bathroom. Lindsey shivered involuntarily, feeling the chill of his cold shoulder. She followed him and waited, watching him at the sink, unsure of how to navigate what was happening.

"Mitchell, what's the matter?" Her voice sounded strangled, probably from the painful lump in her throat.

For the first time he looked up, his scrubbed face dripping water and he pierced her with his gaze. Oh God. It was better when he didn't look at her.

"Did you have a nice day?" he asked dryly, grabbing a towel.

Even though she was now lightheaded with fear, her brain worked at a furious pace, trying to figure out what he knew and what she should say. Finally, she went with the truth. "It was an interesting day. I saw John."

He paused with the towel to assess her for a second before burying his face back into it and finishing up. "Oh yeah? What for?"

She felt the weight of his question, of this make or break moment. Was this it? He obviously knew something. She began slowly, but once she started talking she picked up steam like a locomotive. "Well, you're not going to believe this." His look was so skeptical and distrusting that she hurried past her unfortunate start. "But Jeanie called me yesterday and asked me to speak with John for her. I meant to tell you, but you weren't feeling well and then you were busy when I came down to talk to you after the kids were asleep. Anyway, I was planning on going to my mom's to do my room and all, which of course I did nothing, because I am completely incapable for some reason..." She was totally babbling. "Anyway, I told him to meet me there. We hung out for a little bit, talking more about the house and my parents moving than anything else, and when I realized I wasn't doing anything anyway and there was nowhere to even sit, we went to Small Comfort to talk, where he told me about Jeanie and their marriage and all that." She took a breath and looked at him, her face flushed with nervous energy. "So it was kind of a weird day."

"Wow," he exclaimed flatly, and walked back into their bedroom. But Lindsey perceived less animosity, so she barreled forward.

"Yeah, it was pretty awkward talking with him about his marriage, but Jeanie asked, and I am friends with John, so it was kind of fine, but also kind of weird. John is a good guy, listening to him and his unhappiness, how can I even make a plea for Jeanie? I mean, that's just totally inappropriate, right?"

"Yeah, it is. I don't know why she would ask you to meet with him for her. They've been married for years. If she needs you to intervene on her behalf, they are pretty much beyond help."

Lindsey nodded and sat down on the bed, so relieved Mitchell had actually engaged with her instead of completely shutting her out. "I don't know why either. I think they're beyond help. It's sad what happens in life and marriage." She didn't know if she was speaking of Jeanie and John or of her and Mitchell. "You go in with all this hope and expectations and well, it just doesn't always work out as planned."

Mitchell sat down next to her; his shoulders slumped under an internal weight. They weren't touching but they were close.

"We all want things. We all have expectations for ourselves and our marriages," he admitted quietly. "Sometimes I think we get lost in the image we're creating and miss the big picture."

Lindsey felt the heat of his body and his conviction, as whatever he thought he knew dissolved, leaving just small bubbles of exasperation and uncertainty. He visibly relaxed and put his hand over hers. It made her want to cry with relief and frustration and pain. He squeezed her hand lightly and she looked up at him. It was their first genuine interaction in so long that came close to a real conversation and some intimacy between them, instead of their usual glossing over the surface.

"I really miss talking with you," she said, eyes brimming with tears. She did. She really did. That had to mean something.

Mitchell looked at her, a forgiving smile playing on his lips. He leaned over and kissed her softly. It was nice, sweet and familiar, but more honest than their usual foreplay. She felt a stirring inside which she welcomed. She couldn't remember the last time she felt genuine desire for her husband. It had been a very long time. The kiss opened slowly into something deeper, something more meaningful, when Liam and Riley burst into the room.

"Something is burning in the kitchen!" They yelled, then forcibly grabbed her and Mitchell and pulled them down the stairs. They entered the kitchen and Lindsey immediately covered her mouth. It stunk of over-cooked spinach. She quickly went over to the skillet and saw the burnt, wilted remains of their side dish. When she checked the potatoes, they too, had undergone some charring, and the salmon looked dried out.

"Looks like dinner is ruined." She frowned. She had been so proud of her preparations only an hour before.

"Ohhhh! Too bad!" Liam and Riley both exclaimed with unconcealed glee.

She and Mitchell exchanged a look filled with parental amusement. "How bout we go out to dinner?" Mitchell suggested, and both kids, usually so apathetic about eating out, jumped joyously up and down, hanging on both of them.

Suspiciously, Lindsey wondered if they had homework that needed to be finished, but pushed the anal, controlling thought away.

Looking around at her happy kids and husband in this snapshot moment of perfect family bliss was eye-opening. She hadn't been looking at things from this perspective, only her own.

She hadn't even been able to admit to herself how seriously she considered leaving Mitchell for John until she stood surrounded by her family. She had been so lost in fantasy that didn't really consider their reality, just her selfish needs. Now, like Mitchell had said, she saw the bigger picture, the family picture and she appreciated it in a way she hadn't before.

The day with John lingered like a warm afterglow. The message on the napkin shoved in the back of her underwear drawer but not in the back of her mind. Still, as she grabbed her bag and headed out the door, her family's laughing voices tumbling over each other, offering up their favorite restaurants for consideration, Lindsey knew she had to put her family's needs first. She had to try. It was the least she could do for them.

They went out to Harley's, a local family pub known for the best burgers and fries, which they all ordered, except Lindsey who modified to a garden burger. From where they started; her and Mitchell's dangerous, awkward exchange earlier in the bedroom, the night turned out okay. Better than okay. It was fun, easy and enjoyable. They went out together as a family, eating, laughing, licking dripping ice cream cones. Lindsey concentrated only on them and it worked. They all connected without feeling forced.

When they finally got the kids to bed, she and Mitchell sat together on the couch, opened a bottle of wine and talked to each other. It wasn't exactly revelatory, some light, local gossip, and bits and pieces of the days, but mostly about why in the face of all logic and understanding, Lindsey couldn't seem to clean out her old room. She had been struggling internally for a while with her inability to complete this simple task, which was like a red flag in her obvious refusal.

She usually didn't discuss things like that much with Mitchell, or at least hadn't for years but today had opened up a doorway to the past and she wanted to share. Way back, when they were young and interested in each other to learn more, she had shared about Liam and what had happened but she never told him what her father had said to her the night he died. How he blamed her and how, in essence, she never truly spoke to him again.

Even though her dad had made a number of overtures of apology, Lindsey refused to entertain them. He hurt her in a place that could never heal, and she shut him out and punished him for it. Then she went to college, moved out, got married, had children and they just moved on and never re-addressed it. They got along formally, had dinners together, and attended family functions and all that. They had gotten into the habit of being around each other but not really addressing the other.

Now Lindsey opened up to Mitchell about it all. He was amazed she had kept that in for so long, sensitively suggesting that since she was clearly still having a hard time moving on from her past and letting it go, that possibly she needed some outside assistance, meaning therapy. She was way ahead of him, having already made some calls to therapists in the towns surrounding theirs. Close but not too close.

The night broke some ground for them and they ended it in the bedroom. It wasn't earth shattering and she couldn't honestly say John didn't enter her mind, but she tried to stay focused on her husband and their time together. It was warm, satisfying and emotionally deeper than their routine comfortable sex.

It was a start.

***

The next morning right after the bus left, Lindsey opened the door and found Ellie's face staring back at her. "Gee El, if I'd known you were coming..."

"You would have conveniently been out?" Ellie finished.

"Maybe." Lindsey smiled.

"You can't hide anymore," she chided.

"Because you will hunt me down where I live?" Lindsey took her turn finishing a sentence.

"Apparently." Ellie smiled. "Look. No more secrets okay? You need to tell me what's going on." She looked Lindsey directly in the eyes.

Lindsey immediately averted hers. "I don't know what you're talking about." Lindsey huffed, but it didn't have much air to it.

"Come on, I saw you... and John." Ellie whispered John's name, again becoming her mother.

"Ellie, you're imagining things," she said dismissively, fidgeting with a loose thread on her shirt.

"I'm not imagining anything," she insisted. "I know. Lindsey, I know!"

Lindsey finally looked up with uncertainty. She was ready to crack. Ellie felt it, so she went in for the kill. "I saw you together at your mom's house."

Her face dropped. "What? How?"

"I followed you," Ellie admitted. "I didn't intend to, but I did."

Lindsey let out a deep breath that she must have been holding for months. She nodded, biting her lip, wondering if she should just keep up the ruse but didn't have the strength. "Okay," she finally conceded and let it all pour out in a steady stream, like air from a balloon. She didn't stop till she was empty and deflated, ending with "I am completely fucked."

It was as bad as Ellie thought, possibly worse and she kept shaking her head in disbelief. "Lindsey. You must stop this before it's too late, if it isn't already. Think of Mitchell and the kids, and Jeanie, even if they are getting a divorce."

"Have you seen this?" Lindsey asked and pulled up the post she read on SOS an hour ago. She handed her cell to Ellie to read.

People!! I am both fascinated and freaked out the two bits of gossip I've mentioned, the marriage ending and the affair, were actually.... the same story! Wow. Mind blowing. I am completely WTF over the whole, ahem, affair!! I am trying to be somewhat unbiased and just report the news, but seriously, you can't pee in this town without someone recommending an urologist, how could they think it was okay to step out together? In town?? They appear to be a couple of dumbasses, but hey, I'm not one for appearances. Honestly, I need to talk to this girl. I mean, friends don't let friend's screw other friend's husbands. I'm going to make up tee shirts.

"So I'm double fucked," Lindsey said.

Ellie handed her phone back shrugging. "It doesn't say anything concrete."

"Yeah, but people are already talking about Jeanie and John's divorce. And people saw me and him together out for coffee. It'll only be a matter of time before they start putting the names to the whole business and then it's totally out there. True or not."

"Well it is true," Ellie said, a little self-righteously.

"Well the whole freaking town doesn't have to know it!"

Ellie backtracked. "Of course. You're totally right."

"I mean," Lindsey continued her voice rising, "does this person shouting my business to the town, realize she is screwing with my life and my kids and John and Jeanie's as well? I'm having enough trouble holding it together here, trying to figure it all out. I mean, does she know that Jeanie actually asked me to meet with John to talk to him? That maybe we are just friends and I'm listening to him at a difficult time? No! This points a map directly from his penis to my vagina!"

"I see what you're saying," Ellie said thoughtfully, "but don't get yourself all crazy. It really is just a stupid Facebook page, who takes it so seriously?"

"Kind of the whole town." Lindsey shook her head miserably.

"Maybe it'll just blow over?" Ellie suggested hopefully but without much conviction.

"But more likely it'll just blow up."

They sat with that for a minute, both looking very uncomfortable.

"I've got to tell you something." Ellie began but Lindsey interrupted.

"Hold on. Oh my God. I just got a text from Jeanie."

Jeanie - "So? What happened?"

"What do you mean?" She typed back, even though she knew exactly what she meant.

"I know you met with John."

"I did." Lindsey admitted, wondering how she knew.

"I'll be right over."

Lindsey looked with fear over to Ellie. "She's coming here now."

"I'd better go."

"Yeah, you'd better." She walked her to the door.

"We're not finished here," Ellie said seriously, "There's more we need to discuss."

"Just stalk me tomorrow or something," Lindsey said feebly, trying to be sarcastic but she was too nervous. "If Jeanie hasn't killed me by then."

Within five minutes, Jeanie arrived. She didn't have a bag with her and her jeans were pretty tight so unless she had a weapon hidden in her shoe Lindsey was probably safe; at least physically.

"I guess you're not working today?" Lindsey said in greeting. Jeanie looked so tightly wound that if she took one more turn, Lindsey thought she might snap. She felt really guilty and bad just being near her, but at the same time realized she honestly didn't like Jeanie.

She shook her head, "I took a few days off. I need it. I'm a bit of a wreck getting things in order for the boys and all."

"I'm sure," Lindsey said sympathetically, feeling even worse.

"Plus, I figured I'd mess with John a bit." She gave a short laugh that held no amusement. "You know, since we still haven't resolved the whole house thing."

She didn't feel so bad anymore. She needed to get to business and get Jeanie out of her house. "So, did John tell you we met? I was going to text you this morning, but you beat me."

"No, Caren did. She mentioned that she saw you guys at the coffee shop off Main."

It surprised Lindsey, even though it shouldn't have. It wasn't like they had been hiding. In fact, Lindsey picked a spot in town to off-set suspicion, but the idea that someone actually was watching kind of put her in a whole new defensive place. The SOS poster, Ellie and now Caren - how many other people had seen them?

"Oh. That's right." Her brain was running like a ferret on crack while her body pumped out all kinds of fight or flight hormones. She was sure Jeanie was someone who could smell fear. All of a sudden she was very nervous.

"And did you see the latest tidbit in SOS." Jeanie laid it out there, staring Lindsey down. "Interesting, huh? Kind of coincidental, don't you think?"

"Yeah." Lindsey hesitated. "I saw that."

"So," Jeanie asked challengingly, "anything you want to share?"

"About the Facebook gossip page?" Lindsey somehow managed to sound contemptuous. "Are you kidding me? I'm not even going to answer that." Lindsey could feel herself pale. She was so highly attuned to her heightened stress that she actually could feel her hair falling out, but she maintained Jeanie's steady scrutiny. Finally, Jeanie blinked.

"So," she practically barked, eyes bulging, "just tell me what happened?"

"Jeanie I tried, but I don't think I could tell you anymore than you already know."

"Really?" Jeanie said, pulling back defensively; her eager expression replaced with a bitter one. "Caren said you guys talked for quite a while. That's all you've got for me?"

"We did talk a long time," Lindsey admitted. What else could she do? "But John said you knew the truth about your marriage. That you guys were well beyond any reconciliation and that he was... uh, surprised you asked me to intervene."

"Because he has always had a crush on you?" She taunted, looking almost devious. Lindsey had no idea what was going on in her head. Maybe John was right and she was trying to set them up. She was an interesting girl and by interesting Lindsey meant crazy. Lindsey wanted her out of her house in the worst way.

"I don't know what you're talking about Jeanie, although you keep saying that. It's making me uncomfortable." She needed to get some control here. "But honestly, this is between you guys not me. We just talked for a while. He was worried about the boys and the transition..."

"Oh sorry." Jeanie cut in sarcastically, putting on a mocking apologetic expression full of unconcealed hostility. "I didn't mean to make you uncomfortable."

Jeanie scared her, she really did. This was not a woman to mess with. And yet, mess she did. Lindsey sighed, but was out of patience. "Jeanie, really, I don't know what to tell you."

Jeanie straightened up and composed herself a bit, "You're right, of course." She stood. "I'm going to go now. I've got a lot to do."

Lindsey followed her to the door, wanting to shove her out. "Thanks for talking to him," she said, sounding surprisingly genuine. "I wish I had a good husband to come home to at night, like you do." She said and Lindsey couldn't tell if she was being threatened or propositioned for a threesome.

Lindsey shut the door behind her and took a deep breath of relief. She was so happy that was over with. She closed her eyes and leaned back against the door, enjoying one more satisfying breath before a light knock on the paneled window made her jump. Oh God, don't let it be Jeanie again, she prayed.

She quickly flung open the door and stood face to face with John.

It took a second of them staring at each other before Lindsey realized the implications of him at her door. "Come in," she said hurriedly, looking out the door both ways for any unwanted witnesses. "You really shouldn't be here now."

He stepped through the door slowly. "Don't worry. I watched Jeanie leave."

Lindsey was nervous having him here now. Since Jeanie and John's official announcement, it was no longer as easy to explain his presence at her house, especially without any kids. What if Jeanie was having him followed? Why on earth would he be here? And Mitchell definitely knew something. This wasn't good.

"John, it's really not okay for you to show up here. You know that." He looked hurt. Shit. She shouldn't have sounded so severe. "I'm sorry. I am just all wound up here. It's getting to be too much. I mean, Jeanie was just here freaking me out. And now that the news is out, well, it just doesn't look good. "

"You're right, it is reckless of me. I shouldn't have come. I just couldn't stay away. The thought of you so close was driving me crazy."

Lindsey really didn't want him here. For the first time, she felt conscious that she was in her house with him. Mitchell's house. It wasn't okay. She could see John scrutinizing her a bit, and she softened. "I know this is really hard on you, and I can't imagine what being there with her is like..."

"It is crazy," he acknowledged. "She's crazy." He moved towards her, and Lindsey felt her resolve weaken a little inside, wanting to comfort him, wanting him. Damn, their connection was so strong.

"John, stop. Please don't come any closer to me."

That stopped him. "What do you mean?" he asked slowly. "I thought after the other day..." He drifted off. "I don't know, I guess I thought we were on the same page?" His eyes were so blue, his jaw line so strong, his body so tense. "Aren't we on the same page?" he demanded more forcefully.

"Yes. No. I don't know. Things are going too fast now. Jeanie is freaking me out and Mitchell is suspicious. And I know I keep saying it and it's not fair to you, but I need some time here to think about what I really want. I can't think under so much pressure."

"I know what you want," John said confidently and took a step toward her. Her throat went dry while other parts got wet.

"Don't," Lindsey managed, and he took another step.

"Are you sure?" he asked, smirking a bit. He really wasn't taking her seriously. She hesitated and he took another step, pinning her to the wall. "Are you sure?" he asked again and nuzzled her neck. Now the air was thick with tension. She had lost her position of advantage. The emotional stress of Jeanie had weakened her brain power. She knew she needed to stay away from him and stop all this back and forth to figure out if she could make her marriage work. There was a distant buzzing in her head, drowning out all thoughts. She closed her eyes and felt his body around her, his lips grazing her skin, his hands touching her. It was so good. It was so bad. Control. She needed to find some control.

His lips moved in and she yearned to kiss him. Her body pulsed with need, but somewhere she found the strength to gently push him off. She had no idea how. "No means no," Lindsey said, in a raspy voice that sounded like she had been smoking in a cave for the last thirty years. She gave a small smile.

He stepped back. "Wow. I wasn't expecting that."

"Me either," she confessed. "Your powers are strong, young Jedi." Where did that come from? She was such an idiot. But it lightened the mood considerably and made him smile. "Damn I love you." He looked at her sincerely.

She felt a pang in her chest. She was a horrible person. "John. Please. Give me time. It's gotten too intense too soon. I need to think. I no longer know up from down."

John's optimism this day could not be dissuaded. He pointed to the ceiling. "That's up. But I'd be happy to show you down, if you like." He raised his brows provocatively. She smacked him in the shoulder, and they were good.

"Just some space to think," she pleaded. "There's too much happening. Please. Let's let things settle down a little."

John nodded. "Okay, but we'll talk, right?" He confirmed, nicely mixing a hopeful question with a confident statement. "Please don't shut me out completely. I thought I could take it, but I really can't. I need you. I can't believe how much I need you."

Great, her cynical side immediately griped, one more person who needed her, but it was a knee jerk reaction. "We'll talk," she promised. "But right now, I'm in eye of the storm. Things need to calm down," she said softly but firmly; feeling that old familiarity of holding all the cards in her hands. This was how it always was with her and boys. "And, please don't just show up at my door."

"Bad for business," he joked.

"Just bad, you ass." She laughed.

He suddenly pulled her to him, back against the front door so tight she squirmed a bit in surprise. "John," she warned, but he didn't release her.

"One kiss, my lady. Just one."

It's not like she didn't want to kiss him, but she had been really trying not to. She wanted to do as Ellie suggested, as she knew she should, and put some distance between them so she could concentrate on her marriage, but looking into John's determined, soulful eyes, she sighed and relented. "One. Small one."

"A very, very tiny little one," he promised and his lips toyed with the electric air space around her mouth, drawing it out, drawing her out. He did that for a minute that seemed like a torturous hour, almost touching her lips, gently grazing her cheeks. Fuck, he was killing her.

"Please kiss me," she whimpered softly. "Please."

"Anything for you," he whispered back and then placed his mouth on hers softly first, then pushing deeper with incessant need. When they finally parted, she was breathless and greedy for more, exactly as he wanted her, judging by the smug, amused expression on his face.

She had just dropped some of the cards. Damn. "You've got to go. Now," she ordered and opened the door, half expecting to find Jeanie's face glaring back at them. Thankfully, no one was at there, but she was hyper aware of the bicyclist riding by and the sound of women jogging coming from down the street. She shoved him out, only vaguely registering the unknown car parked across the street.

He didn't say good-bye. He just said, "Remember your promise" and left.

Finally alone, Lindsey leaned back against the door drained. That was way too much morning crazy for her. Having an affair was much more exhausting than she thought, both physically and emotionally. She didn't know how so many people did it. Next time she had an affair, she thought with amusement, she had to remember to do it with someone from work, so much easier.

The phone rang. What now? She wondered and checked the caller ID before picking up. Her mother.

"Hi mom," she said automatically.

"Honey, how are you?" Even in their one short interaction, Lindsey could tell her mom was annoyed, her tone clipped, like her lips were pursed tightly together so that her real thoughts wouldn't leak out.

"Uh good, I guess." She felt a trap and was wary of divulging too much information.

"Really? Good, huh. Well that's great, honey. So why are you trying to give me a nervous breakdown?"

Uh oh. "Is this about my room? Because I swear, I was going to clean it out..."

She cut her off. "Spare me the details. Do I really have to hear from the real estate broker that she went in the other day to give the family another walk thru because their parents were in town or some nonsense, and your room was still untouched? Do you know they are moving in, in less than two weeks? What is going on with you? I swear you don't want to make me come up there. Get It Done!"

Wow, that was a mouthful of vent for her mother. She was obviously seriously pissed with her, but Lindsey went straight to the throwaway just to annoy her. "So you're saying if I don't do it, you'll come up here?"

"Don't mess with me, you rotten daughter. I'm having a perfectly nice time down here with fellow mature adults."

"Mature adults?" Lindsey giggled.

"Yes, that's who we are. Our community had a vote and we don't like seniors, so we're a mature community."

"So I guess you won't be telling people about how your crazy daughter has finished giving you grey hairs and now gives you grey pubic hairs? And what? No more squeezing people's boobs to check if they're real?"

"With an attitude like that you won't be invited to visit," she sniffed.

They were playing, but Lindsey felt really badly about letting her down. How many people could she possibly disappoint this month? "Seriously, mom. I'm sorry. I really am." Then out of nowhere she threw in a bit of honest revelation. "Mitchell says I haven't done it because of Liam."

"Why wouldn't you do it because of Liam?" she asked incredulously, but then she got it. Not her grandson Liam, her son Liam. "Oh."

There was a prolonged silence. Some families talked about their loved ones who've passed almost like they were still with them, theirs didn't talk about him at all. They had an unspoken agreement that Liam was off limits. In the beginning and for a long time after, Lindsey didn't want to talk about him so it was easy to respect her mother's wishes, but then she did and found she had no one to talk with. For the millionth time, she wished Liam hadn't died. He was the one she would have talked to about it.

But it was so long ago. It was time to open up, to heal a little, to laugh and cry and remember. "Mom, I need to talk about Liam." There were some shuffling sounds. She almost half expected her mom to start making fake static noises and claim to have a bad connection before quickly hanging up. Instead, the silence grew to an uncomfortable level until she heard her mother sigh deeply.

"Okay. Not now. But okay."

Okay? Immediately, Lindsey felt lighter. "I'll accept that," she said. "Now when were you planning on coming back?"

"Oh you! Don't mess with me."

She hung up the phone feeling as though she'd made some headway at least in one area of her life. She put another coffee pod in the Keurig. As it dripped into her cup, she thought about Jeanie and John both showing up at her door. Now there was another phone call she needed to make.

She sat down with her coffee and dialed Mitchell's number full of trepidation. Damage control. She didn't want this morning's events to have any negative repercussions on the progress they made just last night. Could it really have been only the day before? So much was happening that each day felt like its own eternity.

Of course Celia answered. "Who's calling?" she asked briskly, all business.

"Celia, it's Lindsey." She sounds so uptight, Lindsey thought. She probably has that waiting room running like boot camp.

"I'm sorry, but the doctor is with patients right now." Lindsey swore she heard her sniff in annoyance.

"Celia, put my call through, please." She definitely heard her mutter under her breath. Did she just call her a bitch? "Celia, did you just call me a bitch?" she asked completely taken aback, but the only response she got were the soft sounds of lite FM playing in the background. What the hell was in the air today?

Finally, after three long minutes on hold listening to the wonderful Debbie Boone singing 'You light up my life,' Mitchell picked up the phone.

"Hey," he answered with more enthusiasm than annoyance. That at least was positive.

"Hey," Lindsey responded, liking his tone. "I hope I didn't interrupt anything too important, Celia was, well, she was kind of a bitch."

He sighed. "I don't know what's up her ass, forget her. So what's going on?"

"I just wanted to tell you this crazy morning I've had. Both Jeanie and John showed up at our door within minutes of each other."

She sensed his hesitation. "No way," he said slowly. She thought she heard him sit down, and imagined him leaning back in his leather chair. "Why?"

Lindsey gave a general account of what happened, spinning the story to suggest that she was the friend somehow sucked into the middle of their marital woes. "So, first Jeanie comes to find out what John said, and then John comes to find out what Jeanie said. It's getting kind of ridiculous. I feel like Dr. Phil," she laughed, and it came out genuine.

Thankfully, he laughed back, "Well, be careful with the meddling, one doctor in the family is more than enough."

"But I might get a talk show," she playfully whined.

"Babe, last night was good," Mitchell changed the subject to a more important one, like Jeanie and John didn't matter at all. Lindsey felt a weight lift. It was small considering the huge burden she was carrying, but it felt good.

"It was," she agreed. "Let's keep it like that. You'll be home normal time?" She asked and when he confirmed added, "I love you."

"I love you back," he said. It was the start of one of their earlier relationship banters, him being an orthopedist and all.

"And what about my knees?" she asked, playing the game, which simultaneously felt awkward since they hadn't done it in a while and sweetly familiar.

"I love your knees," he responded automatically.

"And what about my nose?"

"I love your nose. Although that's not my specialty."

"And my face?"

I love your face. I love your ears. I love all of you."

"I love all of you back," she said and hung up feeling happy, that somehow her slanted world was being righted.

CHAPTER 15

Men are much more likely than women - 48% vs. 28% - to fall in love at first sight.

It had been five days. Five whole days and nights since Lindsey had spoken with John. It was killing her. She did her best not to think about him but she couldn't help it. He was like the irresistible smell of warm cookies. Once he infiltrated her senses, all her thoughts were disrupted and she couldn't get the craving out of her brain, especially when she was alone at night.

Things with Mitchell had definitely improved. Nothing had changed all that much, but Lindsey could tell he was making more of an effort. They sat in the living room (On separate couches but without the laptop.) and talked more after the kids were in bed. They had plans to go out the next night, just the two of them for dinner, kind of like a date night. They were paying more attention to each other, to their relationship, something they had neglected for far too long.

He was still a doctor on call with hospital hours, so there would always be time apart. Early on in the marriage she would question it, question him, question his fidelity, his resolute division between his doctor self and his family self, but she learned to live with the separation and appreciated it. She had never been one to be tied down.

Mitchell's work may have kept him a little less present than other husbands but it had never impacted his ability to be a good father or husband. Sure, there were rough patches, but all marriages have them, she thought. Everyone makes compromises. Everyone accepts things or does things they never thought they would. No matter what, she knew Mitchell loved her and she loved Mitchell. Unfortunately, she couldn't stop thinking about John. It was a bit of a problem.

He was still living a stone throw away, so Lindsey made a point of not driving past their home. She heard from the girl grape vine that he and Jeanie were at a stale mate on what to do with the house, and each person's attorney had advised them not to vacate the premises until they reached a resolution. Lindsey couldn't imagine how uncomfortable it must be for John to be trapped there with Jeanie. It was funny how she didn't even think of them as married any longer. She couldn't even picture them together, even though she had known them as a couple for years.

John texted her each day and asked if she was up for a play date. She responded with a quick, 'not today' because she really was trying to focus on Mitchell and their family. It would be harder in a couple of weeks when Mitchell was set to go to some medical conference upstate. That would be a real challenge.

Outside, she heard the postman and opened the door to retrieve her mail. Noticing the paper on her lawn, she went to fetch that as well. It was then that she noticed the car across the street - an older model, cranberry colored Toyota Camry. With some uneasiness, she realized it was the same one from the other day. She squinted against the sun and saw a man inside. She started to walk over, but then stopped when she realized that she was about to approach a strange car with a strange man in it.

Instead, she did a quick jog back to the house, immediately shutting and locking the door behind her. More than likely that man had nothing to do with her. It could be anyone for any reason, maybe an electrician or someone from the town making assessment. Still, even though she knew her reaction was ridiculous, her internal sensor was vibrating so loud the hairs on her neck stood up.

Peeking out the window through the blinds, she grabbed the phone and called Mitchell.

Celia answered of course. "Celia, it's Lindsey. Put Mitchell on."

"Wow, you're becoming such a devoted wife, checking in almost daily these days, huh?"

"Excuse me?" She was more floored by Celia's retort than the possibility of a killer lurking outside her house. Celia had always been a bitch to her, and Lindsey really never gave a shit. She wasn't new to the party. Lindsey had been a good looking doctor's wife for a long time. Every so often there was a nurse or an aide or a receptionist who crushed hard on her husband and took an attitude with her. But this? This bordered on aggressive. She was almost too stunned to speak. Almost. What the fuck? She thought, and that's what she said, "What the fuck, Celia? Are you kidding me?"

"Oh sorry, did I say something to offend you? It just seems like you're checking up on Mitchell a lot lately and he's checking up on you."

"What are you talking about?" She didn't even care about the car outside anymore.

"I think you should probably ask Mitchell about that. I mean, I don't want to get involved in your marital problems now, do I?" Lindsey could hear her stifling a giggle. Mitchell was going to fire that bitch immediately.

"That's a great idea. Now put my husband on now!"

She was on hold for at least five minutes. By the time Mitchell answered she was vacillating between freaked outrage and insecurity. Every so often, she remembered the car outside.

"Lindsey," he began. "I'm sorry about what Celia said, but she's been very stressed today. Some problems at home and all that. Anyway…"

There was no way he was defending her. No way.

"Mitchell, you need to fire that girl right now. I mean immediately. No kidding." She shook with rage. She couldn't believe the way Celia had spoken with her. Her smug tone offended her in ways she couldn't even begin to address. Ways that opened up doors of denial in her brain that she wanted shut. No question. She had to go.

He sighed heavily. "Babe, she's really good at her job. It's just been a bad day."

Lindsey's blood boiled but her heart went cold and her voice turned to ice. "Oh really, and just what is her job because I'm beginning to think her responsibilities could not be put down on a resume."

"Babe, you're being ridiculous." Mitchell sounded so pompous and cocksure, she wanted to hit him. "Come on, what was the big emergency anyway?"

She was so livid, she almost forgot. Taking a deep, calming breath to put the Celia business aside for a minute, she told him. "I was calling to tell you there's a man in a car stalking our house. I've seen him before and I was going to call the police but I called you first." Suddenly a lightbulb went off in Lindsey head and it clicked. Jeanie.

Mitchell laughed funny. "Really? You think someone's stalking the house? I'm sure there's an explanation. Maybe he's a friend of one of our neighbors?" Now that she thought she understood who the man was and why he was there, Lindsey had no interest in the topic any longer.

Her anger and frustration, her erratic emotions and insecurities all tightened into a ball of determination. She hurled it right at Mitchell. "Listen carefully here, Mitchell. If that girl is not fired, you will have much bigger problems than finding another receptionist." She slammed the phone down hard, her heart pounding.

So much for them being in a good place, she thought. One minute later, the car across the street drove off. Lindsey's brain started to churn and it didn't stop for the rest of the day.

Ellie

Ellie walked around Blue Fin, a local bookstore that also sold specialty gifts, toys, dessert treats, and coffee that made Starbucks seem weak. She glanced distractedly at the books, not really looking, keeping one eye on the door waiting for Diane who had called her out of the blue and didn't ask, more like instructed, her to meet her there at 8:30pm. The impromptu meeting was pretty random, giving Ellie the impression that it was important.

There were only a handful of people in the bookstore store by the time Ellie arrived - two having coffee and two just wandering around, maybe looking for a book or a last minute gift or just killing time. One of the women looked familiar but in their town, everyone looked familiar.

She left the house about an hour early, giving Benny some quality alone time with Conner, and her, the opportunity to just sit with herself and her thoughts. She had a lot to think about and needed a quiet space. But now it was 8:30p.m.. She had eaten an oversized blueberry muffin with a cup of coffee that was going to give her heartburn and had about all the overthinking her brain could take. The door chimes rattled and as if on cue, in walked her friend Diane. She smiled expectantly and strode over to greet her.

"Hey! Di Di, what's going on?" Ellie said cheerfully but her smile stopped short when she saw Diane's sour expression. It was her scolding principal face.

"I'm not here to play games. I'm here for information," Diane said sharply.

Ellie frowned in confusion. "What are you talking about? I'm not playing anything."

"I know," Diane said matter of fact, looking her dead in the eyes and nodding, then repeating slowly with emphasis, "I know."

It took Ellie a minute for comprehension to hit and she still wasn't sure. Carefully she asked, "You know what?

"The Secrets of the Shore posts," Diane deadpanned, sounding almost bored with her exasperation. "Want to tell me about those?"

Her straight-forwardness threw Ellie off her game. Even in yoga pants, Diane was the cool suit in the boardroom. Ellie's eyes widened and she stalled, unsure of what Diane really knew or was bluffing. "Yeah, what about it?"

"It's about Lindsey and John, isn't it?"

Ellie gulped. She was right, the cat was out of the bag, and Ellie needed to declaw it fast. "Hey, why don't we sit down? Let's get a cup of coffee and talk." She led Diane to the small tables and asked the barista for two decaf skim lattes while Diane sat erect in her chair, tapping her perfect nails against the table. Ellie ignored the chocolate muffins that were screaming her name.

"So," Diane asked accusingly, "ready to spill?"

"I don't know what you're talking about." Ellie hedged, wishing she had that muffin to pick at.

Diane sat back smugly assessing Ellie. "I see. So all those posts were talking about someone else?"

"I'm not sure who those posts were talking about. It's not like it says. It could be anyone."

"Really? Even this one from earlier today?" She read out loud,

This is crazier than the Housewives. I swear I'm ready to flip a table. And I'm serious about those tee shirts, guys — Friends don't let friends screw their friend's husband. Come on, I think it's a winner. Who's in?

So far 712 people were in.

"What about it?" Ellie asked seriously, "It doesn't say anything specific about anyone."

"Yeah, that's true," said Diane, deliberately leaning in closer to Ellie. "If you don't know who SOS is, or who her friends are, which I do."

Diane sat across the table calm and cool while Ellie felt the color rise from her chest to her cheeks. She probably looked like a tomato.

"How do you know?" Ellie asked.

Diane waved it off like it was nothing. "I was over one day last year and you were distracted with something, maybe a work call, and I needed to check something on the computer. I don't remember what. I think it was a sale at Bloomingdales. Anyway, it was open on the screen and you were right in the middle of writing an update."

"You've known all that time?" Ellie was floored.

Diane shrugged. "I've known all that time. I thought it was light, entertaining fun. In fact, I'm probably responsible for a good portion of your followers. You didn't have nearly as many back then and I turned a lot of people on to you."

"Did you tell anyone it was me?"

"No. I figured since you never mentioned it to any of us, you wanted it to be a secret. So I kept it for you. No big deal. I can keep a secret. And I liked it. That is, until recently."

They sat for a moment in silence.

"So what now?" Ellie asked.

"You need to close up shop. I think Secrets of the Shore has had a good run but it's over."

Ellie automatically balked. "I spent years doing this. I have over 10,000 followers."

"Yeah, too bad you started messing with your friend's lives. Honestly Ellie, I'm so disappointed in you. I really never thought you'd go there."

Ellie flushed again. "It was totally anonymous!" She justified. "I didn't think anyone would know."

"Oh come on. That's so naïve." Diane sneered. "And we haven't even discussed the fact that..." She lowered her voice. "You knew Lindsey was having an affair with John. I mean Ellie, Lindsey was having an affair with John." It was a whisper with many silent exclamation points.

"I didn't know about that till recently and believe me I was just

190

as horrified."

"You certainly didn't seem horrified."

Ellie refused to defend herself, even though she couldn't have felt more defensive. "Di, I don't need to explain myself to you. The stuff I put up there is random thoughts, gossip, all just trying to be entertaining." A frightening thought occurred to Ellie, which made her gulp down her coffee way too fast, causing an uncomfortable lump in her throat. "Does Jeanie know?"

Diane shook her head and shrugged. "No. At least not yet. It's going to kill her. She's always known John had a thing for Lindsey and to have it confirmed, well that's going to hurt on so many levels."

"Yeah." Ellie nodded sympathetically. "I imagine it will."

"Did you know Sean cheated on me?" Diane declared abruptly, once again causing Ellie to gulp her coffee, this time in surprise.

"No. I didn't."

"Yeah, it was a few years ago with someone in his office. I just knew things weren't right between us, but it's like anything else, you can always find a reason to look the other way, to ignore the signs that are right in front of you. I almost understood that crazy show where the women don't know they're pregnant until they give birth. It really is amazing how you can justify anything in your brain if you want to."

"I didn't know. I'm sorry."

"Yeah well, it kind of devastated me, and it took a long time to get back from that place of bitterness and resentment and distrust." Diane studied the contents of her cup of coffee too hard, avoiding Ellie's eye. "I don't know if I've fully recovered. I probably won't ever. It's hard to forgive. Harder than I thought."

"How long did it go on?"

"Sean said for about four months. A woman from work, you know late nights, big deal going on, all that crap. If I hadn't seen the texts, I probably would have just excused the random all-nighters, the lack of sex and the fact that he dropped ten pounds in a matter of weeks and was looking better than he had in years. When I noted it at the time, he said, and I quote, 'It's nothing. I'm just so wrapped up in this deal that I can't think about anything else, not sleep, sex or even eating.' I totally bought it. What a dumbass I was."

"You were probably so busy with the kids and work and life, you just wanted to believe. That's what it is."

"Yeah. That's what it was. But I did learn one thing. You've got to trust your gut. If you think something is off, you're probably right. And it's not a great idea to just wait and see. You need to address it, immediately. Because once you go down that road, it's very hard to find your way back."

They pondered that thought for a bit. They were at the age where bad things happened. Friends divorced, people unexpectedly died. These were dangerous times. It was important not to act on impulse. Impulse could screw you good.

"So what's next?" Ellie asked, afraid of her answer. "Are you going to out me?"

"I don't have to, if you shut down the page."

Ellie nodded in agreement. "You're right. I really screwed up. I got used to saying whatever I felt anonymously and let it go too far."

"You absolutely did. You let all those little likes go to your big head," Diane confirmed.

Even though Ellie would miss the page she had been writing for almost three years, she was somewhat relieved to have it end. It was a lot of pressure to keep up, to constantly be amusing and entertaining; to be the eyes and ears of her town. With a whopping 10,412 followers and growing, 'Secrets of the Shore' shared all — Style watch, funny stories, light local gossip, observation on humanity, opinions on current events and lately, unfortunately, her best friend's dip into adultery.

It was awesome to have a place to vent and all these followers from her town and all over to interact with who 'liked' her, but that wasn't what SOS was originally about. When Ellie started it, SOS was a page desperately crying for help. It was all about her struggles with infertility. It was a side of her she was embarrassed to share with her friends but desperately needed an outlet for. On line, she found so much support. She could cry and vent. She could be unjustly outraged about girls like Lindsey and others; girls who always seemed to have it so easy, to get everything they wanted with a snap of the fingers or a flip of the hair. She was angry at the world for not giving her what it seemed like everyone else had and what came out wasn't always pretty. So SOS was her dirty secret but when Conner, her miracle arrived, she changed and SOS changed with her. That's when Secrets of the Shore was born.

"Okay," Ellie agreed. "It's over and done. SOS will close up shop with my next update. And thank you for keeping this to yourself. Really." She glanced at her phone, ready to wrap this up and get home. It was only a little after nine but she was exhausted.

"Don't thank me yet. We're not done," Diane cautioned and Ellie felt a new wave of fear.

"What do you mean?"

"Well, I think Lindsey should have to answer for what she's done."

That was not what Ellie wanted to hear and she tried to steer her back over to the side of least interference. "Don't you think that's just adding fuel to the fire?"

"Maybe. But she can't just get away with it. It's not okay."

"I know. I know. But it's over now and I really don't see what help this would be except to possibly destroy Lindsey and her marriage as well." Ellie was totally panicked, frantic in fact.

"Not my problem," Diane said unflinchingly. "Lindsey's problem." She paused and seemed to consider something, "Or, at the very least it should be in Jeanie's hands."

Ellie opened her mouth to protest but Diane held up one of her perfectly manicured nails. A lovely rust color she noted irrelevantly, fabulous for fall. Ellie couldn't stop staring at it. She was transfixed by perfect polish.

"Ellie, don't bother." Diane stopped her before she could even argue. "My mind is made up. There is nothing you can say."

"Fuck!" She exclaimed in exasperation, and the few workers cleaning up momentarily looked over before returning back to the boring business of closing up shop.

Diane gave a small smirk. "Well, you can say that, you just can't do it with someone else's husband." She got up to leave.

"Wait!" Ellie stopped her, panicking. "You don't mean right now, do you?"

Diane's pointed glare was as sharp as her nails. "Do I look like someone who procrastinates?"

Double shit. Ellie gathered her stuff quickly and hurried after her, feeling totally responsible. Lindsey made her choices and mistakes, but she put it out into the world, anonymously she thought, which now in hindsight seemed terribly reckless. What was she thinking? What's the first thing they tell you about the Internet? Nothing you put out there is safe. It can come back to bite you on the ass. Not that she didn't have a nice chunk of ass to spare, but Lindsey did not.

Now it was her words that were going to be the catalyst for whatever shit storm was coming. Lindsey and Mitchell's marriage could very well break up over this and it would be her fault. Well, maybe not really her fault, but she would still be totally to blame.

CHAPTER 16

More than friendship, laughter, forgiveness, compatibility, and sex, spouses name trust as the element crucial for a happy marriage.

8:58p.m.. Lindsey found a panicky text from Ellie on her cell. 'Need to talk. Now!'

9:01p.m.. 'Not kidding!'

9:03p.m.. 'Important! 911!'

Obviously, Ellie needed to speak with her, but the timing couldn't be worse. Mitchell had come home, arms spilling over with Lilies, which were of course her favorite. It was a beautiful explosion of oranges, pinks and whites which would look great on her dining room table, except she was so livid that she could barely appreciate the gesture at all. But then he pulled a Babka cake from Zabar's from his bag. Now that was playing dirty. She couldn't help but notice the crumby chocolate top. Still, even as he handed it to her with his sweet puppy-eyed expression, she brushed the offering away impatiently. She was angry and suspicious, which was sort of like a cosmic karmic payback, but she couldn't appreciate any messages from the universe or gifts from her husband at the moment.

She wouldn't even attempt a discussion until after the kids were in bed, and spent the evening stewing in silent, overly efficient rage. By the time she and Mitchell got some privacy, she was like a loaded gun at a firing range.

"Is she gone?" she asked. She couldn't talk about anything until she knew that disrespectful bitch was gone.

Mitchell sighed long, as if it was his last breath of air which if it were up to Lindsey it very well might have been. "She's gone, but really this is all a big over-reaction."

"Really?" she challenged, feeling herself grow hot with anger. "Are you saying, I'm over-reacting? That the way she spoke to me is okay?"

He quickly backtracked. "No. Not okay at all. She wants to apologize. She was angry at her boyfriend and took it out on you."

Lindsey looked at him carefully. She might be blind but she was not stupid. The way he threw 'boyfriend' in, the way Celia spoke to her, had always spoken to her, his convenient on call excuses, her random calls to the house. Target practice was over. Lindsey felt age old insecurities, questions and resentment simmering on low bubble start to boil, but she put a lid over it and calmly asked, "Mitchell, are you having an affair?"

His eyes, she couldn't pretend she didn't see the truth in that blip of an honest response. She couldn't forget his eyes, but his mouth immediately defended his honor with gusto. "Lindsey! No! I would NEVER do that. You are everything to me. Do you hear me? Everything."

She felt numb all over and turned to walk way, but Mitchell put his hands on her shoulders and looked directly into her eyes. He spoke to her like he was the principle and she was a confused student who couldn't seem to correctly grasp a situation. "I am not having an affair! I can't even believe you'd think it."

Lindsey nodded dumbly, feeling her world swirl around her, but even though she should have expected it, she was completely unprepared when he took out a gun of his own and started shooting. "So now that we've established that I'm not having an affair, are you?"

Slowly, Lindsey turned to meet his gaze and Mitchell flinched.

She didn't care if she was or wasn't. He was not going to turn the tables on her. Not today. "Are you kidding me?" she asked in disbelief. "Are you fucking kidding me? You have the nerve to accuse me of something like that after today? Where do you get off? Wait, don't answer that, I'm pretty sure I know." Lindsey sneered. She could see him deciding what move to play, the sorry, innocent husband or the accusing injured party. It could go either way. It was a tough call.

They were interrupted by a face in the window. Lindsey jumped. "Mitchell!" she yelled. "Someone's outside. I just saw someone in the window."

Immediately, he was in action mode. Mitchell Ryan, doctor, super hero, cheater. He grabbed one of the hockey sticks that Liam had left in the hallway and opened the door.

Ellie stood there with her hand in the ready to knock position. "Uh, hey guys? I know it's late. Am I interrupting?" She smiled guilelessly at each of them, her sweet face emphasized by a dotting of happy freckles over the bridge of her nose and her flowing reddish auburn hair parted in the middle. She looked like an Earth angel. "I'm interrupting, aren't I? I'm sorry. I was just dropping something at Jeanie's and I saw your lights on. I hadn't seen Lindsey and I had this question about Conner and you know..."

Ellie was babbling and Lindsey sensed an urgent desperation that Mitchell would hopefully just confuse with new mom hysteria. "It's okay, Ellie. It's fine, really. Come on in."

"Mitchell," Ellie implored, "I'll only be a few minutes. I promise. Is that okay?"

"It's not a problem. I have some work to finish up."

Mitchell and Lindsey exchanged a glance. Under the circumstances, she didn't think either of them minded the interruption. They were at a really dangerous place.

"We'll be in the kitchen," Lindsey said. "I'll make some coffee." She turned to her husband. "Do you want a cup?"

"Thanks, I would." Somehow the steam had seeped out of their argument. Ellie's distraction allowed them both to retreat back to their corners. They weren't about to shake hands but they hopefully wouldn't be throwing any more punches tonight either.

She headed into the kitchen with Ellie at her heels. "What the hell?" Lindsey mouthed after she powered up the Keurig.

"I'm sorry!" Ellie mouthed back.

This was ridiculous. They couldn't talk at all. Lindsey set a cup of decaf down for each of them and pointed a finger at Ellie. "Wait," she ordered and took a third cup into the living room for Mitchell.

"Here, it's decaf," she said and set it down on the coffee table next to him. He was already set up for business with his laptop ready.

"Thanks," he said, but as she was leaving he grabbed her arm. "Babe, let's not fight. We're happy, right?" He looked imploringly into her eyes.

"I'm not sure," she answered quietly. "I'm a bit confused these days."

"Let's be happy," he pleaded.

"Let's be happy," she agreed wearily, unsure if it actually was possible anymore.

Lindsey leaned down to him on the couch and gave him a light kiss which he readily responded to. They looked at each other a moment for some sort of confirmation that things were okay, or at least might be okay, before she stood up to leave. "We've got a guest," she said and shook her head with a baffled expression.

Back in the kitchen, Lindsey slid into the chair closest to Ellie, opened up the Babka and cut them each a thick slab of chocolate layered goodness. It was the right thing to do. She had company after all. "He's on the couch pretty comfy, we should be fine," Lindsey whispered. "Just remember, inside voice."

"Ha. Ha," Ellie said, but got serious quick. "Listen, you've got a problem. A big one. Diane knows. Don't look shocked. I mean you were dropping clues everywhere. But..." Ellie stalled, looking as though she were in pain.

"What?" Lindsey asked anxiously.

"I kind of accidentally put the icing on the cake. I'm sorry! I had no idea I was... anyway, I'll explain about that later when we have more time. Right now, you just need to know that she is telling Jeanie."

Lindsey stared at her in disbelief.

"Right now," Ellie winced.

"Crap!" she moaned, near hysterical. She was still crapping when Mitchell walked in the kitchen.

"Hey," Lindsey said when she saw him at the doorway.

"Um, you're not going to believe this, but two more of your friends are at the door."

Both she and Ellie sat up straight with attention. "You're kidding," Lindsey said with a raised brow, affecting surprise. She really should have gone into acting. "Is it a full moon out or what?" Oh my God!

"Yeah, I saw their heads through the window popping up and down. They were making more noise than a bunch of drunken teens."

Lindsey and Ellie followed Mitchell back to the front of the house where Jeanie and Diane stood, looking tense and uncomfortable, exactly how she and Ellie looked. They all smiled awkwardly for a moment in a close circle that seemed to be closing in on Lindsey.

Mitchell assessed the lot of them standing in the doorway and made an executive male decision. "Okay, I don't know what's going on, but I'll be on my couch over here while you all work it out."

The women all looked at each other anxiously. It was a boxing match of the eyes and Lindsey didn't feel up to the challenge. "Come on." She gestured weakly, thinking she was going to feel defensive and terrified at this pivotal point where her marriage and life exploded, but all she felt was resigned. "Let's go into the kitchen." They dutifully followed.

The minute they reached the kitchen, Jeanie practically lunged at Lindsey. "You're fucking my husband?" She seethed, yet thank God, amazingly, she was still kind of whispering.

"Jeanie, I'm so sorry. I know that's pathetic. I never expected any of it to happen. I swear." Lindsey felt desperate and under attack, like a trapped animal, fighting for her life. Dying seemed a whole lot easier. "We spent so much time together and it was never there, and then it just was." She felt the tears begin to well.

"Oh no!" Jeanie spat, "You don't get to cry and be the victim. You're not the victim. I am!"

"You're right. I'm sorry." Lindsey put her face in her hands for a moment to collect herself. When she looked up, her tears, although threatening, were in check. "You're right. I did this. I betrayed you and my husband and I deserve whatever is coming. It's all my fault."

Jeanie didn't react or say anything. Her face was a tight mask of anger and hurt. Diane stood behind her, arms crossed aggressively; an underweight, highly-styled bodyguard, ready to intervene for her friend. Lindsey could tell she wanted to. Ellie leaned against the kitchen table, sweating anxiety. She could practically smell her fear.

Lindsey was exhausted and miserable, but a small part of her was actually relieved. They knew. Her friends, if that's what you'd even call them anymore, knew. It had been so hard keeping this to herself and not having their support, or in this case, their judgment. Her grief over Liam was the one thing in her life she couldn't seem to share, but with everything else, she couldn't wait. In a twisted way, this intervention was almost a load off, but then Mitchell walked into the kitchen with a lightly amused smile on his lips, an unknowing deer during hunting season.

"Everything okay in here?" he asked, sauntering over to the refrigerator and pulling out an apple. Lindsey held her breath and looked at Jeanie. They all looked at Jeanie. The air tensed. Mitchell casually rinsed his fruit in the sink seemingly oblivious. He turned to them and took a nice bite. It was a good apple, a Pink Lady, you could hear the crispness. "You know what they say, an apple a day..."

It was all in Jeanie's hands. Lindsey started to feel light-headed and wondered if she might pass out. No one spoke. They all just looked at each other until Mitchell took another bite and said, "Okay then, carry on with your secret club." He walked out of the room as easily as he walked in.

Jeanie finally broke the tension. "I always said you had a good husband." She did, over and over again. Lindsey was beginning to think she harbored a nice sized crush of her own.

They left soon after. There was nothing to say. Ellie at least hugged her good-bye, while Jeanie leaned in toward her and said menacingly, "This isn't over. I don't know what I'm going to do, but I'll do something."

Diane just stared her down full of judgment and disgust.

Lindsey knew this wasn't the end of it. They had just scratched the surface, but it was a deep scratch. After they were gone, Lindsey went in and sat on the couch across from Mitchell. He raised a curious brow. "And?"

Lindsey sighed, too tired to make up any stories, but having no choice. She pulled the one that was closest to the truth out of her ass, "It was mostly Jeanie and John stuff, about the house and lawyers and her anger. She's having a hard time. And there was also an important side discussion on sleep training advice for baby Conner."

"Seemed a little tense," he commented.

"When you walked in she was talking about John and in not such a nice way. I don't think she wanted you to hear."

"So," Mitchell began and Lindsey could tell they have moved on. "Do you want to continue our conversation?"

She really didn't. She was done. "You know, let's table it for now. Okay? I just can't talk anymore. I want to go to bed. Every part of me wants to sleep."

He seemed relieved as well. "Good. Me too. We've got dinner tomorrow night, right? I'll make a reservation."

"Okay. I'm going up." Lindsey rose slowly and they locked eyes, trying to figure out where they stood. Wherever it was, they were still standing. Considering the day's events, that was about as much as they could hope for. "Good night," she said, and sensed a mutual understanding between them.

"Good night," he echoed and Lindsey dragged her ass up the stairs. She couldn't bear to think about anything another moment. She was in two relationships, both in turmoil. Right now, she just wanted to be left alone.

CHAPTER 17

Lindsey – 1987

It took Lindsey's mom a while to agree to send her back to camp that summer. Now watching her small frame as she boarded the bus to leave, Lindsey worried that she had made a big mistake. Would her mom be okay without her?

Her father stood there, one hand in his pocket, the other around her mother's shoulder. If Lindsey didn't hate him, she would think it was a sweet gesture. They hadn't made eye contact when she said good-bye. He just patted her gruffly on the shoulder and distractedly told her to have a nice summer. Lindsey imagined he was thinking, 'Your brother's dead and you killed him, but hey, go enjoy yourself.' She stiffened at the thought. She couldn't wait to get away from him.

When Lindsey had hugged her mom goodbye, she cried almost uncontrollably. She was sure people were staring at this hysterical sixteen year-old girl, but all of a sudden she had an irrational feeling that she would never see her again and she couldn't let go.

Her mother, not big on emotional displays, suffered with her for a bit and then finally held her by the shoulders and told her to pull it together. "Honey, I know this is hard. A big part of me doesn't want you to go but a bigger part of me wants you to. You have to go. It's important for you. Now go, before you drown us both."

Lindsey sucked up her snot, wiping her arm across her nose like a two year-old.

"Pretty." Her mom rolled her eyes and said with a grin, "All the boys are just going to love you."

Lindsey laughed in spite of herself.

"Go," she encouraged. "I'll be right here when you get home."

"You better," Lindsey nodded, hugging her one last time before getting on the bus.

The ride up to Lake Catchacootie in Walla Walla, New York - Seriously? Was a cartoon character in charge of town names? - took about two and a half hours. She spent the ride with her head against the window, tears staining her face, but when the bus pulled into camp and she walked out into the fresh expanse of greenery, kids and counselors with clipboards and whistles running everywhere, she knew she had made the right choice. She needed to get away from the stale, dark place she was in and breathe some clean air.

They gave Lindsey her bunk assignment. She was one of the CIT's for the ten and eleven year-old girls, and she headed over, stopping a few times to say hello to old, familiar faces.

Walking into the small, but tidy sleep space, she saw Ellie was already there, setting up her area all nice and pretty, kind of like her.

"Hey Betty!" she called out, using her nickname for her.

"Veronica!" Ellie squealed, jumping up and hugging her. "I missed you!" Neither of them really looked like the Archie Comic book characters but Ellie was definitely a Betty, and Lindsey was definitely a Veronica.

"I missed you too," Lindsey said. She did. She missed her old friend. She missed feeling young.

"How come you stopped writing?" Ellie asked, her cute freckled nose, wrinkling in question. "I sent you so many letters."

Usually they spent the winters as pen pals, writing back and forth the drama of their other lives; their winter lives. She loved when she got an envelope from Ellie covered in puffy stickers, peepholes for nosy mailmen and a large bubbled SWAK lettered over the front.

Even though Ellie lived in Port Washington, only about a half an hour or so away from her, they were in separate schools, with separate friends and activities. That half hour may as well have been an hour and a half for as much as they saw each other.

"Well," Lindsey flushed. "You know. You know about..."

Ellie didn't need her to finish. She immediately wrapped her arm around her in a hug. "I know," she said. "It's okay. I just hoped to have been there for you more."

Lindsey pulled back sniffling, but resisted the urge to wipe her nose with her hand. "Thanks," she said. "But I don't want to talk about that. Let's just have the best summer."

"Deal," Ellie agreed. "We're definitely the cutest CIT's here."

"Without question, Betty. Shall we go check out the young male offerings of the summer?"

"After you, Veronica." She giggled and followed her out.

It felt so good to be back.

Lindsey spent the first couple of weeks of the summer casually dating every boy in the camp. She'd find one, tire of him, and move on. There seemed a never ending supply, although by her fourth new boyfriend, Ellie threw up her hands. "I'm not even going to bother remembering their names anymore," she chastised. "I think you need to slow down. It's like you're on a mission. Do you even know their names?" she challenged.

"Of course!" Lindsey sneered. Sometimes Ellie really was too much of a mother. She wasn't sleeping with them or anything. She was just having fun. "Maybe you just need to speed up," she challenged right back. "Come on, we're going to find you someone."

Lindsey had Charlie – that was her boyfriend's name – fix Ellie up with his friend David, a sweet, good-looking boy who worked as a lifeguard as well as a CIT. They all had 'other' responsibilities at the camp, like Lindsey was also a tennis instructor and Ellie worked Arts and Crafts, not that she was artsy or crafty. She just looked it.

Ellie and David hit it off immediately. While she got rid of Charlie a week later, Ellie and David stayed an item all summer. Figured. Not that Lindsey let that get in the way of her fun. She was having the best summer. She had no time to even think that she was the girl with the dead brother. Except when she wrote her weekly letters to her mom, which she now dreaded writing since they made her feel miserable and guilty, but still she wrote every week.

It was through David that Lindsey met James. She was down at the pool with Ellie who was waiting for David when she spotted him sitting up on the high lifeguard seat, shirtless with baggy red trunks.

"Hey, Dave? Who's that guy?" she asked.

"Oh no." Ellie was already shaking her head. "Aren't you still with... with... what's his name?"

"That's James," David said.

"I want to meet him. Come on." She dragged Dave over just as James was climbing down from his perch.

"Hey," Lindsey said, but her eyes said more.

"Hey," he responded back, already captivated.

"Lindsey. James. James. Lindsey." Dave and Ellie looked at them and looked at each other and chuckled. "Well," Dave said, having made the introductions, "I guess my work here is done."

She and James stood like that, conversing without words. That was the way it happened at sixteen. When love struck, it knocked you over.

They were an immediate item and Lindsey gave up all the other boys in the field. James was golden and blonde with a big familiar smile.

She tried hard not to think about who he reminded her of, but even if his looks were Liam, his personality was anything but. James was soft and sensitive. They held hands and kissed gently. She felt so comforted by his smile and easy presence that she was just happy to be near him.

They were without question, the cutest couple in the camp, and having been exclusive with him for almost three weeks, they were practically married. It was perfect, until she crossed paths with Max.

Lindsey had seen Max at the tennis courts on and off through the summer, but he worked with the boys and they had just never gotten around to speaking. She had heard he was an arrogant ass, although if she hadn't met James, she probably would have known him by now. His dark curly hair wasn't her usual type, but she had heard he was an impressive player.

The day they met, Lindsey was instructing a bunch of 12 year-old girls and she saw him a few courts over doing the same with boys of seemingly the same age. Somehow a few of the boys' balls landed on the girls' court and when a few of them came over to retrieve them, they started chatting with the girls. Gee, what a surprise.

Max followed. "Hey," he said, using the international greeting of love and sizing her up simultaneously. "What do you say we get a little boy vs. girl game going?" His dark eyes challenged hers.

She felt instantly attracted to him. "You got it."

They set up the kids to compete in rotating doubles matches. It was fun. There was a lot of cheering and booing. The kids loved it and the girls completely held their own. Lindsey snuck a glance at Max, feeling proud but he was feigning indifference.

"What do you say we go half a set?" He suggested, while the kids drank their water and socialized.

"Us?" Lindsey laughed. "Are you serious?"

"You afraid?" He taunted. "I can take it easy on you."

Ugh. He was obnoxious. She grabbed her racket. She wanted to kick his ass. "Let's go!"

They faced off, slamming the ball across the court, back and forth to each other. He was a tough competitor and for the first time in many months, Lindsey felt that need to play hard and to win. It was such a rush, running down those balls, making killer shots, watching his face when she aced his ass to the cheers of the kids watching.

Ultimately, he beat her two games to one. She was secretly thrilled she had gotten a game off of him, but she wanted more. He reached over the net and extended his hand. "Good game," he said. "You're better than I expected."

Lindsey took his hand and shook it. She was attracted to him, but something about him made her want to hit him as well. So she did. In the shoulder. "Huh well, I expected you to be better."

He gave a snort of approval. "Rematch tomorrow?"

"You're on."

They met the next day, and they met the next night. She knew it was a mistake because of James, who wasn't like the random boys of the summer, she really liked him. She didn't want to hurt his feelings or dump him. She felt connected to him in the same and totally different way she felt attracted to Max. One looked like Liam, one acted like him. She knew that sounded sick, but she couldn't help feeling drawn to both of them.

As the weeks passed, she got further and further in over her head. She truly felt in love with them both, but neither knew about the other and she was exhausted running from the courts to the pool, from one bunk area to another. The only saving grace was that Max, being 18, hung out with the older crowd and there was rarely any overlap.

"You can't keep this up," Ellie warned.

"Thanks mom," she'd reply, but she knew she was right. She needed to break up with one of them before the whole thing blew up, but she just couldn't decide which one. James was beautiful and sweet. They would walk hand in hand through the camp and he would bring her little gifts; a necklace he strung together in arts and crafts, an extra chocolate pudding he stole from the mess hall. He wasn't a big talker but his kisses were soft and so were his eyes.

Max captivated her. He was strong and opinionated, older and smart, with that comfortable confidence that was at once off-putting and appealing. Plus, his demands on the court were matched only with the intensity of his need. She had done things with him that she had never done with anyone else.

Lindsey's dual worlds collided one afternoon late in summer when she was at the pool with James. By the time she saw Max coming it was too late. Panicked, she looked at her Swatch. His group's usual pool time wasn't now. Why were they here? Max walked immediately over to her and James. There was nowhere for her to go. She was dead.

"Hey," Max said and touched her lightly on the arm. There was no 'fraternizing' in front of the campers.

"What are you doing here?" she tried sounding casual. "You're not usually here till 2p.m.."

Max looked at her a little funny. Then he looked at James.

"I'm James," James interrupted, probably wondering what the hell was going on as well.

"Max."

They looked at each other with new understanding, and then both looked at Lindsey. She tried to back away, but Max gripped her arm lightly. There was no way they could have a blow-out in the center of camp at the pool.

"You are kidding me!" Max whispered angrily, shaking his head in disbelief. "I can't believe it. I'm so..."

"Max listen, I'm sorry." She really didn't know what to say, but then there was nothing she could say. She was underwater. Max had pushed her into the pool.

She came up and watched him storm off the pool grounds. By the time she reached the ladder to climb out, a hand was waiting. James. "Thanks," she said quietly, shivering a bit. He handed her his towel. "Thanks again." He was so sweet. She felt so terrible. "I'm so sorry, James. I really am. I didn't mean for any of it to happen this way."

He sighed, and looked straight into her eyes. "You broke my heart," he said, and walked away.

Lindsey pretty much spent a week crying on and off. Neither Max or James would speak to her and finally she had given up trying. She became the third wheel with Ellie and David and didn't really mind at all. There was only a week left of camp and she did her best to get through it; busying herself with her group and her girls. Occasionally, at the pool, she and James would exchange a glance. And twice she saw Max on his court watching her intently.

On the last day when they were all set to leave, Lindsey hugged Ellie tight and promised they would be better pen pals this year. "It was a good summer," she said and meant it.

"Don't shut me out, Veronica," Ellie scolded warmly.

"I won't Betty," she said and hugged her again.

Before boarding, James finally did approach her. Lindsey was so happy, she could have cried. "Hi," he said.

"I'm sorry," she bubbled.

"I know. Me too," James said quietly. They stood there like that, silently for a moment, until he dipped his head forward until it was leaning against hers, their noses almost touching, his longish blonde hair falling over into hers. When she pulled back and he smiled, Lindsey felt a surge of emotion that had nothing to do with him, but overwhelmed her.

"I have to go," she stammered and turned for the bus. It was then that Lindsey noticed Max, standing back against a tree with his dark eyes fixed on her.

She really liked them both. She really couldn't be with either. She hurried up the stairs for the bus that would take her back to her broken home and broken life.

CHAPTER 18

72% of women surveyed have considered leaving their husbands at some point.

Secrets of the Shore
FB Post

Words. Words. Words. Just an easy slip of the tongue can change everything. Say something hurtful like, 'You are not my friend.' And magically, you are no longer friends. Say, 'I know you slept with my husband' and watch faces drop, emotions surge, lives alter. Just a few words can transform a relationship - 'I love you,' 'I don't want you,' 'You're not good enough,' 'I'm here'. Saying something like that will make a difference one way or another.

Words. You can use them to hurt or to help. Usually, they're just for chit chat or passing the time. Sometimes, for meaningful dialogue or important conversations, but until we hold someone's future in our hands, we don't see just how much power they wield.

This week, I saw the power of words I had taken for granted. Words I had written. Words that ultimately led to drama and confrontation and possibly severe implications on friendships and marriages. I am appalled to have been a catalyst in any way.

I've used this space for my creative venting. It was by me, for me, but also for you guys. I was trying to be funny, trying to entertain, and I pushed it too far, got wrapped up in the drama. Not intentionally meaning to hurt, but not really thinking much about what I was doing either.

So, I'm sorry. I'm sorry to anyone I've offended. I'm sorry to my friends I've hurt. I'm sorry for putting myself in the middle of something where I didn't belong.

I'm sorry. Just words too, but I believe they mean something. And I hope they matter.

Secrets of the Shore, signing off for good.

Take care, my friends.

***

Friday dawned bright and clear; a beautiful brisk fall day, ripe and full of color, possibility and change, such a contrast to the tumultuous night before. Lindsey stretched lazily in her bed, reading the SOS post with amazement and relief. What happened? She wondered, but didn't care. She was thrilled for the impromptu shut down. It was one less thing to worry about.

She glanced at the clock. 6:48am. Mitchell was already in the shower. He would be heading to the gym before the office. She threw on some gym clothes of her own and walked in to brush her teeth.

His back was toward her and she appreciated the length of his long, lean body; lightly muscled and graceful like a deer. This was her husband, her sexy, doctor husband. Why could she see that so clearly in a steamy shower behind a glass partition? But of course, she knew how easy it was to appreciate an image.

He turned around, catching her staring at his nakedness and smiled like a cat. The view from the front was even better. Damn. Why don't we have sex more? She wondered for the millionth time.

If he were John, she would have stripped down and joined him. But, she guessed if he were someone else, she would be someone else as well. Why couldn't she be that person with Mitchell? She gave a light eye roll at his conceit and started brushing her teeth. That's what they did.

Downstairs, Lindsey busied herself with her morning routine, slicing some cantaloupe and making a turkey sandwich for Liam and a cream cheese and jelly for Riley. She fished around the cupboard and found packs of goldfish crackers for snacks. Good enough for lunch she thought and set about starting breakfast.

"Morning," Mitchell said, walking into the kitchen. He cornered her by the coffee pot, wrapping his long arms around her in a surprise hug. She was taken off guard by the gesture and didn't know exactly what to do with the bottle of Vermont maple syrup she was holding in her hand. Ultimately, she decided to just awkwardly hug back, trying not to let the sticky bottle touch him. It was a good, genuine hug and Lindsey rested her head against the crook of his neck.

She appreciated the warm contact and chose not to think about the reasons behind it, or Mitchell's willingness to seemingly brush everything under the rug. At the moment, she was right there next to him with the broom. Sweep. Sweep. Sweep.

"See you later for dinner," he said into the back of her head, then unclasped her from his grip. "I made 8pm reservations at Sweet Honey. We'll have a nice night out. Talk."

"Okay," she agreed and mourned the loss of closeness for a second.

Within minutes, he was gone and she went about starting her day. She needed to be prepared. After last night, who knew what *or who* today might bring.

She got the kids off to school as usual but instead of racing to the gym or running outside, she sat down and sipped her coffee contemplatively. Waiting. She just knew it wouldn't be long before there was a knock at the door.

She wasn't disappointed. Within 15 minutes, Ellie appeared. She barged in like she just jumped a train as it was pulling away.

"Oh my God, Lins! Last night was crazy! I couldn't even sleep."

"Coffee?" Lindsey asked, weirdly calm, as if all the drama last night hadn't completely revolved around her. Ellie declined, holding up a cup from Dunkin Donuts.

"Brought my own." Her brow furrowed. "Sorry, I should have brought you one too." Lindsey waved her off. "So," Ellie began tentatively, "There's so much to discuss but before we get into anything, I need to come clean about Diane." She took a deep breath and continued, "She found out because of me... and my posts on Facebook."

Lindsey looked at her in disbelief. "What posts? I never saw any."

Ellie grimaced. "Secrets of the Shore."

Lindsey just looked at her uncomprehending.

"I'm SOS." Ellie admitted sheepishly. "It was supposed to be anonymous. I originally used it to vent about my fertility issues and adopting Conner but then it turned into the page you know it as. I never meant to hurt you. I never used any names and I truly thought no one knew, but I got carried away. I'm so sorry."

"You're Secrets of the Shore," Lindsey repeated, her mouth hanging, her face crumpling with understanding. "How could you, El? How could you talk about me?"

Ellie grit her teeth and looked miserable. Her eyes welled with tears. "I'm such an idiot. I am so sorry! Really beyond sorry. I got sucked into the online drama and never thought it would come to this. I wasn't thinking." She started to cry.

Lindsey took it all in. A few months ago, the idea that Ellie could be the administrator behind Secrets of the Shore would have blown her mind, but her mind had already been blown.

"How could you keep what you were doing a secret from me all this time?"

Ellie shrugged weakly, "I don't know. When it started as an infertility thing there were things about myself I didn't want to share, but then I think I got used to keeping my secret a secret. It became a habit and I kind of liked it. Although, I swear I almost told you about it a million times." Her eyes pleaded with Lindsey for understanding.

"But you didn't. And instead you used me." Lindsey put her head in her hands. "I don't know if I can take it. There's too much going on for me to deal with this. And your betrayal..." She shook her head in sadness. "You were the one person I truly trusted, have always trusted."

Even being a miserable wreck looked good on Lindsey, Ellie noted in shame, wondering if she subconsciously sabotaged her oldest best friend because she was jealous of her perfect life, looks, fertility. Because she was always the popular one who got away with everything. What had she done? There seemed nothing to do but to admit the truth and beg forgiveness. "I got addicted to the thrill. It was exciting watching my numbers go up and having people hang on my every post. I am so beyond sorry. I know it doesn't matter but I really thought it was anonymous." It was such a pathetic excuse but it was all she had.

Lindsey looked at her best friend with new eyes. These days, she was seeing so many people more clearly, including herself, and it wasn't necessarily a good thing.

"How did Diane find out about it?" Lindsey asked, summoning her inner calm.

"She found out inadvertently when she used my computer. I didn't know she knew until last night when the shit hit the fan."

"Yup," Lindsey agreed, feeling as flattened as her voice. "The shit is everywhere."

They sat for a moment in silence.

"I don't know Ellie. So much has happened that I can't seem to get properly outraged. I mean I am completely thrown by this. That you, of all people. I must be in shock because I know I should be livid and I am, but I honestly can't deal with you right now. One wrong word from

Diane or Jeanie or anyone and my marriage could end but it's not as though I'm not considering that every other minute anyway. I just feel so tired."

Ellie looked so full of emotion she might burst. Lindsey remembered the day they went to lunch and she had first revealed to Ellie that she was having an affair and she was the one who couldn't seem to form words, now Ellie was flushed, tear streaked and speechless. Lindsey noticed grey hairs shining at her part, flecks of white sprouting against the tawny red. She wondered if they were there yesterday before this fiasco.

"I think it's time for you to go," Lindsey said and stood up and started walking toward the door.

"Lins, I really am truly sorry for this."

"You should be. You screwed me here," she sighed exhaustedly. "I know I really screwed myself but you... well what you did was almost as unforgiveable."

"I know, but I hope you forgive me."

"I hope so too," Lindsey agreed. "I'm running out of friends."

Once the door shut, Lindsey went directly for the Babka loaf, ripped off a hunk and inhaled it, chewing furiously. After a few stress releasing seconds, the sugar hit her blood and she felt soothed and a bit more in control as she pulled off another piece, got fresh cup of coffee and sat down at the table. Slowly sipping as she delicately peeled layers of chocolate bread and placed them ritually bit by bit into her mouth, she tried to work through the million feelings and judgments crashing in her head. John. Mitchell. Ellie. Jeanie. Her kids. They overlapped and like the strings of a bunch of balloons, they tangled together making it almost impossible to extract a single thought.

She really didn't know how she felt about anything anymore. She didn't know what she wanted, or who. She wasn't sure how she felt about her needs and the needs of her family, or how the two might be at odds. She struggled thinking about things that before recently never even crossed her mind - Is this what I expect from my life? Is this who I want to be? Am I satisfied?

All of a sudden, she acutely understood the mid-life crisis concept. Time was running out. After years of compromise and putting her needs on the back burner, she felt somewhat validated in taking control of her life. But of course she wasn't just an individual any more, she was part of a family with wants and needs that possibly trumped her own. And there were the lesser, more dirty logistics of financial security. No one talked about it, but it couldn't be ignored. Could she withstand the change? Possibly selling the house? Moving?

A knock at the door interrupted her. She was not surprised.

John.

They locked eyes and her heart did a little leap. She loved him, she thought. She really did, but she couldn't think about that. Don't look too happy, she commanded herself and for God's sake keep your damn distance. "Come on in," Lindsey gestured for him to follow her. She concentrated on accomplishing one step at a time, overly conscious of his presence behind her and trying not to think about the sharp line of his jaw completely in contrast to the soft expression in his eyes. "Sit." She pointed to the same kitchen chair recently vacated by Ellie.

"I heard about what happened last night," he said. "I didn't know what they were up to until after they went to see you. Diane came over and after a bit of them talking in loud hushed voices, Jeanie shouted that she was going out and they abruptly left. It was only after they came back that Jeanie confronted me. If I had known I never would have let her go."

"But how would you have stopped her?" Lindsey asked.

He had no answer for that. Once Jeanie was on the runway, there was no stopping her take-off. "I guess I would have used duct tape," he joked, and then turned serious. "She wouldn't tell me what happened, only that she and Diane had come over to confront you. Did she? Does Mitchell know?"

Lindsey shook her head. "It was bad, but it could have been worse. She didn't tell Mitchell. She only threatened to." It might have been her imagination, but for a second she was sure he looked disappointed. She understood that as well. In some ways, it would be easier if it was all out there. Then the cards would just fall where they fell and although she might be in hot water at least she'd be out of the madness of the spin cycle.

"She raged at me," John said, "but honestly, it was more subdued than I expected, no broken dishes or anything. It's like she really knew already and this was for show."

Lindsey raised a brow, "Should I expect her at my door next?" They really lived way too close.

"I don't think so." He turned suspiciously toward the bay windows. "I hope not. I waited till she was gone before I walked over." They sat in the quiet for a minute before he continued, "I told her it that was my fault. That I pursued you."

"I'm not exactly innocent," Lindsey admitted.

"Yeah, but I opened the door."

"And I walked in, again and again." There was another moment of silence where they each contemplated their 'again and again'. Then Lindsey asked, "How are you doing over there?

John exhaled big. "It's far from ideal. I'll say that, but we're being civil for the boys. I should be able to move out of the house in a week or two. The financial thing gets tricky. I don't want to pay her any support since she makes a solid income, but I'll do anything for my kids. We'll figure it out. She may not admit it, at least not for a while, but she knows this is the right thing."

More silence, until finally he asked, "How are you doing?"

Lindsey gave a small shrug. "I really don't know." A swell of unexpected sadness surged in her chest. She had been so unemotional throughout the whole ordeal last night, but here it all was now, filling her with empty confusion.

John placed his strong hand on her face and she leaned into it, feeling safe, letting a few tears slide down his fingers. "I'm sorry," she sniffled a bit. "The last thing I want to do is cry. I don't even know why I'm crying. I mean I know why, I just don't know why now." He looked at her so tenderly, that she automatically pressed her lips to his hand. It was a reflex. "I'm sorry," she repeated hopelessly, gently pushing his hand away, afraid she might do it again, or worse.

"I'm the one who's sorry." He grabbed back her hand. They apparently could not stop touching each other even when they wanted to. "Everything is my fault. You were perfectly happy with your life and I screwed it all up."

Her fingers twirled in his. They should not be doing that. Lindsey had a momentary realization that they were both using their emotions to stay connected, to find reasons to lean on one another, but because she wanted to, she pushed the thought away. "Yeah," she agreed, "you kind of did."

"Hey!" He chuckled and his mouth broke into a grin. "You're not supposed to say that."

"And you're not supposed to be here," she teased, her heart pumping life in her chest.

"I'm addicted to you. I can't stay away." His eyes darkened with intensity.

"I'm addicted right back. But you have to." Her eyes pleaded with him to stay back, while her body opened wide like a yawn, drawing him in.

"I just can't," his voice deepened and he moved in closer.

"John." Her body tingled. She felt outside of herself.

"Lindsey," he mocked.

"Don't," she quietly implored, but her lips parted.

"I'm going to kiss you." His face was inches from hers.

"Don't," she said again, waiting breathlessly.

His lips grazed hers lightly, gently pressing them in a soft, delicious kiss that simultaneously filled her with hope and despair.

When he pulled back to look at her, every part of her wanted to pull him back in. She desperately wanted more, but one kiss was one too many. She tried to pull herself together instead. "You have to go," she said gruffly. "I can't be near you."

"And I can't be away from you," he responded. "It's a problem."

"One of many," she agreed.

Sighing, he lifted himself from the chair. She waited a beat until he made a move toward the door before she followed. She didn't trust herself at all.

"I'll see you round," he said casually, even though there was nothing casual about their situation. Before he walked out the door he asked, "Maybe, we can set up a play date soon?" He was half-joking.

"We'll see." She smiled. "Now go."

He left and she watched him walk down her pathway almost skipping. Before he reached the sidewalk, he turned and spread his thumb and pinky finger out and held them from his ear to his mouth, making the universal symbol for 'call me'. Lindsey beamed stupidly, like a young girl in love, forgetting she just was an old, foolish married woman.

Quickly, she caught herself and checked her spontaneous response. She needed to get in control here. It would be better when he moved. These little surprise drop-overs were not good. Every time she saw him her heart exploded and she did what she clearly wanted to, but didn't want to do. If she truly intended to work on her marriage which was an open question, she couldn't do it with him popping by. Just seeing him conjured up too many feelings, intense good feelings that made her want to forget all this thinking and drama and just be with him. No matter what she told herself, if she saw John, she lost all resolve and she lost Mitchell and her family. If that was going to happen, Lindsey wanted to be the one who decided. She didn't want her life decided for her.

She went inside and retrieved her cell from the charger. Before she had time to change her mind, she found his number and dialed it quickly. He answered immediately.

"Wow, if I knew how quickly you'd respond, I would have just told you to call me a lot sooner." His voice carried the same skip as his step. She hated what she had to say.

"John..."

"Uh oh." Immediately, he sensed the shift. "I don't like the sound of this."

"I'm sorry. I know I just gave you the idea that we might... play soon. But I really can't see you." She hedged. She couldn't help it. "At least not now, not for a while."

"Well, that's the last time I ask you to call me," he joked lightly, but she could tell he was wounded.

"It's just that, when I see you, I don't want to be with anyone but you. I can't think straight. I can't think at all."

"That might be the best kiss off ever. Takes, 'It's not you, it's me' to another level. Not bad." His words were lined with sarcasm.

"John, please. That's not fair and you know it." She didn't want to cry, but felt her voice quivering. "I told you. You know how hard this is."

"I do. I really, really do. Remember, I'm in this too. I'm completely in this." He was angry. Lindsey felt it in her gut like a punch.

"I know. But, I need time."

"I know what you need." He stopped just short of a bitter laugh. "And it's not time, but take it if you want it." She felt him closing up, could almost see his eyes retreat behind a veil of hard blue granite. She desperately wanted to soften him, to bring back the man who just left her house only minutes before. She wanted to make him happy, for him to continue loving her the way he did, but she couldn't. She let him have his anger. It would be cruel of her not to.

Salty tears streamed down her face and she tasted them on her lips. "I'm going to go now," she said, and even though staying on was torture, hanging up was the last thing she wanted to do. She bit her lip to keep the cry at bay.

"So am I," he said it gently, sadly. It hurt more than if he would have yelled because then he clicked off and was gone. She held on to the dead connection feeling just as dead inside. Not knowing what to do, she walked to her living room and sat down on the couch, closed her eyes and sobbed. Why did doing the right thing feel so utterly wrong? She remembered that first day, that first time, right where she sat. She allowed herself the pleasure of the memory still so potent in her brain.

After some minutes, she breathed deep, released herself from her misery and her fantasy, which were one in the same, and went to splash some cold water on her face. This was turning out to be some day, and it was only 10am.

CHAPTER 19

86% of men and 85% of women don't think they have any friends who tempt their partners.

Now that she was all cried out for so many reasons she couldn't even settle on one, she was just empty. She hadn't moved much, just from one room to the other, fussing around with no rhyme or reason. On a whim, she called Mitchell at the office just to see if Celia would answer. She didn't, so Lindsey hung up. Now she was just killing time before the kids got home from school.

At least she wasn't cooking dinner. She and Mitchell had plans to go out and the kids could choose where to order in from. Even though she knew they needed to talk, the idea of going out to dinner with Mitchell filled her with dread. She didn't know if they could handle alone time. There was so much to say and so much not to. It could be very uncomfortable.

The squeaky wheels of school transportation sounded outside, and Lindsey hefted herself up from the kitchen chair and went to the door to meet the kids. As usual they barreled in, both knocking into her and completely ignoring her at the same time.

"Hey guys!" she greeted. "How was school?" She bent down to pick up the backpack Liam automatically had tossed and placed it on the hook on the wall next to Riley's. No one answered her and she follow the trail of Liam – sneakers, a water bottle, a pencil – into the kitchen where she found them both getting a drink.

"Hey guys!" she repeated.

"Hey, mom. Is Jacob coming over?"

Lindsey almost forgot he had a friend coming. "Yep, in about half an hour. You guys have any homework?"

"Just some reading," Liam said. "I can do it over the weekend."

"Same," Riley chimed.

"Okay," she consented. "Do you guys want a snack?"

They didn't answer even though she was two feet in front of them, yet perked their ears and twisted their heads like dogs at the sound of a light knocking. Immediately, they raced toward the door. There were excited voices, and the screen door opening and slamming shut. "Well, okay then," Lindsey said to herself. "Nice chatting with you guys too." She made her way toward the front to see who was there and what the kids were doing. Clearly, they were playing with someone, since the sounds of voices laughing floated through the hall.

She was about to push open the screen and stopped. Liam and Riley were on the lawn with Trevor and Elliot. Panicked, she stepped out on the porch, trying to find the parent attached to the kids. Was it John? Would he come by after their conversation? It didn't seem likely, unless the kids begged which was possible. It was more likely Jeanie. Her chest tightened.

"Hey Lindsey." Somehow when she was looking left, Jeanie came up from the right causing Lindsey to jump back in surprise. Jeanie smiled wide in a way she rarely did even when she was genuinely happy and amused. Since she was neither, the result on her tight, thin lips resembled the Joker from Batman.

"Uh hi," Lindsey's heart hammered and her brain was totally freaking out. She could not be more uncomfortable at this moment. She needed to get a real estate agent pronto.

"The kids wanted to walk by, so I said why not?" She might be high, Lindsey thought. Her eyes looked cartoon crazy. "I wasn't going to let a little sex between you and my husband stop me." She looked at Lindsey sideways, assessing her reaction.

Lindsey wanted to say something, but she was kind of speechless. Regardless, she made an attempt at reason. "Jeanie, I really don't know what to say. I know there's nothing I can. Everything I think of sounds so pathetic and insincere."

"Yeah, that makes sense." Jeanie looked her up and down coolly. Lindsey automatically felt self-conscious. Appearance-wise, it wasn't her finest moment. She was in gym clothes with her hair in a ponytail, exhausted from crying and not sleeping, while in contrast, Jeanie's blonde hair looked recently blown out and her smart trousers and blouse were the picture of chic sophistication. Lately, low key grunge was Lindsey's new look. Keeping up with any fashion or beauty maintenance had become increasingly less important.

"Boys!" Jeanie called out. "We're going now." They ignored her, but in about a minute when she used her tone that took no crap, they would jump to attention. She was small, but her presence was fierce. "Good seeing you. We should do this more often," she said nastily.

Lindsey was so relieved that she was going that inadvertently a smile came to her lips. She watched as Jeanie's face turned red, then her ears, and her eyes burned fire. She had just ruined Jeanie's exit moment which meant she needed another good one. Lindsey braced herself.

"Tell Mitchell I stopped by. I'll try to come back later when he's around," Jeanie snapped threateningly, before stomping off in some very trendy camel colored ankle boots.

Lindsey's involuntary grin was immediately erased from her face.

The morning with first Ellie and then John, followed by the afternoon with Jeanie left her wiped and emotionally unstable. She couldn't think. She could barely function. She let Liam's complaints that

Riley was ruining his play date go unheeded. At least she was annoying someone other than her.

Riley even comically noted her unusual inefficiency. "Mom," she said, coming down for a drink, "You're just sitting. You never do that." She may have looked idle, but her internal system was working overtime, swinging wildly from confusion and fear to anxiety, excitement, and love. She was a melting pot of insanity with Mitchell, John, Jeanie and her as the soup.

Lindsey looked at the clock. Just before 5pm. Even with everything going on in her head, there was something gnawing in the back of her brain. She picked up the phone and dialed.

"Uh, hi there," she said, assuming a slightly comical southern accent that came from God knows where. "Can I please speak with Celia. I'm her friend, uh, Jeanie."

Her heart pounded in her chest as she waited for the woman to reply, and then her heart stopped beating all together when she answered, "Hold on a second, I think she's in the back."

Lindsey held the line for a minute unable to breathe. Then the woman picked up the line and it was her voice as clear as Lindsey's new awareness. She quickly hung up, glad that the office didn't have caller-ID.

There were no words. Her melancholy anxiety and confusion transformed into a storm of anger that roiled about inside her, gathering weight like a snowball. So it was really true. He was having an affair with Celia. She couldn't even process that and on a very superficial level was highly insulted that he would even be attracted to her. She was low class, gum chewing, tight clothes, too much make–up, the whole bit.

But maybe she was getting ahead of herself. Just because he didn't let her go like he said, didn't mean he was sleeping with her, did it? A million tiny red flags in her head all of a suddenly brightened and burst into flames. She knew it did, just like that quick look in his eye when she confronted him, and all the dozens of small inconsistencies that separately meant nothing but together meant everything.

Lindsey wanted to kill her. And him. She wanted to kill them both. Those red flags were burning a fire in her belly. She headed to the wine cabinet. She needed something to help put them out.

Around 6pm, she ordered a pizza and garlic knots for the kids and got ready for her dinner out. Mitchell called to say that he had changed his mind about Sweet Honey, and instead made a 7:30pm reservation at this little French place by the water that had good food and a decent atmosphere. He reminded her to confirm the sitter and asked if she picked up his dry cleaning.

Lindsey bristled when she heard his voice lightly discussing the mundane, but she managed to sound neutral instead of telling him to shove his dry cleaning up his ass. Thank goodness, she had started drinking.

How was she going to sit across from him and look him in the eye for two hours? What would they talk about? Would they address anything? Would she bring up Celia? She didn't know and she couldn't stress about it. Right now, she could just drink her drink, put on a pair of jeans and go with it.

Downstairs, she heard Mitchell come in and the commotion of kids crashing into and over each other for his attention. There was a woman's voice as well and she figured the babysitter had come a little early.

The sound of high laughter traveled up to her. It wasn't the babysitter. She listened more carefully. It was Jeanie. Panic erupted in her brain, making her more sober and drunk simultaneously. She needed to get down there immediately, but she was rooted to her spot. Part of her just wanted to leave them and let it all come out, but the thought was fleeting. She didn't want Jeanie in control of anything in her life if she could help it.

Lindsey walked carefully down the stairs, holding the bannister, afraid she would trip from her nerves. Jeanie stood in the foyer, chatting easily with Mitchell. Their eyes met. Jeanie's danced merrily while Lindsey's retreated to the back of her head in fear. If she were a cat her tail would be defensively puffed and her ears flat as an instinctive reflex to danger.

"Hi Jeanie," she said. Her mouth felt like it was filled with cotton. "What are you doing here?"

"Oh, Trevor thought he left his little soccer ball when he was playing on your lawn earlier, so I came over to look and bumped into Mitchell." She ran her hand down Mitchell's arm like she was one of those models on the Price is Right and Mitchell was a brand new dishwasher. "Mitchell was telling me you were going out for dinner. Where are you going?"

"That French place by the water. I can never get the name right," Mitchell answered casually, saving Lindsey from the torture or small talk. It was all that she could handle just standing there. "In fact, I'd better go change. Reservations at 7:30p.m.. The sitter should be here any minute."

"Thanks for the impromptu check on the back." Jeanie smiled coyly, clearly flirting with Mitchell. "I just might need to make another appointment."

"Of course." Mitchell nodded, seemingly oblivious. "Come whenever you need to. I'll fit you in."

"Thanks. I will."

Jeanie's eyes glistened as she watched Mitchell head up. This was getting weirder by the minute. Jeanie was either totally messing with her or definitely had a major crush on Mitchell. Probably both. Then as if she read her mind Jeanie hissed, "Maybe I should just sleep with your husband. We'll see how you like it."

Lindsey didn't like it and hissed back. "Are you going to tell him?" She couldn't take much more of this. She was on the verge of a nervous breakdown.

"I'm not sure," she said contemplatively with a touch of malice. "But I'm having fun figuring it out."

Lindsey was so tired of games, but she knew Jeanie wanted to see her humbled, even kind of deserved it. "What do you want me to do, Jeanie?" She begged desperately, "Tell me. What can I do? Please. Anything."

"There's nothing you can do. This is about what I can do," Jeanie warned and walked out. "Have a real nice dinner." Then she yelled behind her, up the stairs. "Bye Mitchell! I'll call you!"

Would this day never end?

The phone rang.

Apparently, it wouldn't. She checked the caller-ID. Her mother.

She answered immediately, desperate for a familiar, loving voice. "Hi mom."

"Honey, how are you?"

"Been better. There's a lot going on here."

"Is that your way of telling me that you haven't gotten to the room yet?"

"Well no it wasn't, but now that you mention it..."

"Lindsey!" she shouted in frustration, "You better stop this bull crap right this minute. Stop being a rotten daughter, get over there and do it."

"Mom." She couldn't take another person attacking her. She felt like she had been shot at so many times already today. Boom, she took one in the heart. Boom, she took one in the head. Boom, she took one to the body. "Stop shooting me!" she yelled and in the momentary silence that followed, she could almost see her mother's arched brow.

"Okay, honey," she softened. "I don't know exactly what's going on with you, but I want to. I'm flying back up there next week. We can talk about things." She paused and added tenderly, "We can talk about Liam."

"Really? You're going to come up?" Lindsey almost cried. She was so happy. She noticed Mitchell had come into the room and was ready to go.

"Yes, you crazy rotten, daughter. There are some loose ends that need tying. So I'll see you next week."

"Now that I know you're coming, I'll bake a cake," she chuckled, all of a sudden lighter.

"I'm wise to your game, missy. You can't sweeten me up."

"We'll see," she said, enjoying for a small moment the sensation of being happy, of something positive. They hung up as the doorbell rang. The baby sitter had arrived and the night was just getting started.

"Do you know what you're getting?" Mitchell asked. He looked extremely attractive in a new soft green polo shirt and haircut. His hazel eyes shone with flicks of gold and green.

She shrugged. "Maybe the lamb chops? And a salad." Her stomach was in knots. It wasn't like she was going to eat much, except maybe the bread basket. "I would definitely like a drink." Mitchell beckoned to the waitress and placed their drink orders while Lindsey picked at the brioche roll in front of her and thought about their basically silent car ride over. What was he thinking about? What was going on in his head?

With the waitress gone, he turned his attention to her. "So," he started, but then trailed off, not knowing where to go.

"So," she responded, feeling exactly the same. Their small table was crowded with wine, bread and secrets.

He took a visible deep breath and jumped in. "So, Jeanie's been around a lot more lately."

Okay. Breathe. Speak. "She's taken some days off with the divorce and all. I don't know, I guess she's reaching out a bit."

"How's she doing?"

She had no idea, but she shared what she could. "She seems to be doing okay. I guess, there's a lot of semantics to deal with, financially and legally, and then John hasn't moved out yet and there's the kids to think of."

"Divorce sucks," Mitchell said, knowing first hand. His parents had divorced in a messy way, leaving permanent scars on his psyche. It had been part of their early bonding, neither of them was a big fan of marriage or commitment. They were alike back then in so many ways.

"It does," she agreed.

They sat quietly with the implications of divorce hovering around them like bees waiting to sting.

"Have you seen John?" Mitchell asked. His tone was neutral but his eyes darkened to a greyish color.

Lindsey took a sip of her drink and lied. "Not since that last time I mentioned."

"Maybe I should give him a call," Mitchell suggested, his eyes a question mark. "We were always friendly. Just to see how he's doing? That's the right thing to do, don't you think?"

The idea of Mitchell calling John made her physically sick. Although, Lindsey was pretty confident he didn't know anything for certain, she was just as sure that he had his own little red flags waving like mad. "Yeah. I guess," she casually answered. She was sure John could handle a check-in from Mitchell. "That would be nice."

He nodded, more to himself. "Maybe I'll get the husbands together to go out with him."

Now that was truly a bad idea. She didn't think Benny knew about her and John or would say anything if he did, but it was likely Sean, Diane's husband did and who knew about Marnie and Bradley. Getting the bunch of them together, probably with some heavy drinking could only lead to disaster. "Maybe, you just call and check in. Don't make it seem like a party yet. It could get awkward with Jeanie."

"Okay," he agreed. "You're right."

Thank God.

She went to sip her wine and realized she had emptied the glass already. That was fast. Too fast. Where was that waitress? If she was going to open up a can of worms, she needed more wine to wash them down. Unfortunately, the waitress was at another table and Lindsey would have to wait, but the discussion couldn't.

She had spent that silent car ride figuring out how to best approach the Celia matter and decided to just ask innocent questions and see where it went. "So," Lindsey began, nervously grabbing another piece of bread. Their interaction was more of a back and forth interrogation than conversation. Now seemed a good time to take up smoking. "I feel a little bad about having you fire Celia. How did she take it?"

So much lying and manipulation, she thought, feeling like they were two actors in a show, instead of her and Mitchell sitting there.

"Not great," he admitted. "You know her. It was a small scene and all, but at least it was after office hours, so there were no patients around."

"What happened?" she prodded, wide-eyed with interest. If he was going to lie, she wanted him to dig his hole deep.

"I just told her that the way she spoke to you was unacceptable, no matter what had been going on in her day. That I was sorry, but she had to go. She didn't take it well. She cried and said some nasty things, but ultimately she just went."

"That sounds like pretty dramatic behavior for a receptionist," she said. "Don't you think?"

"That was just part of her charm," Mitchell shrugged off-handedly. "She certainly knew how to keep the difficult patients in check."

Did he really just say charm?

Without Lindsey even saying anything, Mitchell corrected himself. "I don't mean it was charming. I just meant that was her personality. She was always a dramatic girl but she was a good worker."

"So you'd like her back?" she asked.

Mitchell sensed a trap and gave a cautious, reassuring smile,

"Not if it upsets you. If you don't want her there, then I don't want her there. What she wants doesn't matter, only you."

Oh God. He was killing her with these lies. She wanted to scream and shake him. She wanted to throw her glass of wine in his face – but damn it, it was empty. Where was that waitress? Oh, what to do? What to do? Should she call him on it? Should she blow this fish right out water?

She assessed him across the table. Back when they were courting, he had admitted that he was the guy who always had a girl on his arm and another in his back pocket. He told her he was never satisfied, was afraid he could never settle down and be happy. He told her flat out. Why was she even surprised?

Was their seemingly happy marriage for almost fifteen years this much of a sham? It was all too much. Maybe the two of them really deserved each other.

She came back to the present to answer the question hidden in his supposed comforting statement of loyalty which was pathetically thin.

"Well good, because I don't want her there at all. In fact, I don't ever want to see or hear her name again. She could go cry a river with all that mascara somewhere else, but not near you." It was a succinct tirade, but it was strong and effective.

Mitchell looked startled for a second. He just realized there was more to this line of questioning than it seemed and that they might be on thin ice. Still, he quickly recovered. "Your wish is my command."

The food came and the distraction helped. They relaxed in the time and attention it drew away from them. They were in too volatile a place, talking about too many things that they weren't actually addressing. Lindsey didn't know about him, but she needed to regroup and have a meeting with herself. So after cutting up her food, and getting her wine refilled, she started in on a safe conversation, one that talked about the kids and her mother's plans to visit next week.

He seemed relieved as well to be on more comfortable ground. There were some huge issues to deal with, but right now they both silently called stale mate. Amazingly, they actually enjoyed the rest of the evening. With the return to normal conversation, the tension lifted and they chatted easily, even a bit flirtatiously. The whole night was extremely surreal, and when they walked to the car, it seemed bizarrely natural for his arm to be the steadying force around her waist.

On the car ride home, quiet tension once again filled the space between them. What they knew or didn't know or thought they knew was the loudest presence in there, but for some strange reason, it bound them a little. Neither wanted to separate, and in desperation they denied, denied, denied.

Before they exited the car to go back inside, Mitchell took her hand and they shared a strange moment of understanding. She couldn't begin to think about what it meant. She wanted to be happy that his hand was on hers, but she wasn't.

How could she when she finally was beginning to grasp what they were dealing with as a couple? They were both liars and cheaters, who wanted to have their cake and eat it too. How long before they fell apart, regardless of how they tried to hold the pieces together? It just seemed inevitable and maybe for the better.

Later, after the babysitter was gone and they were tucked into their warm, comfy bed, Mitchell turned to her as naturally as he had done a thousand times before and they made love sweetly and a little desperately as the tears ran down Lindsey's face.

***

Brisk and sunny October was typically Lindsey's favorite month. She found the change in the air rejuvenating. Just the smell of it filled her with possibility. After the crazy of back to school in September, the kids were now nicely transitioned into the school year. They each had consistent playdates and lucked out with good teachers who gave enough homework but not too much. Their fall schedules were in place. There was school, sports and homework. There was playtime and dinner, washing up and bedtime, and in that easy way the days passed, one after another. And today her mother was coming.

It had been over a week since that horrible day that Lindsey liked to think of as Black Friday. That next morning when she woke up, she immediately felt anxious and apprehensive. She had been given a brief reprieve the night before and had actually enjoyed an uninterrupted night of deep sleep, her first in so long. But then, Lindsey kept waiting for Jeanie to show up at her door, or to hear the whispers through the grapevine that Diane had shared the gossip with half the town. She couldn't shake the feeling of doom all that day or the next, but nothing happened.

Somewhere along the way, she just got too busy with the kids to dwell on it. Each day that passed gave her a small breath of hope that somehow things might be okay, even if they weren't.

She and Mitchell resumed a kind of heightened auto-pilot purgatory. He went to work, came home for dinner, played with the kids and sat on the couch with his laptop. He engaged her in safe conversation and after a few minutes she was happy to retreat to the bedroom with her thoughts. There was no more sex and a lot of denial but things weren't bad. One might actually call them pretty good, depending on what you were looking for in life.

While she had managed to steer clear of all the women who used to be her friends, with the exception of Ellie, and also stay away from John, there was one person Lindsey was subtly obsessed with and could not stay away from. Celia.

She had developed this dysfunctional little habit of calling the office at random times and asking to speak with Celia. If she was lucky, they automatically transferred the call. But often they asked who was calling and Lindsey would make up a name. No matter what way she got to Celia, she always hung up when she answered. It was a strangely satisfying kind of punishment that Lindsey felt the need to constantly subject herself.

However, she now sensed trouble. The last time she called, the receptionist who answered sounded suspicious and started asking some questions. "What did you say your name was again? How do you know Celia?" Apparently, her stalker hang-ups were attracting some attention. She needed to steer clear a bit, but it was a struggle.

She distracted herself by going for a run, which she had done compulsively, every day this week. The combination of fantastic weather and need to expel some energy while clearing her mind, made running a meditative gift. She had 45 minutes to run her body and her brain to exhaustion before she needed to get home and get ready to pick her mom up at the airport. She couldn't believe she was due in just a few hours. She was so excited. The only thing dampening that excitement was that they were set to drive straight to her old house to complete what Lindsey had failed to start.

Lindsey had suggested lunch or just hanging out for her first day back waiting for the kids, but no, her mother was adamant. "We have some work and some talking to do. Might as well multi-task for the few hours we have."

As Lindsey ran, she thought about the conversation they might have about her brother Liam. She thought about sharing what was going on in her life. She thought about Ellie and the SOS posts. She thought briefly that she needed to go to the bank and pick up milk. But mostly, she thought about John. Block after block, she re-lived their affair, going over each delicious moment together, exciting herself, torturing herself. She remembered the intensity of his eyes; how deeply and sweetly he kissed her, how perfectly they moved together. She remembered laughing and talking, teasing and joking, feeling so wanted, connected and happy.

Her runs ended far too quickly and she always finished by passing their block. She didn't have the nerve to actually run down it, but from the corner across the street she could see their house. Today, she saw piles of stuff left out by the curb; giant garbage bags, pictures, an old gym bench, an ugly chair. John must be pretty close to moving out, she thought, ignoring the sadness aching in her chest. She wanted to see John. She just couldn't.

Slowly, she padded towards home, but picked up the pace when she remembered she needed to shower and hurry to the airport.

"Mom!" Lindsey cried when she saw her petite form making her way towards her car. She really cried, tears streaming down her face.

"Honey! You know we're not the type of family who displays emotion." She laughed and hugged her. "Stop this nonsense."

With her carry-on bag stowed in the trunk, they drove off and immediately got lost in the airport trying to follow the exit signs. After a half an hour driving in circles, giggling like school girls, they finally made their way out to the highway and headed towards their old house.

During the ride, she forgot all her troubles listening to her mother's stories of crotchety old people cheating at cards and stealing spoons from the community room. She made fun of everyone but genuinely seemed happy there. Her skin glowed with sunny health.

"So, I guess you're not moving back," Lindsey pouted.

"And miss Wednesday Bingo night?" She stared as if Lindsey just suggested passing on wine with dinner. "Come on. I could win dinner for two at Dennys!" She patted Lindsey's hand unconsciously. "So you see, we can't."

"Well, I'll just take you," Lindsey joked, but something flickered in her mother's eyes, and she turned serious.

"Yes, that's something we need to talk about as well."

They pulled up to the house that she and her brother grew up in, and both Liam and her childhood died in, parked in the driveway and sat. It could have been twenty-five years ago coming home from a tennis match. Time is a funny thing. In that driveway with her mom, the years disappeared. She almost expected to walk in and find Liam casually sitting on the couch, his feet propped on the coffee table, a bag of Fritos on his lap watching a rerun of The Odd Couple, which was one of his favorite shows.

Lindsey sighed, not wanting to go in and ruin the memory with the reality.

"Are you thinking of Liam?" her mom asked tentatively, almost shyly. Lindsey couldn't remember the last time she heard her mother speak his name, and she nodded.

"Me too," she admitted. "I think about him all the time."

"I didn't know that. You never speak about him with me," Lindsey whispered. It felt like they were discussing a sacred topic, which they were.

"I know. In the beginning it was just too hard. I couldn't talk about him to anyone, and then as time passed I got used to holding him inside, keeping him quietly with me. I almost couldn't share him. It hurt me too much."

"I know what you mean," she agreed. "I felt kind of the same."

"I'm sorry if it seemed like I shut you out. I'm sorry for a lot of things, honey. But now, if you're okay with it, I want to talk about him. I hope you'll share some of your Liam with me and I can share some of mine with you. Like, I'll bet you didn't know that before every one of your tennis matches he went into your room and rubbed your racket with his lucky tee-shirt?"

"The green one with the yellow stripe in the middle?" Lindsey looked at her wide-eyed, tears starting to rise. "Really?"

"Yup. He was your biggest fan."

Lindsey sniffled a little and the tears fell. "He was my best friend."

"I know, honey. I'm really sorry I wasn't there for you."

She nodded in acknowledgement. They gripped hands and both stared straight ahead openly crying. It felt so good.

They stayed like that for a while, sniveling and sniffing, wiping snot away with their hands, until they laughed, openly and uncontrollably.

"This moment brought to you by Cardak."

Lindsey snickered. "Mom, is Kodak even a company anymore?"

"Hmm. I don't know. That's so sad."

"More sad than us right now?" Lindsey smiled and her mother squeezed her hand more tightly.

"This sad makes me happy. Let's do this more often."

"Promise?" Lindsey asked. The door finally was open and there was so much to talk about.

"Yes." She turned more serious. "But we also need to talk about your father."

All of a sudden the car got a bit claustrophobic. She wanted to get out. "Okay, mom. But not now. One emotional family breakthrough is enough for one day."

"But we will deal with it. It's been too long. Your father has suffered as well. It's time to forgive."

Lindsey expected more tears and a bubbling pot of emotion to overwhelm her at the mention of her father, but she was surprisingly calm. She didn't know if that meant she didn't care or that she was ready to move on and forgive, but her mom was right. It was time to deal. "Okay. I promise."

Her mom gave her hand another squeeze. "You ready to go in?" she asked, eyeing the house.

"Let's get to it," Lindsey said with forced enthusiasm.

They opened the car doors and stepped out into the brisk, sunny day. Their house looked beautiful to Lindsey. A standing memory. Here, she would be fifteen forever. Here she was happy. Together they walked in.

Lindsey braced herself against the cold emptiness that was at odds with the warm memories coursing through her system. They went directly to her room and her mother took a moment to assess the perfectly intact monument to her daughter's youth.

"Well, looks like you've been very busy," she snipped sarcastically, flipping a tassel from her graduation cap which sat on her desk.

"Yeah," she sheepishly looked around, "Sorry. But I'm glad we can do it together. There's some other stuff I need to talk to you about;

some stuff that has been going on with me recently."

She felt ready to open up on all levels. This was her mom, her best friend. She didn't want any secrets from her. She wanted to share. She wanted her to know who she was and what she was going through. She cast a glace toward her bed and had a warm flash of her and John. She took a deep breath. She was ready.

"I'm glad to hear it," her mom said, looking at her with interest. "And it looks like we've got some time here."

They got to work; stacking up photo books and memories into cardboard boxes. Placing beloved objects of youth away for posterity, for maybe Riley and Liam to one day discover. Lindsey noticed the roller skates with the giant rainbow laces and pompoms and set them aside. Riley would love those, she thought and then noticed the Hello Kitty clock winking at her. For more than one reason, she put it aside as well.

As she placed each item in a box, Lindsey appreciated them and let it go. The hardest boxes to fill were for her tennis trophies and some mementos of Liam. Putting them away felt like putting him away and she cried with her mom the entire time until the box was sealed.

"Stop it!" her mom affectionately scolded. "I'm ruining my make-up. I'm going to look like Tammy Fay soon."

By 2pm, they had made quite a dent, but were exhausted and the bus was coming in an hour. They called it a day.

"I think we accomplished a lot," Lindsey said, looking around.

"We accomplished more than you know," her mother said solemnly, and she knew she wasn't talking about the packing.

Opening up about Liam was a momentous step for them, and Lindsey started telling her about what was going with Mitchell and even about John. Not everything, but an inside view on how she was feeling about her marriage and her husband and her ex-friend's husband. Her mother listened carefully and while she wasn't happy about what was going on, she didn't attack her either.

"What you're going through is tough but sometimes this stuff happens in life," her mom said, "Growing older ain't easy, but .I'm grateful that you're here to make these mistakes." She was thinking about Liam. "That's enough nonsense for today," she concluded with finality. "Tomorrow we'll continue. Now, let's go home and see those fabulously rotten grandchildren of mine."

CHAPTER 20

45% of men and 26% of women are attracted to friends of their partners, and are tempted to act on it.

The week with her mom passed too quickly. They finished packing up her room and put her furniture in storage. One day, who knew, maybe she'd use it for Riley's room. She already had Liam's furniture there, in wait for his namesake.

She and her mother always had a solid relationship, but it was further strengthened by their constant closeness this week. They opened up so much and shared in ways they never had. Like adults. All of a sudden, her mother became a real person, not just her security blanket. She was a woman who lost a son, had a reasonably happy marriage and dreams of her own. She was a woman in her sixties with strengths and weaknesses; a woman who made mistakes, carried burdens and carried on. Lindsey learned a lot about her, about Liam and about herself.

By the time they left the old house completely empty, Lindsey had left a lot of her baggage behind. She felt like she had emptied herself as well.

She was so busy that it was reasonably easy to distract from the things that nagged at her, namely, John and Celia. For some reason, she couldn't completely explain to herself, she was less and less concerned with Jeanie or Diane or the damage they could inflict. In many ways, she welcomed it. It might be easier than doing it herself. She still felt bad about Jeanie and was afraid of her, but she was in line behind her passion for John and her rage for Celia, as despicable, contrary and ironic as those feelings were. Mitchell hovered somehow in the center of it all, and she vacillated wildly between anger and regret to love and attachment.

John. She thought endlessly about John. He consumed almost every minute of her brain. It had been more than two weeks since they had contact and it tortured her days and kept her going at night. She worried that he had forgotten about her, had moved on; that she was nothing but a momentary distraction. She missed the strong lines of his face and of his body. She missed his playfulness and his arms around her. She missed feeling special.

Yesterday, she thought she saw him during her run and it made her almost trip and fall. Her legs went bendy, her heart raced, and her brain immediately emptied of oxygen, causing her to sway with dizziness. Regardless, she sped up and tried to catch him, but she had lost him.

The day of her mother's departure was sad but happy. They had accomplished so much. With many hugs, lots of kisses, a suitcase full of drawings from the kids and a promise of a visit down to Florida for Thanksgiving, her mother was safely sent off, back to her Canasta games, tennis doubles and wine parties, and Lindsey was alone again feeling both settled and unsettled.

She and Ellie touched base a few times, or more accurately Ellie tried like a maniac to get in touch with her but Lindsey continued blowing her off. She just wasn't ready and still nursing her wounds. It's crushing when you think you know someone and realize that you really can't know anyone completely, even those closest to you. She never thought Ellie would surprise her like this, would have bet the house on her loyalty and was almost more stunned by her betrayal than Mitchell's. But even though it was difficult to get past, she would forgive her; she pretty much already had in her head. They went too far back and there were too many ways she had screwed up to hold a grudge. Still, she didn't want to see or speak with her just yet.

Lindsey wondered a bit what was being said in their inner circle, if Ellie, Jeanie, Diane and Marnie were out at this very moment having lunch at Yaki and talking about her. It was possible, but probably not with Ellie there, or Jeanie, who would probably have returned to work. Maybe she should call Ellie, Lindsey thought yet again, but changed her mind immediately. She wasn't up to a long conversation and was still unresolved.

She settled on a text instead. "My mom just left. We'll catch up later this week."

Ellie responded immediately. 'When?'

'Whenever'

'When?'

Lindsey sighed and typed. 'Thursday?'

'Great!'

With that settled, Lindsey realized it was lunch time and now that she thought it, she craved sushi. She called Yaki and placed an order. Twenty minutes later, she walked in and stopped cold. They were there just as she imagined and Lindsey gulped hard as she took in the table of Marnie, Diane, Jeanie and Caren, her replacement she presumed. She breathed a small sigh of relief. No Ellie. Her chest swelled with tenderness. There was the loyal dog she knew and loved. She hadn't abandoned her.

There was about a half second before the table noticed her where she could have backed out quietly, but Lindsey stood gaping for that moment too long. Marnie saw her first and caught her eye. Lindsey was relieved to see that there wasn't hardness in her stare. She didn't hate her, but the disappointment she saw was almost as bad.

As if they sensed the energy of the room change, Diane and Jeanie both raised their eyes to her at the same time. She watched their surprise happen, then she watched Diane's gaze turn into any icy aloofness, and in Jeanie she saw something resentful and a little malicious. Sweating and afraid, like her life was under attack, Lindsey backed away and almost tripped into the giant fish tank.

Their stares suffocated her body like a rash and she quickly paid for her take-out order, placing her credit card back in her wallet with shaky hands. The group of them was so intimidating and painful that she wanted to run and hide.

She was one of them Lindsey thought and noticed an open seat at the table. She used to sit right there. She could see herself there now, shooting daggers at the bitch who dared to betray one of her friends. She almost embraced their attack because she deserved it. She couldn't expect them to forgive her or accept her ever again. She couldn't expect them to understand what was unexplainable to her. Something she would have harshly judged from anyone else. Something so unbelievable, that she almost felt as if someone else had done it. It couldn't have been her who cheated on her husband with her friend's husband. That would be unthinkable.

Lindsey cowered toward the door; their stares on her never wavering. It was only as she was just about to walk out that she saw her, Ellie, coming back from the bathroom. The empty seat. Their eyes connected and Ellie looked truly devastated to see her. The hole in her heart was ripped open anew, but Lindsey couldn't blame her. How could she blame anyone for this mess but herself?

She stumbled out of the restaurant in complete nervous breakdown mode; crying, choking, hyperventilating. She felt like she was having a heart attack; more likely it was a panic attack, but it was a panic attack of the heart.

Leaning up against the store front, she tried to catch her breath and stop the heavy heaving of her heart. She never expected seeing them around town to be easy, but she didn't realize it would be traumatizing. She didn't know if she could do that on a daily basis. Even if they didn't gossip about her to the town, even if it just stayed in that circle, it was too much. They seriously might have to move, she thought with dread. A wild idea came to her. Maybe they could move into her parents' old house. They could buy it from whoever the new owners were. They haven't even moved in yet.

She was figuring out the logistics of this implausible plan when Ellie walked out and approached her, putting a steadying hand on her shoulder. "Are you okay?"

Lindsey nodded and snorted at the ridiculous question, snot running into her mouth. She was in front of a popular restaurant in town. It was only dumb luck that no one had passed by to gawk or stopped to help during her public nervous breakdown. "Not really, but I'll manage."

"Yeah, that was rough," Ellie agreed. "It's probably going to be like that for a while."

"I know," she accepted, sucking up her face to hold in her emotions. "I deserve it, but I don't know if I can take it."

"You'll take it," Ellie soothed. "You're tough and it will get better."

"They really hate me. They were my friends."

Ellie tentatively reached out for her hand, seemed unsure but then grabbed it anyhow. "They should hate me too. I don't know why they don't."

They held hands for a minute until Lindsey pulled hers away to wipe her nose. "Do they all know?"

Ellie nodded.

"What about you, do they know about you?"

"Yeah, they do. Diane and Jeanie spilled the whole story quickly to Marnie and Caren. I can only guess who else knows, but I think it'll stay pretty tight. Jeanie isn't interested in any of this spreading around."

Ellie grabbed Lindsey's hand again.

"Ew El, I just wiped my nose."

They laughed for a second then turned serious. "Listen. It will get better. Just give it some time. And no matter what, I'm your friend. I know I fucked up. And I also know that just because you fucked up worse, I've gotten off easy, but I know Lindsey. I know. And I swear I'm your friend before I'm their friends. So whatever it takes, I'll do it. I'll touch your snot covered hand. I'll never go to Yaki with them again. You can even sleep with Benny."

Lindsey shoved her lightly. "Not funny." But there was a warm smile on her lips.

"You want me to walk you to your car?" Ellie asked. "You need to go home."

Lindsey pointed to it and she walked her over. "I'll see you on Thursday." Lindsey said confidently, just as aware of how important Ellie was to her, how devastated and alone she would be without her.

"Of course. I'll see you Thursday," Ellie confirmed and gave her a good hug. "BFF's forever remember?"

"I think BFF now means Best Fucked up Friends."

"Yeah, that'll work, but just for now," Ellie agreed. "Best Fucked up Friends?" She asked hopefully, extending her pinky finger for Lindsey to grasp.

"Best Fucked up Friends," Lindsey returned, linking her finger with hers.

She head home but at the last minute made a quick, completely asinine decision and turned in the other direction. She couldn't stop herself. The itch in the back of her brain had grown to a full on rash. She had to scratch it. She headed directly towards Mitchell's Great Neck office.

She was driving too fast, feeling completely destructive, manic on negative energy, when she pulled into the parking lot. Throwing the car in park, Lindsey leapt from the car for the building. She didn't want to think. She just wanted to do.

She strode into the office purposefully, ignoring the people waiting, and marched right past the receptionist she didn't know, who opened her mouth in protest. She swung open the door that led to the patient rooms and headed right in, not looking, not stopping. Somewhere in the background noise, she heard the hubbub from reception and the light chatter identifying her as Mitchell's wife. It wasn't like she was there often, but obviously someone recognized her.

Lindsey walked through the back office maze, peering into the open doors of patient rooms. Random people sat waiting, some with a nurse or assistant. She saw Dr. Fields, who shared the practice with Mitchell. One of the nurses she knew greeted her as she moved quickly past, but she was nearing the back of the offices, and was too focused to stop or acknowledge.

She overheard Mitchell's voice in a room she was passing and stopped to peer through the window. Sensing a presence, he turned mid-conversation and saw her. For a split second his eyes smiled in surprise, but then quickly look troubled, then panicked.

She hurried on before she lost her chance. "Lindsey!" he shouted, emerging from the room behind her, but she kept going.

"Lindsey," he called after her. "Lindsey!"

But it was too late. She had already reached the back office and saw her sitting at a desk, some patient folders spread out in front of her, her dark hair loose on her shoulders, her skirt riding high up her infuriatingly nice thigh. Celia.

They looked at each other; Lindsey's face, a mask of cold rage, while all the make-up in the world couldn't cover Celia's anxiety.

"Lindsey baby, I can explain!" Mitchell stumbled over himself, rushing up to her.

For years, Lindsey had dismissed the little warnings in her head. She had chosen to believe her husband wasn't a cheater when deep down she knew the truth. Had known it all along but wouldn't admit it.

"I really don't think you can, honey," she said filled with contempt, and looked at Celia who actually had a small smile of triumph on her face. Lindsey snapped and lunged at her. Shocked, Celia moved sideways to get out her way, and fell off her chair, while Mitchell grabbed Lindsey back. "Don't fucking smile at me, bitch," she yelled and pushed Mitchell off.

Taking a deep breath, closing her ears to Mitchell's pleas and apologies, she gathered up her shattered dignity, turned around and walked back out.

"Fuck!" Mitchell cursed, loud enough for the workers in the back room and a passing nurse to raise a brow, but not loud enough to disrupt the office. "Fuck, fuck, fuck!" He fumed under his breath, pacing in a tight circle. He had successfully maintained the balance of his work and home worlds for over a decade and now it was all fucked. He needed to talk to Lindsey, to somehow get her to forgive him. He pushed a shaky hand through his hair and breathed deeply to steady himself. It was still a work day. He had patients to see. He would have to deal with this disaster later. Lindsey needed some space to cool off anyway. "Fuck!" he spat one last time because he knew he was.

Lindsey didn't stop till she hit the street. She didn't know who said, 'Knowing is better than not knowing." But she was pretty sure they didn't know what the fuck they were talking about.

She drove home like a crazy woman; her cell buzzing and ringing continually. Finally, she couldn't stand it anymore and in a fit of frustrated fury, threw it to the back of her car. She really wanted to dramatically toss it out the window like they do in the movies, but it was a $600 phone with a pretty silver rhinestone jeweled case with her initial that she loved. She just couldn't.

Having suspicions was a whole different ball game from having confirmation. With suspicions, you can justify and validate. You can allow yourself the illusion of your life and continue on, but once the spell was broken, once the truth was thrown in your face, there was nothing to do but react. There was no hiding anymore.

From nowhere, Jeanie entered her brain. She was her Celia. No. She was worse. She and Jeanie were friends. Lindsey got a sick feeling in her stomach. She might throw up. She made horrible choices without thinking much about Jeanie at all. She only thought about herself. Was there any excuse in the blindness of love and passion? Was there any way she could justify her behavior? She didn't think so.

Once home, she paced her house, wearing out the wood floor. She had so much energy, anger and confusion. She was exploding with emotion and needed an outlet. Her brain kept going back to that moment of discovery, seeing Celia's smug smile and her husband's weak, ineffectual pleading.

She really wished there was someone she could talk with, but there was no one except maybe her mother. But the thought of sharing this with her right now was the last thing she wanted to do. Maybe another time when she wasn't so emotional and literally standing on a ledge.

Ellie was out of the question as well. She was probably still lingering at lunch with her ex-friends. Besides, she didn't think she could speak of it yet, even with her. It was humiliating, and many might say, karmic.

There was no one. For now, this was her secret, her business, her mess. She needed to work through it on her own.

Having nothing to do, nowhere to go, no one to talk to, and an hour before the bus, there was only one thing she could do that served as any sort of therapy. Run. Even though she had already gone that morning, she needed a release. She went upstairs and quickly changed into running clothes, pulled her hair back in a ponytail and tied up her sneakers.

Even before she began, the weight in her chest lightened. Just having something to do relaxed her. She stepped outside and the air invigorated her. Breathing deeply, she hit the road, her mind moving faster than her feet.

She passed Jeanie and John's block and in another demented move, decided to run up it. With the day she was having, she felt justified in this minor indiscreet pleasure.

As she came to their house, she saw a bunch of garbage and packed belongings piled up outside. There was a small moving truck there as well. She slowed to a stop. Two movers emerged from the house carrying boxes of stuff and laid them heavily in the back alongside a few other cartons and some furniture.

So this was it. He was leaving, she thought sadly, experiencing an abnormal urge to open his boxes and touch his things. It was then that she saw him walking out of the house as well, casual in a long sleeved jersey and loose fitting jeans. His eyes found hers and she immediately felt nauseous with longing. Unsure of what to do and completely confused, she stepped backwards and started running up the block.

It was purely instinctual. She didn't know why she was running when she wanted desperately to see him, but her thinking wasn't straight and she forged ahead. She registered his steps behind her and even though she knew inside her confusion that she was thrilled, she automatically picked up the pace. It was around the next block that he caught her, grabbing at her arm. But still she pressed on, pulling him forward with her, until they both tumbled and fell on the front lawn of somebody's house who she didn't know. Panting, they laid there, eyes to the sky.

They stayed a few minutes watching the puffy white clouds move slowly across the expanse of blue, catching their breath, collecting their thoughts.

"We've got to stop meeting like this," Lindsey said softly, still not looking at him.

"I just couldn't let you run off."

"I wanted you to catch me," she admitted for unknown reasons. With him, she was as open as the sky.

"You move pretty fast for someone who wants to be caught."

"You never heard of playing hard to get?" She was being flirty and playful, when really all she wanted to do was cry.

"I think you've been doing a pretty good job of that," he said seriously.

Still lying on the grass, she turned to face him. "I haven't been doing a good job at all."

His blue eyes pierced her, flashing with pain. "We haven't had any contact in over two weeks, since you needed some time to think, remember? I've been hoping every day to hear from you. Two weeks is a very long time."

"I've thought of you every day, mostly every moment. It has not been easy for me."

Like spiders in the grass, their fingers moved slowly over and lightly touched, playing with each other, intertwining.

"Are you moving soon?" Lindsey asked.

"Today."

"Far?" she asked, suddenly more breathless than when she was running.

"Not far."

"Okay." Relief filled her. He would still be close.

"Will you see me?"

"I don't know," she confessed. "I want to desperately."

He inched closer to her, so that now they were lying side by side. So far, no people had passed, but this was bordering on deranged self-destruction. All it took was one person who knew them, and in this town almost everyone knew everyone. Lindsey couldn't believe she was being so brazen. She didn't want to get caught, yet she didn't care enough to move. She was so happy in this moment next to him. Like a stubborn child, she wanted to stay and not think about the consequences. But if she'd learned anything she knew there were always consequences.

"I want you to desperately," he whispered. She felt her insides liquefy, melting into the grass like crayons in the sun.

"Come on, you're going to be an eligible bachelor soon. The gals will be lining up." There she went again, talking like an idiot.

"I'm not going to even respond to that," he said flatly, his eyes hardening a little.

Dummy, dummy, dummy. She reprimanded herself. "I'm sorry," she said. "Sometimes my mouth is bigger than my brain. I say stupid things. It's nerves."

In one quick motion, he rolled over on top of her. She felt a flutter of panic, but it was crushed by the weight of his body, the smell of him and his closeness. "You're the one I want," he whispered hoarsely. "I don't want you to think I'm not in this for real. I don't want a line-up of girls. I want you. I've always wanted you." He looked at her and into her, their faces inches apart. He nuzzled her nose and her cheek, his eyes intense and earnest, "I love you, Lindsey. I really do."

This felt so good, so right. How could it be wrong? How could her entire body and brain be wrong? She loved him. She did. Desperately, like a seventeen year-old, experiencing it for the first time. He felt more right than anything she had ever felt in her life. Her bubble of happiness right now was so inflated, tears leaked down the sides of her face, and he kissed them each away.

"Me too." It came out muffled and small. And then she said it for real, "I love you." Her words stopped him and he studied her searchingly with unconcealed tenderness and happiness. "Kiss me," she whispered. "Please kiss me."

Right on the lawn of some random neighbor, he did, opening his mouth softly, slowly. Her heart raced against the slow workings of his kiss, wanting more from him. But as quickly as he rolled on, he rolled off. The air hit her body, making her shiver. Without him on her, she felt empty and cold. She felt like nothing substantial, like she could float away with the wind if he didn't harbor her.

"Come on," he stood up, and put his hand out for her to grab. As he did, a car zipped down the road. "Let's go. We've just about pressed our luck here."

John pulled her up, looked around, and seeing only a desolate, tree-lined block, pulled Lindsey to him, running his hands through her hair, cupping her face. They kissed deeply, hungrily, and again when they parted, she wanted more. He was the force of their restraint.

"Two weeks," he repeated, accusing and absolving simultaneously.

"I'm sorry," she muttered softly.

They had only been together a short while, but their chemistry

253

was so strong, it was like he knew her from another lifetime; like they had been waiting for each other for years. Soul mates. Or, at least that's what Lindsey kept telling herself. She didn't know if it was true or not. She was a pretty good bull shit artist.

They walked back toward his house together, resisting the overwhelming urge to hold hands. When they reached his lawn, they lingered for a while out front. Warmed by the young October sun, they spent the next fifteen minutes in perfectly respectable conversation, talking about how he was doing and how she was doing and how the kids were doing. They didn't talk about Jeanie or Mitchell, and Lindsey didn't tell him about Celia. They just talked about safe things like school and his new place and her mother's visit. When it was close to bus time, he took her cell and plugged in his new address. Then they were like two lovers at a departing train.

"So I'll see you?" he asked hopefully.

"I've got your number." She smiled sadly.

"That's not answering my question."

"I know. I know." She hated when he steeled himself, when she so craved his affection. Could she be more selfish and unfair to any more people? "I promise I won't wait as long to get in touch with you."

"Don't. Or I'll come get you and I don't think you want that." She didn't, but the thought of it gave her a secret thrill; her cowboy coming to rescue her. "Oh you like that idea?" John said reading her not so private thoughts.

She blushed and shook her head in embarrassment. Twenty minutes ago she might have entertained the idea of sex on a public front lawn, but now she was self-conscious. A yellow school bus passed down the adjacent street. It was time to go.

"I promise," she said.

He grasped her hand one last time and held it possessively. "I'm not sure I trust your promises. I wish I could."

"Then, I swear," Lindsey said, gazing up at him with big puppy eyes. He smiled and gave a tolerant shake of his head.

They looked at one another not wanting to break apart, but knowing it was past time. "I guess I'll just be moseying on now, cowboy," Lindsey said and pulled to leave, stretching out their arms. But he didn't let go. She half expected half hoped that he would pull her in one last time for a kiss, but he just held her hand. Instead it was Lindsey who rushed in and pulled him to her, throwing her arms around his neck and hugging him close. She rested her head on his shoulder and held him to her tightly. They stood like that for a minute not moving, just hanging on to their last moment together. Finally, they parted and Lindsey slowly walked away, not able to maintain enough dignity not to look back. Three times. All of which found him watching her go.

She turned the corner and instantly was back in her normal life. She jogged the four blocks to her corner and waited the few minutes till the school bus arrived. She watched fondly as one of her kid's bounded off and the other one lumbered.

Somehow the time with John had given some perspective to Mitchell and Celia. Not much, but it was hard to be so full of fire when you're sitting on your own hot plate. Maybe this all happened for a reason. Maybe Mitchell should be with Celia and she should be with John. It seemed pretty convenient. You take this one, I'll take that one and we'll call it even and move on. Maybe it would work out and they'd all be happy. Lindsey didn't want to rush her brain in any one direction. Acting quickly was acting foolishly. She knew that, yet she hadn't exactly been practicing what she preached.

She knew she loved John and wanted nothing more than to be with him, but issues notwithstanding, she also loved Mitchell, had made a life with Mitchell. Could she love them both at the same time? Immediately, she knew she could. It was like with the kids. You didn't run out of love because you already had one. You loved them all the same, but differently. Each had their own uniqueness to appreciate. Sure, occasionally there were favorites. But it was cyclical and usually, at least with the kids, it was whoever happened to be listening better at the time.

Without a doubt, she knew John could make her happy, although she wasn't naïve enough to think it wouldn't change if they were actually a couple without restriction. There would be no clandestine meet-ups, no secret rendezvous. There would be kids and exes, schedules and responsibilities. There would be real life. Could they stand up to real life?

She lived real life with Mitchell and until recently they had done a pretty good job together. Their marriage was always comfortable, easy, happy, the kind that required no real effort on either end, because it just worked.

Still, he was absent so much with work that honestly, who knew how many affairs he had had. There had been a number of bright red flags she chose to ignore along the way. They were at a stage where they took their relationship for granted. It was hard not to after so many years.

Being with John was like a clean slate. Get out of this town. Start fresh. Start over. Be in love. She could picture them as a couple and being happy. They would eat out and drink wine. They would laugh a lot and be playful and affectionate. They would seek out each other's company. They would talk and their conversations would be continuous and meaningful. They would have fantastic, amazing sex. They would -

"Mommy, what are you thinking about?" Riley asked, her head cocked like a puppy, the side pony tails enhancing the effect even more.

Startled, Lindsey looked at her daughter, so innocent and perfect, gazing up at her with expectant eyes. She looked at her son, sitting at the kitchen table, writing in his reading journal for school, his tongue hanging from his mouth in concentration, and her fantasy dissolved.

How could she do it to them? It was one thing to change her life, but it was another to uproot her kids from their family; to change their entire lives and perspectives; to make them children of divorce.

They had always been a happy family. It never quite even left them. They could be that again. Maybe. She just needed to figure out how not to be miserable. Lindsey lovingly fixed Riley's pony tails a bit, feeling a sudden rush of protective instinct, a need to touch her.

"Nothing, honey. Hey, you guys want to go on a bike ride

around the neighborhood or something? Maybe we'll make it to Dunkin Donuts?"

Lindsey was expecting cheers of joy, but then she remembered who she was dealing with.

"Nah," Liam mumbled, "sounds boring, but could you give me a snack."

"I'm too tired," Riley chimed in, "but maybe you can have them delivered!"

"Dunkin Donuts doesn't deliver DoDo," Liam teased.

"Mommy, can get anything delivered," Riley pouted. "Can't you mommy?"

"She can't," Liam insisted.

"Kids, let's forget about Dunkin Donuts, okay. I just thought you'd like a nice bike ride. It's not a big deal. I've got Goldfish crackers or Pirate Booty. Let's just finish up your homework and get outside in the sun for a bit."

They both got back to work, but Riley looked back at Lindsey expectantly and she winked in answer. Riley smiled knowingly and hurried back to her paper. Yes, mommy can do anything.

In the other room, Lindsey called Mitchell's cell. He picked up on the first ring.

"Lindsey! I'm just waiting for the last patient to leave and then I'm coming home. I don't know what to say. I'm so sorry about today. Can we talk about it? Please? I really did let Celia go this time. I don't know what I was thinking. It was a mistake, I know that and, I can only imagine what you're thinking." He was actually babbling. The good doctor never babbled.

"Yeah," she answered calmly, interrupting his admission and apology and overflow of words. She was the cool one now. "We can talk about it later tonight. Do me a favor and pick up two rainbow tie-dyed donuts from Dunkin. I promised the kids."

"Sure," he answered, sounding perplexed at her strange reserve in light of what had happened. "No problem."

"Okay, I'll see you soon."

She hung up right after, not wanting to linger on the phone. There would obviously be a lot more talking later. She had thought it would take all her composure to keep it together and not lose it on him, but she was strangely calm and controlled. After being in the eye of the tornado, things looked different on the other side. She needed some more of the debris to clear but somehow though the mess, a path was forming. She knew what she wanted and what she planned to do. It wasn't a perfect plan by any stretch, but at the moment it was the only one she had. For the longest time everyone thought she was the picture perfect wife with the picture perfect husband. Lindsey even bought into the fairy tale herself and worked hard to maintain the image, but perfect was no longer something she aspired to be.

When Mitchell came home not too much later to the overwhelming smell of chicken cutlets cooking, he was completely thrown off.

"Hey," he said cautiously, walking in the kitchen where Lindsey was in the middle of the dip, bread, pan fry, flip routine. He didn't even attempt to walk toward her, but instead stopped a safe distance away and leaned on the island in the center of the room. He had flowers, a fresh Babka and a bag from Dunkin Donuts in his hands which he set on the counter.

"Hey," she repeated. The gravity of their situation pulled them down; a wall they couldn't climb.

"Where are the kids?" he asked.

"Liam is upstairs working on a Lego set and Riley is watching a show in the basement."

Mitchell gripped the countertop and she saw the stress in his face. He was worried. Very worried.

"Is she gone?" Lindsey asked quietly.

"She's gone." He swallowed audibly.

"For good?"

"You'll never see her again. I promise you." His hazel eyes entreated her to believe him.

"But will you never see her again?" she asked coldly.

The slight hesitation was telling. "I will never see her again," he lied. He totally lied to her face. She knew it, as she knew herself.

"Do you love her?" Despite herself, her voice cracked. She couldn't believe they were having this conversation. This would be completely unthinkable a few months ago.

She could see him fighting with himself to answer, not knowing how much to reveal.

"I love you," he pleaded with her. "You!"

She wasn't letting him off that easy. "And her?"

His shoulders slumped, and he ran his hands through his hair, and held them to his forehead like he had a severe headache. "No. I don't love her. I just liked the way she made me feel." He confessed and then seemed horrified that he had.

He fell all over himself to recover. "Lindsey, I've only ever really loved you. You're my wife. I don't want to lose you. Please."

Tears streamed down Lindsey's face but she returned to her chicken that needed to be dipped, breaded, fried and flipped, finding comfort in the process. Mitchell tentatively walked closer. Standing behind her, he whispered in her ear, "Lins? I promise. It's only you."

"You humiliated me. You let her humiliate me." That part really stung. That Mitchell allowed her to have such power in their lives, that he defended her.

"She's gone. I made a mistake. Please forgive me." He nestled his head in the crook of her neck and Lindsey let him stay, even though she was tormented by the idea of forgiving him and not forgiving him. If he hadn't been having this affair, it was possible she never would have started hers with John. If she hadn't been so unconnected to her husband, sexually and emotionally, she might not have been as vulnerable. Who knew really? A part of her wanted to go back to when it was easy, before she knew things about herself, about Mitchell.

She sighed. There was no going back. Going back was never having experienced love and passion with John, going back meant returning to a superficial existence. No. There was no going back only forward, and which direction they went in would be up to her.

"I don't know if I can," she said. "I don't want our kids to come from a divorced family. I don't want them to suffer or know anything different at all but I don't know if I can get past this."

"Do you hate me?" he whispered.

She couldn't find the words to answer but shook her head. No. Despite this, she didn't hate him, and a big part of her worried that soon he would hate her.

Mitchell wrapped his arms around her and gave her one tight hug from behind, and even though she was the one being squeezed, she swore she felt the relief seep out of him. Such was the power of temporary clemency. She broke from his hold and put some distance between them. "No hugs. No nothing right now. It's too much. It's hard enough just being here right now."

He backed off respectfully, "Of course. I'm sorry. Lins. I'm really, really sorry. The last thing I ever want to do was hurt you and put our family in jeopardy."

"I know." She nodded. "Me either."

Either Mitchell didn't understand it or just let the comment pass without question. It didn't matter which. It wasn't like she was going to explain herself.

They were interrupted by Liam barreling down the stairs and a few minutes later Riley came up from her show. The whole of the Ryan family filled the kitchen and the happy noises of the kids seeing their dad filled the empty space between them.

They sat down to chicken cutlets, sautéed broccoli and spaghetti. Lindsey had a glass of wine at the ready and another waiting in the wings. This was a day she would never forget, although she was having quite a bit of those recently.

Liam talked excitedly about a soccer game he and his friends had played at recess, while Riley shared her dramatic heartbreak over her friend Lucy choosing to have a play date with another girl, Julie, over her. Mitchell caught Lindsey's eye with amusement, and she smiled before she could stop herself. It was hard dismissing fifteen years of habit. Their natural dynamic was too comfortable and easy to be ruined so quickly. They had always been good friends. Lindsey wondered if she would be taking this as well if she didn't have her own secrets. She supposed not.

Dinner ended and the kids went upstairs to wash up and do some reading before bed. "I'm going to go supervise them," Mitchell said, as Lindsey started rinsing the dishes to put in the dishwasher. Lindsey nodded okay and continued with the job at hand. "Are you okay?" Mitchell asked standing at the doorway, leaning a hand on the frame. It was nice of him to ask. She thought, maybe he even really cared about the answer. She was being a bitch. She knew he cared. He was a cheater, but he cared. She knew exactly how that worked.

"Remains to be seen," she said, feeling kind of numb and picking up the statement he had used on her a few weeks ago. She felt close to crashing from this ridiculously long day, and the two full glasses of wine weren't helping. Or they were. "One day at a time." She suddenly had an urgent need to be alone, to end this conversation.

"Do you think we'll be okay?" he asked.

"I hope so," Lindsey admitted honestly but unsure of in what way she hoped.

He seemed to accept that. "Me too." He hit the frame twice as a sort of farewell and went off to help the kids.

Alone at last, she rinsed the same dish over and over, not really thinking of anything, staring into space, floating on the haze of Shiraz clouding her brain. Giving up, she left the dishes in the sink and headed up to help with the kids. Lindsey knew as soon as she got them to bed, she was soon to follow.

By 9pm, after an exhausting marathon of book reading to Riley – really, Ri? Every Mo Willems book we own, with voices and effects - and pleas for more time from Liam, they were both down for the count.

"You ready to talk?" he asked immediately when she finally escaped from the kids' rooms, but she shook her head.

"Let's let it ride." She had no fight left and no interest in the argument. She needed a cocoon where she could process and change in solitude before reaching out to the world anew.

"Going to bed?" Mitchell asked, taking one look at her eyes, swollen from exhaustion and crying.

"Yeah. I'm done."

"I'm going to do some work downstairs on the couch." Ah seems like old times already, she thought a little bitterly. She almost said, you like the couch so much, maybe you should stay there awhile, or at least for tonight, but it wasn't necessary. She would just be saying it for effect. They had slept next to each other plenty without having sex. She didn't need to put him out of his bed.

"Okay, goodnight," Lindsey said and did the mixed sigh shrug thing that happened when they were weary and without words.

"I love you," he called out as she walked away from him toward their bedroom. It came out a little desperate, spoken as much out of the need to say it as the need for her to hear him say it.

"I know you do," she said instead of, 'You have a funny way of showing it'. Those in glass houses and all that.

"Goodnight."

She stripped off her clothes, brushed her teeth and crawled into bed. Within minutes, she fell dead asleep.

CHAPTER 21

Many people find a more suitable mate (someone they love more than their spouse) after they are already married.

Morning came and Lindsey didn't even hear the alarm which was so unusual that Mitchell gently shook her awake before he walked out. She never overslept on a weekday morning; rarely on weekends, for that matter. There was always too much to do. Apparently, her brain needed the rest.

When she walked downstairs her coffee was already steaming in her cup, waiting on the counter. A slice of Babka rested next to it. She smiled involuntarily. Touché, Mitchell.

She didn't have time to linger on any thoughts because there were lunches to be made and backpacks to check. She remembered Liam needed to be woken early. He had homework to finish. Life went on as usual. Go figure. Life didn't care about her drama.

With the kids safely on their way to school, she took her time, showered and dressed casually in a pair of jeans and a cozy sweatshirt, putting on only tinted moisturizer and pulling her hair into a loose pony tail. Losing her social standing was in many ways liberating.

She called her mom who entertained her with her latest stories from the 'the people who haven't yet passed but sure do pass a lot.' "I try not to stand too close to anyone, because I am one of the few with a functioning nose," she said with mock pride.

They confirmed travel plans for the next month and somehow Lindsey evaded any serious discussion by cutting her off. "Oh, sorry Mom, what's that? I think I hear the bus coming."

Her mom did insist on putting her father on the line for an extremely awkward forty-five seconds. It seemed hard to believe that she could successfully not have a relationship with her dad all those years having lived in his house, and then having spent so much family time with them, but it was surprisingly easy to avoid someone standing right next to you, especially after years of practice. They were masters at civility and avoidance.

"Hi Lindsey," her dad said a little gruffly and a lot uncomfortably. Besides the brief inadvertent pickups when she called before he handed her off to her mom, she couldn't remember the last time they directly spoke.

"Hi dad," she responded.

"Your mom thinks it is a good idea for us to talk."

Blame mom. She liked the tactic. "She's usually right," Lindsey said.

"That she is," he agreed and she could almost see him nodding and scratching his head, which was a habit of his when he was at a loss for words. A momentary silence followed and Lindsey thought that was all he had, but then he surprised her by following up with a question. "So, how are you?"

"I'm in the thick of things, dad," she admitted, although it was unconnected and meaningless.

"You always were a popular girl," he said not really understanding her plight, yet somehow making perfect sense.

"I guess I was," she agreed.

"I'm looking forward to seeing everyone here next month." And then he amended gently, but coughed a bit to hide his emotion. "I'm looking forward to seeing you next month."

Lindsey suddenly realized she was talking to an older man. The person who had accused her that night, who had turned on her in a desperate horrible moment was no more. She had spent years hating him and then many more years ignoring him. She now realized the stupidity of it. The lost time. The past needed to stay in the past. It was time to move on.

"Me too, dad."

She hung up feeling happy. That was a good start to the day. Now she had list of things to accomplish. She grabbed her bag and sunglasses, but when she reached for her bling covered cell she looked at it with interest. All of sudden it was amazingly ugly and obnoxious. She snapped the case off and tossed it in the trash before heading out.

First stop, dry cleaners to pick up Mitchell's clothes. Just because they were in a questionable place didn't mean he had to look like a mess. The next stop was to CVS. Riley insisted she needed a new folder for school and it absolutely had to be purple. Not pink like she had already purchased – purple. CVS didn't carry purple folders. The best she could come up with was one from Target; a purple folder with a unicorn on the front cover. She hoped it would work or she was just taking a crayon to the pink one later. Of course she couldn't be in Target without spending over $100. It was funny how once you were there you realized you needed everything... paper towels, Goldfish crackers, a new sports bra, a Lego set, Halloween decorations, fuzzy slippers...

She didn't buy any perishables because she had a few hours before she needed to be home, and she still had one more stop to make. She put the address in the GPS and followed the annoying woman's voice till she came to a sweet little block in Glen Head, two towns or so over from her. The house was blue-shingled and not too big, but it was charming with a sweet wrap-around porch. There were even wind chimes hanging by the front door, a surprising touch.

She knocked quietly and heard the weight of his step as he got closer and opened the door. The moment she saw the lightly lined, sharp features of his face, she felt at home.

"Hi," she said a little nervously.

His eyes sparkled happily. "I'm so happy to see you. I didn't know if I would."

"My mom always says, you've got to keep the mystery in a relationship," she joked.

"Well then, I think we're good."

Lindsey looked around, noting the porch, complete with a swinging chair. "Charming place you've got here."

"Thanks. I really like it. And it's close to the kids, but enough of a distance away that I can feel like I can have some privacy."

Lindsey raised a brow. "Privacy, huh? For what?"

He moved closer, wrapping her in a hug. "Oh, any number of things," he remarked suggestively.

They stood close together, arms wrapped around each other, and Lindsey leaned into his chest, like they were dancing at a Prom. They stayed pressed together for minutes, swaying lightly to the music in the wind. It was so liberating to just stand in the open air and hug. Finally, he lifted her up off her feet and squeezed her to him like a bear.

"Oh my God!" She laughed. "Put me down."

"Maybe I'll just carry you in," he joked, but something about the idea of being carried over the threshold of his new home stopped her.

"Let's just stay out here for a bit. I really like your porch," she said, then nodded to the rocker. "Can we sit on the swing?"

"Of course." He set her down on the chair, and then sat down next to her. She pushed the chair off a little with her feet and they relaxed there slowly swinging in silence, her head resting on his shoulder.

"This is so nice."

"This is perfect."

As they sat enjoying each other's company, a man and a woman walked past, obviously out for a late morning stroll. They waved amiably and Lindsey and John waved back. Such a pretty lie they were. Just like her and Mitchell, she thought and immediately pushed it away.

"This is so nice," Lindsey repeated.

"This is perfect," he repeated back.

"I don't know what's going to be." She sighed. She wanted to be honest. "Things might get uncomfortable and messy but I'm not willing to give you up. It's very selfish and I don't know if you're okay with that. I don't know if you should be."

He nodded thoughtfully. "I don't know either."

They talked for the next hour, stopping only for John to go inside and bring out some peanut butter sandwiches and iced tea which they ate while gently swaying.

"I love this day," Lindsey said happily, finishing the last bite of a sandwich she never would eat in her real life of sushi lunches and chopped salads. But John wasn't her real life, he was her dream life. "I only have about an hour before I have to head home." Lindsey gave the pouty lips.

"That's okay." He swung an arm around her, pulling her closer. "That's sixty whole minutes of rocking pleasure."

"I can think of a more rocking pleasure," she not so subtly suggested.

He looked at her with a raised brow. "I didn't think we were going to go there?"

"Oh, we're going to go there." She slid a hand in between his thighs.

His expression was conflicted, and for a second Lindsey felt self-conscious. "Unless, you don't want," she flushed pink, and went to pull her hand away. Immediately, his hand covered hers and kept it in place.

"I want." He brought his face close to hers. "I want too much." He kissed her, deep, slow and sexy. She felt it in her toes and everywhere else. The chair moved to their rhythm and she wanted to climb on top of him. Even though they were partially concealed by shrubbery, she didn't think it was the best way to say hello to the new neighbors.

They kissed again and this time he pulled her body tightly toward him. She felt every muscle in his body against her. She touched his chest and wanted to rip his shirt off. She was ready to go inside, but he just continued kissing her. Sweet, tortuous kisses that made her heart pump and pulled her nether region into a tangle of desire. She tilted her neck back against the rail of the chair as he nibbled at her ear while his hand gently rubbed her inner thigh.

She closed her eyes to the sensations swelling inside of her. This was the most connected and sexually satisfying relationship of her life. She felt young and sexy. She felt present and pulsing with power, energy and happiness. She felt so God damn alive. It was brilliant.

For the last eleven years, she lived in a world of babies and lunches, school functions and home making. She got the right pink Uggs for Riley, played Uno and Trouble, went to soccer and gymnastics. She made semi-healthy meals, fresh baked goods and volunteered at the school. And for the most part, it was good. Really good. It was what people did after they got married and had babies, but it wasn't living, feeling, experiencing. It wasn't about her. She was invisible. It was about her children and husband and about being the good Doctor's wife. It was about appearances and sacrifices that she only now was allowing herself to fully understand. It was about getting through the day in a distractedly enjoyable way which she did very well; until that moment, that one small moment when her eyes opened. And once you see light, you just can't go back into the darkness again.

She opened her eyes and saw John's face looking down on her; blue eyes intense, and a lightly amused expression on his lips. She smiled back leisurely, like a lioness taking a morning stretch, then got up from the chair and headed toward the front door.

It was then that she noticed his house number 27, ornamented in Kelly green above the mailbox, next to the door frame. Underneath the number were two brown, crisscrossing tennis rackets. Lindsey fingered them lightly.

John noticed and hurried an explanation. "It was a housewarming gift from the guys I play with at the club." She didn't know he played. It was a sign, she thought, an extremely obscure one, but a sign nonetheless.

He watched until she put her hand on the door knob and looked back at him flirtatiously from over her shoulder. "Well, what are you waiting for, cowboy. I ain't got all day."

She didn't have to ask twice.

***

When Mitchell arrived home that evening, she was preparing a dinner of meatloaf, baked potatoes and roasted Brussel sprouts. It all looked delicious. Lindsey thought even the kids might like it, except of course the Brussel sprouts, which were her favorite part.

He walked into the kitchen to greet her as he always did, but stopped short of kissing her, opting again to lean against the counter. "How was your day?" he asked, making the usual conversation.

"It was fine. Ran a bunch of errands. Nothing exciting. You?"

"It's work."

They were tip toeing around each other. "I'm getting tickets to visit my parents in Florida for Thanksgiving," she said.

Mitchell hesitated and looked at her carefully. "Am I invited?"

"We'll talk about it," she said softly.

"Okay. We'll talk about it." He had lowered his voice to a more intimate level. Even though this interaction would normally be filed under, random things to run by Mitchell to check off the list, these days everything took on deeper meaning.

"Dinner looks good," he complimented.

"Hopefully it tastes good." She offered a small smile.

"I'm sure it will."

He seemed encouraged by her smile and Lindsey wondered if they typically interacted like this. It felt so... Stepford. "Well, let's find out. It's ready."

During the meal, the kids took the lead, talking over each other for the floor. They were just so fun and entertaining and gorgeous, except when they started yelling at each other over whose turn it was to talk next. Then they were annoying, obnoxious and frustrating. Just like that. The switch flipped.

"Can we watch America's Got Talent?" Liam asked. "Please!" The 'ask' reverted to a 'beg'.

"Please!" Riley echoed. Now she was his partner in crime. They both start jumping up and down. "Please???"

Lindsey looked over their heads to Mitchell who shrugged affably.

"Okay guys, here's the deal." She took Mommy control. "You can but you need to go wash up now and change into your PJ's, make sure your backpacks are packed for the morning and when the show's over, it's right up to bed. No nonsense."

They nodded like bobble heads in the breeze. "Can we have an ice cream sundae while we watch?" Liam asked while Riley jumped. "Please, please."

She nodded right back.

"And..." Riley interjected, "Will you and daddy watch it with us? All together?"

Now Liam jumped for Riley. She couldn't help but smile. She loved when they worked together, brother and sister, partners, friends, rivals. Mitchell gave another look of easy acceptance.

They washed up while she and Mitchell silently cleaned up the kitchen together. It was both awkward and nice having him help. When they were done, she made four bowls of ice cream. Mitchell and Liam were doing plain vanilla with rainbow sprinkles, whipped cream and M&M's, while she and Riley had chocolate mixed in with chocolate sprinkles, mini-marshmallows and whipped cream. When it came to ice cream, the Ryan family didn't mess around.

At 8p.m., she and Mitchell took their regular spots on their adjacent couches while Liam sat with her and Riley cuddled her dad. They laughed together at some of the terrible acts and oohed and aahed over the great ones. They ate their ice cream and bet on who would go through and who would get X'd off. Lindsey watched Riley almost drip ice cream onto her rug and saw Mitchell catch it just in time.

She sent him over silent thanks to which he silently answered, you're welcome. He gave her a wistful glance of appreciation. It was so nice sitting together as a family, which was what they were. For all the pleasure John brought her, she couldn't deny the pleasure Mitchell did. She was surrounded by comfort, security and happy contentment. They were gifts that she had no intention of returning.

When the show was over, Lindsey ushered the kids upstairs to bed.

"I'm going up too," she told Mitchell. "I'll get them to bed and then I'm going to bed myself. I'm tired."

"Of course. I'm going to stay here and do some work."

"Sure. Of course."

"And in case you forgot, I have that medical conference this week. I'm going to be pretty much gone till Sunday."

Immediately, little red flags pop pop popped in her head.

Mitchell laid his hand out on the armrest of the couch, palm open, an invitation. With only slight hesitation, she slipped her hand in his.

"This is our family," he said, with quiet seriousness. "I'm not going to let us fuck it up."

"I don't want to fuck it up," she said.

He smiled grimly and pulled a large manila envelope from the pack of work papers by him on the couch. Lindsey took it from him with trepidation. Slightly shaking, she pulled the contents out and immediately sucked in her breath. They were pictures of her and John. There were shots of them talking at their front door, ones of them at her parents' house. There were a few of them hugging outside in front of John and Jeanie's house. And there some taken today on the swing of his porch. Fuck.

She couldn't look at them, but she couldn't look away either; especially the ones from this afternoon. They were so intense, she blushed. The thought of Mitchell seeing these horrified her to her core.

"I know. They're tough to look at," he said with sadness.

"You had me followed?" she asked dumbly, the reality of his knowledge settling in.

"I'm not stupid. I've known." He was more gentle than angry. "It just took a while to get proof. You know how the saying goes. It takes one to know one." He gave her a small, apologetic smile.

Speechless, she slid the photos back in the envelope and automatically sat down on the couch deflated.

"I don't know what to say." The envelope hung in her hands like her head.

Mitchell put his computer down and moved to the couch beside her. She couldn't look at him, yet he took her hand in his. She was still holding the offending envelope and she let it drop to the floor. It made her hand in his feel dirty.

"We've both made mistakes," he said gently, much more conciliatory than she would ever expect.

"Yeah, we have," she agreed and her eyes started to well.

"But we've been happy. I know we've been happy. I've been happy. Have you been happy?"

"I have," she sniffed. She was on the verge of major emotional breakdown; tears rolled down her face. "But I don't think I'm happy anymore."

"I've spent a lot of time thinking about this, about us," Mitchell reasoned. "I think we should just move forward, and I think we should stay how we are."

Lindsey looked at him funny. What was he saying?

"I'm just saying," he continued as if to answer her thoughts, "that we both deserve to be happy and I still want us to be together."

"And how do you propose that might work?" Lindsey asked tentatively. "Could you clarify, please?"

His look said it all.

"Seriously?" Lindsey shook her head in disbelief and almost laughed. "You're kidding me? You want us to have an open marriage?"

"It's not that crazy." He squeezed her hand. "I love you Lindsey and I know you love me. I do. We have a good marriage, but maybe we're not conventional. Our marriage is our marriage and we can do with it what we like, as long as we both agree. It has to be mutual. I don't want the secrets and I don't want to lose you."

She was trying to breathe from the shock of what he was suggesting. Of all the things she considered, the thought of having her cake and eating it too never crossed her mind, even while she was doing it.

"No matter what, we're a family first. That's the most important thing," he pressed, "We certainly wouldn't be the only experimental couple on the north shore."

Was she breathing? Were they really having this conversation like they were discussing what to watch on television? "Mitchell," she stammered. "I don't think that 'arrangement' is going to work. I really don't."

He pulled her to him and hugged her. "I really love you. It never meant I didn't. None of it ever did. You've given me everything I've ever wanted, a beautiful family, a life. You and the kids are everything."

He was saying what she had been thinking but realistically for a million reasons it wouldn't work. She knew it wouldn't work. No marriage could stand so much truth.

She heard stomping and turned around to see Riley standing there. "Come on, you guys!" She giggled. "Stop that."

"Stop what?" Mitchell played along. "Stop this?" He kissed Lindsey on the lips, on the cheeks, on the head.

"Mitchell, stop!" Lindsey giggled a little too.

"Mom!" Riley complained, hovering over them. "You said you'd come up like ten minutes ago!"

"Okay, I'm coming honey. Give me two minutes." Riley remained fixed in her position with her arms crossed. "Go child," she warned, "or I'll make it three."

Mitchell took the opportunity to kiss her face, her neck, her nose, and her head. "Stop it!" She laughed. Riley rolled her eyes, but then her glance took in the envelope lying on the floor.

"Hey, what's that?" She bent to pick it up and as she did, both Lindsey and Mitchell almost fell off the couch to retrieve it first.

"Nothing honey, just Daddy's work," Lindsey said, a little too excitedly, clutching the envelope possessively. "Now go. I promise. Two minutes."

Riley looked at them skeptically. "Two minutes!" she said with finality and stomped heavily back up the stairs.

"What are you feeding those feet?" Mitchell remarked, and she playfully slapped him.

"That was close," she said.

"Yeah," he agreed, running a hand through his hair. "Listen, I'm going to shred them. Some things you really shouldn't ever see."

"I've been working with that principal for years," Lindsey jabbed. Her years of denial done, she couldn't help herself.

"I'm sorry," he said sincerely. "I never meant to hurt you."

"I'm sorry too." Lindsey rose from the couch. "I've got to go up there, or soon they'll be back down here."

"I know. Just think about what I said. We're good together babe. We work. I love you and I love our family."

Lindsey was still trying to process that he knew about her and John. The idea that he could live with it was both insane and intriguing. She had lived with her blinders on in a one-sided open marriage for many years. She could only guess how many 'Celia's' came and went while she busied herself leading the perfect life. Could she turn away knowingly?

She couldn't. She had deluded herself for too long. They had spent the last few months in an emotional tug of war trying to pretend and ignore, trying to keep their marriage together instinctually, against all odds and reason.

"Just think about it," he coaxed. "I'll be gone most of the week," he added in a horse whisper, the implications hanging out there for both of them. "We can talk more afterwards."

"It's not going to work," Lindsey said suddenly and sharply. The thought of him spending the week with Celia made her skin crawl, but she would probably feel the same with anyone. Now that it was all out there, she could not openly accept them having other relationships and being married. "In so many ways I wish it could but it won't. And it's because we love each other."

He nodded slowly, holding her gaze. "So what do we do?" Mitchell extended his hand once more and she accepted it. They held together, eyes locked; the most raw, honest, precarious moment of their marriage. And they discussed a separation.

CHAPTER 22

"It's never too late to start over again and to be happy."
— *Anurag Prakash Ray*

"Would you put that dang thing down already? I'm not getting any younger you know." Lindsey's mom shook her head disapprovingly.

Lindsey gave her a smirk, typed one last word and placed the cell phone down on the table where they were sitting outside at Xpresso Yourself, Lindsey's new favorite coffee house. "You're just jealous because you don't know how to use yours."

"Pffft!" Her mom waved her words away like she was swatting at the fly that buzzed around their muffin. "Remember the good old days when you were begging to see me? Now I come in from Florida and you don't even give me the time of day." She sighed dramatically and sipped her coffee.

Lindsey glanced at her phone. With its unadorned case, it still took a moment to realize it was hers. "It's 9:27a.m.."

"Don't be such a smartass," her mom replied. "Now who were you texting with? Was it... John?" She cocked her already arched brow comically.

Despite herself, Lindsey blushed just a little. Even six months later, she couldn't help herself. Her feelings for John made her shy and excited and embarrassed in front of her mother or anyone for that matter. She didn't like talking about him and just wanted to stay nestled alone with him in his house and in his bed; bubbled in a secret cocoon of satisfaction and happiness that she hoped would never pop.

"Maybe," Lindsey hedged coyly.

"So am I going to see my boyfriend this trip?" her mom asked, doing the eyebrow thing again.

Her parents had gotten to know John a little better on their last visit, where he and her mom had laughed together like old drinking buddies, often at her expense. Lindsey didn't mind. Watching them filled her with happy and allowed her father and her, who were clearly on the outside of every joke, some tentative bonding of their own.

"If you do a good job helping me with the move today, I'll consider it," Lindsey bargained.

"I'll be on my best behavior," her mom promised, eyes twinkling.

"Uh oh." Lindsey laughed. "How about you just behave?"

Her mom smiled. "Rotten daughter," she said affectionately and added a serious note. "I'm so proud of you."

"Mom!" Lindsey scolded but looked wistfully at her. "Stop it."

"You've really grown up. Look at you. You've made some mistakes and you've made some tough decisions but you've taken control of your life. And, you're so beautiful."

"Mom! Don't cry!" Lindsey teared a little. "You're going to make me cry! And I'm a total mess."

She tugged her pony tail tighter. She was wearing workout leggings and a fitted pullover. Her face glowed naturally with just a little secret Orgasm Blush. Not that the real thing hadn't already done wonders for her complexion. She had even gained a few pounds of happiness, and had lost all, well most of, the designer pretense and need for outer approval. The clichés don't lie. Beauty comes from the inside out.

"Okay." Her mom dabbed at her eyes. "You're right. You are a mess."

"Hey!" Lindsey laughed and gave her a little kick under the table.

"And what about Ellie?" her mom asked, changing the subject. "How is she?"

Lindsey shrugged. "We're okay. I've forgiven her, sort of. It's that kind of thing where you know you have to move on and you do, but it still lingers and changes things. It's subtle but I can feel our trying too hard and pretending to be normal. You know, just wanting it to be the 'us' from before."

"If I've learned anything," her mom said, "it's that you can't ever go back to the 'before', but you still can go forward."

Lindsey nodded, and pulled a piece of muffin from the plate between them. "I still keep some of those old SOS posts of hers saved to remind me, which is unnecessarily twisted, but I'm not ready to delete them. I'm sure I will someday, but I don't want to let it go yet. So I guess we're good and we're working on it."

They finished their coffees and shared blueberry muffin, leaving only licks of crumbs on the plate and headed over to the old house to supervise the movers already in progress.

After everything that happened, Lindsey only briefly entertained the idea of staying in Shore Point. She loved living there, but that was another Lindsey and another life. She needed a fresh start and a fresh town. If she stayed it would have been much harder. She had to let it go. The truth was there had been much harder things she had to let go.

Lindsey watched the movers emerge from the house that used to be hers and Mitchell's, steadily heaving box after box, chair after chair and heading in separate directions, one towards a white truck reading, We Move it but don't Shake it, and the other into a truck that said simply, Minelli Brothers Movers.

There was an artful systematic beauty to their work that created a clump of emotion in her chest that threatened to overwhelm her. She felt split in two as well. Of course, it was exactly what was supposed to happen. She wanted it to, needed it for closure and to move forward, but as always, knowing it and seeing it are very different animals. This was her old picture perfect life literally being dismantled.

These past months, she and Mitchell worked extremely hard at being amicable and making the transition as easy as possible. There were tense moments of course, but overall, things ran smooth as the crisp sheets on a fresh bed, their slight hesitation when they looked at each other creating the most noticeable ripples.

They focused on the kids, including them in most decisions, being overly attentive, putting them all in therapy – something Lindsey should have done for herself long ago - deciding all together to move within a mile of each other to a small town called Bay Cliff which was close to Shore Point but completely different with a vibe more Magic Garden than Dynasty.

The men were carting out their bed, heading toward the Minelli truck – Mitchell's, not hers, she wanted no part of that - when Lindsey felt a presence besides her.

"So this is it," Mitchell said and when Lindsey looked at him she wanted to cry and smile simultaneously. So that when he extended his hand to her, she grabbed it and got the opportunity to do both.

They hugged and she cried. "We're going to be okay," Mitchell said warmly.

"I know," Lindsey agreed, sniffling a little. "I know. But will the kids be okay?"

"The kids will be fine," Mitchell assured her. "They are fine. As long as we're good, they'll be good."

"Am I interrupting something?" Lindsey's mom asked, making a loud coughing sound.

Lindsey broke away from Mitchell with a smile and hit her mom in the shoulder. "All yours," she said and stepped to the side while Mitchell and her mom talked.

"I think we should get back to the house," Lindsey said after a bit. "Our truck is getting ready to head over."

"See you at their camp open house next week," Mitchell reminded as she walked away, impressing her with the knowledge of his fatherly schedule duties. He never would have remembered that a year ago. Maybe it would be okay, Lindsey thought hopefully.

They left Mitchell looking winsome, standing on their sun drenched green lawn. She held that last picture of him and her house and gave a small wave before disappearing into the car. Mitchell would like that. He always appreciated a good exit.

***

"Well, here we are," her mom exclaimed as they pulled up to Lindsey's new home, a reconstructed and renovated arts and craft style bungalow with a ton of windows and open spaces but still modest and homey. Lush trees surrounded it making it feel private, like a cabin the woods.

Her mother jumped out to supervise as Lindsey watched with excitement as the movers began the meticulous and tedious business of pulling things from the truck. She watched her half of the couch, the one she always sat on across from Mitchell make its way in. She watched both her old childhood bedroom set and her brother Liam's come out, having been picked up from storage, ready to be settled in the kids' new rooms. She loved this house; had loved it on first site and could barely contain herself. She wanted to squeal with delight.

When his car pulled up, she waited impatiently for the engine to shut down, the car door to slam and to hear the click of his steps on the pavement. Finally, John's arms slid around her waist and she melted back into him. "Looks like someone needs to release some pent up energy." He nuzzled her neck.

"Are you suggesting a quick run?" Lindsey tempted, turning round for a sexy, playful kiss that still made her almost weep with desire.

"I'm suggesting..." He put his lips to her ear to whisper.

"Hey you there," her mother called from the house. "What are you doing with my boyfriend!"

They broke apart, reluctantly, happily. The way they connected made almost every other relationship in Lindsey's life fade into the background. With him she fantasized about running away to an island, another world, another life, a closet, anywhere, anything, as long as his strong arms circled her waist, his lips greedily met hers and his blue eyes twinkled with happiness and need when they saw her. Not that she was going anywhere. They were firmly planted in a reality that at the moment was better than any fantasy she ever envisioned because it was real and he was hers.

"Mom!" Lindsey giggled, taking John's hand and leading him up to the house. "Not so loud. Don't want to start the whole town talking."

***

No More Secrets
A Blog

Hey y'all, whoever you are and welcome to my blog and very first post. Let me introduce myself. My name is Ellie.

I have an eighteen month-old baby, who my husband and I adopted after a long and miserable stroll on Infertility Road. My baby is the sun, moon and stars to me. Every poop I change I appreciate. Every yogurt stain on my shirt I appreciate. Every exhausting moment chasing his toddling, crawling, climbing, never want to nap ass all over the place, I appreciate. That's me, up to my eyeballs in appreciation And laundry. I have a husband who is wonderful – funny, supportive, hot. I can't say enough good things about him, except when he gets on my nerves which, lucky for him, is not right now.

Like everyone, I live a complicated, fascinating, boring, exciting, beautiful, frustrating, crazy life. I've decided to start this blog because I really like to write and connect with people, so I'm hoping you guys are the connecting type. There's so much in life that needs discussion. I want to share my shit. I want you to share your shit. But what I won't do is share other people's shit. Recently I made a really poor decision and shared a friend's shit and I'm very lucky and grateful that friend is still my friend. (Shout out to friend! Hey girl!)

It has gotten me thinking deeply lately about a lot of things and that's what I'd like to discuss in my maiden post - choices.

Everything we do in life is a choice. From the moment we wake up, to the moment we go to sleep, we make choices. Simple things, like whether we wear the funky heels or comfortable shoes says something about who were are at that moment.

Are we choosing a donut for breakfast or an egg white on an English muffin? Or did we choose the donut then feel guilty and get the egg white muffin, and ultimately wind up eating both? That one just might be me.

There are also slightly more complicated choices each day, like should you avoid that nice person in the neighborhood who just talks too much? Do you agree to help someone out even if you don't have the time? Do you go back into the supermarket when you realize you accidentally didn't put a tub of cream cheese on the checkout aisle, thus stealing it? Again, that one might just be me.

Then, there are all those big life choices early on. Who do you marry? What do you want to be when you grow up? Do you have kids? What do you make a priority in your life?

I remember two choices in my life that left a major impression, one small and one big. The first was when I was six years-old. I was on the playground with my class behind my best friend Terri, in line to go down the slide. I followed her up the steps and when she reached the top, just before she sat down to slide, I lifted up her skirt so all the kids could see her panties.

I have no idea why I did that. I probably thought I was being funny, or showing off for my classmates. I can't say, but at the time, I didn't realize the consequences of such a seemingly small action. First, that I would hurt Terri's feelings. Second, that she would never speak to me again.

I felt bad about the moment for the rest of that year when Terri refused my apology or to play with me. Terri could have turned out to be a good friend in my life. I'll never know.

The second choice I made was when I was sixteen. I was drinking wine coolers with a bunch of friends, and having no tolerance or much experience with alcohol was completely in over my head, and off my feet drunk. That's when someone suggested a drive. I followed along like a chicken to slaughter. I remember lying in the backseat, my head spinning, feeling the engine of the Trans Am roar. We were going fast. Too fast. Somewhere in the buzzing of my head, I thought, 'Wow, this wasn't smart. I might die.' But it was a distant thought, up in the clouds, somewhere touching the corners of my brain but just out of reach.

Thankfully, we didn't crash and die that day, but we very well could have. I easily could be dead.

Just to balance it out and give you an example of a good choice, to show you that I am indeed capable of making a good choice. I'm going to go with the obvious, right off the top of my head and say, I married Benny, the most solid, giving, strong man who has made my life and my every day a gift. Except when he annoys me, of course, but overall..."He lifts me up, when I am down. He is ti ta ni um!" Sorry, the song is stuck in my head and it actually makes sense. It does! My point is that those are only a few of my choices in my lifetime, so far. I've made thousands and thousands, but most of the choices we make on a daily basis are typical. Safe. Where to eat? What to buy for a gift? Where to send your kid to camp?

And even these seemingly innocuous choices could have big consequences. What if your kid meets the person they love at camp and later marries them? What if your kid hates the camp you chose and then they refuse to go to camp ever again, becoming somewhat of a social recluse and ultimately living in your basement at 35. It can happen, people.

And those are almost throwaways compared to some serious decision making...

Will we confront a friend when she hurts our feelings, possibly putting the entire friendship in jeopardy?

Will we put our parent in a nursing home because they are old and bitter, and in need of a lot of attention?

Will we allow flirting to go a step further, even though we are married, because we are lonely and feel invisible and have met someone who all of a sudden makes us feel special?

Will we take the keys from a friend who swears they are fine but we have seen drinking a bit more than appropriate?

Will we end life support for a loved one when it is their wishes, but not our own?

All this is to say, we won't know what we will do until we are in those positions. We might make choices we may not have expected. Done things we couldn't believe we would.

One choice. Good. Bad. Indifferent. They all matter and can completely change our lives; often in unexpected ways. You never know what wheels you have put in motion. What subtle or dramatic change you have made to alter the course of your life.

One moment is all it takes. So choose carefully people.

I, for one, have just decided I am totally getting that donut tomorrow and not feeling guilty.

So there you have it. What's new with you guys?

Book Club Discussion Points

What if Lindsey was your friend? How would you react? Would you drop her? Or would you stick by her? Can a relationship survive infidelity? Can a friendship?

Why is the SOS FB page so alluring? What attracts us to gossip?

Is Shore Point an accurate reflection of the suburbs?

Do you feel like you know your neighbors? Do you feel like you know your friends? Do you feel like you can truly know anyone?

Do you know people like Lindsey and Mitchell? People who present themselves and their lives as perfect?

The lives of Lindsey and Mitchell, Jeanie and John are clearly affected by the affair. But how does it affect the dynamics in other relationships?

Is Shore Point a main character in the book? Is a small town almost like a living entity?

In the end, Lindsey chooses to leave the town she loves. Can you live in a town after committing the ultimate taboo?

For Lindsey, John's attention mixed with an absent husband and unresolved issues in her past led her to give in to temptation. What is it that ultimately makes people cross that line?

Lindsey carries heavy baggage from her childhood. How much of who we are in the past determines our futures?

Lindsey's mom turns inward to deal with her grief. How does this lack of communication change Lindsey? Do you think that if Lindsey dealt with her guilt and her grief in the past, she would have made different choices?

Do you think the fact that Lindsey was 'middle-aged' had any bearing on her choices?

Ellie is really Lindsey's one true friend. Are the suburbs an isolating and lonely place? How many people can you really trust in life?

Lindsey ultimately chooses to leave her husband and her family and take a chance on a new life. Do you judge her for her choice? Do you think she should have stayed?

How realistic is happily ever after?

At what point should someone decide to make their own life and happiness a priority? Are moms allowed to be selfish in that way? Does society allow them that choice?

Chapter subhead citations

The Normal Bar. Copyright © 2013 by Chrisanna Northup, Pepper Schwartz, and James Witte.

Harden, Seth. "Infidelity Statistics." *Statistic Brain*. Statistic Brain, 31 Dec. 2014. Web. 18 Aug. 2016. <http://www.statisticbrain.com/infidelity-statistics/>.

"26 Surprising Statistics on Cheating." *HRFnd*. Health Research Funding, 07 Jan. 2015. Web. 18 Aug. 2016. <http://healthresearchfunding.org/26-surprising-statistics-cheating-spouses/>.

"Truth About Deception." *Truth About Deception*. N.p., n.d. Web. 18 Aug. 2016. <https://www.truthaboutdeception.com/cheating-and-infidelity/stats-about-infidelity.html>.

Lake, Rebecca. "Infidelity Statistics: 23 Eye-Opening Truths." *CreditDonkey*. Credit Donkey, 18 May 2016. Web. 18 Aug. 2016. <https://www.creditdonkey.com/infidelity-statistics.html>.

About the Author

Alisa Schindler lives in the wild, wild suburbs doing extremely exciting things like picking up her children from school, schlepping to baseball practice and burning cupcakes. She lives dangerously by rollerblading on her street and eating far more ice cream than any middle-aged person should. Her free time is spent at the computer writing, which makes her husband happy because it keeps her from shopping and her kids happy because they're eating chocolate bars while running with scissors. She loves and truly appreciates her three boys, her husband and her friends who keep her sane and smiling.

Catch up with her at Facebook.com/authoralisaschindler/ or at Twitter.com/icescreammama, or on her blog at Icescreammama.com where she occasionally hangs out with a story and an ice cream cone.

Other titles by Alisa Schindler

Murder Across the Street

Made in the USA
Middletown, DE
21 March 2017